THE HOPEFUL ROMANTIC SERIES

Blue Eyes, Red Dress

STEPHANIE JACK

Blue Eyes, Red Dress
The Hopeful Romantic Series
Stephanie Jack

Published by:

Mary Ethel
Mary Ethel Eckard
Frisco, TX

Library of Congress Catalog Number: 2024918927 ISBN (Paperback): 979-8-9910210-1-2
ISBN (Hardcover): 979-8-9910210-3-6
ISBN (E-book): 979-8-9910210-2-9

To contact the author: sbjack2022@gmail.com
Follow on Facebook: thehopefulromantic and Stephanie Butterfield Jack
Follow on Instagram: @sbjack2011
Follow on Tiktok: The_hopeful_romantic
Follow on Threads: @sbjack2011

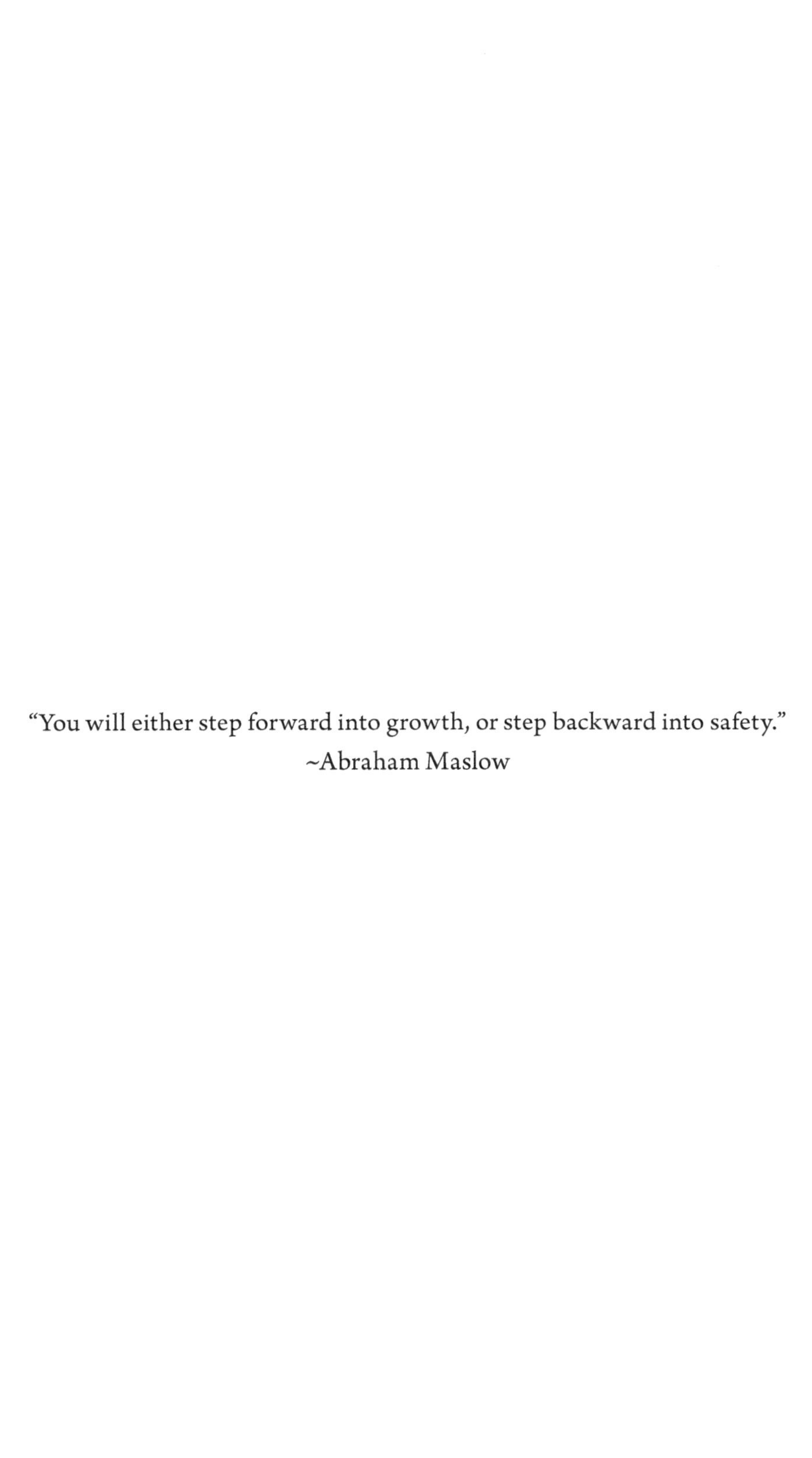

"You will either step forward into growth, or step backward into safety."
~Abraham Maslow

ALSO BY STEPHANIE JACK

Food for Thought: Energizing the Busy Professional
The Day the Train Stopped
The Secret in the Letter

CONTENTS

1

THE RED DRESS

In Denmark when a loved one nears the end of his or her life, there is a simple act, a swift gesture, that says so much: the opening of a window so the soul of a loved one can pass through.

A warm, gentle breeze flaps at the curtain that hangs over the raised windows in room 113. A golden glow bathes the room in sunlight before twilight, the welcoming guest, transitions the day's harshness into magical minutes of pure glory when it is neither day nor night. An interlude when the universe paints the sky in pinks and oranges with a hint of yellow before deep maroons and purples waltz across a black canvas stretching as far as the eye can see.

A nurse pauses before shutting the windows, remembering a conversation from a few days earlier. "Open the window, my dear, so I may travel to them with haste."

Lottie was restless; had been all day, Kristen noted. The patient wasn't agitated but conveyed through her limited use of body and speech that she needed to be somewhere other than in her bed.

"Miss Kris, I've got to get into that boat," she insisted.

"Lottie, is there someone in the boat?"

"No, but I can see someone across the water, on dry land, waving to me."

"Do you know that person, Lottie?"

"Looks like my Jeremy."

The air had turned cold from the fog creeping in from the ocean, so Kristen closed the windows. Lottie wasn't going anywhere this evening, or was she?

Not everyone was called to care for the sick and dying. Kristen Warner loved her vocation, seeing it as an honor and privilege to take care of her patients and their families when they were most vulnerable. One of her patients had called her a "mid-wife for souls."

For most of Kristen's patients, this solo journey was a leap of faith: a destination unknown to the physical world. Her job was to support and provide palliative care and to travel on their journey as far as they needed her to go. She had come to recognize the consistent pattern in each of her patients as they traveled their journey. She could not always say where the destination ended, and what she believed was not always the same as her patients' beliefs. However, as she observed while tending to her current patient, Lottie, the end of the road could be vastly different for each one.

Kristen never referred to her patients' visions as hallucinations, even though some of her colleagues removed from hospice care, did. The patients who recognized a loved one waiting for them on the other side were rarely agitated and seemed overjoyed to see someone they had loved. Many times, her patients became lucid before they took their final breaths. Sometimes a patient's family member would insist the visions were hallucinations and demand that Kristen give a sedative to their loved one.

At times, a family member might become frightened when their loved one experienced a rattle in their lungs. These were times when a sedative was necessary, as this eased the breath when the patient's lungs stopped functioning. Kristen reassured the family their loved one was not suffering but was in transition. Just like a transition during childbirth. She attended to the soul as it made its way into the spiritual realm.

If a patient suffered because of extreme pain from their illness, Kristen had orders to give a heavy sedative to ease their suffering. This passing was peaceful, and that was the norm. The patient's breath would become shallow, one or two long breaths followed by a length of no breaths, until one final breath and the patient was gone. No fanfare, no wave, just a peaceful passage into the arms of their loved ones who had gone before and stood waiting.

Kristen reassured the family that their loved one was more in control of their life's end than they realized. Her experience was that, if a patient said they were going to die on a Tuesday, they did. The patient's dignity, respect, and comfort were her main concern.

While Kristen held Lottie's hand, a soft chime sounded on her watch. She looked at the time, remembering the gala. Lottie's death was not eminent, but it could progress rapidly. If she did not have to attend the gala, she would have preferred to stay with her patient, but she was the face of hospice and had to make an appearance.

"Lottie," she said. "I have to go now; I am taking my pager with me. Nurse Kelly will stay with you. I will be back, I promise."

Kristen whispered into Lottie's ear as her patient struggled for her hand. "Don't make Jeremy wait. Goodbye, Lottie."

Something inside Kristen's viscera told her she would not see her patient again. This was the cycle of life. Birth and death were a continuum of mystery. When Kristen worked with families to help alleviate their fears of the unknown, she felt rewarded. This was her job; one she could do over and over again.

Not all hospice patients died. Some of Kristen's patients recovered and went home. Theirs was a need to be validated and cared for as well as to feel loved. They needed to feel human. No matter the reason for hospice care, Kristen loved her patients.

Hospice care had been an easy choice. Sylvia Warner was concerned that her daughter might be making a mistake in choosing this vocation. Although Kristen never said, Sylvia suspected her daughter was running away from something.

"Are you sure you want to work in hospice care?" she asked on more than one occasion.

"Yes, Mom, I am certain," was all Kristen offered. She didn't need to give her mother a reason. Her reasons were valid enough, and it was far easier to love people who would not hurt her. And even though hospice patients' lives were short, it was easier to accept their deaths. She didn't need anyone complicating her life.

Over the years, hospice care had become her only life. When she felt particularly grieved, she would sink into a dark place from the past, so she tried to stay busy with work to keep her from falling that low.

When the opportunity to attend the gala was presented, Kristen was reluctant and excited. She did not want to leave her patients, but she knew she needed balance in her life. The gala was an opportunity to get out of her work routine and socialize.

There was only one slight problem. The invitation stated that the gala required formal attire. The last formal function Kristen had attended was a colleague's wedding. For that event, her choice was a long red, strapless gown that hugged her hourglass figure. There wasn't time to buy another gown or have the red one altered, so she hoped the dress hanging in the back of her closet would fit.

After clocking out, Kristen hopped into her car and drove the short distance from the hospice facility to her house. Once inside, she raced upstairs and searched frantically for the red dress, pushing aside the clothing in her closet until her hand touched the plastic that covered the dry cleaned gown. Taking it out of the bag, she held it over her body. If anything, the dress was a tad big. Better than being too small, she surmised.

While the water heated in the shower, Kristen quickly changed out of her work clothes and put on her white terry cloth bathrobe, tying it closed with a knot. Thinking about appropriate jewelry, she decided on a double strand pearl chocker with complementary drop pearl earrings. After placing the jewelry on top of her dresser, she checked the water in the shower, elated it was sufficiently hot.

Kristen untied her bathrobe, letting it slip off her right shoulder, then the left, and fall to the floor. As she stepped into the shower, she realized she was still wearing her watch. Removing the watch, she stepped out of the shower, laid it on the bathroom sink, then returned to the hot water where she lathered her body and washed her hair with eucalyptus and sweet herbs, which revived her for the evening ahead. The complementary shampoo and body wash were just enough fragrance to feel and smell fresh. It wasn't that she didn't like perfume; she just didn't give it a second thought. She rarely wore perfume because she felt patients in transition didn't need to be distracted by such earthly scents.

After the shower, Kristen quickly dried her long, blonde hair and coiled it into a bun at the nape of her neck. Then she secured the bun with tiny pearl hairpins. After stepping into her dress, Kristen clasped the necklace around the back of her neck and inserted the pearl earrings in each ear. Surveying her ensemble in the full-length mirror hanging on the inside of her closet door, she said, "This will have to do." She tucked a strand of hair that had fallen out of her bun behind her ear. It was then Kristen realized she had forgotten her watch. That would not go well if it chimed at the gala, and she did not answer. Besides, she promised Lottie she would be with her at the end.

Forgetting where she had placed the watch, Kristen searched the top of her dresser, thinking she had left it there. Beginning to panic, she remembered where it was. After retrieving it from the bathroom sink, she hastily turned her left wrist up so she could clasp the watch band with her right hand. Then she applied a shade of red lipstick that closely matched her dress. A final glance at her face in the bathroom mirror revealed her shade of lipstick was perfect. Out of habit, she pursed her lips together, then left for the gala.

2
THE BANKER

Lime County Savings and Loan was a magnificent building that could be distinguished from a distance as it rose above the violet mist that settled around the middle of its dark, red stone, like the tulle on a ballerina's tutu. The bank was located on the corner of Avalon and First Avenue. Its Corinthian columns were an image that came to mind when patrons of the bank described the landmark as a temple.

The bank's reputation for security was the reason it retained its clients, notwithstanding the fact that Lime County's patrons had deep pockets with diversified portfolios. They knew the bank was FDIC insured, and that was the reason for their loyalty.

As an officer of the bank, Tim Hurst had passed several securities licensing requirements. It was not surprising that he landed a job as vice president of Lime County Savings and Loan. He had a talent for reading the stock market. Money, the use of money, the way money could make money, fascinated him. Occasionally, he entertained the thought that he would like to have a client wealthy enough to own an emerald mine.

The bank expected Tim to sell products that did not always sit well with him. Some of these products included risky stocks. If the bank's clients proved to him why they wanted to invest in said stocks, he would write copious notes in their files before investing their money. After reviewing his notes in the portfolio of his client, Helen Trenton, Tim leaned back in his black leather swivel chair, wondering if she would attend the Hospice Gala Fundraiser that evening.

Before placing Helen's portfolio on top of the pile on his desk, he noticed a set of plans he had drawn up for a custom motorcycle. Sure, Tim owned a bike. He had several even though his mother objected to his riding. His love for bikes came from his dad who said, "Nothing like the feeling of wind, speed and vibration, to set your mind at ease." That's why Tim chose his Norton Commando. It was a good bike for easy riding on days when he wanted to clear his mind. So when he thought of a custom bike, he wanted something special. His design was not your everyday off-the-showroom-floor model. It was well thought out, and it would be a bike no one else possessed. It might come with a high sticker price, but that was expected for a custom bike. He had no sooner started to pick up the plans than his head teller, Shelly, tapped on the clear, glass window separating Tim's office from the bank lobby. Tim looked up, acknowledging Shelly.

"Tim, don't forget the gala tonight."

"What gala?" he teased back at her.

"Don't act coy with me! You know how much I wanted to go with you!"

"Oh, that's right, the fundraiser gala. I believe it benefits a new hospice center for kids."

"It's black tie, Tim."

"Maybe next time you can go with me."

Shelly turned on her heel and muttered, "Like that will ever happen."

"I heard that," Tim shouted through the glass. "Not my choice kiddo. This was an executive decision, and I drew the short straw."

Shelly turned around and walked back into Tim's office. Looking him in the eye, she said, "You loathe these events."

Tim paused before he replied to her comment. "Not entirely. I have an engaging personality. This is an opportunity to hunt."

"That's terrible, Tim. Referring to your clients that way."

"Truth be told, Shell, that is how corporations relate, not me."

"Enjoy your hunt then," Shelly mocked, then turned and walked away.

Tim rolled his eyes as he grabbed his motorcycle plans before tossing Helen's portfolio on top of the pile on his desk. He thought he should retire. He did not have a wife; he did not have a dog or kids. He didn't know where his father was or if he was still alive. Other than his mother, who lived in a nursing home about an hour away, he had no responsibilities. Furthermore, his life was uncomplicated, and thus far, he liked it that way. Tim's friends, however, thought he should have a companion. They would plan elaborate dinner parties and barbecues, invite Lime County's most beautiful women, and Tim would find himself seated between a blonde with a smile that dazzled, and a brunette with lovely, brown eyes. Once they opened their mouths to speak, all that remained was a vacuous package.

It wasn't that he didn't appreciate women, he did; all kinds of women. If he were to settle down, he wanted someone with a brilliant mind and not just a beautiful face. As an unmarried man, Tim wanted what he wanted, and he was not about to make compromises. He enjoyed his friends' attempts at matchmaking and he played the game well. After all, he knew he was not a scoundrel, but if at the end of the evening, his dinner partner expressed more than a casual interest in him, he would invite her for a nightcap. If the nightcap turned into passion, then all the better. A vacuous package had its benefits.

In the grand scheme of things, upon retirement, Tim planned to take an extensive cross-country motorcycle trip, which is why he had tinkered with a design. He also thought about a companion who would share the ride, but increasingly, this looked like it would be a solo trip. It wasn't that he required much in a companion, and yes, he did want someone to share the scenery with. Maybe that individual would point out something he didn't see and that would be magical. That was the plan, anyway.

When he thought about the reason for the gala, Tim shuddered. He had clients withdraw funds from their retirement accounts to pay for hospice care. To him, hospice felt like the end of the road, and that was not a road he wanted to go down anytime soon. The gala, however, provided him an opportunity to find new clients. He would use the platform that end-of-life care was expensive and that he could help them fund their care before they exhausted their retirement savings. It was a win-win for all involved. That is what the bank expected Tim to do; find new clients with deep pockets.

Tim looked at his watch just as Shelly walked over from her station to lock the bank's front doors. He tapped on the glass to signal her attention because his driver, Terrance, would pull up in front of the bank at any minute. While Shelly secured the doors, Tim pulled down the shade between his glass window and the bank's lobby. He grabbed his black tux, white shirt, and black tie from inside the closet in his office and quickly changed.

When he came out, Tim caught sight of Shelly looking at his window, and, having been discovered, she turned a deep shade of pink. He knew what kind of effect he had on her, and this was not the first time she was betrayed by her thoughts. Shelly was an easy read that Tim enjoyed. He turned to her and said, "Have a good night," as Terrance pulled up in front of the bank. Then he winked at her before he pushed the interior doors open and let himself out.

Terrance had gotten out of the driver's side and opened the passenger door on Tim's BMW M6G Power Hurricane CS. He loved the car as much as Tim did, but tonight would not be a leisurely drive on circuitous Highway 1 along the Pacific Ocean. Terrance enjoyed that route when Tim was not in a hurry to be anywhere. They would pull over on the side of the road and watch the sun's fiery flames shoot into the sky before disappearing over the horizon.

After Tim got into the car and secured his seatbelt, Terrance, out of habit, asked, "Where to this evening, Sir?"

"The Jackson Hotel, please, and step on it if you don't mind. I don't want to be late."

The Jackson Hotel was equidistant between Los Angeles and Culver Heights where Tim had grown up. Even though it was past rush hour, Tim didn't expect any delays in his travel to the gala.

"Yes Sir," Terrance replied.

"You've heard that proverb, Terrance. The early bird catches the worm."

"Yes Sir, I have. It means it's important to start early to maximize a potential outcome."

Tim looked at Terrance, "Tonight is one of those occasions."

"I will get you to The Jackson in plenty of time. You have my word."

Tim had no doubts his driver would get him to The Jackson; as they drove along without a hitch for twenty minutes. When they were a few blocks from the venue, Terrance turned onto Marquis Boulevard and saw that all traffic in that direction had slowed to a snail's pace.

"Sir," Terrance said as he looked to his left and then to his right and straight again. "There appears to be some sort of standstill up ahead."

"I can see that," Tim responded impatiently. "Call one of your friends; maybe they know what the holdup is."

Terrance wasted no time calling Roger, another driver. "What's the holdup on Marquis?"

Roger replied, "Looks like some sort of accident. Can't make out much. Fools don't know how to drive."

"Thanks, I'll find another route to The Jackson Hotel."

"Good luck with that, Terrance."

"What do you mean?"

"There's that gala going on at The Jackson tonight. I hear lots of high society folks are going to be there. Maybe some of them have already started their cocktail hour. Should not be driving. That's my opinion, anyway."

"Ok, thanks. Maybe I'll have better luck on Broad Street."

Terrance hung up the phone, then expertly maneuvered the car in the opposite direction of the standstill as he turned onto Broad Street. He no sooner entered onto Broad than he came to a screeching halt one quarter of a mile from The Jackson Hotel. Up ahead he could see flashing red lights.

"Oh, for Pete's sake," Tim shouted.

"Sorry, Sir. I can't go anywhere."

"I'll walk, you can pick me up later."

"Whatever you say, Sir."

The traffic jam irritated Tim. He was not concerned about the reason for the traffic jam; just that it would make him late for the gala and he did not want to arrive after the introduction of the guest speaker began. Without looking behind or to the side, Tim violently shoved the car door open, and heard a voice shout, "Hey buddy, look out!" Tim turned to the sound of the voice, shocked to see he had knocked a motorcyclist off his bike. The car door hit the gas tank on the motorcycle so hard that it made a dent and ruined its deep blue, metallic paint. He didn't know the condition of the motorcyclist. "You ok?" he asked.

"No, I'm not ok. Look what you did to my bike!"

"I'm sorry," Tim stammered.

"You should be! This is not your everyday, run of the mill, stamped, and delivered showroom model. It's a custom bike. Nobody has one like it." The motorcyclist paused, then blurted, "DAMN."

"I'm so sorry," Tim repeated. "My insurance will pay for the damage. This was an accident."

"Forget it, I can fix it myself," said the motorcyclist.

"I'd like to pay for the damage."

"You can pay for the part and the paint. But it is not going to be easy matching up that paint. Took me forever to get it right."

"How much?" Tim asked, as he pulled out his wallet.

"I'll let you know. Name's Kaos, by the way."

"Nice to meet you. I'm Tim. Tim Hurst. No hard feelings?"

"No hard feelings." Taking in Tim's formal attire, Kaos added, "Looks like you have somewhere important to be."

"Yes, The Jackson. I'm already late."

"I can get you there, hop on."

"Thanks," Tim answered. He was grateful not to be stuck in traffic.

3

KISMET

 Hotel hosted its first guests in 1895. Prior to that, electric lights and hot and cold running water were left to the imagination. Entrepreneurs of the late nineteenth century had the foresight to provide guests with an extraordinary experience. The Jackson was the first of its kind, boasting breathtaking architecture and imported French chefs. Guests could linger over patisserie, sip espresso, and marvel at rich tapestries and fabrics. Live plants and deep soaker tubs with a separate walk-in shower were luxurious amenities. It was a predilection of the upper class, while those less fortunate lived vicariously from the tales retold by someone who knew someone who stayed at The Jackson.

The bank had given Tim a voucher for overnight accommodations in one of the hotel's most coveted suites, which was his to be used as he wished. However, the unspoken rule was to give the voucher to a client with the deep pocket.

After being dropped off at The Jackson, and before entering the stately doors, Tim patted his pocket to make sure the voucher had not been misplaced. Reassured, he entered The Jackson Hotel. The lobby had high ceilings with gold patina arches separating bounteous spaces from one area to another. In that vast space, Tim found himself in a sea of black tuxedos milling around in front of the ballroom doors. He was used to these kinds of events where women attending wore long, black gowns, accompanied by their tuxedoed counterparts. Tim had never noticed how black tie events were so colorless until a flash of red caught his eye. The distracted banker almost forgot to check in with the receptionist until a lilting voice from behind the high concierge desk cleared her throat.

"Sir, may I be of assistance?"

While Tim tried to keep his eye on the woman in the red dress, he did not want to be rude to the concierge.

"Yes, I believe you have a reservation for me, Tim Hurst, in the Fairmont Suite."

"Yes Sir, I do." After locating the room access keycard, she handed it to him. "Here is your key. The Fairmont suite is on the ninth floor, elevators are to your left and down the hall. Enjoy your evening," she said.

"Thank you," Tim responded. He tucked the key into the inside pocket of his tuxedo jacket, then left in haste to look for the woman in the red dress who had disappeared into the ballroom. This woman, whoever she was, seemed to hold a power over him, and he was not used to feeling like this. Tim's purpose for attending the gala had shifted from seeking new clients to finding the woman in the red dress. He imagined unpinning the neat bun at the nape of her neck and letting her blonde hair tumble down her shoulders. It was enough to drive him mad; the only word that came to mind to explain his feelings was *kismet*.

Kristen, completely unaware of Tim or his emotions, found her name card on table 10. She was happy her table was close to the exit, in the event she had to leave. She laid her black clutch purse on the table between her assigned seat and a seat assigned to a name unfamiliar to her. Looking over the other name cards, she realized she didn't know any of the guests assigned to table 10.

As she turned toward the cocktail station, Kristen recognized a bevy of big named cameos in the medical field circle. Before she could step away from her table, a white gloved butler offered her an aperitif from a silver tray.

"Thank you," she said, as she took a fluted glass from the offering.

"My pleasure, Ma'am."

The champagne's tiny bubbles rose to the top of the flute and tickled her nose as she sipped the sparkling gold liquid. "This is delicious," she said to the butler, smiling. After another sip, Kristen remembered her purpose at the gala. She was the ice breaker for the main speaker because she was an expert in the field of hospice care and could field questions posed by attendees. She would also encourage benefactors to give generously to the new hospice center for children and their families.

Remembering why he was at the gala, Tim's eyes followed Kristen while he glanced around the room for potential clients. He was handsome, unmarried, and every available person's idea of the perfect man, and he did not have to try hard to find conversation or, for that matter, wealthy divorcees. Tim felt a tap on his shoulder that made him jump. Turning to see who had intruded on his thoughts about the woman in the red dress, he recognized divorcee Helen Trenton. Her settlement from her husband, Howard Trenton, owner of Jungle Securities, provided for her philanthropic pursuits. She was wealthy enough to own an emerald mine.

"Hello Tim, I thought I recognized you. How have you been?"

Tim shuddered. Even though Helen was an endless font of cash, he did not want to have a conversation with her. She was clearly interested in him for more reasons than money management, and their meetings were awkward, to say the least. When she made an appointment at the bank for a review of her investments, she would invite him to her home to look at her "etchings." The sun had not been kind to Helen. Endless rounds of golf, tennis lessons, and sitting by the swimming pool watching her pool attendant, while most likely having amorous thoughts, had aged her more than she cared to admit. The mirror, however, did not lie. Plastic surgery and Botox injections left her with a characteristic permanent uplift across her cheekbones that looked like her face would crack if she smiled. Nothing short of surgery could be done to eliminate her creped skin.

"Hello, Helen, it's good to see you. What brings you to this event?"

"Why, you do, dear!"

"How did you know I would be here, Helen?"

"I always know about fundraisers. My personal assistant keeps me informed. I know why you attend these events."

"Is that so."

"Absolutely I do, Tim."

"It's my job, Helen."

"I know, dear. That's why I write you big checks."

"It's not me you write those checks to, Helen. It's the bank's money."

"Yes, but you do benefit from my generosity. I know you get a percentage of my investment. Did I neglect to tell you I own an emerald mine?"

"No, Helen, you didn't divulge that. Was this a recent purchase or a holding you just found out that Howard kept from you?"

Helen chuckled, then replied, "I don't own an emerald mine. I just wanted to see your reaction."

At some point during Helen's attempt to hold the attention of the handsome banker, Kristen came dangerously close to Tim. His head spun around, away from Helen, as his eyes connected with the woman in the red dress. There was something about the way her eyes seemed to pierce right through him, but before he could give it any thought, she quickly turned and walked away, disappearing for a second time, into a sea of black tuxedos and gowns. Tim tried to follow her with his eyes, much to the chagrin of Helen Trenton who was not daunted in the least. What she lacked in looks was made up in money.

"Tim, dear," Helen said sweetly, "I plan to write a large check for the hospice cause. I could be induced to split the difference between you and hospice, if you know what I mean."

Tim turned to face Helen, then asked, "How much of an inducement?"

"A cool half million, Tim, dear."

"Very well, Helen, I will find you at the end of the evening."

"Not if I find you first, dear."

Tim turned away from Helen, rolling his eyes. At least for the moment, the pressure was off to make money since he secured a half million dollars in the first thirty minutes of the gala. Now he could turn his full attention to the woman in the red dress. Before he could wade through the crowd in search of her, a woman in a long, black gown approached the podium at the front of the ballroom. She pulled the microphone closer to her mouth so everyone in the room could hear her.

"May I have your attention. Will everyone please take your seats at your assigned tables?"

While the woman spoke, Tim watched Kristen walk to table 10. He had not located his table, nor did he care; he would find a way to sit at the same table, if not beside her. He didn't think he had competition for her attention until a stocky man with thick fingers tried to approach her. Tim beat him to the table just in time to pull Kristen's chair out before the stocky man did. Then he sat next to her, unaware the name card assigned to that spot had his name on it.

"Thank you," she said, turning her face toward him. Tim was instantly smitten by the exquisite blue eyes looking back into his. Women, in general, did not affect him this quickly. But this woman had charmed her way straight through his heart with a glance. Leaning closer to her hair, he helped her scoot her chair closer to the table. Her fragrance was intoxicating. Tim knew he had to ask questions, find out who she was, and he was not going to share her with the stocky man who was still desperately trying to get her attention.

They had no sooner sat down than a tiny chime sounded. Kristen looked at her watch, then at Tim, then at the stocky man. She looked back at Tim once more and said, "Please excuse me," as she scooted her chair away from the table. She stood up, retrieved her purse and name card, and said, "Enjoy your evening. I hear this benefit is for an exceptionally good cause." Then she quickly disappeared from their sight, using the exit door closest to table 10.

"Well, that's a shame," said the stocky man with thick fingers. Tim's heart sank. He turned to his competitor and asked, "Do you know who that was?"

"Sadly, no," the stocky man said. "I had hoped to before you did, since you were my competition. Looks like we both missed out. It's going to be a long night." Tim sighed, then in one gulp, he polished off the champagne in his glass.

A tap on a glass at the head table made a pleasant ring as it summoned the guests' attention. Tim turned to see who made the announcement, but it did not register because his mind was consumed with thoughts about the woman in the red dress.

The same woman in the long black gown who first addressed the attendees approached the podium. She stood behind the microphone until the room quieted. Then she began. "Tonight's presenter is Dr. Eli Christensen, Co-Founder of Hospice International. All proceeds from tonight's gala will benefit Rory's Place, Hospice International's newest project. Without further ado, and it is with great pleasure I introduce to you, Dr. Eli Christensen."

A round of applause echoed around the ballroom as Dr. Christensen arose from his chair and walked to the podium. He faced the crowd, then turned to the woman in the long, black gown who had stepped toward the back of the dais.

"Thank you, thank you," he said, as he acknowledged the guests. "I have to say, this is a beautiful ballroom. Before I begin, I would like to thank all the benefactors and coordinators of the gala. Your generosity toward Rory's Place is deeply appreciated. Let's give them an applause to show our appreciation." Another round of applause reverberated throughout the ballroom. When the applause died down, Dr. Christensen extended his hands in front of him, signaling the guests to sit. When they were all seated, he began.

"Why is hospice care important? Has anyone seated in this room experienced hospice care in one form or another? Perhaps hospice care is familiar to you because you have had a family member or a friend benefit from this care, or you would not be here. Equally, there may be those who have never experienced hospice. So, I thank you for giving up your evening for this noble cause."

A thunderous applause reverberated again throughout the ballroom. Dr. Christensen waited for the applause to end, then began to speak a second time. "Thank you. Tonight, I will give you some background and historical information about hospice. First of all, hospice is based on two principles. Dying people should have a say in how they want to spend the rest of the time they have left. They should be as peaceful and as comfortable as possible. Secondly, Hospice treats the whole family, not just the patient. It is difficult to see a loved one die while hooked up to tubes and monitors, bells, and whistles. Every move they make signals a nurse, and in the case of a child, they may be frightened and need their parent to hold them. Until they are ready to leave us, all patients have the right to feel loved in an environment where they are most comfortable, surrounded by those they love and those who love them. We think of family members as anyone the patient chooses to be such, and they are not necessarily blood relatives. Hospice is not a place. It is a group of people; it is a concept of care."

Tim's mind wandered in and out of Dr. Christensen's presentation. He could not get the woman in the red dress out of his mind. He barely heard Dr. Christensen say, "Hospice is not a job, it is a philosophy that has a profound effect on the nurses lives as well as their patients' lives," when a waiter asked, "Sir, would you like coffee?" Tim didn't drink coffee late in the evening; however, the thought of Helen Trenton made him accept the beverage. "Yes, thank you," Tim replied, as he took the cup of strong black coffee from the waiter.

After Dr. Christensen left the podium, the lady in the long, black dress returned to thank the guests and attendees for their participation in the evening, encouraging the benefactors to dig deeply into their pockets and make a generous donation to hospice and Rory's Place. She then encouraged everyone to stay for a while and enjoy music and drinks to close out the evening.

Wishing he could call it a night, Tim glanced up to see Helen making her way across the ballroom.

"Tim, dear, I have looked everywhere for you," she said in her sweetest voice.

She sat down in the chair where the woman in the red dress sat earlier in the evening. Tim's perfect memory of her was marred by Helen's presence.

He winced when she said, "I have something for you, or have you forgotten?" Tim put his cup of coffee down, turned to Helen, and said, "No, I did not."

Opening her handbag, she made a dramatic presentation of the half-million-dollar check before handing it to him.

"I believe I promised you this?"

"Yes, Helen, you did."

"What do you have for me, dear?"

Tim removed the Fairmont Suite access card and placed it on the table in front of her.

"Oh Tim…is this what I think it means?"

He hesitated before answering. "It means you have a luxurious suite for the rest of the evening. All night if you want."

"Will you join me, Tim, dear? I did give you half a million dollars."

"That you did, Helen. You should go up and get comfortable. I will join you shortly."

Helen could not contain her excitement, "Do not tarry, dear!"

After Helen left the ballroom, Tim signaled the waiter. He had no intention of sleeping with the rich divorcee. As far as Tim was concerned, he was off the market. He felt a soul connection to the woman in the red dress even though he had barely met her, if you could call it that. He wasn't about to lose hope as he recalled something he had read from his mother's favorite author Kahlil Gibran. "Is it wrong to think that love comes from long companionship and persevering courtship. Love is the offspring of spiritual affinity. And unless that affinity is created in a moment, it won't be created." He had to hold on to hope, even though he had reason enough not to.

As the waiter approached, he asked, "What may I get you, Sir?" Tim replied, "Two magnums of Lamborghini Oro Vino Spumante to the Fairmont Suite."

"Yes Sir.".

Tim winked at him, "It is exactly what you think."

The waiter turned to Tim, "Not my place to think, Sir. I will deliver the champagne."

4

TIM

Tim left The Jackson Hotel shortly after midnight. Helen's tolerance for champagne was as he expected; worthy of two magnums. She definitely liked her champagne, even though she had passed out and would not remember what transpired between them, and Tim would not bring up the subject. After she passed out, he laid her in the bed, covered her, and left. He knew his behavior toward Helen was unscrupulous, but she would forgive him. She always did. And if she inquired, he would reply, "Helen, you don't remember?" That would be it. Nothing more, nothing less.

Helen, of course, would search her mind in an attempt to ascertain whether something magical took place. Tim played the game well. She liked any attention she could squeeze out of him and did not mind throwing money his way, as long as it was a legal transaction. Tim knew that was one important lesson Helen had learned before her divorce from Howard Trenton: the value of money. The banker was all too aware that she would try to satisfy her need for his affection while making money for herself.

Terrance was waiting patiently for Tim in front of The Jackson Hotel, even though the hour was late. The driver was amused by and used to Tim's lifestyle. He was a loyal friend, not just Tim's employee. When he saw Tim emerge from the hotel, Terrence got out of the car and opened the passenger door.

"How was your evening, Sir? Anything exciting to share, other than the usual?"

"Oh, about the usual, Terrance. Can you swing by in the morning and pick up Helen Trenton? I have no idea when she wakes up. She is bound to have one heck of a hangover. The concierge will call when she is ready to check out."

Terrance turned his eyes toward Tim.

"I saw that look, Terrance."

"What look? You didn't, did you, Sir?"

"You know very well what I meant, Terrance, and I know what you think. And no, I didn't sleep with Helen. She might think I did."

"I don't think anything, Sir. You got a guilty conscience?"

"I know it's terrible of me to play games with Helen. She did write a large check!"

"You gonna let her think amorous thoughts about you two?'

"I do feel some remorse about that, but I don't feel guilty because I took her money. It is a win-win for all concerned parties."

Terrance looked at Tim. Something was amiss. He was not his usual self-confident, cocky employer.

"Did anything exciting happen tonight, Sir?"

Tim let out a sigh.

"Spit it out, Sir."

Tim confessed, "An exquisite woman bewitched me."

"That is not like you, Sir."

"She took my breath away."

"Did you talk to her, Sir?"

"No."

"Why not, Sir?"

"Because she left before I could. I had to bolt away from Helen to get to her before my competition did. I only had time to help her with her chair as she sat down at a table. Her perfume was intoxicating. Then, before I could introduce myself, her phone chimed, and she excused herself and quickly exited."

"That is a pity, Sir."

"I think she was affiliated with the gala, but no one at my table knew who she was. She took her name card when she left."

"If it is meant to be, she will show up when you least expect it, Sir."

"What do I do in the meantime? I can't get her out of my mind. Our eyes met for a second. Hers were the most exquisite shade of blue I have ever seen."

"What color hair, Sir?"

"Blonde."

"What was she wearing?"

"A red dress! You are not helping me, Terrance."

"She must have been something special since you cannot forget her. That's not like you, Sir."

"No, it's not."

Terrance drove in silence while Tim escaped into his thoughts about the woman in the red dress. The night sky had blackened and was full of stars, glittering in the distance. Tim came out of his reverie when Terrance turned the engine off. He didn't realize they had arrived at his home.

"Here we are; home, Sir. Do you want me to put the car in for the night?"

"I don't think it's going to rain. I might take a drive."

"As you wish, Sir."

"Thank you, Terrance."

"You're welcome and goodnight, Sir. I won't forget about Ms. Helen."

"Good night, Terrance."

Tim opened the hammered steel front door of his contemporary, ultra-modern home. A geometrically designed dwelling, composed of two rectangular stories cantilevered over each other. At the opposite end of the second floor was a garden Tim accessed from his bedroom. Two glass, double doors swung open from inside the bedroom. He liked to sit among the shrubs and trees as he listened to the birds sing their first notes in the morning and their last at night. When it rained, which was not very often, Tim liked to hear the rain splatter on the pea gravel paths that meandered around his flower beds. Sometimes, he took a walk in the rain, enjoying the sound the small pebbles made as it scrunched under his feet on the saturated paths.

As he stood inside the foyer, and for the first time in his life, Tim felt lonely. He didn't realize how lonely he was until tonight. His brief encounter with the woman in the red dress was an epiphany he would not take lightly. Now, the house felt empty, and he wanted her to be with him to fill the void. He walked over to his wet bar in front of a dry stack rough stone wall. The stones were various shades of neutral browns. In front of the stone wall was a white, tiered shelf that held opaque, frosted glass wine bottles and an assortment of tall and short beverage glasses. Underneath the shelf was a cabinet that housed bottles of bourbon, scotch, and whiskey.

Tim took a bourbon bottle from the cabinet and placed it on the countertop of the wet bar. He took a shot glass off the shelf and poured the measured bourbon into it. For a moment, he swirled the amber liquid in the glass before knocking it back in one gulp. When he finished, he set the glass in the sink, turned off the overhead light, and checked the security system camera that showed all was exactly as it should be.

Then he trudged up the open slated staircase to the second floor. At the top of the stairs was a long hallway that led to a guest suite. Tim's bedroom was to the right of the stairs, a huge open room with a separate bathroom. In his bedroom, the double glass doors that led to the lanai were floor to ceiling in height and provided light in the daytime and moonlight at night. On nights when the moon disappeared, the room was pitch black.

Tim turned on a floor lamp in the corner of the room that cast enough soft light so he would not trip over a corner of the oriental rug that covered most of the hardwood floor. He flung his black tux jacket over a chair in the same corner of the room where the floor lamp stood. Then he strolled over to the glass doors and took off his black tie. While he stared through the clear panes into the dark night, he instinctively folded his tie in thirds. Then he turned away from the window before putting the tie in the top right dresser drawer. Tim started to unbutton his heavily starched white shirt, then stopped. He patted his pants pocket locating his BMW's fob, aware that he was too restless to relax.

Leaving his bedroom, Tim proceeded to walk down the stairs into the kitchen. He turned on a light just before he opened the hammered steel front door, then closed it behind him. Tim stepped onto the gravel path, his feet crunching on the pea gravel as he strode toward his car. He opened the door, sat down in the driver's seat, and before pushing the ignition switch, he leaned back in his seat and closed his eyes.

After what seemed like an eternity, Tim started the car, and its engine sprang to life. He let the car idle as he listened to the engine, then zoomed off into the black night. The roar of the engine sounded powerful as he shifted down, then accelerated around the curves of Highway 1. The car responded to his touch. Driving was the only thing that gave him control in a situation wherein he had no control.

Throughout his life, thus far, control had been an issue, mostly a lack of control over his parents' failed marriage. Ultimately, Tim realized he was not responsible for their divorce but, as a kid, he blamed himself, which gave him a reason to believe as to why his parents were no longer together.

Tim loved his dad. Never stopped loving him, even though his mother had. In the early days of his childhood, he remembered his parents had loved each other. But something changed when his dad embarked on a new career involving motorcycles.

Perhaps Tim's exhilaration for speed came from his dad. They would go for rides at top speeds that cut around curves so sharp the bike almost laid on its side, forcing his dad to take a knee inches from the macadam road. These adventures scared the life out of Mary Jane Hurst. If Bud Hurst wanted to kill himself, so be it, but she would not stand for her son being hurt, or maimed, or killed.

One night following a father/son ride, after Tim had gone to bed, he woke to his parents arguing. The yelling stopped after he heard the kitchen door slam. In the morning, his dad was gone.

From time to time, Bud would let Tim know when he was in the area. This usually occurred after Bud wrecked one of his bikes in his traveling thrill jump show and he was in town so the mechanic at Slim's Garage could repair the bike.

Bud was known as the greatest motorcycle daredevil. Mary Jane did not want to be a part of the traveling circuit. She preferred a house and stability. This was important to her because she wanted her son to go to the same school every day, not just for a few months. Bud barely escaped death after his second harrowing accident. While attempting to break a world record jump, his back tire caught on the hood of the last car he tried to clear. He was tossed over the handlebars and landed on his back in a sandpile. His ribs were crushed, his spleen ruptured, and several vertebrae in his back were broken. Luckily, the spleen could be stitched, and the vertebrae cemented back together, but he would have a long twelve-week recovery.

Mary Jane got word of the accident and rushed to the emergency room to see her husband. Bud sat up in his hospital bed and patted the left side of the mattress. Relieved to see he was alive, but worried about the future of their son, Mary Jane sat next to him and confessed, "Bud, I can't keep doing this. You need to think long and hard if you want to keep up with this insanity. Choose wisely. I am not going to nurse you back to health every time you have an accident, and I spend more time worrying about your life than I do for myself."

He took her hands in his and reassured her, "Sweetheart, you don't have to worry. I promise you this is the last time I will get hurt."

But that was not the case. A short time later, she received a phone call from Bud letting her know another accident had left him with a broken left arm and leg. Mary Jane, realizing her husband had no intention of easing up on the thrill of the risks he took with his new sport, was furious. How could he continually put his love for thrills and motorcycles over his love for family? It was time to end the drama before it completely broke her. It was time for her to take care of herself and leave Bud to the consequences of his decisions. "That's it, Bud! Don't come home!"

Tim was horrified that his mother would forbid the man he looked up to and the man who showed him what exhilaration felt like, to come home. He felt his mother abandoned his dad. In reality, it was Bud who abandoned them. He sent his alimony and child support, so Tim never went without, but the young boy missed his dad. So, when Bud called or had someone else call when he was in town, Tim would sneak out of the house and meet his dad at the track or at Slim's Garage.

5
KRISTEN

Culver Heights was a quiet, small town about an hour's drive east of the Pacific Ocean; a picturesque community with trees that grew equidistantly on either side of the streets. Neat, well-kept houses surrounded by white picket fences boasted an array of pink, yellow, and red wild roses. Their fragrant blooms filled the air with delicate notes of perfume.

In the late summer, trees provided a canopy of shade for children playing endlessly from breakfast to a brief pause at noon, when their mothers called them home for a light repast and brief interlude during the hottest time of the day.

Culver Heights also boasted several denominations of churches for their citizens, but it was the steeple of St. Ambrose that crowned over the tiny community; the all-seeing eye over every action carried out by the citizens, whether early in the morning or late at night.

St. Joseph's Hospital and Kauffman's Funeral Home were the guardians of the living and the dead. St. Joseph's Hospital was the institution of birth on the morning Harry Warner discovered his father in the kitchen instead of his mother.

"Where's Mom?" he asked.

"She's at the hospital. The baby came last night."

"Oh…"

"Aren't you curious to know if you have a brother or a sister?"

"I hope for a brother, Dad."

Harry put on the dark blue windbreaker his dad had taken out of the hall closet. The day was windy, and his dad didn't need him to get chilled, so when Harry tugged at his jacket, Virgil helped with the zipper. Harry obediently followed his dad through the kitchen door and got into the family car, looking out the window of their sedan as they passed houses with white picket fences enroute to St. Joseph's. He kicked the seat in front of him and said, "I hope for a brother." Since he was too little to ride his bike with the older kids on the block, he had been wishing someone his age would move into the vacant house across the street. Now, instead of a friend, he had a sibling, and even though he was five years old, it wouldn't be that long before he had someone to play with.

"I heard you the first time, son. You will have to wait until we get to the hospital."

Harry sighed as his dad turned into the parking garage, circling the first two floors, looking for an empty parking space. He circled up to the third floor, where he found a car pulling out of space number four. After parking the car, he looked at Harry in the back seat and said, "Try to remember this parking spot. We are on the third floor, space number four. Does that remind you of something?"

"Hey… that's my birthday, March fourth."

"Then it should be easy for you to help me remember where we parked."

"Yeah!" shouted Harry from the backseat.

Virgil unbuckled his son. "Are you ready to meet your sister?"

"My sister! Oh no…I thought you said I had a brother."

"No, I did not say you had a brother. You said you hoped for a brother. I think you will be surprised."

"If you say so. I want to see Mom."

"Alright, she will be happy to see you, too."

Virgil took Harry's hand as they entered the doors that revolved in front of St. Joseph's. He looked perplexed because the floor moved even though he was standing still. The doors took a one-hundred-eighty-degree rotation before they opened into the lobby.

The first thing Harry noticed was the highly polished floor. He lingered so long, mesmerized by his reflection, that Virgil tugged on his hand. Harry didn't notice that his dad had stopped until he bumped into his backside. He heard the reception ask, "May I help you, Sir?"

"I am here to see my wife on the maternity floor. My son is a big brother today."

"You can take elevator three to the second floor, turn right. You will see signs pointing to the maternity wing."

"Thank you," Virgil replied.

Before the receptionist could ask another question, Virgil took a few steps away from the information desk, then turned around and said, "Room 207. I was here last night."

"Some fathers don't remember," she said. "I'm glad you did."

The elevator doors across from the receptionist desk dinged. Harry stood in disbelief as the doors automatically opened. After he and his dad entered the elevator, Harry pointed to the lighted buttons next to the door.

"What are these for, Dad?"

"They tell you the floor numbers. We are going to floor number two. Can you press that number?"

"Sure," said Harry as he pushed the button with the number two on it.

He felt the elevator move upward. It stopped with a tiny jolt, then the doors dinged twice before opening. Virgil took Harry's hand as he walked out the elevator, turned right, then stopped in front of Sylvia's room and let go of his son's hand.

Harry was delighted to see his mother and started to run into the room, then stopped. He suddenly realized he was no longer an only child. Here was a tiny helpless creature in his mother's arms. The older brother walked over to his mother and kissed her, peering down at the baby. As if on cue, the baby girl opened her eyes and looked into Harry's eyes. That's all it took. Harry was head over heels in love with his new baby sister.

Virgil watched the interaction between Harry and his new sister. He had no doubt Harry would be smitten with her and that he would be a good big brother. Virgil kissed Sylvia, took the baby in his arms, then turned to Harry and said, "I will not be around forever. I want you to look after your sister."

"Yes Sir."

"I'm serious son. Eventually there will only be the two of you." Harry looked wide-eyed at his dad.

"Don't worry, I will be around for a while. I just want you to know that Kristen will need her brother and you will need her."

Harry frowned. "Oh, so that's her name. Why couldn't I pick out her name?"

"Well for one thing, we didn't know if you were having a brother or a sister. Your mother and I decided on Kristen for a girl and Carl for a boy."

Just then the baby sneezed. Harry laughed because her whole body shook. Virgil carefully handed Kristen back to her mother. Harry put his arms around his mother and hugged her tightly. Looking up at her, he said, "Mom, I didn't want a sister." Then he kissed the top of his sister's fuzzy head. "I'm glad I have a sister now." Sylvia smiled. She knew Harry would love his sister. "Can I hold her?" Harry asked.

"Yes, you can sit next to me on the bed, but let me put some pillows around you first."

Harry climbed onto the bed and sat very still while Virgil tucked pillows around him. Then his mother carefully helped him hold his sister. About thirty minutes later, a maternity floor nurse poked her head inside Sylvia's room.

"Mrs. Warner, is there anything you need? I can take your baby back to the nursery if you'd like to rest."

"Thank you," she said, looking tenderly at her new daughter. She knew the baby would be in good hands with the nurse and she also realized just how much rest she needed. She continued, "I am tired."

The nurse took the baby and placed her in the bassinette. Noticing Harry's disappointment, she smiled and asked, "Would you like to help me push your sister back to the nursery?" Harry looked at his mother, "Can I?"

"Oh course, dear. Your dad will meet you there. Now, before you go, give me a hug. I need to rest but I will see you in the morning."

Harry smiled from ear to ear as he helped the nurse. He was an official big brother.

Over the next five years, Harry and Kristen were inseparable. He doted on his little sister, read to her, and made-up stories about adventures they would go on when she was older. His favorite game was making a fort out of sofa cushions and then rescuing Princess Kristen from a mean ogre who held her prisoner in the fort. He would gallop around the wall of cushions reassuring her, "Princess, I will rescue you! Stay away from the wall. I have to knock it down with my sword." Kristen would giggle and clap her hands in delight. Then her knight would lead her out of her prison cell.

When Harry turned ten, he no longer played with his sister. He preferred riding his bike as fast as he could down the gravel driveway. Just before the driveway became the street, his tires would skid in a woosh as they dispersed tiny pellets of gravel into the air.

One day when Harry raced down the driveway, Kristen ran out in front of him. He slammed on his brakes, but the wheels just spun on the gravel. Losing his balance, Harry fell off the bike, landing on his arm with the bicycle laying on top of him.

Sylvia was washing dishes at the sink when she heard Kristen's screams. The plate she had rinsed clattered as she dropped it on the floor. Luckily, the plate didn't break, but when she looked through the window and saw Harry laying beneath the bike, she wondered if something else had broken. The dishtowel she was holding barely made it onto the drainer board before she ran out the back door to assess the damage. Trying to stay calm for Kristen's sake, she managed to gently ask, "My goodness, what happened?"

"Harry's hurt, Mommy," Kristen sobbed.

Harry winced when he saw his mother. Sylvia lifted the bike off her son. The position his arm was in confirmed her suspicions.

"Does your arm hurt?"

Harry tried to hold back tears because he did not want Kristen to see him cry. Sylvia calmly said, "We need to get you to the hospital for an x-ray to see what's wrong with your arm."

She knew it was broken and carefully helped him stand up. Kristen put her arms around her brother in an attempt to be of assistance. She didn't know what exactly was wrong but knew he was hurt, and she helped him, along with her mother, get into the car. Then she buckled herself in the seat next to him and held his hand.

The drive to St. Joseph Hospital's Emergency Room did not take more than fifteen minutes. It seemed like seconds from the time she registered Harry until he went back to the ER. He bravely walked with the nurse to get his arm x-rayed. Forty-five minutes later, he emerged wearing a shiny white cast. He looked at his mother and said, "I'm tired, Momma. Can we go home now?"

"Yes, my love, we can go home."

As Sylvia drove home, she listened to Kristen tell her brother a story in the back seat of their car. "Once upon a time, there was a brave knight named Sir Harry. His princess, Kristen, got locked up in a castle by a mean ogre." As Kristen's voice trailed off, Harry fell asleep.

The drive home felt longer to her than the drive to the hospital. When she noticed her brother had fallen asleep, Kristen kicked the driver's seat in front of her.

"Kristen!" Sylvia responded sharply. "How many times have I told you not to kick the seat!"

"When are we gonna get home?"

"In about five minutes. Do you have to go to the bathroom?"

"No, but Harry is asleep."

"That's ok, Kristen. Don't wake him."

Kristen stared out her car window. Just before her neighborhood came into sight, she dozed. Her mother let her sleep until she parked the car and turned the engine off.

"Kristen, it's time to wake up. We're home." Sylvia unbuckled her daughter's seat belt and helped her out of the car. Then she unbuckled her son and touched him gently.

"Harry, we're home. I need you to wake up."

He didn't want to wake up, but he was too heavy for his mother to pick up.

"Harry, you have to wake up. Do you want to spend the night in the car?"

"Ok, ok I'm awake," Harry said groggily. Then he stumbled out of the car. His mother grabbed his arm and guided him along the walkway while Kristen trailed behind, up the front steps and onto the porch.

"Kristen, I need your help. I can't unlock the door and hold onto your brother at the same time. I don't want him to fall again. You are a big girl now. I need you to do this for me," she said, handing the door key to Kristen.

Kristen looked confused because the door was slightly ajar. In her haste to get to the hospital, Sylvia had forgotten to lock it. "Oh, my goodness," she said. But Kristen did not open the door further because she heard noises coming from the direction of the kitchen. She tugged at her mother's sleeve.

"Kristen, please open the door."

Kristen balked. Calmly, Sylvia asked, "What is it, dear?"

"I hear noises in the kitchen. I am afraid to go in."

"That's Daddy. I told him we were at the hospital, and we would meet him at home. It's fine, go on in."

Kristen pushed the front door open for her mother, letting her step over the threshold and into the living room. Virgil came out of the kitchen when he heard the front door open.

Harry, barely awake, mumbled, "Hi Dad." Virgil scooped up his son and carried him to the sofa. Sylvia was about to ask Kristen to get her a blanket, but when she turned around, Kristen had already disappeared into her bedroom. Virgil looked at his son resting on the sofa. "How bad is the break?"

"Not as bad as I thought it could be, Virgil. The break could have been worse."

"How long will he be in the cast?"

"The doctor said about four to five weeks."

"That's good, still Harry will have to take it easy."

"Yes, the doctor said the same thing."

While Sylvia and Virgil talked softly, Kristen emerged from her bedroom wearing her nurse's costume from Halloween and carrying her favorite nap blanket with blue satin binding. She sat next to her brother pretending to take his blood pressure just like the nurses did in the ER. Sylvia smiled as she watched her daughter act so grown up.

"Perhaps this is a good omen," Sylvia said out loud. "She will be a good nurse."

6
HARRY

By the age of 13, Harry Warner knew he was an adrenaline junkie, pure and simple, no two ways about it. From his first bicycle ride down the driveway, he was addicted to the thrill of going fast, even when the outcome was broken bones, a bump to the head, or scratched knees and elbows.

The house directly across the street from the Warner's on Arlanda Drive stood vacant. It seemed to Harry that, as much as he wished for a boy his age to move in, it was just never going to happen. It was a sad little house that needed a family. Rumors had been circulating that a tragedy occurred in the house. No one knew why, but the rumor became increasingly embellished as time went on.

Then the impossible happened. Harry watched the moving company pull up in their long trailer and unload the family's few possessions into the vacant home. He was elated to see a boy about his age sitting on the front porch, reading a magazine. Curious and excited, Harry strode across the street and walked up to the porch.

"Hey, what are you looking at?"

The boy answered without looking up. "It's a motorcycle magazine. I'm gonna get one of these when I turn seventeen."

Harry was bewildered. "Not a car?" he asked.

"Nope, I want a fast bike." Looking up, the boy added, "My name's Mitch, by the way."

"Mine's Harry, I live across the street."

"I know who you are. You're that kid that almost got killed the other day trying to make daredevil jumps off homemade ramps. I saw you."

Without hesitation, Harry said, "I like to jump and go fast."

"Yeah, fast is good," Mitch said, then turned the magazine so Harry could see the motorcycle.

"Take a look at this bike."

"What kind is that?" Harry asked.

"It's a Kawasaki ZZ-R1100. She's a beauty."

"How fast is it?"

"Top speed, 175 mph."

"Whoa, that's a lot of power, Mitch."

"Yeah, too much for a kid like your age."

Harry winced, "How old are you?"

"Fifteen. And you?" Mitch asked, looking directly at Harry.

"Thirteen!" he replied.

That was all the motivation Harry needed. Once he saw that Kawasaki, his heart belonged to the motorcycle. In the meantime, he rode his bike even faster down the driveway. His tires spun out when he made a sharp turn before he flew out into the street.

Mitch recognized a kindred spirit in his new adrenaline junkie friend and knew he could feed into Harry's desire for speed and thrills. He knew his young friend wouldn't back down so, after his dad would go to sleep, and after Harry's parents' bedroom light had turned off, Mitch would throw a rock at Harry's bedroom window and challenge him to dangerous escapades. Harry would give the thumbs up and sneak out of the house, leaving the front door unlocked so he could sneak back in and not disturb his parents.

The boys would ride their bikes a few blocks until the hill on Maple Street came into view. Maple had a big drop halfway down before a stop light, so they rode to the top of the hill and stopped. Mitch counted one-two-three- as they peddled as fast as they could down the hill. They flew through the intersections until the road came to a dead end; then they would go back home.

These shenanigans continued until Mitch turned sixteen. That was when he started working in his dad's garage on Saturdays. He would sweep the floor and organize his dad's tools. He answered the telephone and booked appointments for car repairs and inspections. This gave Slim, Mitch's dad, time to work on his favorite mode of transportation: motorcycles. He had manuals for all makes and models.

One Saturday, Slim found Mitch engrossed in a repair manual. "Son," he said, "there are two kinds of people. There are Harley people and everyone else."

"What do you mean, Dad?"

"Let me explain. You have European bikes and Japanese bikes."

"I want a fast bike."

Slim continued, "Harley has made some nice bikes; they have been around for a long time."

"Really…like how long?"

"Since 1903, Son."

"So, where did they build them?"

"The Harley Company started in a shed. But bikes have been around longer than that."

"You mean before 1903?"

"Yes."

"You know a lot about bikes, Dad."

"Yes, I do. I love motorcycles. I often wonder what it was like to ride the first motorcycle."

"Why?"

"Because it was made of wood. It had a 265-cc single cylinder four stroke engine. They were made in Germany."

"Sounds kind of clunky."

"Yes, they were cumbersome. Took nine years before a 1500-cc twin cylinder engine was made to sit in a steel frame. That was the brainchild of Hildebrand and Wolfmüller; a liquid cooled engine."

"When was the wooden one built?"

"1885, I believe."

"Wow! Impressive."

"Yes, then France started building bikes, like the De Dion Bouton."

"What was so special about that one?"

"Well, first, bikes motors were positioned above the front wheel. They didn't look like bikes of today."

"Oh."

"Now here is a history lesson for you, Mitch. About 1901, I read that the engine was moved from above the front wheel to between the wheels in the triangular frame."

"Did the same people from France build it?"

"No, the Werner brothers, another French team, designed it."

"You said Harley Davidson started in 1903."

"Yes, but before that, in 1901 in the United States, two guys, George Hendee and Oscar Hedstrom, built the first Indian motorcycle. That's a cool bike. Shortly after that," Slim continued, "Milwaukee boasted the first Harley-Davidson. That was in 1901."

"Dad, you should have been a history teacher. I might have remembered important stuff."

"Listen to this, Mitch. By the end of the decade, motorcycle production took off in Europe and in America."

"Yeah, but in America it seems like a lot of people ride Harleys."

"There is a reason they do. It's their V-twin motorbikes. That's what they were called anyway. Through trial and error and perseverance, the model 11F was born in 1915. Anything worth having is worth doing. Stick to your dream and plan. Because the V-twin was Harley Davidson's trademark. Engines are important."

"I always took engines for granted. Like they were basic, I didn't think about how they were cooled."

"Mitch, the 11-F engine was air cooled. It had a four-valve inlet over exhaust 45-degree twin. Looked pretty in a frame."

"How fast did it go?"

"Top speed, sixty mph. That was fast back then."

"How did they stop?"

"That is an interesting question because we always think about brakes but, in the beginning, they didn't have front brakes! A part was invented called an expanded band in the rear that helped the 11-F stop. They have front brakes now."

"That's a relief, Dad. I know how much I depend on my bike's front brakes."

"One of my favorite Harley's is the V-Rod. I think it's a pretty bike. Has lots of power and speed. One burst from standstill can rev to 9000 rpm, redline through its five-speed gearbox in seconds."

"Like how?"

"Acceleration, Son. That bike accelerated cleanly from 200rpm and 30mph. Once over three thousand rpms made for a hell of a ride."

"I want a bike like that, Dad."

"You can when I approve."

"What's not to approve? You *love* motorcycles. You would be a hypocrite if you said no."

"Mitch, you must learn safety first."

"Like what?"

"To start, you have to be sixteen years old. And you have to be a resident of the state where you want to get your license."

"I am sixteen, is that all?"

"No, there is a lot more. You have to complete the motorcycle learner permit application. You must pass the DMV test. You must take the vision and screening test and the motorcycle knowledge test."

"I thought you would teach me all that."

"If you want to ride, Mitch, you have to take this seriously. You will take a class to learn how to ride. I will teach you the knowledge part."

"Ok, Dad. That's a deal."

"I mean it, Mitch, this is serious. No sneaking off on your bike before you get your license."

"I don't have a motorcycle. You talk like I do."

"You can save up for one. I plan to pay you more, and I want you to educate yourself so that you know what kind of bike you want and how to fix it. I will teach you motorcycle repair."

"I want something fast!"

"We shall see…" Slim replied to Mitch's emphatic desire to have a fast bike.

Several months passed, almost a year to be exact, since Mitch had begun working for his dad at the garage. Harry usually stopped in by himself. As of late, he was doing more and more without his sister. One Saturday afternoon, Kristen watched her brother stroll through the kitchen to the back door.

"Where are you going, Harry?"

"To Slim's Garage."

"Can I come too?"

"NO!" Harry answered sharply.

Kristen started to cry; big silent tears rolled down her cheeks. One look at her in tears softened his heart. "Ok, you can come with me, but don't touch anything! I mean it, Kristen."

"I won't touch anything, I promise."

Harry usually rode his bike to the garage in a matter of minutes, but today the trip took longer because he had to walk with his sister in tow. He purposely walked so fast that Kristen had to run to keep up. She didn't complain; she was happy to be with her big brother.

They arrived at the garage fifteen minutes from the time they left their house on Arlanda Drive. When Harry pushed open the door to the garage office, Mitch looked up from the motorcycle magazine he was reading and noticed Harry wasn't alone.

"Who's this?"

"This is my sister, Kristen."

"Oh, hi," said Mitch staring at her. He was taken by the color of her eyes; they were not blue nor were they green. They were the most exquisite shade of blue he had ever seen. Kristen felt slightly uncomfortable and mumbled, "Hi." Harry noticed the exchange and spoke up.

"I told her not to touch anything."

"As long as she does exactly as I say, then she can come back with you. I shouldn't let either of you back here, but I want to show you something special."

Harry squeezed Kristen's hand. "Don't touch anything!"

She pulled her hand away from his tight grip shouting, "I won't!"

Mitch led the way through the office and into the service bays of the garage. Slim had gone to lunch, and that was the only reason Harry and Kristen were allowed back. She noticed the garage smelled like engine oil and gas and rubber. It wasn't unpleasant as she looked around at all the tools hanging on peg boards on the back wall of the garage and the shelves lined with cans of oil, headlights, fuel pumps, and timing belts, spark plugs and tires. Her eyes followed the scent of oil and stopped at a rag laying on a work bench that looked like it had cleaned up a large oil spill. The garage was magical to her because her brother was happy there. Mitch interrupted her thoughts when he nudged Harry in the ribs.

"Ow...what did you do that for, Mitch?"

"I want to show you something. Look at that outrageous bike in the back near the tools. What do you think about that?"

"Looks kinda plain."

"I like it, looks like a spy plane."

"If you say so, what is it?"

"It's a Super Blackbird. Honda makes it, and it's named after a spy plane."

Harry walked around the bike looking at it from all angles. He stopped in front of the bike taking note of the narrow nose.

"Looks like a shark's nose."

"I know," said Mitch. "Look at these piggyback headlights. I've never seen twin lenses set above the other on any bikes before."

"Yeah, that's cool. But how fast does it go?"

Mitch explained that the bike could accelerate to 5000 rpm as it sent the rev counter needle around the dial to 10,000 rpm redline. "It's FAST, Harry."

"Sure would be fun to take it out."

"Don't tempt me, Harry. I know how to ride. I've been taking classes.

"You have?"

"Yeah, that was the deal I made with my dad. I would take classes and learn."

Harry walked around the bike again, then looked at Mitch. "I know you're tempted."

"I don't need much incentive, so be careful what you say next, Harry."

Kristen looked at her brother in disbelief. When he saw the look on her face, he knew that if they took the motorcycle out, it would be a bad decision. "I got to get going, Mitch."

"Ok, see ya." Mitch looked at Kristen and said, "Nice to have met you, kid."

Kristen waved, then walked back through the garage office, out the door, and stood on the sidewalk waiting for her brother. She kept her thoughts to herself until Harry had exited the office. She turned to face him. "I may be younger than you, but I think that Mitch is up to no good. Don't even think about getting on that motorcycle."

"Aw, you worry too much," Harry said, but he couldn't get the Super Blackbird out of his mind.

That evening after Slim had gone to bed, Mitch sneaked out of the house and went to the garage. He wanted to look at the Super Blackbird again, but after seeing the bike, he realized that just a look was not enough. Fate had tempted him. A little spin wouldn't hurt, he thought. After all, he was sixteen, almost seventeen, and he had finished his classes. Surely, he could manage the bike. He quietly rolled the bike out of the bay before locking the garage door.

Mitch thought about the midnight bike races he challenged Harry to not that long ago. He knew if Harry was still awake, he wouldn't have to twist his friend's arm to go for a ride. Mitch jumped on the bike and headed toward Arlanda Drive. When he was about a block away, he turned off the engine and rolled the bike until he turned onto the Warner's driveway.

Unbeknown to Mitch, Harry had just turned off the light in his room. He had been reading an article about the Super Blackbird in his Motorcycle Madness magazine and had not changed his clothes from earlier in the day. Mitch picked up a piece of gravel and threw it at Harry's window. Accustomed to hearing that certain ping sound, Harry got off his bed to see what Mitch was up to. Down below, on the gravel driveway, he saw Mitch sitting on the Super Blackbird, motioning for him to come down.

Excited, Harry picked up his shoes and quietly crept downstairs. In his haste to get to the bike, he forgot to latch the front door. He walked around the house to the driveway where he found Mitch, grinning from ear to ear. "Wanna go for a ride?"

"Of course, what do you take me for, a sissy?"

"Help me push this bike down the street. You don't want the ride to be over because your parents woke up, do you?" Harry's emphatic, "No," removed any doubt Mitch might have had about taking the bike out. When they were two blocks away, Mitch showed Harry the start-up procedure.

"First, ya got to unlock the forks. This next step is important, Harry, so pay attention. You got to be in neutral to engage the clutch. See this switch here, that's the power switch. Oh yeah, you got to wear a helmet," Mitch said as he handed Harry a helmet. "Make sure it's strapped on tight."

After Harry put the helmet on and adjusted the straps, Mitch asked, "You good?" Harry gave him the thumbs up; he was ready to get on the bike. Then Mitch pushed the power switch and let the motor idle. He kicked the bike in gear and off they flew on the Super Blackbird into the still, dark night.

The boys had an exhilarating ride racing through the quiescent streets as the trees on either side of the streets blurred into a dark wave. They flew past their neighbors' houses and past St. Joseph's Hospital, then under the all-seeing steeple of St. Ambrose.

Mitch stopped the bike and turned around to face Harry. "Wanna go on the highway?" Harry gave him the thumbs up. Then Mitch said, "You better hold on tight."

Mitch fired the throttle, then cycled through the gears that sent the rev counter needle around the dial to 10,000 rpms redline in seconds.

On the highway, the bike had too much power for a novice driver. Failing to commit to it, Mitch went too hot into a curve. In a panic, he stabbed the back brake, causing the bike to high side. Mitch was thrown from the motorcycle and sent flying through the air, landing in a trash-filled ravine that ran alongside the road. He had broken his neck.

Harry was pinned underneath the motorcycle, which was heavier than the bike that landed on him when he was ten years old. When Mitch went flying through the air, the bike crashed onto the road and skidded to the curb, taking Harry with it, scraping his limbs as they were dragged across the pavement. Unaware of what had happened to Mitch, Harry was unable to move, quickly losing consciousness.

Bud Hurst, a motorcycle enthusiast, had been driving on the same highway for an hour when he saw the crumpled bike on the side of the road. He stopped his travel RV a distance from the wreck and got out. As he approached the carnage, he saw Mitch's lifeless body a few feet from the motorcycle, laying in the ravine, and thought he could hear moaning from underneath the bike. Bud tried to pull the motorcycle off Harry, but his feet slipped on the oily surface, and he almost lost his grip on the bike. Getting a stronger stance, he tried again and was able to successfully grip the handlebar with one hand and the back of the seat with the other hand and heave. After a few attempts, the bike was upright, and the now-shaky kickstand managed to hold it in place. Bud checked to see if the young boy found underneath had a pulse and was still breathing. He was relieved to find the boy alive. Then he stepped into the ravine to check on the other boy, not knowing which one had been driving, and which had been the backseat rider. The second boy was not breathing and, by the look of how the body landed, it was probably for the best. "Such a waste," he said out loud, before dialing 911.

Bud felt anguish for the boys and their parents, thinking one of these boys would not grow up, get married, or have a family. He thought maybe even both boys' lives could end tragically after such an accident.

Then, it dawned on him why his wife, Mary Jane, was always furious when he took their young son, Tim, for a ride on his motorcycle. He never had an accident those times, but what if he had? Is this what Mary Jane would have to deal with? He was selfish with his traveling thrill jump show that ended his marriage. But it was too late to repair the damage that had already been done. The accident, while tragic, was an epiphany that, if he had made better choices, he would still have his family.

The ambulance flashed its red lights as the deafening blare of the siren woke Bud from his thoughts. When the ambulance came to a halt, a paramedic threw open the double back doors and jumped out.

"Did you see what happened?"

"No," answered Bud.

"Did you run these boys into a curve?"

"I told you, no. I was driving and saw the wreckage so I pulled over to see if I could help." The paramedic quickly assessed Harry. Bud stood by, helplessly listening to the paramedic call for an evac helicopter. His partner, the driver, got out and covered Mitch's body with a sheet. The partner looked up and asked, "Any ID on these boys?"

He looked at Bud and asked again. Bud stuck to his story. He had been driving on the highway when he came upon the accident and hadn't checked for ID. Then the paramedic told his partner to call Kauffman's Funeral Home because Mr. Kauffman could probably identify the boys.

Within minutes Mr. Kauffman arrived on the scene as the whirling of the evac helicopter's blades sounded in the distance.

The first paramedic asked Mr. Kaufman if he could ID the boys. "I'll try," he responded.

He looked at the bodies and immediately recognized Harry. "That's Virgil and Sylvia Warner's boy, Harry."

"What about the other boy, can you ID him?"

Mr. Kauffman walked over to Mitch's lifeless body lying in a heap. When he pulled the sheet off, he instantly recognized the body as Slim's boy, Mitch, from the garage.

"I'll tell Slim. These calls are the worst," he said, as he pulled the sheet back over Mitch's body. The paramedic asked, "Do you want me to notify the Warner's that their son was in an accident and has been evacuated to St. Joseph's?"

Mr. Kauffman, dreading the task of telling Slim his son was dead, answered, "They live on the same street, across from each other. I'll stop by and tell the Warner's first so they can get to the hospital. Then I'll go tell Slim about his son." Mr. Kauffman loaded Mitch's body into the hearse thinking how nothing else could be done for the boy except to make him look as normal as possible for the funeral.

For the moment, Harry was alive. How long, Mr. Kauffman could not say. But, based on the extent of his injuries, he did not think the boy would be alive much longer. He did not want to deliver this news to the Warner's either.

Kristen tossed and turned. She could not get to sleep. Something inside her heart made her feel sad. Usually when she had nights like this, Harry would let her drag a blanket into his room. His rule: she could lie on the floor next to his bed but not get in it. That was all she needed and would fall back to sleep. But tonight felt different. Kristen crept into Harry's room and stood next to his empty bed. She didn't know what to do in her panicked state other than rush downstairs into her parents' bedroom.

On her way past the living room, she noticed the front door ajar. Just as she was ready to shut it, a car pulled up in front of their house. Kristen shrieked! Her mother heard her distress and ran out of her bedroom, tying her bathrobe around her waist. Her husband was not far behind. "Kristen!" What is all this hysterical shrieking about?" her mother demanded. Kristen could not answer her mother and started to cry. Sylvia crouched in front of her daughter, then opened her arms. All Kristen could do was stand there motionless.

Mr. Kauffman knocked on the front door just as Virgil turned on the porch light. When he opened the door, he gasped at Mr. Kauffman. This was not a social visit at this late hour and could only mean one thing, although Virgil was clueless as to why Mr. Kauffman was there. Before Mr. Kauffman could speak, Sylvia pulled Kristen close to her breast. Mr. Kauffman acknowledged Sylvia before turning to Virgil, motioning for him to step outside. No need for the child to hear this kind of news from him; that would be better handled by her parents. After stepping several yards from the listening ears of mother and daughter, Mr. Kauffman explained the reason for his late night visit.

"There is no easy way to say this. Harry has been in an accident. He was flown to St. Joseph's Hospital."

Virgil was stunned. "How can this be, I thought Harry was in bed, asleep."

"Best I can tell, Mr. Warner, is that the accident involved a motorcycle."

"Was he alone?"

"All I can say at present is, no. I am sorry to have to deliver this news."

Virgil stood motionless as he watched Mr. Kauffman get into his vehicle and drive away. He walked back to the porch in wide-eyed shock and said, "There must have been a fatality or Mr. Kauffman would not have been called to the scene."

"Virgil! Is it Harry?"

"Yes, but thank God, he has been flown to St. Joseph's Hospital. He's been in an accident. I don't know any other specifics about what happened or who he was with. I need you to stay here with Kristen. There's no need for her to hear or see anything until we know what's going on. I'm going to the hospital; I will call you as soon as I know something."

Sylvia squeezed Kristen tightly. "Mommy, I can't breathe. You're squishing me."

"Honey, I'm so sorry," Sylvia said, as she released her tight grip on her daughter.

Kristen noticed her mother's distress and asked, "Is Harry gonna die?"

"Your brother has been in an accident. That is all I know."

Kristen started to cry, "I…I don't want him to die."

"Neither do I. We should get dressed so we are ready when Daddy calls."

"Ok," murmured Kristen.

Virgil returned to the house to grab his shoes, wallet, and keys, and headed to St. Joseph's. Sylvia and Kristen began dressing. Sylvia tried not to pace around the house too much while she waited on the call from Virgil. They did not have to wait long. Sylvia had just finished getting dressed when the telephone rang in the kitchen. Before she could say "hello" her husband began to speak. "Sylvia, Harry is in bad shape, does not look good. I will pick you and Kristen up in fifteen minutes. I don't know what to tell her."

"We will tell her the truth, Virgil. Harry has been seriously hurt and is sleeping."

Sylvia no sooner finished her sentence than Virgil hung up. She instructed Kristen to finish getting dressed, to put on her jacket, and wait by the front door. When her dad drove up, Kristen ran out the front door, got into the back seat, and buckled her seatbelt. Her mother closed the door behind them, then got into the car.

The drive to the hospital felt like an eternity to Kristen. She noticed her mother's tears and that her parents said very little to each other. Her dad pulled up to the front entrance to the hospital and stopped the car.

"You go on in while I park the car. I have already seen Harry, but you two need to go now." He didn't know if Harry would be alive. He hoped for their sake he would be, as he was barely breathing when he left to pick them up at home.

Sylvia wasted no time going through the revolving doors of the hospital, but Kristen balked. "This is no time for silliness, Kristen. You will not get stuck. Take my hand," she demanded. With Kristen in tow, Sylvia moved through the revolving doors and into the lobby, grateful there was not a line at the front desk.

The receptionist looked up. "May I help you?"

"My son, Harry Warner, was admitted earlier this morning. Can you please tell me where I will find him."

"First, I need some verification. What is his birthdate?"

"March 4, 1965."

"Address?" The receptionist continued without showing any emotion to the obviously bereft mother in front of her. Sylvia was exasperated.

"Don't you already have this information. My husband was just here."

"I'm sorry, Ma'am, it's protocol."

"If you must," Sylvia complained because every second she wasted checking in was one less she would have with her son. "1215 Arlanda Drive, Culver Heights."

"Thank you, your son is in bay 3. A nurse will be out shortly to take you to him. You may have a seat in the waiting room."

Kristen walked with her mother to the waiting area. She observed many people in various states of illness and, for some reason, felt their pain and anguish, even though she was not prepared to see her brother. While she was absorbed with her thoughts, a nurse in blue scrubs called out, "Sylvia."

"I'm Sylvia," her mother said. She stood up and took Kristen's hand and followed the nurse into the treatment area of the Emergency Room. The nurse stopped in front of bay 3, pulled aside the curtain that surrounded Harry's bay, and looked at Sylvia.

"Here is your son. Are you ready to go in?" as pleasantly as she could under the circumstances. As a seasoned ER nurse, she never got over the death of a child. These were the worst. She turned to Sylvia a second time and said, "I am so sorry," then left.

Sylvia nodded, but she wasn't prepared for what she saw. Her husband told her Harry was in bad shape, but nothing could have made this any easier. There lay her son, wrapped up in white gauze with tubes under his skin, hooked up to monitors that beeped every five minutes. Harry was miraculously breathing on his own.

The nurse came back in and pulled up a chair for Sylvia next to the bed. Before sitting down, she bent over Harry and kissed him on the cheek. The she leaned close to his ear and whispered, "Mommy's here." Kristen stood on the opposite side of her brother's gurney. She picked up his other hand and noticed it felt warm. She wished her brother would open his eyes.

Meanwhile, Virgil could not find a parking space on either of the first two floors. He circled to the third floor noticing a car pulling out of a space. After he parked the car and turned the engine off, he took out a piece of paper and pen from the glove compartment and wrote down the floor and space number. As he wrote, he repeated out loud, third floor, space number 4. Then it dawned on him that was Harry's birthday. "You'd think I could remember that" he said out loud, but his mind was on other things, as time was of the essence.

Harry had sustained massive internal injuries and may not be alive when he returned. Taking the stairs instead of waiting for the elevator, he flew past the receptionist as he flashed his visitors badge from earlier that morning. He didn't need an escort since the nursing staff was expecting his return. Virgil paused before he pulled the curtain open to Harry's bay. He took a deep breath, then went in. He bent over his son and kissing him on the forehead, said, "Your mother and sister are here."

Harry opened his eyes. "I love you, son," Virgil said. Harry blinked. Sylvia wiped her eyes.

"Harry, my son, my beautiful boy. I love you."

He blinked again and turned his eyes toward Kristen. His breath became shallower but did not set off any alarms. Kristen climbed up on the bed and laid next to him. She turned her mouth toward his ear and began to tell him a story. "Once upon a time, there was a brave knight named Sir Harry. His only purpose in life was to rescue Princess Kristen who had been locked up in a castle by a mean ogre. Sir Harry heard the Princess's cries from her prison cell. He followed her voice, but the mean ogre tried to stop him. He wanted the Princess all to himself. Sir Harry drew his sword and shouted at the ogre, 'Get out of my way or I will run you through with my sword.' The ogre was afraid of Sir Harry. He grabbed the key that the ogre held in his hand to the Princess's cell. Sir Harry pushed him aside and unlocked the cell door. Princess Kristen ran out of the cell toward Sir Harry. He took her hand in his and guided her out into the sunshine."

Kristen had no sooner finished her story than the alarm on Harry's monitor went off. Nurses rushed into Harry's bay and started to run a code, but Virgil put up his hand to stop them. When he looked at the monitor, there was a flat line where there should have been a heartbeat. He nodded to the nurse that she could turn the monitor off; Harry had passed away peacefully surrounded by his loving family.

Kristen continued to lie next to her brother. She didn't realize what had happened until she saw her mother sobbing into a tissue. The nurse left the room and returned a few minutes later with an attending doctor who approached Harry's bed and took out his stethoscope, placing it on Harry's chest. He listened but heard no heartbeat. Then he quietly called it. "Time of death: 9:06 a.m."

7

TWO KINDS OF PEOPLE

A cool breeze floated eastward across the Pacific Ocean, stirring the fog that clung to the cliffs overlooking the dark water, as a thin beam of light rose on the eastern horizon. Tim didn't know how long he had been driving. His thoughts were consumed with the woman in the red dress and wondering why he felt so drawn to her. All he knew after his drive was that she would haunt his dreams until he found her.

Usually after a late-night function, Shelly didn't schedule any appointments for him the next day. He knew he should not drive around with a half million-dollar check in his pocket, and sometime during the day he should make the deposit. Until then, he decided to return home and get some sleep.

After a five-hour deep sleep and a cool shower, Tim put on clean black slacks and a freshly laundered white shirt. Even though he was not conducting business, he decided he should wear a tie. He walked over to his dresser, opened the top right drawer, and let his eyes roam over the neatly folded stacks of ties until they fell on a conservative one with black, burgundy and forest green stripes. He put the tie around his neck, under his button down white collared shirt, and let it dangle on either side.

A gnawing feeling and deep rumble coming from Tim's stomach

reminded him that he hadn't had anything to eat since the day before. Hoping he had something in his refrigerator, Tim rummaged around until he found a chocolate protein shake in the back. The carton showed that the drink hadn't reached its expiration date. Satisfied, he shook it, unscrewed the cap, and consumed the shake in three gulps, then threw the carton in the trash can under his kitchen sink. Quickly brushing his teeth in the half bath off the kitchen, he inspected his pearly whites in the mirror before realizing he hadn't tied his necktie.

The drive to the bank felt like minutes because Tim's thoughts once again turned to the woman in the red dress. He pulled up to the bank and parked in the parking spot designated for the bank's vice president. He could see Shelly through the glass doors, watching him from her head teller position behind the counter. When he entered through the bank doors, she pretended not to see him as she counted the money in her cash drawer. Tim stopped in front of her station, but she did not look up. Instead, she made him wait until she had finished counting the stack of money, then nonchalantly asked, "How was your evening, Tim?"

"Interesting," he replied.

"Was your admirer there?"

Tim responded to her inquiry, "Of course she was."

Shelly blushed; she could not fathom, nor did she want to know, how her boss managed to secure such large checks from his client. Tim winked, which made her turn a darker shade of scarlet. Without hesitation, she asked, "Did you have a nice time?"

"Not really."

"You would have if I had been your plus one. I would have made sure of it."

"You think so, Shel?"

"I know so, Tim."

"I listened to a boring speech. If this is your idea of fun, then maybe the next time you can go with me."

Tim looked intently at Shelly. He leaned over the counter so that no one else in the line that had formed behind him could hear, "I am certain you would look stunning."

Shelly blushed from her cheeks, down her neck, and across her cleavage.

"Excuse me, my throat is dry. I need some water," she said.

Tim winked as he turned away with a smile. He knew Shelly had a crush on him and that he shouldn't play with her emotions. On occasion, he thought about asking her out for a drink, but never did. He surmised that if he mixed business with pleasure, that could be a recipe for disaster, and he really wasn't that interested in her.

Disappearing into his office, he thought his first order of business should be Helen's check. He sat the briefcase on top of his desk and opened it, expecting to see his client's file. Instead, his motorcycle drawings lay on top of it.

Distracted, Tim started thinking about motorcycles. He didn't know if he was going to buy one or build one, as each had its own set of problems. He picked up the drawings, discovering Helen's check underneath. Thoughts about the bike would have to wait. His first order of business was to process the check; that involved several steps. He wrote up a sales slip that contained pertinent information. He was careful not to let his mind wander to the bike or the woman in the red dress.

The bank had strict policies that required his full attention: where he received the check, who the check was from, what was purchased and how much, and the date and personal information about his client. He then made three copies of the sales slip; one for Helen, one for her file, and one for the back office.

With the sales slip in hand, Tim walked out of his office and stood in front of Shelly. She looked up from her computer where she had been reconciling business accounts and inquired, "How may I help you?" She knew Tim needed her to buzz him in so that he could make the deposit in the back office. She enjoyed the suspense she created, since she could play the game just as well as he did.

After Tim made the deposit, he walked across the lobby and back into his office. He sat at his desk and stared at the motorcycle plans in front of him. He liked speed, particularly the Ducati 916. There was something about the 916's eight valve engine that was charismatic. It was a majestic machine. Its midrange response rocketed out of corners. Its high rev acceleration sent the bike to 160 mph in no time. It was not a machine for riding in town but on the right road it was pure magic.

If someone were to ask Tim why he liked the Ducati, he would say, "That's easy, it's beautiful!" The Ducati was a contender, but it had one significant drawback. It was not for long-distance rides. Long distance was a key factor in the creation of a high-performance machine. Tim reasoned, if he were to take a cross-country trip when he retired, he must have a motorcycle capable of not only being comfortable, but also a joy to ride and one that could go fast.

He remembered how his dad talked about a BMW R90S when he had the brilliant idea to become a stunt rider. Bud said that taking a leisurely ride on that bike would help clear his head after a show, provided he had not killed himself. There were features he found appealing, such as a large gas tank and a second front disc brake. But did he really need an excuse?

"Tim," Bud would say when they talked about the BMW R90S, "This bike manages well despite its soft suspension. Don't let it fool you. It is an incredibly special bike and it's not cheap. Costs twice as much as other bikes on the market. Only a select few can buy a bike like this. It can be fast; it handles well, and its comfortable."

Tim remembered a sign on the wall of Slim's Garage where his dad's mechanic worked.

THERE ARE TWO KINDS OF PEOPLE.
HARLEY PEOPLE AND EVERYONE ELSE.

"Aw the V-Rod, a very exciting bike," his dad had said when he found Tim staring at the sign. That was not the only memory that suddenly surfaced. He remembered Slim's son, Mitch, talking to another boy about the same age as himself and there was a little girl waiting on the sidewalk outside the office door. He only saw her the one time. She was about ten years old and wore blue jeans, a t-shirt, and red Ked sneakers. He remembered she had long blonde hair and briefly saw her exquisite blue eyes. He had never seen anyone with eyes that shade of blue.

"No, it can't be!" Tim said out loud. "No-way! Maybe? I'm imagining things."

But that was not the case. He could not get the woman in the red dress out of his mind. What use would it be for him to brood over the fact that he had no idea who she was, where she worked, or if she lived in the same town. He could ask Helen Trenton, she knew everyone. But that might not be in his best interest, business wise. If Helen thought he was romantically interested in someone, she might not be his client. No, he surmised, it would be better to continue to play the game with Helen.

Tim had not thought about the house he grew up in for decades, and this woman in the red dress made him think about those years.

When his mother needed an assisted living residence, he sold her house to help pay for her living arrangements and never gave his childhood home, or Culver Heights, for that matter, a second thought. Because of her failing health, Mary Jane soon forgot who he was, but that didn't matter to him. She was his mother, and he wouldn't abandon her just because she didn't remember him.

He visited her once a week on the same day of the week and at the same time. He thought consistency in his visits might help her remember him. He brought her a new bouquet each visit from the nearby florist. He would make a grand presentation of the flowers as if she were his queen. Mary Jane would smile and blush. She perked up whenever he brought her a new bouquet.

One day, he surprised her with plumeria. Mary Jane ooed and awed over the flower's delicate, pink blooms that were outlined in fuchsia with a pale-yellow center. Their fragrance filled her room with notes of jasmine and coconut.

Sometimes the blooms he brought her reminded him of cinnamon and citrus. He tried to bring different scents to pique her memory. Sometimes when his mother was arranging her flowers in a vase, he thought she remembered him. He never gave up hope that one day she would.

That was the main reason he had not retired, even though he had the means to do so. If someone asked why he was still working, he would say he liked his job, and he liked to make money for his clients and for himself. But deep down, he knew the truth. He stayed at the job so he would be able to stay close to his mother, just in case she needed or remembered him.

As for his father, Tim had no idea where he was. One day he simply disappeared, left no forwarding address, nothing! At first, Tim felt betrayed, but then he reconciled himself to the fact that his father would resurface sometime, if he had not killed himself.

During his reverie, Tim did not see or hear Shelly knock on his office door. "Tim, have you finished your notes for Helen Trenton's file?" The sound of her voice quickly brought his sensibilities to the present.

"Yes, I have finished. Thank you for asking."

Shelly smiled, then said, "That's my job, to keep you in line."

Tim got up from behind his desk with Helen's file in hand, following the head teller to the front counter, wherein she produced her key and opened the half door between the lobby and the other teller's stations. After he made the deposit, he returned to his office and attempted to call on his clients. He would start to dial a number, then hang up. He stared out his window for several minutes thinking about the woman in the red dress until he decided to call it quits for the day. He walked to Shelly's station and announced, "I'm going to take the rest of the afternoon off. I will be in tomorrow. You have my cell number if something comes up."

Shelly secretly hoped Tim would stay at the bank. She liked him. While he flirted with her, she was not about to let him know how she felt. She took a deep breath and casually looked up from her computer, "Have a nice afternoon, Tim."

"Thanks Shelly."

The banker turned and walked back into his office to collect his motorcycle plans and briefcase. Whether he would work on the drawings was questionable, as his mind was on something else. He waved to Shelly as he proceeded to walk through the lobby, through the glass doors, and to his car.

The sky was a brilliant blue and the air crisp and clean. He unlocked his BMW and lowered himself into the driver's seat. Tossing his briefcase onto the passenger seat, he loosened his tie and rolled up his shirt sleeves before depressing the button that retracted the convertible roof somewhere behind the back seat. Once the roof was secured, Tim pushed the ignition, and the car sprang to life as it made deep, guttural purrs of a contented large feline. Tim shifted into gear and then accelerated like a shot from a cannon reaching seventy mph in seconds.

The quiescent streets at high noon were a rarity for Tim, since Terrance drove him most of the time, and rush hour extended well past five o'clock in the evening. It was a moving parking lot, murderous for clutch driven vehicles, and merciful to the automatic transmission drivers. Tim sped onto Marquis Boulevard, then took a quick right-hand turn that put him on the expressway. The air that had been crisp only minutes earlier suddenly changed. Warm, dry air swirled around him as his shirt sleeves fluttered in the breeze.

Culver Heights, where Tim grew up, was about an hour's drive from his house in LA. He had not thought much about going back until a quiet nudge tugged at his heart that said, "Go home." While he drove, Tim thought more and more about his dad. Bud was the reason he had fallen in love with motorcycles. By his example, Tim understood why his dad would suggest to his mechanic to take certain components of a particular model and marry that part or parts onto the frame of another model to create something unique and special. One motorcycle Bud never tampered with was the Honda CB750, a superbike all its own in rank and design. When Tim asked his dad why, he would say, "Wind and vibration, a perfect balance."

Tim depressed the accelerator that skyrocketed him out of his motorcycle thoughts. He glanced over his shoulder and marveled at the Pacific Ocean on his left. Myriads of diamonds danced and sparkled on the surface of the water. He temporarily forgot about the woman in the red dress, as he became one with the car, the road, and the sunshine. Wind and vibration were magic.

The drive along the coast to his old neighborhood did not take long, as his mind emptied of the things that were completely out of his control. Before he realized, his car was suddenly in front of Slim's vacant garage. Tim got out of his car and stood there while remembering a conversation he had with his dad about his first bike.

"Dad, why can't I have a CB750?"

Bud thought about how he would answer his son without nixing the CB750, which had entirely too much power for a novice. "Because you need to take a class on a bike that will not intimidate you the first time you get on it."

"Oh, like what?"

"Son, I think you would do well with a Norton Commando."

"Then I could upgrade to something else, like the CB750?"

"Don't get ahead of yourself, Tim. You haven't sat on a bike, let alone driven one."

"What's it like, riding a motorcycle, Dad?"

"It's kind of like the feeling you get when you ride a bicycle."

"Yeah, I get it…but like fast!"

"Tim, while a motorcycle is an upgrade from a bike, it is different. You must respect the machine. You must be aware of your surroundings.

You are more vulnerable on the street because motorists don't care about motorcyclists."

"They should, Dad."

"I know…but they don't. So that's why I suggested a Norton. You will be able to put your feet on the ground, be comfortable in the seat, and not have too much power. Maybe … maybe once you have mastered that, you can get a Velocette Venom Thruxton."

"That name sounds wicked."

"It's a little quirky, Son. Like it's not the easiest to live with, but when it is running well, it delivers a thrilling blend of long-legged and high-speed cruising."

"Sounds interesting, Dad."

"If you want a bike that looks good, I suggest a Kawasaki Zx-12R. It is a handsome bike. But if you are into long distance rides, you can't beat a BMW R90S."

"Why?"

"As I told you before, it is great for long distance. The kind when you are not in a hurry to be anywhere. The kind you can take out on a sunny day. Go for a ride along the coast, take in the scenery. Maybe a stop at a lakeside winery for a leisurely bottle of cabernet sauvignon or shiraz with someone whose company you enjoy. Then, after the wine has settled, get back on your bike and ride to the wharf. I hear they have the best seafood. While you are savoring your Dungeness crab, watch the sun sink into the ocean. But don't take your eyes off the horizon for a second or you will miss the sizzle of the sun's fiery flames in the black water. Sounds like the perfect day to me, Tim."

"Why didn't you take Mom on a ride like that?"

"She was afraid to ride. Nothing I could say would convince her otherwise."

"Oh … you could have had fun."

"You know that, and I know that, but your mom and I fought too much over the motorcycle."

Tim shook his head sadly, thinking about the conversation. He didn't hear footsteps approaching from behind.

"What are you shaking your head for?" Tim heard a voice ask. "Do you want to buy the place?"

Tim turned around to see who was speaking.

"I didn't know it was for sale." He suddenly recognized Kaos, who was just as surprised to see Tim.

"Hey, you're the guy that tried to kill me last night! And no, the place isn't for sale because I bought it."

Tim mumbled, "Yeah that was me."

Kaos didn't say anything for a few minutes. Then he asked, "You want to see the place? It's been vacant for a long time. Not sure what we will find in there. Nobody wanted to buy the place after Slim closed shop and Bud took off."

"WAIT, hold up there, Kaos. You know somebody named Bud?"

"Yeah, used to ride the roads with him. I would fix his bikes after he wrecked them. He was popular and didn't back down from a challenge. Always had to outperform his last stunt."

"Do you know where he is?"

"First of all, who are you and who is Bud to you?"

"Bud is my dad! I take it you haven't seen him in a while."

"Oh, I've seen him."

"What do you mean?"

"His last stunt was his last stunt. He should have retired long before this. I must warn you; Bud is banged up pretty good."

Tim was both elated and angry that someone other than him knew where his dad was.

"Where is he, Kaos?"

"He is in critical care at St. Joseph's. You need to know, he's in a coma. I can take you; you seem pretty shook up."

"Wouldn't you be? I haven't seen nor heard from my dad in years, and now you tell me you have been with him all this time! I'm his son, I should have known where he was and what he was doing, not you!"

Kaos, realizing the stress of the situation, calmly asked again, "You want me to drive you?"

"Yeah, I don't trust myself. Truthfully, I'm overwhelmed."

The only person Tim allowed to drive his car was Terrance, but now, he didn't care who drove. He just wanted to get to his dad.

The trip to the hospital felt endless, longer than it should have since the hospital was near Slim's Garage. Kaos barely stopped in front of the main entrance to the hospital before Tim pushed the passenger door open and jumped out.

There's something about that man and car doors, Kaos thought, remembering the day before and how Tim almost knocked him off his bike. He didn't say that. He started to say, "I'll be here," but he knew his words would fall on deaf ears.

Tim pushed through the revolving glass doors with the moving floor, then stopped in front of the receptionist's desk. As soon as she looked up from her computer, he blurted out, "I'm here to see my dad, Bud Hurst." He didn't wait for her to respond before shoving his ID in front of her face. "I'm his son, Tim Hurst."

"I can see that; you may put your ID away."

Tim put his ID back into his wallet and started to walk away until the receptionist reminded him that he had no idea where to find his dad.

"Mr. Hurst," she called. "You need to put this visitor's badge on. Your dad is in intensive care. I will call an escort for you."

Tim took the visitor badge from the receptionist and clipped it to his shirt muttering, "Thanks." While waiting for the escort, he paced back and forth in front of the elevator. Just when he turned to ask the receptionist to check on the escort, the elevator doors opened. A nurse in navy blue scrubs emerged, looking straight at Tim. "You must be Mr. Hurst."

"Yes, yes I am."

"I'm Cheryl, I have been taking care of your dad. You can follow me; I will take you to him." On their ride up to the Intensive Care Unit, Cheryl informed Tim of what he already knew. "Your dad is in a coma in the

Intensive Care Unit and has been agitated today. I am extremely glad for his sake that you are here."

"Oh? Why is that?" Tim asked.

"He is waiting for someone. I trust that is you. He can't speak, but he can hear you. You should know he has a DNR order."

When the elevator doors dinged open on the fifth floor, Tim turned to follow Cheryl to his dad. She stopped in front of Bud's hospital room and, taking a deep breath and comforting voice, said, "Take all the time you need."

Tim nodded. As they entered the room, he saw his dad, vulnerable and frail, hooked up to bells and whistles with monitors flashing. All of Tim's pent-up anger, disappointment, and frustration disappeared when he stood by his dad's bed. Tim spoke the only thing he wanted his dad to hear "I love you, Dad." Bud's eyes began to flutter.

Tim turned to Cheryl, "Does he know me?"

She paused before answering. "I can confidently say he does. As I said before, he has been agitated all day. When I told him his son was here, he settled down. I didn't have to give him a sedative. He knows your voice."

Tim didn't know what he would say next. In his mind, he had rehearsed over and over what he thought he would say when the occasion presented. For some reason, none of that mattered anymore.

Bending over to kiss his dad on the forehead, Tim whispered in his ear, "I love you Dad, and I forgive you." He had no sooner finished his sentence than Bud drew a final breath. He exhaled one more time. Tim waited for him to take another breath, but there wasn't one.

Suddenly the waves on the monitor screen flatlined. Cheryl took out her stethoscope and placed it on Bud's chest. She listened intently for a faint heartbeat, but it was absent. Then she walked over to the monitors and turned them off. She removed anything that would restrict Tim from getting close to his dad. Turning to Tim, she said, "He's gone. I am so sorry for your loss. Take all the time you need." Then she left and closed the door behind her.

Tim sobbed as he laid his arms around his dad's lifeless body. When he felt like he had cried rivers of tears, he opened the door to his dad's room, surprised to see Kaos standing there.

"He's gone, Kaos. How can I thank you?"

"You can't," said Kaos "because there is no such thing as coincidence."

"I guess I should make some kind of arrangements," Tim muttered.

"There's no need, Tim. Your dad gave me POA over his affairs and final requests. I will take care of all of that for you."

Tim quickly regained his composure as he thought of his mother. "Kaos, would you mind driving me over to State Street? My mom is in a nursing home there. I should tell her about my dad."

"Not a problem, Tim. I am here at your service."

Tim noticed Kaos was non emotive, especially since Bud just passed.

"Kaos, don't you feel anything? Aren't you sad?"

"I said goodbye to Bud. I feel sad for you, though. You ready to go now?"

"Yes."

In the meantime, Mary Jane Hurst was having a difficult day. She had been restless, which was uncharacteristic of her usual good nature. Her nurse, Angela, wrote a note in her chart. She turned to her co-worker at the nurse's station.

"I hope her son shows up today. I know he is good about visiting and today is not his usual day, but maybe he can calm her down. I don't want to restrain or medicate her unnecessarily."

The other nurse thought for a moment about Mary Jane's behavior, then asked, "Has she been saying anything differently today that is not like her?" Angela reported that Mary Jane kept repeating the name, "Bud," over and over. "Who do you think Bud is, Angela?"

"I don't know. I believe she was married at one time, but Tim Hurst, her son, is the only contact we have for her."

Suddenly, the alarm in Mary Jane's room pierced the quiet nurse's station, causing Angela to jump unexpectedly. Without hesitating, she ran to Mary Jane's room in time to see her leaning over the rails, stretching out her arms, repeating over and over, "Bud, it's you, I knew you would come back for me." Then she fell back on her pillow, closing her eyes.

Tim's cell phone rang while Kaos was driving him to State Street. He didn't feel like answering, hoping it would stop. But when it rang persistently, he looked at the number and recognized it as his mother's nursing home.

"Hello, Tim speaking."

The voice on the other end identified herself. "Mr. Hurst, I'm Angela. I have been taking care of your mother. I think you should come today."

Alarmed, Tim inquired, "What's wrong?"

"Your mother has not been herself; she is extremely agitated."

"I'm actually on my way over now," Tim replied. "I'll be there in about five minutes."

"Ok, good. We will be waiting for you.

Tim wondered if the phone call was a harbinger. He had already lost his dad. What now, his mother, too?

Kaos pulled up in front of the nursing home. Before Tim could get out, Kaos reminded him, "Take your time, she's your mother." Tim nodded, then jumped out of the car walking briskly into the nursing home, not knowing what had transpired.

He stopped at the reception desk and signed his name alongside his mother's room number in the visitor's log. When he looked up, he saw Nurse Angela. She had a worried look that told him something was not right. She motioned for him to follow her. As soon as he stepped into his mother's room, the fragrance of plumeria filled his senses. He looked at her, lying peacefully in her bed.

"I'm so sorry. We loved Mary Jane," was all she said.

Tim demanded, "What do you mean, loved?" Angela wiped away the tears that had fallen down her cheeks. "Your mother, Tim, she's gone." Startled, Tim stammered, "Gone…as in dead?"

"Yes," Angela replied.

"Was she alone? Tell me she wasn't."

"Mr. Hurst, all day long she kept repeating the name Bud."

"Then what happened?" Tim demanded a second time.

"I called you after I caught her trying to get out of bed. I saw her stretch her arms toward someone, but no one was there. The last thing she said was, 'Bud I knew you'd come back for me.' She didn't die alone. I know that doesn't help much; I am terribly sorry."

Tim bent over his mother and kissed her goodbye. She was with his dad. In his heart he knew his mother had loved his dad. Now she was with him. Was she the bride of her youth? Was he the husband of her youth? Tim wished he knew for certain they were together. When he was ready to leave his mother, he kissed her one more time, then walked out of her room. He stopped at the nurse's station.

"I believe you have instructions on file. I will be back tomorrow to collect my mother's few possessions." Angela wiped her eyes and nodded. Then Tim walked out of the nursing home.

Kaos was in the same place he had dropped Tim off. When he saw the look on Tim's face, he knew better than to ask questions. After Tim got in the car, Kaos drove away in silence, back to Slim's Garage where he had found Tim earlier in the day. He stopped the car, turned off the engine.

"You've had one hell of a day. Want to come in for a beer?"

8
STAN

Kristen never got over Harry's death. A part of her heart was broken beyond repair. From time to time, she thought her heart had healed, if only temporarily, as reminders of Harry resurfaced. Sometimes, she thought she saw her brother in line at the grocery store. There were other instances when she was in the movie theatre, and she would feel his presence. Grief would consume her, and she'd have to leave.

Her grief was unpredictable. It would come upon her in waves. Each wave built into a crescendo, then slowly rolled to the shore until it became bits of foam that fluttered on the sand.

Sylvia's grief was just as valid. Even though her length of days with Harry exceeded her husbands by nine months, that didn't make her sadness any less.

Virgil would become vehement and agitated when he looked at Slim's house across the street, and he would have angry outbursts at the dinner table. Once he sat down, and before he placed his napkin on his lap, he would look at Kristen shouting, "Don't you ever think of riding a motorcycle by yourself or have a boyfriend who rides one." He lost his son; he was not about to lose his daughter.

"Virgil!" snapped Sylvia. "Don't go scaring her to death. Give her some credit for having common sense."

These incendiary conversations upset Kristen. Her dad constantly drummed into her head his alarming statistics about the evils of motorcycles. One evening six months after Harry's death, Virgil looked up from the newspaper he had been reading, "Another fatality."

"Of course there are fatalities, Virgil."

"Says here that motorcycles account for 14 percent of all crash related fatalities of vehicles on the roads."

"Dear, you are exaggerating. It is only 3 percent. There are more car fatalities than motorcycle fatalities."

Virgil continued to argue. "No, Sylvia I don't think I am exaggerating. Listen to this: motorcyclists are twenty-eight times more likely than passenger vehicle occupants to die in a car crash."

Exasperated, Sylvia exclaimed, "Oh Virgil … no one knows the day nor the hour. When it is your time, it is your time."

Virgil churlishly contradicted his wife. "More than 80 percent of these types of crashes result in injury and death. *Motorcycles are dangerous!*"

When he finished his outbursts, Kristen would cry and ask to be excused from the table. After their daughter was excused, Sylvia would boldly reprimanded her husband, "Why do you upset her? You know Kristen hasn't moved passed her brother's death."

"I don't want to lose another child, Sylvia. I couldn't take it. Seems so easy for you to say."

"It's not easy, Virgil. I must go on living for Kristen's sake. Harry is gone. How would it be for you and Kristen if I moped around all day? Yes, I am sad. No parent should expect to bury a child, but that is our cross to bear. We are not the only parents who lost a child."

"I can't help it, Sylvia. I am still so angry! Every time I look across the street and see that house where that boy Mitch lived, I get so angry."

"Virgil, are you angry at the dead boy or at yourself?"

Virgil didn't like the question because it sent his mind to the true grief in his heart. "I should have been a better parent."

"You are a good father, Virgil." Then, sitting in silence, dinner would be finished, the table cleared, and the evening would proceed with both Sylvia and Virgil dealing with their own brand of sadness.

During these episodes with her father, Kristen would sneak out of the house and visit Slim across the street. She was not angry with Mitch, and she felt sad for Slim. Sometimes they would sit together quietly on the front porch steps with nary a word spoken between them. When Kristen sensed Slim felt better, she'd say, "I best get on home, Mr. Slim."

"Yes, Miss Kristen, I expect you do. Thanks for coming by."

She would get up from the porch, smile at Mr. Slim and bound across the street. Once she was safely on the sidewalk, she waved to him. He'd wave back and she would sneak back inside her house before her parents realized she was missing.

One day, when Kristen came home from school, there was a FOR SALE sign at Slim's house. She ran across the street not even looking to see if cars were coming. She bounded up the steps to the front porch and paused in front of the door, wondering if she should knock. Instead, she peeked in the windows to see if her friend was there. Everything had been packed up. The house was dark and empty. Slim had left without saying goodbye.

That night at dinner, Virgil reported that Slim's Garage was for sale. "Good riddance," he shouted out loud. Kristen felt even more distraught. Any ties to Slim that had brought her comfort were now gone, just as both Harry and Mitch were gone. They were never coming back.

During the summer of the year Kristen turned fourteen, her mother thought it would be a good idea for her daughter to take a civics class during her freshman year at St. Ambrose Academy. School wouldn't start for another month and, if any changes were to be made to her schedule, this was the time to do it.

"Kristen," Sylvia called from the bottom of the stairs. "Please come down, I want to talk to you about your classes."

"Really, Mom," Kristen replied, as she lay face down on her bed, reading a book with her head hung over the side. "I already have enough on my mind without thinking about adding more to my schedule."

"Just come down, please."

"Oh fine," she muttered, as she threw the book onto the floor, hitting with a horrendous thump.

"That better not be a library book, young lady!" Sylvia called out, looking at the top of the landing.

"No, Mother!"

"Books are treasures, Kristen, not something to be thrown about."

Kristen came out of her room and plopped down on the top step. Sylvia knew her daughter was nervous about starting high school even though Kristen hadn't voiced it. Culver Heights was a small community; everybody knew everyone and, while that had its benefits, there were some things that were never forgotten. Such as the horrible motorcycle accident that took Harry and Mitch's lives. Sylvia was aware that the nuns who taught at St. Ambrose had Harry as a student, which could be why Kristen felt anxious.

Grief, Sylvia knew, took a long time to reconcile itself. A well-meaning comment by one of the nuns could scratch open the wound that Harry's death caused. Sylvia also knew that the civics class would open up opportunities for her daughter to heal. She remembered the nurse's uniform Kristen had begged her to buy for Halloween and how she sat next to Harry and pretended to be his nurse after he broke his arm. Civics class, Sylvia hoped, would be a well-intended catharsis for her.

"I have been looking through your course catalog. I see there's a civics class."

"Mother, why on earth would I take a civics class?"

"For one important reason. One should learn to be a good citizen and that includes volunteer opportunities."

"Like what?"

"Give it a try, Kris. If you don't like it, you can drop it."

"Whatever you say, Mother."

Kristen got up from the top step plodding to her room without a backward glance at her mother, who couldn't possibly know what she was talking about. "Civics, humph…" Kristen muttered.

September's weather was always hot and dry because the Santa Ana winds chose to make their appearance during standardized testing week. Kristen hated this week. She tried to convince her mother she was sick on the first morning the tests were given. She got up and ran into the bathroom quickly filling a jar with water from under the sink that she had conveniently placed there the night before. She slowly opened the bathroom door so her mother could hear her gagging and vomiting. Sylvia smiled at her daughter's attempt to feign the flu.

"Give it a try, Kris," her mother started to say before she was interrupted with, "But I'm sick."

"It's your nerves, Kristen. Don't make such a fuss."

Kristen slammed the bathroom door, frustrated her mother didn't fall for her faux illness. Sylvia called again from the bottom of the stairs, "You have five minutes to pull yourself together. I'll wait in the car."

Kristen splashed cold water on her face and patted it dry. Then she brushed her long, blonde hair and pulled it back into a ponytail. Satisfied, she looked in the mirror and opened the cabinet where the cosmetic bag was kept and took out a light pink frosted lipstick. Kristen applied it to her lips, then smacked them together, blending the lipstick. She looked around the bathroom thinking she had brought her bookbag only to discover she had not. She went back into her room and found it in a corner where she had absentmindedly thrown it the night before. After checking to make sure she had sharpened number two pencils in the backpack, she resigned herself to making the most of testing day, as it was the first day of the new school year.

On her way through the kitchen, Kristen noticed a brown bag with her name on it. She smiled because her mother had, from the time she was in kindergarten, packed her lunch every day. Now that she was in high school, she thought after today she should do it for herself. But on this day, grateful for her mother's kindness, she grabbed the bag on her way out to the car, slamming the kitchen door behind her.

After Kristen had secured her seatbelt and placed the brown bag lunch on her lap, her mother remarked, "I see you remembered your lunch." Kristen looked at her mother with a smile. "Thanks, Mom."

Sylvia put the car in reverse and backed out of the driveway onto Arlanda Drive. She drove in silence as Kristen looked out the window. When they were a block away from St. Ambrose, Sylvia turned to Kristen.

"Do you want me to let you out here or in front of the school? Harry never wanted me to let him off where his friends could see him get out of the car."

Kristen winced, "In front is fine, Mom."

Sylvia drove the remaining block, then stopped in front of the main doors of St. Ambrose. Before Kristen opened the car door, Sylvia gently reminded her, "It's a half day. I'll be here after your test. Good luck, dear."

Kristen took a deep breath before getting out of the car. "Thanks Mom," she said, as she turned to wave. Sylvia watched until Kristen disappeared into a sea of uniformed students before driving home.

The room at St. Ambrose where the freshmen were to take their test was stifling hot. As she walked through the halls and into her homeroom, Kristen thought about the rumors the school would be torn down and rebuilt to include central air conditioning the year after she would graduate.

She was shocked to see Sister Mary Agatha. Sister's reputation proceeded her. She could strike fear at any moment at any given time. Kristen decided after seeing Sister Mary Agatha that she was not going to be intimidated. She took a seat toward the back of the classroom, as far away as possible from Sister Mary Agatha's piercing glare. She had no sooner sat down than the first bell of the day rang, signaling the start of the dreaded test.

Before Sister passed out the test booklets, she walked over to the windows, opening them as much as she could. Turning to her students, she said, "If you think this is hot, think of the poor souls in purgatory." A boy sitting across the aisle from Kristen nudged her elbow and rolled his eyes. Nothing escaped Sister Mary Agatha's glance that shot through him like a hissing, burning arrow.

"There will be no talking," she barked.

"Sorry, Sister," he mumbled.

She passed out the booklets and instructed no one to open them until she said they could. Setting the timer, she instructed, "You have four hours to complete this exam. You may open your booklets now and begin."

Half-way through the exam, Kristen's mind started to wander. She was bored and tempted to alternate her answers until she discovered those would be incorrect. Besides, her mother would be furious if she found out she had thrown the tests; her score on the entrance exam to St. Ambrose was the highest in the history of the school. If she failed, the Academy would lose its reputation as superior in academic excellence, and she would lose her scholarship.

When Sister Mary Agatha's timer chimed, she looked up from her rosary beads, "Pencils down, close your booklets whether you have finished or not and pass them to the front of the room."

The boy seated across from Kristen elbowed her again, "Did you finish?"

"Yes," she replied, "Did you?"

"No, I had half a page left. I was tempted to fill in any random answer."

"Why didn't you?" Kristen asked.

"My mom would kill me."

Kristen smiled. "I was tempted to do that myself because I was bored but thought better of it since I am on academic scholarship."

"Oh, so you are one of those academically gifted!" he said, rolling his eyes again.

"It's not that," Kristen mumbled as she turned her attention back to the front of the room.

"Then what?" he asked.

"My mother would be terribly disappointed in me, wouldn't yours?"

"All my mom said was, 'Do the best you can.' And I did."

The lunch bell rang in the hallway, signaling the underclassmen that it was their time slot in the cafeteria.

"We better get in there," the boy said.

"Yes, I guess so. Did you bring a lunch?"

"No."

"You can have half of mine or all of it, if you want. I don't feel like eating. It's too hot."

"Thank you," the boy answered. "My name's Stan Becker and you are?"

"Kristen Warner. It's nice to meet you, Stan."

The cafeteria was crowded by the time they arrived. Stan looked around, spotting two seats near the water fountain. Not the best seats but being close to the water fountain was a gift. "We can sit over there," he said, pointing to a table.

"I'll follow you Stan, lead the way."

The decibel level in the cafeteria made it difficult for Stan to talk to Kristen, so they ate in silence until the bell rang, signaling the end of their first day. Stan walked Kristen to her locker and waited for her to collect her bookbag. When she closed the metal door, she was surprised to see him standing there.

"I'll see you tomorrow, Stan."

"Sure, see you tomorrow," he said as he lightly touched her arm. "Thanks again for sharing your lunch."

Kristen felt her heart pound unexpectedly in her chest. She started to say something to Stan, but he had already disappeared into the sea of underclassmen in the hallway. She lingered for a moment before she left the building in search of her mother's car.

Sylvia was parked in front of the school's main entrance just as she said she would be. As Kristen got closer to the car, she noticed a bloom on her daughter's cheeks, the kind that was not produced by hot weather. After Kristen got in the car, Sylvia asked, "How was your day, dear?"

"Mom, it was fantastic!"

Remembering Kristen's antics from earlier that morning, Sylvia inquired, "So, the test wasn't as bad as you thought it would be?"

"Truthfully, I was bored, and the room was hot. I was tempted to randomly fill in the answers."

"Kristen! You didn't did you? What would Monsignor say if you failed the tests? You are on academic scholarship."

"Oh, Mom, I didn't say I did. I said I was tempted. Besides, I noticed if I randomly filled in the answer key, those answers were definitely wrong. My conscience would not let me do that. I have my pride."

"I am relieved to hear that Kristen, and I'm sorry you were bored."

"Mom, the room was so hot, and Sister Mary Agatha showed us no mercy. You'd think she would let us get a drink at the water fountain right outside her door. But no…she said, 'Offer it up for the poor souls in purgatory!' Geeze, Louise!"

"I hope you kept that comment to yourself."

"I did."

The lively banter between Kristen and her mother filled the heavy gloom that had hung like a shroud, always a reminder of Harry.

Every time Kristen looked at the empty house across the street, she felt sad for Mr. Slim. She didn't know what had happened to him nor would anyone purchase the house. It stood there all those years vacant, empty, lonely. Someone mysteriously mowed the grass, but that was it. No shrubs or flowers grew anywhere on the property. It was a sad, empty little house, always a remembrance of the lives that were lost too young.

Sometimes Kristen wondered what Mitch would have been like if he had grown up. She could only imagine. Sometimes she thought about Harry. It was easier to think about Mitch, but to her, Harry would always be fifteen years old.

Sylvia let Kristen sit in the car as long as she wanted on those days. She watched her stare at the house across the street. Grief took a long time to process and there was no magic time to recover from a death; however, there was a reasonable amount of time to accept it and move on. As far as Sylvia could tell, her daughter was doing ok. She never saw her daughter cry and she never spoke about her feelings.

Sylvia, on the other hand, had her moments. What parent who lost a child didn't? Her grief came in waves. In moments when her grief was unbearable, she would shut herself up in her bathroom and take a long shower. Her tears would fall into the black abyss of the drain, traveling miles until they comingled with tears shed for reasons known only to the bearer. Together, those tears emptied into the sea as its restless tides retreated somewhere into its vastness on the other side of the world.

"Kris," Sylvia whispered, "Are you coming in?"

"Yeah," she said as she turned her face away from the house across the street.

Harry's accident and death changed Virgil. Prior to the tragedy he had been kind and loving to everyone he met, including his clients where he practiced law, but especially to his family. Afterward, he had bursts of anger, then apologized for the outbursts. If anyone needed counseling in the family, it was Virgil. In the wee hours of the morning, Kristen could hear her parents' conversations through the vent that led from their bedroom to hers.

"Virgil, Monsignor has suggested that you come in to talk."

"What does he know, Sylvia? He never lost a child."

"He has been educated in ways we have not."

"Like what?"

"One time I asked him what happens to a person after they die?"

"What did he say?"

"He said they have things to do; they have jobs. They don't stick around. I can imagine."

"Well, I can't! Good night, Sylvia."

Kristen would close her eyes and try to imagine Harry and Mitch in heaven, but all she could see was black.

The next morning, Kristen sprang out of bed before her irritating interruption of dreamtime shocked her into reality. She was anxious to get to school to confirm that Stan was a real live human being, not just a dream. She quickly put on her uniform, scarfed down a carton of yogurt, and made another sandwich for her lunch while her mother waited in the car.

Sylvia dropped Kristen off in front of the main doors of St. Ambrose. It was easier that way because the upper classmen were allowed to park near the football field where they collected in groups before the first bell rang. Kristen got out of the car and waved to her mother before walking down the sidewalk and into the school. She wasted no time getting to her locker in the freshmen wing, waiting for what felt like an eternity before slamming her locker. Caught off guard, Stan was standing on the other side of the metal door. His sudden appearance caused her to gasp.

"Stan, you scared me!"

"Aw, I'm sorry. I didn't mean to scare you. I told you I would see you today."

Kristen smiled. "You are forgiven."

"I'm glad to hear that. I can't imagine you staying away from me because of a little scare. Anyway, what electives are you taking? I ask because that will depend on whether I see you throughout the day or only after school."

"I'm taking French and civics."

"No kidding!"

"What are you taking, Stan?"

"Carpentry with Father Robert. You know Jesus was a carpenter. If that was good enough for him, it's good enough for me."

Suddenly the first bell rang. Kristen took the extra sandwich out of her lunch bag and placed it on the top shelf of her locker. Then she handed Stan the brown bag lunch her mother had packed. She shoved it toward him. "Here take this, in case I don't see you until after school."

"That's not why I wanted to eat lunch with you," said Stan. "But thanks anyway. If I don't meet up with you in the cafeteria, I will meet you here after school. And for that matter, every morning."

Kristen blushed. "Ok, see you later." He squeezed her hand, "See you later."

The second warning bell rang. Stan took off for the shop wing and Kristen the academic where her civics class was scheduled. She arrived just in time, as Sister Mary Agatha shut the door behind her. If she had been a second later, she would have had to go to the Attendance Office for a late admissions pass. Kristen was flabbergasted to see Sister Mary Agatha. It was one thing to have her proctor the exam the day before, but to have her teach civics?

Nobody liked Sister Mary Ag, as they called her. Most feared her. Kristen wasn't sure how she felt other than she was not about to let a nun intimidate her. She slithered into the nearest available seat in the classroom, proceeding to take a new notebook out of her book bag when Sister Mary Ag walked over to her desk.

"Miss Warner, why are you taking this class?"

Kristen swallowed the lump that had been rising in her throat. Truth of the matter, she didn't want to take the class; her mother strongly suggested that she take it.

"Miss Warner, please stand when I am addressing you."

Kristen slowly rose from her chair, "Yes, Sister."

Sister Mary Agatha took several steps away from the desk. "I am waiting for your answer."

Kristen didn't want to make up a fancy excuse. She took a deep breath then let it out slowly. "I didn't want to take the class, Sister."

"Then why did you?"

"My mother suggested it. She made me take it and said if I don't like it, I can drop it."

Then she sat down in her seat without Sister's permission. Sister Mary Agatha turned on her heel walking toward the blackboard, smiling. She esteemed students who could hold their own. That was part of the reason she came across as stern. She knew what students said about her, and she felt it was her responsibility to prepare them for the world outside the hallowed walls of St. Ambrose. Life was not always pleasant; people were not always kind; they could be mean and hurtful. If one grew a thick skin, the insults when they occurred wouldn't be so traumatic. That was her philosophy. She wanted her students to stand up for themselves in a way that, while polite, was serious, leaving no room for discussion. She wrote on the chalkboard,

"LET YOUR YES MEAN YES AND YOUR NO MEAN NO."
~ JESUS

Throughout the first weeks of school, Kristen learned that civics covered a wide range of subjects. One could participate in politics, health care, or other real-world experiences. Sylvia Warner knew what she was doing when she suggested Kristen take civics. The class and experiences would serve her well.

Before the end of the marking period, Stan had become an affable companion. Kristen enjoyed his company before and after school. One day after class, he stopped by her locker, as usual, but instead of going in the opposite direction when the bell rang, he lingered.

"Kristen, there is something I want to ask you."

"Oh?"

"It's not enough to see you in the morning for a few minutes and after school for a few minutes at your locker. I want to see you outside of school."

"I would like that, Stan."

"Where do you live?"

When Kristen told him where she lived, his jaw dropped.

"You live across the street from the house everybody says is haunted!"

Kristen laughed, "It's not haunted; I will prove it to you. Are you coming over later or not?" Kristen demanded.

"I'll be over; I have to go home first. See you in about thirty minutes."

"Great. See you soon, Stan."

Sylvia had been reading a magazine while she waited for Kristen. Her head spun around when she heard the car door open.

"Mom, we have to get home fast!"

"Why? I planned on running a few errands first."

"Well, you can't because Stan is coming over."

"And just who is this Stan? Not an upperclassman, I hope."

"No Mom, he is in my grade."

"Alright, the errands can wait. Let me meet your Stan."

"MOM! You don't have to say it like that."

Sylvia smiled. She knew better than to ask anything more. First boyfriends were special, one never forgot their first love.

They drove home in silence. Sylvia had no sooner pulled up to the front of the house than Kristen jumped out of the car. She didn't wait for her mother to come to a complete stop. Her heart was racing, and she didn't know what she was feeling: exhilaration… excitement… that a boy could be interested in her? Someone who eased the pain of Harry's death? That was a lot to put on Stan.

Kristen raced up the stairs and threw her bookbag into a corner in her bedroom. She quickly changed out of her uniform, tossing it on top of her bookbag. She finished putting her sneakers on as the doorbell rang. "I'll get it, Mom!" Kristen shouted from the top of the stairs. When she opened the door, she was surprised to see Stan not wearing his school uniform. She liked his casual t-shirt and blue jeans.

"Hi, Kris," he greeted.

"Hi Stan, please come in," Kristen said excitedly.

Out of the corner of her eye, Kristen saw a motorcycle pull away from the curb in front of her house. She didn't mention the motorcycle to Stan. Ignorance is bliss, she thought, because she didn't want to know if Stan was involved with motorcycles. Her dad had traumatized her and that was terrifying enough.

Kristen shut the door. "Did you have trouble finding the house?"

"No, my brother dropped me off. He knows this street pretty good."

Kristen didn't need to wonder. Everybody knew the street because most people thought the vacant house on Arland Drive was haunted. "Oh…well come meet my mom, Stan."

Sylvia had been occupied baking chocolate chip cookies, which was something she used to do when Harry brought Mitch over to their house. Stan stood in the kitchen inhaling sweet notes of creamed butter, sugar, vanilla, and chocolate with a pinch of salt. "Smells good in here, Kristen. Does your mom bake a lot?"

"No, it has been a long time since she did."

Sylvia wiped her hands on her apron. Something about Stan reminded her of her son. Then Kristen spoke up, "Mom, this is Stan Becker, he is in my class."

"Pleased to meet you, Mrs. Warner."

"It's nice to meet you too, Stan. I've just baked chocolate chip cookies. Would you like some cookies and a glass of milk?"

"Sure, thank you Ma'am."

Stan sat at the kitchen table while Kristen poured two tall glasses of cold milk, then brought them to the table. Sylvia took a plate of warm cookies off the top of her stove and walked to where Kristen and Stan were seated. She put the plate in front of them.

"Help yourselves."

"Thanks Mom," Kristen replied.

After Stan had consumed a cookie and a gulp of milk, he turned to Sylvia. "These are delicious. I haven't had home baked cookies in a long time."

"Thank you, Stan. May I ask why?"

Kristen suddenly chastised her mother. "MOM!"

Stan spoke up. "That's ok, Kristen. Your mom can ask me anything she wants."

Kristen interjected, "You do have a mom, Stan, don't you?"

"Yes, I do, but she works a lot. Doesn't have time to bake cookies anymore."

"You may have cookies anytime you would like." Sylvia said, smiling at him. It was nice having someone Harry's age in the house again. She cautioned herself not to get used to him.

After Stan finished his third cookie and polished off his glass of milk, he turned to Kristen. "Hey, did you forget you said you would prove that house is not haunted."

"Kristen!" exclaimed Sylvia, "Have you been spreading rumors?"

"No, Mom. It seems rumors get started on their own. I'm going to prove to Stan that what people say is not true."

"Kristen, I don't know if you should go poking around that vacant house."

"Oh, Mom, really!"

"I guess it's ok, just be careful. Someone keeps an eye on the property because I see that the lawn is always mowed."

With her mother's permission, Kristen grabbed Stan's arm. "Are you coming?"

"In a minute," Stan replied, standing to take the empty glass and plate to the kitchen sink. "I'll take those," Sylvia said, as she reached out for the dirty dishes.

"Thank you for the milk and cookies, Ma'am."

"You're welcome, Stan."

Kristen was becoming impatient. "Stan, are you coming or not?"

"I was saying thank you to your mom."

Sylvia turned her attention to the kitchen sink. She smiled as the back door slammed. There was a temporary air of happiness in their home, something that had not been present since Harry died.

Kristen stood on the curb outside her house facing Slim and Mitch's house. "Doesn't look like a haunted house to me, just a sad, little house is all I see."

Stan stood alongside her. "Now that you mention it, Kristen, it does look sad. Let's check it out anyway." Kristen looked at Stan with a gleam in her eye. "Race you across the street."

She barely looked both ways before sprinting away. Stan struggled to catch up. He didn't realize he had winged feet for competition, and he was out of breath by the time he reached the other side.

Breathlessly Stan whispered when he caught up to her, "How'd you get to be so fast?"

"I didn't know I was! Want to look in the windows? Maybe you will see a ghost?"

"Very funny," Stan retorted.

"I'm dead serious, maybe you will. You said people say it's haunted. See for yourself."

While Stan peered into the windows, Kristen snuck around the corner of the house, picked up a pebble that had been lying on the porch, and gently tossed it behind Stan's back, where it landed with a thump. Startled, Stan jumped, and Kristen doubled over with laughter. Embarrassed, Stan said, "That's not funny Kris, not funny!"

"Oh Stan, you should have seen your face."

"I am glad you are having a laugh at my expense."

"I'm sorry. I didn't think you actually believed in gossip."

"Truthfully, I was curious."

"Now you know it's not haunted. It's sad, that's all. I hope it stays vacant because I like to think about the last time I talked to Mr. Slim."

"What was so special about that? Did he live here?"

"He did, his son Mitch was killed with my brother, Harry. They had an accident riding a motorcycle."

Stan didn't know what to say. The rumors he heard told a different story. While this was sad, he was glad someone wasn't murdered in the house.

"So, tell me, what was special about your last visit with Mr. Slim?" Stan asked again.

Kristen paused before explaining, "It wasn't that we said anything. It's what we didn't say, didn't need to say."

Stan was confused, then asked, "Like, what do you mean?"

"I left my house because my dad was in one of his tirades about Mitch, Mr. Slim's son, and the evils of motorcycles. He was the reason Harry died. I didn't think Mr. Slim deserved to be talked about like that. He lost a child, too. So, I'd come over and sit with him. We didn't need to say anything because our hearts talked to each other."

"But he didn't say goodbye to you, did he?"

"No, he didn't. That hurt a lot, but I think Mr. Slim wanted me to remember him like the last time I saw him, all peaceful and quiet."

"That's a nice thought. Let's look around back."

"Are you sure you want to?"

"Yes, Kristen. There are no ghosts, like you said. Maybe there's some interesting stuff back there."

"Maybe, but I have never been in the back yard. What if someone see us?"

"Let 'em see us. I don't know why that's such a big deal."

"It's a big deal, Stan, because we are trespassing."

"Nobody lives here, I didn't see a NO TRESSPASSING sign. Where is your sense of adventure, Kristen?"

"I'm adventurous sometimes."

"Well, let this be one of those sometimes."

Meekly, Kristen responded, "Ok."

Stan jumped off the porch offering Kristen his hand, which she didn't hesitate to take. It felt nice, but he let go of it too soon.

The back yard left much to be desired. No one had mowed the knee-high grass, but there was a small circular clearing in the middle of the yard that looked like it had been used for a fire. Stan quickly surveyed the yard, scouring every inch until his eyes fell upon a stack of wood. He found two pieces that he could use for seats. Without a word, he set to the task of making his queen her throne. He laid two long boards across two tree stumps, then pushed down on the flat boards, making sure they were supported sufficiently. He turned to Kristen, extending his hand for her to take, guiding her to her throne.

"For you, my Queen," he said. "Your throne is ready."

Kristen blushed as she let Stan help her step over the boards before sitting on them. Stan sat next to her, holding her hand, as they stared into the circle of nothingness. Was this what Kristen meant when she said their hearts were talking? he wondered.

"This is nice," Stan said. "I could sit here all night. I really don't want to go home."

"Why not?" Kristen asked.

"Because I like it here with you."

"I like being here with you too, Stan."

When Kristen said she liked him, Stan felt comfortable asking her a question that had been on his mind.

"There is something I want to ask you. You heard about Homecoming?"

"Yes, but I haven't given it a second thought. Why do you ask?"

"I would like it if you will go to the dance with me."

"I didn't know freshmen were allowed to go."

"We can. It is our only dance of the year. So, will you go with me?"

"I would love to. Thank you for asking me."

Stan was relieved and happy. Relieved that Kristen had not been asked to the dance by anyone else, relieved she had not asked him about his breathlessness when he ran after her, and happy she said yes to the dance.

He leaned into her, lightly brushing her lips with his. Kristen didn't pull back or push him away. His lips lingered on hers, tasting chocolate and savoring their softness. Then he withdrew from her even though he wanted to drink of her kisses again and again.

"I think we should get going. Your mother is going to wonder what we have been doing."

Stan held Kristen's hand until they crossed the street. When they reached her house, he turned to her saying, "I'll see you tomorrow, Kristen."

9
CANDY STRIPERS

Kristen waited for Stan the next morning. When the second bell rang, she slammed her locker door, wondering what was going on. Stan had never missed a morning with her, and she was accustomed to him meeting her every morning before class.

His absence caused her to have feelings of sadness that stung, like pouring salt into a wound. She ran to her first class of the day, civics, because if she lingered any longer, she would have to get a tardy slip and her mother would not be happy. She barely made it into the classroom before Sister Mary Agatha started to take attendance. By the time Sister came to the end of the roster, Kristen's thoughts were far away and didn't hear when her name was called.

"Miss Warner," Sister called, "are you present or not?"

A girl seated behind Kristen nudged her in the back, waking her out of her melancholy.

"Yes, Sister, I am here."

"Next time, please answer the first time I call your name."

Sister Mary Agatha closed her roll book. Then she made a foofaraw of opening her teaching manual that had been lying underneath. When she finished her unnecessary fuss with the manual, she looked at her students for a minute before beginning the lesson.

"Now class, I want to talk to you about volunteer opportunities in the field of healthcare." Kristen's ears perked up. "How many of you have heard of Candy Stripers?"

A girl in the back of the classroom let out a giggle. Nothing escaped Sister Mary Agatha. To the shock of the other students, Sister singled out the girl who had giggled.

"Miss Sullivan, did I say something humorous?

"No, Sister."

"Then why are you giggling?"

"I…I thought you said stripper."

"Quite the contrary, young lady," Sister Mary Agatha replied. Getting up from her desk and turning toward the blackboard, she wrote in capital letters STRIPER and STRIPPER. Turning to face the class, she said, "You can see, Miss Sullivan, striper has only one P." Embarrassed, because Sister had called her out in front of the class, Miss Sullivan meekly responded, "Yes, Sister."

Sister Mary Agatha returned to her desk yet remained standing. "As I was saying, how many of you know anything about Candy Stripers?" None of the students raised their hands. "That is what I thought. Gather your things. We are going on a little walk."

After the girls packed up their bookbags, they followed Sister Mary Agatha in single file out the classroom and down the hall to the Home Economics room. When they arrived, a jolly little nun greeted them at the door. When Kristen saw Sister Benedict, she immediately regretted taking civics.

"Ladies, please come in," she said cheerfully.

When all of Sister Mary Agatha's civics students had accumulated in front of the room, Sister Benedict began, "You may take a seat anywhere you would like, just make sure you can see the front of the classroom. If you cannot, you may stand along the wall. I trust you will find a seat," she said with a smile.

Kristen looked for a seat but could not find one that gave her a view of

Sister Benedict. She chose to stand along the wall with another girl who was as height challenged as she was. When all the girls were either sitting or standing, Sister Mary Agatha turned to her students and sternly suggested, "Be on your best behavior." Then she nodded to Sister Benedict and said, "I will take my leave now." As Sister Mary Agatha left, Sister Benedict closed the door then turned and smiled at her new students.

Kristen looked around the Home Economics classroom. She did not have a full appreciation of the room until she had taken it all in. The atmosphere was pleasant, a welcome contrast to Sister Mary Ag's stark civics class. The room was a double lab that provided a complete kitchen and a sewing room with several sewing machines lined up against a wall of windows, opposite the yellow wall where Kristen stood.

Sister Benedict walked over to a shelf of neatly folded colorful fabrics. She opened a stepstool that was next to the shelf, and climbed up so she could reach the pink and white striped fabric on the top. One of the girls closest to the shelf stood up to receive the bolt of fabric Sister Benedict handed to her. When Sister had climbed back down, she folded the step stool and placed it back in its original spot next to the shelves of fabric. Then she took the bolt of fabric from the girl holding it and asked the students, "Ladies, do you know why I have this fabric?"

"No, Sister."

"No idea at all?" she prompted them.

Kristen raised her hand. "Yes, dear," Sister Benedict acknowledged. "Please share with the rest of the class your experience."

Kristen swallowed the lump that had risen in her throat. The fabric reminded her of the night her brother died.

"The night my brother Harry died, I saw a girl in a pink and white striped uniform."

The mention of Harry's name and the fabric brought uncontrollable tears to Kristen's eyes. Huge tears rolled down her cheeks and, as fast as she wiped them away, they continued to rise in her eyes. Sister Benedict put the bolt of fabric down on her desk and picked up a box of tissues, then walked to Kristen and handed it to her. Sister Benedict leaned in close to her and whispered, "You are a brave girl."

The staff at St. Ambrose Academy knew about Harry's accident. Several of the teachers had him as their student. His death was tragic and raw and sad for all of them. They also knew that his sister would be attending the Academy and that it might be difficult for her, so they were all in agreement that they would be vigilant for any opportunity to help her through her grief, whomever got the chance first.

After the exchange with Kristen, Sister Benedict resumed her questions about the fabric. "As I was saying, this pink and white striped fabric is worn by junior volunteers in the hospital. Their job is to make the patient's visits as pleasant as possible. They are a friendly face, and friendly faces make their stay happier."

A girl in the back of the classroom raised her hand and spoke out before Sister Benedict could acknowledge her. "So not everyone in the hospital dies?"

"No dear, most get well and go home. Some are there recovering from lifesaving surgery. Others are new mothers on the maternity floor who go home with their babies. And some are there for treatments of one kind or another."

Another girl raised her hand. "You mean like cancer?" Sister Benedict thought for a moment before answering her question. "Sadly, yes. Childhood cancers are the hardest. It takes a special person to be able to work with those patients. It is not to be understated; it is an honor and a privilege."

Kristen raised her hand. "Yes, dear," Sister Benedict said looking straight at her.

"I think I would like to do that."

"I will make a note of that. But first I want to tell you a little bit more about where and when and the history, if you will, of the Candy Striper.

Close your eyes and travel back in your mind to the year 1944. You are in the East Orange, New Jersey high school civics class. The classroom is very much like the classroom you are in right now. Not much has changed except hair and uniform styles. Americans were very patriotic because, as you will learn in American History, WWII was in full force. Americans sacrificed for the boys on the front and at home. They did not waste resources and they gave up luxuries. For example, Christmas cards were rare because paper was used for the war effort, but I digress. Girls made their uniforms out of this pink and white striped fabric that reminded them of a candy cane. Thusly the name, Candy Striper."

Sister Benedict paused for a moment, letting the girls envision the history lesson. Then she continued, "Candy is sweet and makes people happy-go-lucky. So, the Candy Striper's job is to be pleasant, no matter what the patient's demeanor. Also, they provide an extra pair of hands that the nurses will require from time to time. Taking out the trash with a smile, no matter how unpleasant the smell may be is another quality we look for in our junior volunteers. But that is not their only duty. In the early days we are envisioning, the Candy Striper assisted the nurses in changing beds and retrieving documents. Now they can do much more because nurses have become busier, which gives them the opportunity to deliver mail and meals to patients.

"Sometimes a Candy Striper will help feed patients, read to them, and help at discharge time. There may be other duties they will be required to carry out. These are especially important tasks and must always be done with a smile. It is not always pleasant and can be sad. So, if you decide to volunteer in this way, you must be incredibly careful not to get too attached to your patients."

Kristen raised her hand again. "Sister Benedict, how old do we have to be and how long can we be a Candy Striper?"

"I believe one must be fourteen years of age to start and usually stop at age eighteen when the young lady graduates from high school."

"Sister," Kristen interjected, "do any Candy Stripers go on to become nurses?"

"Yes, dear, some do, and some have had enough of the hospital environment and do something entirely different. But those who are called stay on to become nurses and even doctors."

Something inside Kristen made her heart leap when she thought about taking care of sick people. She smiled thinking about her nurse's uniform that she wore for Halloween when she was four years old.

Five minutes before the bell rang to signal the end of the period, Sister Benedict reminded the students to see her after class if they were interested. When the bell rang, Kristen lingered while the other students filed out of the classroom. When the last student left, Kristen approached Sister Benedict and announced, "Sister, I would like to be a Candy Striper." Sister Benedict smiled, "If you are genuinely interested, I will make all the necessary arrangements. But first you need to talk to your parents and have them sign this form."

Kristen took the piece of paper Sister Benedict was holding out for her. "Thank you, Sister," Kristen replied.

"Kristen, bring this form back as soon as you can. You must make your uniform; I will provide the fabric. Oh, before I forget, that was brave of you to talk about your brother in front of your classmates. That must have been hard. You are welcome to come and talk to me anytime. I have been around for quite a long while, and I have been told that I am a pretty good listener."

Kristen brushed away a tear rolling down her cheek brought on by the kindness and understanding of the nun. "Thank you, Sister. I best be going."

The excursion to the Home Economics class took up most of the morning. When the class ended, it was lunchtime. Kristen didn't think much about Stan's absence, as she was used to eating lunch without him. It was not until the end of the day at her locker when she thought something was wrong. She waited and waited, but he didn't show up. When it was obvious he was not going to meet her at the locker, she slammed the door.

The hallway had emptied by the time she left the building. Students rarely tarried; they had extracurricular activities such as football practice, band practice, Latin club, French club and chess club. Kristen purposely walked past Sister Benedict's classroom and peeked in the door. She noticed a group of girls working on a project with the Sister. She paused, trying to decide if she should go in. Sister Benedict looked up from the group of girls and smiled. Kristen waved, then hurried out to meet her mother at their usual spot.

When Kristen approached the car, Sylvia noticed something was amiss with her daughter. She decided to make light of her mood. "Hi honey, how was your day?"

Kristen looked away, reluctant to divulge her thoughts. Sylvia didn't pry, as this could lead to "heaven forbid" an argument which they had not had since Stan entered Kristen's life. They drove home in silence. As Sylvia parked in front of their house, Kristen blurted, "Mom, Stan wasn't in school. He said he would be."

"Did you ask any of his friends where he is or why he's absent?"

"No."

"Why not, Kristen?"

"Because I don't know any of his friends. He is usually alone when he meets me at my locker."

"I see," said her mother. "Maybe he will be in school tomorrow. I'm sure there is a reasonable explanation."

"There better be, Mom. I don't know what to do if he isn't at school tomorrow."

"Do about what, Kristen?"

"Homecoming, Mom."

"When were you going to tell me? You should have a new dress."

"I have my Easter dress, it still fits. I probably won't go anyway."

"Why?"

"Because Mom, I already told you, Stan wasn't in school today."

"Maybe he will be there tomorrow, Kristen."

10
ST. JOSEPH'S HOSPITAL

Kristen trudged upstairs to her bedroom; her heart felt heavy. She missed her friend. She didn't realize how much she liked Stan until he wasn't in school. Her whole day felt off because she was used to his company. Then, she remembered the permission slip to have signed so she could become a Candy Striper. Fortunately, it was in a folder and not wadded up at the bottom of her bookbag.

"Mom," she called, as she walked into the kitchen, "I have a permission slip I would like you to sign."

"Oh?"

"I want to be a Candy Striper."

Sylvia smiled to herself because she knew the civics class would provide volunteer opportunities at the hospital and, if Kristen truly was interested in a nursing career, this was a good place to start.

"I'm old enough, Mom. Sister Benedict said she would make all the arrangements; you just need to sign the permission slip."

"Do you wear a special uniform?"

"Yes, it's a pink and white striped fabric. Sister told us the history of the Candy Striper today."

"I didn't know Sister Mary Agatha taught Home Economics, Kristen."

"She doesn't. She took us to Sister Benedict's Home Economics room."

"Sister Benedict must have made an impression on you."

"She did. I found myself blurting out that I saw Candy Stripers at the hospital when Harry died. Sister was so kind to me. She said I could talk to her anytime."

Sylvia smiled, then changed the subject. "Did Sister Benedict tell you where we could buy the fabric?"

"She said she would give us the fabric. There is a bolt of it in her classroom."

"That is very generous of her, Kristen. Will you make your uniform at school?"

"I think so because I saw a group of girls working on something with her after school today. That is part of the reason I was late coming to the car."

"I didn't think anything of it, Kristen. I was young once too."

"So, you will sign the form, Mom?"

"Of course, dear."

Kristen handed in the permission slip the next morning. She was excited to make her uniform so she would be ready for her first day as a volunteer at St. Joseph's Hospital.

The staff at St. Ambrose was aware of the impact of Harry's death on Kristen, and they were also aware of the reason behind Stan's absences, but they were not allowed to talk about certain matters. They had seen Stan's interaction with Kristen and were pleased she had a friend. They also noticed that she was making great strides by talking about her brother. They wanted her to stay on this momentum of healing, and Sister Benedict didn't want Kristen to have any reason not to stay on that course. So, unbeknown to Kristen, Sister Benedict, certain Mrs. Warner would sign the permission slip, took the liberty of estimating Kristen's size and cutting out the pattern pieces for the uniform ahead of time.

After the dismissal bell rang at the end of the day, Kristen stopped by Sister Benedict's room. "Hello, Sister."

"Hello, Miss Warner, I have something for you."

"You do?"

"Yes, let's hold these pattern pieces up to see if I estimated your size correctly. I have never been wrong."

Sister Benedict pinned the pieces together so that the pinafore, once slipped over Kristen's head, fit perfectly. "See, I have a knack for estimating sizes," Sister Benedict said with a smile. "Do you have a sewing machine at home?"

"Not that I know of Sister. I don't think my mother sews."

"No matter, I will have these pieces stitched together in no time. You can have your pinafore by the weekend. I have you scheduled on the volunteer roster for this Saturday."

With that news, all thoughts of Homecoming disappeared from Kristen's mind. Stan had not been in school, even though he had asked her to the dance. They had not made any plans. She was excited to have something new in her life that would fill the void created by Stan's absence.

"Thank you, Sister."

"You are most welcome, Kristen. Stop by after school on Friday. I will have your uniform ready. There are a few items you will need to purchase if you do not already have them. You will need a Peter Pan collared white shirt."

Kristen's brow furrowed, then she remembered, "I have one or two from last year that I think fit, Sister Benedict."

"Good, you will also need white stockings and white shoes. You will be on your feet a lot."

"I will make sure my mother and I buy those things before Saturday. I am so excited to start volunteering." Sister Benedict smiled, then waved her off, "Don't keep your mother waiting."

Sylvia had parked in front of St. Ambrose in her usual spot and had brought along a magazine to read while she waited for Kristen. She often arrived earlier than she needed because she enjoyed the peace and quiet before the dismissal bell rang. She also enjoyed the lively banter that took place among the students as they departed the hallowed halls of St. Ambrose.

She no longer felt sad thinking about Harry. Of course, she missed him; she carried him in her heart and believed he was only a breath away. Sometimes she thought she felt his presence in the car while she waited for Kristen. It was not anything tangible; he was present without being physically there. It was as if she could hear him say, "Hi, Mom." As soon as Sylvia recognized his spirit, he was gone.

Sylvia desperately wanted to share these experiences with Virgil, but his heart had turned ugly, and he was not going to believe her. She suggested a talk with Father Robert would help, but when she brought up the subject, he walked away.

Motorcycles were another taboo subject that neither she nor Kristen talked about. Sylvia did not want her daughter to be afraid of motorcycles, but Virgil was no help when he reacted to each motorcycle fatality he read about in the newspaper. "What did I tell you, Sylvia! There's another motorcycle fatality." Then he would glare at Kristen and say, "Do not get on the back of a motorcycle, EVER!"

Sylvia did not hear Kristen approach the car and was startled by her daughter's cheery greeting of "Hi, Mom."

"I'm sorry, dear, I didn't hear you."

"You seem far away, Mom. What were you thinking about?"

"Oh, nothing important. How was your day?"

"Exciting!"

"Do you want to tell me about it?"

"Yes, I stopped by Sister Benedict's after school and guess what?"

"What?" Sylvia replied excitedly. Kristen's enthusiasm was contagious.

"Sister is making my Candy Striper uniform. She had me try on the pinned pieces. My uniform will be ready on Friday because she scheduled me to volunteer for the first time on Saturday."

"Did Sister say you will need anything else?"

"Oh…yes, I will need white stockings and white shoes. Sturdy shoes. Sister Benedict said I will be on my feet a lot."

"What type of blouse do you need? I assume the uniform is a pinafore and you wear a blouse under it."

"Oh Mom, it's not a little girl pinafore. Of course I will need a blouse. One that has a Peter Pan collar. I think I have two from last year that still fit."

Sylvia smiled at Kristen as she waited for her to secure her seatbelt before putting the car in drive. The afternoon was sunnier than usual and the air around them felt clean and crisp. Sylvia was not in a hurry to go home, so she took a longer route than normal. When Kristen realized they were not going directly home, she questioned her mother.

"Mom?"

"What is it, dear?"

"Can we go by McGinn's? I still need a pair of shoes and white stockings."

"We can go tomorrow."

"Why not today?"

"I guess we can, Kristen."

McGinn's shoe store was a family-owned business that had been in Culver Heights for one hundred years. It was the first and only family shoe store in the community where parents bought their children's first pair to the last pair purchased as an aged adult. McGinn's had a friendly staff who took their time with each family member in need of new shoes. They had practical shoes that parents could pass down to siblings because they never wore out. There were occasions, however, when a child was exceptionally hard on a pair of shoes; but that was a rarity because most children's feet grew so fast the shoes didn't have time to wear out.

The excursion to McGinn's took much longer than Sylvia thought it should because Kristen could not make up her mind. There were several styles of nurse's shoes on display. To Kristen, they looked like a white version of the sturdy shoes the nuns wore and she was certainly not going to wear those.

A woman who worked at McGinn's approached Kristen after she saw her looking at a pair of shoes, try them on, then put them back on the shelf, only to come back to the first pair, and then put those back on the shelf as well. "Is there anything in particular you are looking for that I may help you find?"

"I'm looking for a pair of sturdy white shoes because I will be on my feet a lot."

"I see," said the saleswoman. "What kind of work will you be doing?"

Kristen replied, "I'm not working, I'm volunteering at St. Joseph's Hospital as a Candy Striper. I'm having trouble finding shoes that don't look like shoes the nuns wear at St. Ambrose Academy."

The saleswoman smiled, then walked to another section of the store that had shoes more in style for a younger person. She picked out a pair of white leather Mary Janes that had a slight wedge heel and strap across the middle. They were practical and cute. "What do you think of these?" she asked Kristen, handing them to her. "What size do you wear?"

"These are cute. I hope you have a size six."

The saleswoman smiled; "I believe I have a size six in the stock room. They will look stylish with your Candy Striper uniform. You do wear the pink and white striped pinafore, do you not?"

"Yes Ma'am, I will be wearing the pinafore."

The saleswoman disappeared behind a charcoal-colored curtain and reappeared from the stockroom within a few minutes with a size six pair of white leather Mary Janes. Then she handed them to Kristen just as her mother walked into that section of the store with two pairs of white stockings in her hands.

"I see you have made a decision, Kristen."

"Yes, Mom I did. I like these Mary Janes." Sylvia looked at the youthful shoes in Kristen's hands. "They are cute, are they comfortable?"

"They are. What did you find?" Kristen asked, as she looked at the packages of stockings in her mother's hand. "These are for you; white stockings with a little support."

"Thanks Mom, I think this is all I need. I am ready to go home now. Can we go the long way?"

"I think that is a splendid idea, Kristen." They completed the purchase, thanked the saleswoman for her help, and made their way back to the car. Sylvia was happy they were finally able to settle on a pair of shoes, and Kristen was glad to have all the clothing pieces she needed to complete her uniform. Getting into the car, they buckled into their seatbelts and started their trek home.

Sylvia drove through Culver Heights, past houses with white picket fences and children playing in their yards. They drove past St. Ambrose Academy and St. Joseph Hospital where Kristen would be volunteering. The sight of the hospital did not sting as much as it had a few years ago. Kristen, Sylvia was certain, would come home bubbly with excitement after her first day there. It was something to look forward to.

As soon as they arrived home, Sylvia was surprised to see her husband's car in the driveway, knowing he wanted her to be there when he came home from work. "Oh my, I didn't realize where the time went." Kristen noticed her mother's sudden change in temperament, then reminded her, "We were having fun, Mom." Sylvia smiled; it had been a long time since she could honestly say she had fun. "Yes, Kristen, we did have fun, but I best get dinner on."

Sylvia parked the car in front of the house. Kristen didn't wait for her mother to get out. Instead, she dashed into the house and raced up the stairs to her bedroom. She was excited to find her white Peter Pan collared blouses, which she found in the back of her closet. She hung them on the closet door and put her shoes and stockings underneath. All she needed was her pinafore and Sister said it would be ready on Friday.

In the meantime, Sylvia started to prepare supper when Virgil opened the back door and walked through the kitchen.

"Hello, dear," she said. "This is a surprise. What brings you home so early, not that I mind. It's nice to have more time with you than usual."

"No special reason," he said. "I just wanted to be with my girls. Take your time; I'm not in a hurry for supper."

He kissed Sylvia on the cheek, picked up his evening newspaper, and headed into the living room to read the news. While he was reading, he heard a rumbling motor idle outside their house. When the motor stopped, he went back to reading the paper and did not give it a second thought. That is, until the doorbell rang. Kristen heard the doorbell from upstairs in her bedroom and shouted loud enough so her dad could hear, "I'll get it!" She secretly hoped Stan would be standing on the porch when she opened the door, but it was someone else that Kristen thought could be his brother. She recognized his motorcycle.

"Hi," she said, after opening the door.

"Hi, I'm Mark Becker, Stan's brother. He wanted me to tell you that he will not be able to take you to the dance on Saturday. He is deeply sorry. Ok, then, I will be going."

That was all he said; he didn't stick around for Kristen to ask any questions. He had no sooner finished his sentence than he turned away from the house and walked off the porch, got on his motorcycle, and started it up. He revved the engine a few times before taking off down the street without any explanation as to why Stan couldn't take her to the dance. Kristen was heartbroken. Why didn't Stan tell her himself? Where was he, she wondered.

Sylvia heard the doorbell but continued preparing their meal. She waited until Kristen closed the front door before asking, "Who was that, dear?"

Kristen was barely able to utter the words, "It was Stan's brother," before she broke down in tears.

"What did he want?" Sylvia asked.

Kristen didn't answer. Virgil, who had been reading his newspaper, overheard every word of the conversation, and marched out of the living room shouting, "What kind of boy sends his brother to deliver a message like that? Certainly not one I want dating my daughter." Sylvia tried to diffuse the all-too-familiar onslaught of her husband's rants. "Now, now, Virgil. I'm sure there is a reasonable explanation."

"It's just as well because that boy rides a motorcycle. You know how I feel about that," he roared. "As a matter of fact, I just read about another motorcycle fatality." Virgil glared at Kristen, "I'm glad that boy, Stan, isn't taking you to the dance. The sooner you forget about him, the better. I forbid you to have anything to do with anyone involved with motorcycles."

"Oh, Daddy," Kristen wailed. "You are so unfair. You don't know Stan. How can you say things like that?"

"Because I am you father, that's why."

Sylvia's ears prickled. Her face turned scarlet when she heard Virgil shouting at Kristen. She'd had enough of her husband's negative behavior. She and Kristen had a lovely afternoon together; the first one that didn't include Harry in her thoughts. She felt they were moving in a healthy way while still holding him in their hearts. But now, any thoughts of happiness quickly evaporated.

"Virgil, that is entirely ENOUGH!"

Sylvia's tone of voice left no room for a retort from her husband. She rarely contradicted him and never in front of their children. But today, after his outburst when Kristen was clearly upset, was unforgivable. "She is sad, Virgil. Don't you feel anything anymore? Where is your empathy?"

"I don't know anything about this boy, Sylvia, other than his brother rides a motorcycle, and that makes him guilty by association."

Sylvia was livid. "You are so unreasonable, Virgil. Save your lawyer jargon for your clients!" She stormed out of the kitchen while untying the apron she had been wearing and tossed it over a chair in the dining room. Glaring at her husband, she said, "I need a moment; you can fix your own plate."

Virgil was gob smacked. His wife had never yelled at him. Oh, he knew she could hold her own as they had lively discussions from time to time, but when it came to her only child, she was a force to be reckoned with. He thought better of the situation than to add fuel to the flame.

Sylvia listened to Kristen slam her bedroom door. She waited at the bottom of the stairs until she heard Kristen crying, sobbing into her pillow.

Stan had broken her heart. It wasn't about the dance, which made Sylvia sad; there would be others. But there would never be a first dance with Stan. Why didn't he tell her himself, she wondered. He just disappeared without communicating a reason. This felt almost as bad as the day Harry died.

Sylvia knocked softly on Kristen's bedroom door. "May I come in?" Kristen didn't want to talk. She half-heartedly uttered, "Sure," as she got up from her bed and opened the door for her mother. It pained Sylvia to see her daughter's swollen, red eyes. She knew first loves were hard to forget and hoped there was a reasonable explanation for Stan's unexplained behavior.

"Come here, dear, let me give you a hug."

Kristen sobbed into her mother's shoulder. When she stopped crying, she looked up and asked, "Why is Daddy so unreasonable?" Sylvia paused before answering, even though she was still angry with her husband.

"He is afraid something will happen to you that he can't prevent. He has not made peace with Harry's death."

Kristen frowned, "Mom, just because Harry made a bad choice doesn't mean I will. Besides, I don't think Stan even knows how to ride a motorcycle."

"Your father has opinions and there is nothing we can do to change them. I suggest that when you and Stan go on a date, please go in a car."

Kristen rolled her eyes, "Oh, Mom, I don't know where Stan is. Maybe I don't want to go out with him, anyway."

"Stan didn't strike me as the kind of boy who would intentionally hurt you, Kristen. He was polite and very gracious."

"I didn't think that of him either, until his brother delivered the message."

"Perhaps there is a good reason for his absence."

"I hope so, Mom, because I really like him."

"I know you do. Now dry your eyes, everything will be ok, you will see."

"Mom, how can you be so certain?"

"I had a few boyfriends before I met your father. So, I know a thing or two."

"Thanks, Mom. That is reassuring. Speaking of Dad, I hope the dad I knew before Harry died comes back. I don't like this version of him."

"All we can do is pray that he does. He needs to decide he needs God's help."

Kristen hugged her mother. "I think I can eat now. Is dinner ready?"

"Yes, dear, almost. I just need to get everything on the table. Come downstairs with me."

Kristen followed her mother down the stairs and into the kitchen. Sylvia was surprised to see that her husband had set the table and was waiting for them. She looked intently into his eyes, then turned away to finish preparing the tossed salad. The oven timer chimed, signaling the casserole had finished baking.

While Sylvia put the finishing touches on the salad, Virgil turned to Kristen. She noticed he no longer appeared angry and had somehow softened a little, even though there were lines on his face she had not seen until now. "Kristen," he began, "You know I love you very much, and I am sorry I have been conflicted. Losing your brother was something I never imagined would happen. I couldn't stand the thought of losing you to anything I could prevent from happening. I am truly sorry your young man can't take you to the dance. When were you going to tell me you had been invited to the dance with a boy?" he asked with a grin.

"Oh, Dad," Kristen mumbled, as she hugged him. Sylvia smiled. She glanced heavenward murmuring, "Thank you!"

On Friday, the halls of St. Ambrose were filled with happy voices and loud conversations about the homecoming football game and dance. Kristen tried not to pay attention to any of it, since her plans had fallen though. She wanted to go with Stan and now that wasn't going to happen. It would not be in her best interest to waste time thinking about what might have been. She had something on her mind that was more important than attending a football game and dance. Sister Benedict said her uniform would be ready and this was the day to pick it up.

After the final bell rang at dismissal, Kristen stopped by the Home Economics room, thinking Sister Benedict would be available. She blurted, "Hi, Sister, I have come for my uniform," before she realized that Sister Benedict was engaged with another student. Sister looked up from a garment she had hemmed for the girl sitting beside her. "Just a moment, Kristen, I have a few more stitches to put in this hem. You aren't in a hurry, are you?"

"No. Sister. I can wait. I apologize for barging in like that. I am excited for tomorrow."

"And so is Miss Reed," Sister said with a smile.

After a couple of final stitches and the thread knotted and snipped, Sister Benedict handed the Homecoming dress to Miss Reed. "There you are," she said. "Enjoy the dance."

"Thank you, Sister," Miss Reed said, as she took her dress and scurried out the classroom door.

Sister Benedict turned to Kristen. "Come for your Candy Striper uniform, have you?"

"Yes Sister, I am very excited to start my volunteering at St. Joseph's tomorrow." The nun smiled and said, "I think you will be an asset to the program. I have no doubts about you, Miss Warner. Do you have all of your uniform?"

"Yes, Sister. I am ready."

"That's good because you need to be at the registration desk by 9:00 a.m. tomorrow. The supervisor of the volunteers will meet you there. I believe her name is Nurse Maloney."

"I will be on time, probably before 9:00 because my dad says, "If you are on time, you're late." Sister Benedict smiled. She could tell Kristen took this opportunity seriously.

"Kristen, you may want to pack your lunch. I believe you will have a locker. If not, there is a refrigerator in the break room."

Kristen frowned. She never considered that she would have a break time. "Oh, I will be too busy to eat, Sister."

Sister Benedict looked at her squarely in the eyes. "Kristen, you will need your break time, take it. I don't want to hear you have skipped it. You will need your strength and nourishment for your job, trust me."

"Thank you, Sister. I will make sure I eat."

Sister Benedict nodded and then turned to the closet where she had Kristen's uniform hanging next to clothing items she had worked on for other students. Her job was to teach the girls basic sewing skills, like hemming. She also offered garment construction to those who wanted to learn more than the basics. She didn't mind hemming a dress or two when the task overwhelmed one of them. This gave Sister Benedict an opportunity to get to know her students in a more casual way outside the classroom.

There were times when a student approached her in tears because she needed help with a dress for a special occasion, like Homecoming. Sister often put more of her time into the dress than the student had. She lived vicariously through them, a surrogate mother who appreciated their youthful exuberance.

As for Miss Warner, Sister Benedict referred to her as a delicate flower. Not like a flower that after a day of blooming wilted and faded, but a rose, whose petals could easily bruise while still effusing a delicate scent, despite the injury. She would blossom as a Candy Striper.

"Miss Warner," Sister called after her, "enjoy your first day. I expect to hear all about it on Monday."

Kristen smiled, tuned around, and answered, "Yes Sister, I expect you will. Thank you for this opportunity." She left the building with her pinafore in hand, moving to the next task of locating her mother.

Sylvia arrived early, parking in her usual spot. She couldn't help listening to the students chattering about Homecoming as they came close to her car, wondering if her daughter felt left out.

Kristen, however, was naturally optimistic so her disappointment over Stan was short lived. As Sylvia watched her daughter approach the car, any reservations she may have had about the dance dissipated.

"Hi, Mom!"

"Hi, dear, I see you have your uniform. The Candy Striper fabric will look so pretty on you."

"Thanks, Mom. I'm excited about tomorrow."

"You should be, Kristen. This is an opportunity to see if you absolutely love nursing."

"I have always wanted to be a nurse, Mom, since I was little. Remember how I begged you for a nurse's costume for Halloween?"

"Yes, I remember. I also remember you taking care of your brother when he broke his arm."

"I did, didn't I."

"You were only five, but you showed compassion. It's a gift, Kristen, don't forget that."

"I won't."

Kristen woke up early the next morning. She hardly slept a wink, or so she thought. Hers was not the sleep of babes, but intermittent periods of wakefulness and light sleep as her mind was going a million miles a minute thinking about her first day. She had just fallen back to sleep when the sun peeked through her bedroom window and woke her up.

After showering Kristen twisted her wet hair into a bun at the base of her neck and secured it in place with bobby pins. She applied a touch of dark brown mascara and pink lip gloss, which was all she needed to look professional. After lingering to gaze at her uniform hanging over her closet door, she took it off the hanger and laid it on her bed to inspect it one final time before pulling the pinafore over her head. At the front of the pinafore was a square bib that she would attach to a full skirt with two big pockets. Kristin put a little pad of paper and a pen into one of the pockets, in case she needed to remember room numbers or other important information she would need to know for her job. Then she took a deep breath and headed downstairs to pack her lunch.

Sylvia had been up and moving around long before Kristen came downstairs. Much to Kristen's surprise, her mother had made breakfast and packed a lunch for her. "Thanks, Mom," she said when she saw the prepared food. As she sat at the kitchen table to eat her breakfast of pancakes and bacon, her mother asked, "How did you sleep, dear?

Pausing a moment to swallow her mouthful of food, she finally answered, "I don't know if I slept at all, Mom. I must have, though; just not a sound sleep. Tonight should be better."

Sylvia smiled, then said, "It is normal to be a little anxious on your first day. You have not been in St. Joseph's since…" Sylvia paused because she suddenly could not say what she was going to say next.

"Oh Mom, you can say it, since Harry died."

"Yes, I know. I don't know why I couldn't bring myself to say his name."

"I will be coming home, Mom. I'm not a patient."

Sylvia turned away from Kristen and cleared the breakfast plates from the kitchen table. Then she said, "I know, dear. Are you ready?"

"Yes, Mom. I thought Dad was driving me?'

"No, he is not ready to go by the hospital, yet." She took a breath, assuring herself she would be able to pull into the hospital parking lot without remembering the last time she was there. Then, turning to Kristen, she said, "I will be waiting in the car for you. I am sure you will want to brush your teeth again."

After brushing her teeth and reapplying fresh lip gloss, Kristen got into the car. Sylvia waited for her to buckle her seat belt, then backed out of the driveway and drove down Arlanda Drive to St. Joseph's Hospital. The drive took fifteen minutes but, to Kristen, felt like seconds. Her mother pulled up in front of the doors to the hospital and let her out. "Have a great day, dear. I will pick you up at five."

Kristen got out of the car and closed the door. Waving to her mother, she turned away from the car and headed toward the hospital

As Kristen walked through the revolving doors with the floor that moved into the lobby of Saint Joseph's Hospital, the first thing she saw was a sign hanging behind the reception desk that read:

"WE ARE THE HANDS THAT HEAL."

Kristen pondered, "We are the hands that heal, the hands that hold, the hands that feed, the hands that change, the hands that cuddle, the hands that love. We are the hands…" Her musings were interrupted when she heard a voice ask, "May I help you?" Kristen turned to the sound of the voice.

"Yes, I am looking for Nurse Maloney."

The nurse behind the receptionist desk smiled. "You are in luck; I am Nurse Maloney, and you must be Miss Warner."

Kristen immediately felt at ease with Nurse Maloney. "Yes, I am," she replied. Nurse Maloney came around the receptionist's desk. "It's nice to have you here. I will show you where to put your things. Oh, I see you brought your lunch, but if you ever forget, we have a cafeteria with food that, despite what you hear about hospital food, is delicious." Chuckling, she added, "Some patient's diets leave a little to be desired." Then Nurse Maloney gave Kristen a rundown of where to find patients rooms, the cafeteria, the gift shop, and the nursery. She gave the new Candy Striper instructions on what needed to be done first, which was to deliver fresh flowers to patients.

Kristen was busy all morning. She particularly loved the nursery with the newborn babies and stopped to gaze at them. Some, she noticed, were not sleeping but crying. A nurse saw Kristen outside the nursery and motioned for her to come in. The nurse was trying to calm a baby when several others started to cry. She turned to Kristen, "I know this may not be protocol, but I need your help. Will you take baby Ellis to his mother in room 265?"

Kristen was surprised she was asked, since this was her first day.

"Of course, I will take him for you."

The nurse was relieved that an extra pair of hands became available. "Thank you," she said, "but first I want you to write Ellis's ID number on a piece of paper. You will find it on his bracelet. When you get to room #265, check the mother's ID bracelet to make sure they are a match. You must never give the wrong baby to the wrong mother. That is protocol."

Kristen nodded, "I will make sure I do that."

The nurse put baby Ellis in his bassinette, then showed Kristen where his ID# was on his wrist band. She no sooner finished instructing Kristen than another crying baby needed her attention. Kristen wheeled the tiny baby down the hall to his mother in room 265, knocking on the door before going in.

"Mrs. Ellis, I brought your baby."

The tired mother looked at Kristen. "Oh…that time already? All I do is feed him."

Kristen didn't know what to say. She didn't babysit nor have younger siblings. It was just she and Harry until he died. She had baby dolls, but they were not real, even though she had pretended they were.

Kristen imagined picking up a real baby was not unlike her dolls. Before she handed the baby to his mother, she checked Mrs. Ellis' ID band. After she confirmed the numbers were the same, she picked up the baby from his bassinette, supporting his head and neck with one hand while cradling his body in her other. Then she put him in the outstretched arms of his mother. After the baby began to nurse, Kristen offered, "There are some diapers in the bassinette, if you need to change him. If you would like to rest, I can come back for him after he has been fed. Just push the call button." Then Kristen left the new mother with her baby.

On her way back to the nursery, Kristen passed the pediatric wing. She did not have a reason to go in but was curious about the patients. When she got back to the nursery, the nurse, wanting to confirm everything was handled properly, asked Kristen to explain the details of what had transpired when she delivered the baby to his mother. After going over the conversation between herself and the mother in room 265, Kristen asked, "Nurse, how old are the kids on the pediatric wing?"

The nurse, wondering why she would ask, didn't hesitate, "They are anywhere from infant to fifteen years old; I believe."

Kristen asked, "Is there anyone as old as 15 on the wing now?"

"Kristen, I can't tell you that. Patient confidentiality is SOP." Kristen was slightly embarrassed, so she decided it was a good time to excuse herself. "Oh…ok, I understand. Do you need anything else? The babies are all sleeping."

"No, I am fine now. Thank you for your help."

"You're welcome. I enjoyed holding a real live baby." The nurse smiled, then said, "Holding a baby is like holding a piece of heaven in your arms." She added, "Anytime you are not needed elsewhere, you may come by. Babies always need to be rocked."

"I would like that, thank you."

The nursery nurse smiled again, then turned her attention back to her charting. Kristen left the nursery turning to walk down the hallway past the pediatric wing.

She no sooner turned the corner when her Supervisor, Nurse Maloney, approached.

"I have been looking for you, Kristen."

Suddenly, Kristen's heart stopped beating. She was certain she'd be dismissed on the spot since she hadn't been told to help in the nursery.

"I'm so sorry, Nurse Maloney. There were so many babies crying, I stopped in to see if I could be of help." While that wasn't entirely true, she didn't want to be the cause of someone else getting into trouble. Nurse Maloney paused. "Ordinarily, I will give you your assignments. I do like initiative in my volunteers. You came highly recommended, so I will excuse you this one time. If this happens again, just have Nurse Mary or another staff member page me."

Kristen was relieved she wasn't put on report and that she had prevented Nurse Mary from the same.

"Yes Ma'am," Kristen responded.

"We have procedures that must be followed, Kristen. I can't have you roaming the hallways unaccounted for, understood? It's for your own safety in the event of an emergency."

Kristen looked at her shoes, "Yes Ma'am," she repeated a second time.

Nurse Maloney held a stack of mail. "Good," she said "Right now I need you to take this mail to a patient on the PEDS wing. He is in room #285."

Kristen took the stack of mail from Nurse Maloney then turned toward the pediatric wing. When she arrived at the nurse's station, she announced that she had mail for a patient in room #285. The nurse looked up from her charting. "Do you mind delivering it for me?"

Kristen was ecstatic but didn't want to betray her inquisitiveness. As calmly as she could, Kristen said, "Of course not. I don't mind at all."

"Thank you," the nurse replied. "Room 285 is down the hallway, the last room before the window."

Kristen nodded, then left the nurse's station in search of her patient's room, locating it at the end of the hallway just as the nurse had said. Before knocking on the door, she stared out the window, mesmerized by the low hanging clouds in front of her that appeared as though she could walk on them.

After a minute, the Candy Striper remembered the mail and knocked on the door of room 285. "Come in," the voice responded. Startled, Kristen thought she recognized the voice, but logic told her she was just imagining, even though her heart told her something else. Then the patient, lying in his bed, turned his face toward the door.

"Kristen!" he exclaimed.

"Stan?" she gasped, both confused and excited at the same time. "What are you doing in here? Is this why you haven't been in school? Is this why your brother delivered your message about the dance?"

"Yes, and I'm so sorry I couldn't tell you myself. Things happened so fast."

Perplexed, Kristen asked, "What do you mean?"

"I've been sick for a while. I didn't want to worry my mom, so I thought if I kept it to myself, I would get better. But as you can tell, that wasn't such a great idea."

"That's crazy, Stan. What kinds of things were happening to you?

Stan looked her in the eyes and answered, "I had some chest pains and my heart felt weird. I got short winded trying to sprint after you when we spent the afternoon together. I was surprised and relieved that you didn't notice."

"Stan, I didn't notice your shortness of breath, but I did notice when you disappeared. I waited for you by my locker for a few days and was so disappointed when you didn't meet me there. Then, everybody was talking about their plans for Homecoming, and I felt left out because I didn't know what happened to you. And then, when your brother came to the house and told me you wouldn't be taking me to the dance, I was so confused and sad. And I was worried! I was beside myself. Nobody knew what happened to you or, if they did, they weren't talking about it. I felt so alone and forgotten."

"I'm sorry I worried you, Kristen. I didn't want Mark to tell you I was sick. I like you, Kristen, and I didn't want you to think of me as weak. And now, you are here, and you know what's been going on, so you don't need to worry anymore."

"Stan, I don't think that about you at all. I am so relieved to know where you are and why you are here."

A chime suddenly went off on Kristen's watch. She winced because she wanted to linger a bit longer with Stan. Looking down, she remembered she was wearing her uniform and she wanted to tell Stan all about her new volunteer position, but she had a job to do.

"I'll be back, Stan. I have to help deliver food trays to patients. So maybe after that I can take my lunch break and eat in your room with you. I have so much to tell you."

Stan smiled, "I would like that, Kristen. I would like that a lot."

11

KAOS

Kaos unlocked the office door to Slim's Garage, and he and Tim stepped over the threshold. Tapping the light switch on the wall behind him, the old office where Slim once worked was instantaneously illuminated. It was dusty from years of neglect, but some of the comforts, like the orange leather couch, was still in the same spot it had been for decades. The sofa needed some cleaning but, other than that, was still serviceable. It was one less thing Kaos would have to buy new.

Next to Slims desk was a metal file cabinet with three drawers, and on the desk was a rotary phone, typewriter, and a stack of ledger cards. A small file cabinet was next to the desk which held service records of clients who came to Slim's Garage for oil changes, tire rotations, inspections, and general upkeep and repair of their vehicles. Kaos thought these were worth saving because he could use them to get the word out that Slim's was again open for business.

In the front windows of the office facing the street hung metal Venetian blinds covered in dust and grime. After Tim's eyes adjusted to the bright light, he noticed a stack of old telephone directories. "Would you look at that!" Kaos looked puzzled, "What am I supposed to be looking at?"

"Look at all those dusty old phone books. What are you going to do with them?"

"Probably throw them out. Why would I want to keep them?"

"Because Kaos, some of the names may still be active. You know, use as a cross reference for marketing purposes."

"You got the time to help me go through those, Tim?"

"I might want to use them for my own purposes. You know, like finding people with deep pockets."

Kaos chuckled, "In this town? Look around you, Tim. I don't think you will find that type of clientele here."

"You would be surprised, Kaos. In my experience, those you least expect have the most money."

"I guess I will keep a few; probably the most recent. The older ones, depending on how old, are kind of a novelty."

Kaos walked to the refrigerator and pulled out two beers. The caps made a hiss as he twisted them off the brown bottles, then he handed Tim a bottle, holding up his beer bottle to clink it against Tim's. "Here's the beer I promised. Cheers!"

They drank in silence, easily downing the beer in a couple of gulps. Kaos heard Tim's stomach rumble. "You want a pizza?"

"Sure, sounds great. Maybe that will shut down these deafening stomach growls." Kaos looked at Tim, who was obviously exhausted.

"By the way, Tim, I don't think you should drive home, wherever your home is. I never asked you."

"Probably not. It has been a day I'll never forget."

"You can stay at my place."

"Oh… and just where is your place?"

"It's not far from here. Just down the road a piece. I got a great deal. The garage and house were owned by the same person, and nobody wanted to buy either one, so they came as a package deal. I heard rumors that the house was haunted. Imagine that."

"What kind of rumors?"

"I heard a kid who lived there died in a motorcycle crash. People say the weirdest stuff. Do you believe in ghosts? You're not afraid, are you?"

"No. I'm not afraid. The nursing staff today told me my mom kept asking for my dad, and when she passed, it looked like she was taking the hands of someone she knew. So no, I don't believe in hauntings. Maybe there is more to the afterlife than we know."

"Ok, just checking, Tim, because you really are in no shape to get behind the wheel. I'll drive us to my house. It's clean, not like this place."

"That would be great, I am tired, and I don't want to drive back here in the morning."

"Do you have anything like appointments you need to get back for?" Kaos asked.

"Even if I do, they can be rescheduled. I'll call my head teller in the morning and have her reschedule my clients. I need a few bereavement days anyway."

Tim was tired, but he was not ready to sleep. The gnawing in the pit of his stomach told him he was hungry.

"Kaos, how far is the pizza joint?" Tim asked.

"It's not far, I'll have them deliver it. We can sit out back and eat, if that's ok with you."

"Sure."

"By the way, there is a nice fire pit behind my house. Somebody made a bench; looks like it's been there a while, weathered and all."

Tim thought the idea nice, but he didn't respond right away. Kaos, realizing Tim was still in his suit offered, "You can borrow a pair of my jeans. I think they will fit."

"Thanks Kaos, I'd rather not snag my suit pants on a distressed wooden bench. Let's get out of here," Tim said, handing his fob to Kaos.

They rode in silence down the quiet streets of Culver Heights, passing the all-seeing eye of the steeple on top of St. Ambrose Church. Kaos stopped the car a block from the church. Turning to Tim he said, "I got to show you something."

Tim snapped, he was tired and hungry. "What am I supposed to be looking at?"

Kaos pointed to Maple Street. "Look at that incline, must be a 21 percent grade. How fast do you think you could go in this car? That is, if the clearance weren't so low we'd bottom out. We would fly!"

Tim looked out the window at the steep grade. "I wonder if any kids rode their bikes down this hill? I would imagine a change of clothes would be in order once they maneuvered the drop and survived."

"No kidding. That is a crazy drop; just had to show it to you."

"Thanks, but are we close to your house? I'm starving."

"We are about two blocks from Arlanda. It is not on an incline like this. Maple Street is the only street in Culver Heights like that."

Within minutes, Kaos pulled in front of his two-story craftsman style home that was covered in white stucco. On either side of the black door were two floor to ceiling windows framed in the same black color as the front door. The front of the house boasted a wide covered porch. Tim remarked on the simple elegance of the home, "Nice place you have, Kaos."

"I enjoy it when I'm here," he said as he unlocked the front door, moving aside so Tim could enter.

Before Kaos entered, he handed Tim the fob to his BMW. "I expect you will need this tomorrow."

"Yes, I probably will. Thanks."

Tim was surprised to see how neat and orderly Kaos liked his things. The inside of the house was light and bright and cheerful. If any ghosts inhabited the house, they were sure to be peaceful ones, as Tim did not get an eerie vibe, nor did he believe in ghosts.

"Make yourself at home, Tim. There is a closet in the hallway where I keep my jeans; help yourself to a pair. I'm going to call in the pizza."

"Thanks," Tim said, as he walked down the hallway toward the closet.

While Tim changed, Kaos called the pizza shop placing their order. Then he went to the backyard and started a fire in the firepit. Kaos smiled when he saw the bench that was fabricated out of stumps and logs. He was grateful to whoever had the foresight to make the extra seating, knowing it would be nice if he were to have guests. For now, Tim was his only guest, and Kaos much preferred sitting in foldable camping chairs.

Within fifteen minutes the pizza arrived. Tim heard the doorbell just as he was coming out of the bedroom, wearing a pair of Kaos' jeans. Deciding on a pair took him longer than necessary, not that he had so many choices, but the magnitude of the day's events finally caught up to him. He sat with his thoughts about his mom and dad and how they were no longer a part of his life. They would soon be dust, scattered on the winds, free. Then Tim remembered a poem his mother liked, especially the words, which resonated in his mind. "And when the earth shall claim your limbs, then shall you truly dance."

Kaos heard the pizza delivery car pull up, and he came inside only to find Tim paying for the pizza. "Thanks, Tim. I didn't expect that."

"No problem, it's the least I can do since you are putting me up for the night."

Kaos dismissed Tim's remark. He was happy to have company since Bud had also been a part of his life. He asked, "It's nice outside, how about we eat out back?"

"Sounds good to me."

While Tim carried the pizza box through the kitchen, Kaos grabbed two more beers from the fridge near the back door. Then he turned to Tim and asked, "Not to get into your business, but don't you think you should leave a message at the bank? You are taking a few days off."

"Thanks for the reminder. I did forget about that."

When they were outside, Tim put the pizza on the bench next to the firepit, pulled his cell phone out of his jeans pocket, and dialed Shelly's number, knowing it was after hours and voice mail would pick up.

"Shelly, this is Tim. I won't be in tomorrow or, for that matter, the rest of the week. Sorry for the short notice, but I need some personal time. I will be in touch. Thanks." He put the phone back in his pants pocket declaring, "I'm starving."

Kaos chuckled, not that this was funny, but the way Tim had said it. It was as if he were relieved that he made the call and wouldn't have to explain anything to anyone. The message got right to the point that he would not be at the bank for the rest of the week.

"You're probably famished by now. Did you eat anything today?" Tim started to say "No" until he remembered the chocolate protein shake from earlier in the morning. They sat in the camping chairs while Kaos reached for the pizza box on the bench, opening it for Tim. Then he took a large slice out for himself and put the box down on the ground between their feet. He took a bite of pizza, savoring the sweet tomato sauce and melty cheese. "Pizza tastes great, by the way. Help yourself."

The pizza wasn't anything spectacular, as in exotic toppings. It was plain cheese and pepperoni. The crust was light and airy, and the sauce tasted like it had been made in the shop owner's grandmother's kitchen, simmering on the stove all day until there was a perfect marriage of sweet basil, garlic and onion, rosemary, and heat from chili peppers.

Tim took another slice out of the box, folding it in half before he took a generous bite, savoring the flavor of the sauce, the heat from the pepperoni, and the light airy crust. He followed it with another beer, then sat back in his camping chair staring at the fire in the fire pit. Life could not feel any better than this moment, albeit temporarily. Kaos noticed the faraway look in Tim's eyes. "Where did you go? You look miles away from here."

"I was wondering how you got involved with my dad. It wasn't like he didn't have a family; he did. He had me and Mom."

"Truthfully, Tim, I wasn't looking for adventure. I had been working for Slim for about a month when your dad came in with his beat-up bike."

"Did he say how that happened?"

"Slim told me he was your dad's mechanic; had been for years. But he was getting tired of fixing Bud's bike every time he wrecked it. He said no one in their right mind would do so much damage if they loved their bike."

"My dad loved bikes, Kaos. He used to take me to Slim's Garage. I remember this one time, there was a kid running the office; I think it was Slim's son. He was talking to another boy about the same age who brought his kid sister in. Even now, remembering back, I can see that little girl. It's funny, I had no reason to think about Slim's until now."

"So, you don't remember much about the boys in the garage, but the little girl stuck with you? She must have been memorable."

"She was a kid, Kaos. Maybe ten years old, but she had the most exquisite eyes I have ever seen. So yes, that would make her memorable." Tim frowned because thinking about the girl at the garage reminded him of the blues eyes of the woman in the red dress from the gala.

"I'm just busting on you, Tim. Hand me another beer, will ya?"

"You didn't answer my question, Kaos. How did you end up traveling with my dad?"

"Slim had special bikes in his garage. One was a Honda Super Blackbird, an awesome looking machine because it had headlights stacked one on top of each other, not side by side. It was fast, top speed 180 mph."

"Whoa, that's a lot of power."

"Too much for a novice rider."

"Both Slim and Bud were experienced drivers, so why did you say that?"

"Bud told me he was coming home from a show, hauling another wrecked bike to Slim's Garage. It was about midnight when he came upon a horrible motorcycle accident."

"That's awful. Cars should be more respectful of bike riders. They have road rights, too."

"Yeah, but this was particularly sad."

"Why?"

"These were boys, maybe fifteen or sixteen years old."

"Kaos, I wonder if those were the boys I told you about that I saw at the garage. When I saw them, they were in the bay area looking at a Honda motorcycle Slim had just brought in. I remember because my dad was really impressed by the bike, and I could tell the boys were too."

"From what Bud saw, he said that one boy didn't have a chance and probably died as soon as he hit the ground. I heard the other boy died later. What is really tragic is that one of the boys was Slim's son, Mitch. He and the other boy apparently stole, maybe borrowed is a kinder word, the bike. Still, they had no business riding a bike like that. Sadly, it was their first and last ride on the Super Blackbird. So, to answer your question, maybe."

"My God! That is tragic, Kaos."

"Yep."

Tim and Kaos took a synchromatic sip of beer, then another. The magnitude of the accident reeled in their minds until Kaos spoke up. "After the accident, Slim lost all interest in fixing motorcycles. He said I could if I wanted to, but he didn't want to fix another crumpled bike. It was too painful."

"You fixed my dad's bike?"

"Yeah, Slim wasn't going to take on any new work. He never said what he was going to do. So when Bud asked me to travel with him, I accepted his offer." Tim shouted, sarcastically, "Good for you." Kaos waited for Tim's ire to pass. Then he patiently explained, "I can understand why you would feel that way. But you should know that Bud always talked about his family. And after the novelty wore off that he was a superstar with groupies, he didn't bother with women anymore. He loved his wife he would say, but didn't think his marriage could be salvaged, and he felt drifting in and out of your life would do more harm than good."

"I didn't think he loved me. I never forgot about my dad. I just tried to hang onto the good memories." Tim paused for a few minutes, taking a sip of beer, then another, as he gazed into the atmosphere seeing nothing there but pondering on something. Then he continued, "Now that I think about it, building a bike in his memory would be a legacy."

"That would be Tim. Got any ideas for a bike?"

"I have some drawings that I look at every now and then. I have been planning to take a cross-country trip once I retire."

Kaos thought about all the days he traveled with Bud across the country and back, then asked, "Is it going to be a solo journey?"

"Not so much anymore. I would like to have a companion. Funny how you don't think you need anyone until you don't have anyone."

"Yeah, Bud was my family."

"How so, Kaos. What's your story?"

Kaos paused, took another long swig of his beer, not wanting to think about his early childhood. "My biological father ran out on my mom once he found out she was pregnant with me. It was Mom and me for the longest time. Then she got involved with a miscreant and it was all downhill from there. Social Services intervened many times, but Mom died from a drug overdose a few years later and I ended up in the system. So, when I finally met Bud, he was like a dad to me. Guess he made up for losing you."

That statement made Tim livid, knowing Kaos had spent quality years with his dad when it should have been him. "He didn't lose me, he chose to!"

Kaos again waited for Tim's anger to subside. When it did, he gently reminded him. "Like I said, Bud never stopped talking about you." To ease the sting of the years Kaos had with his dad, Tim joked, "I'm grateful I ran into you, literally!"

"Tim," Kaos said, "I am of the firm belief that there is no such thing as coincidence."

Looking directly at Kaos, Tim said, "If what you say is true, maybe it's in the cards that I will connect with the woman in the red dress."

"No maybe about it, Tim. I believe that."

Then Kaos turned his attention back to the glowing embers in the firepit. Every few seconds the logs that had hours before snapped and crackled in violent protest had been transformed by the intense heat. A soft thud could be heard from a log as the wood shifted and pulsated with a heartbeat that glowed and dimmed in the simmering ash. When the embers turned from red to white to black, Kaos asked Tim if he was ready to turn in for the night, which, in reality, was the early morning.

"Yeah, I'm ready. It's been a long day. I think I can sleep now, Kaos."

"Alright, grab your empties on the way in, will you? I have a recycle bin outside the kitchen door."

"Sure, no problem," said Tim as he gathered his collection of the amber glass bottles that had provided him with a mind-numbing respite from the events of the proceeding day. Kaos turned to Tim asking, "You ok sleeping on the couch?" At this hour, Tim didn't care where he slept as long as he could just lay down.

"I could sleep anywhere. Toss me a blanket and it's lights out for me."

When Tim woke up, it was high noon. He couldn't remember the last time he had slept that late. He didn't remember much about the day before in those first waking moments, but as the wisps of his dreams faded about the woman in the red dress, his memory suddenly became clearer. Mom.

He had to make sure Kauffman's Funeral Home had gone to the nursing home to take his Mom's body away. Her only request when she was lucid enough to discuss her end of life wishes was to be cremated. She wanted her ashes transformed into a blaze of glory like the setting sun over the ocean, becoming ashes that floated on the breeze. Mary Jane had said little until she and Tim had a conversation about what to do in the end. She had been adamant that she wanted her ashes cast through the whispering pine trees overlooking the ocean. She distinctly said, "Make sure it is a bright day, Tim. I want to dance with the sunbeams on the water."

Kaos had awakened before Tim. He was used to a few hours of sleep, having traveled with Bud. If the show was good, they might stay on. If it ended in a disaster, they would pack up and be off to the next town to recuperate. Bud would promote himself handing out flyers for the next show while Kaos repaired his beaten-up bikes. For a while this was an exciting life, traveling the circuits with Bud. But Kaos was getting tired of moving around and wanted permanence somewhere he could call home.

When Bud had his final accident, while tragic, it also provided Kaos the opportunity to buy a place. As luck would have it, Slim's Garage and house were on the market. The FOR-SALE sign looked weathered, like it had been tossed on its hinges by the wind and assaulted by pelting rain for years until the telephone number for the realtor was barely visible. The house and garage stood empty; a collection of gathering dust and peeling paint.

Kaos asked the realtor, "How long has the property been up for sale?"

"A very long time," she responded. Then mumbled something about being superstitious.

Kaos continued with his questioning. "Oh, like how long? Is it in bad shape?" I mean will I have to sink a lot of money into it before I can start to make a living there?"

The realtor didn't respond immediately. After a few minutes she said, "It is in good condition, other than some dust removal and new paint."

Kaos thought that something as minor as paint was an odd reason for the house to have been on the market for so long. "Then, why is it still on the market? I also noticed there are no other garages around here so business should be good."

"That is correct," she answered. "This is the only garage for miles."

"You didn't answer my question," Kaos reminded her.

The realtor couldn't find a way out of his line of questioning, resigning herself to tell him the reason the property was vacant. "Kaos, people are… superstitious."

"Superstitious about what? Did somebody die here?"

The realtor responded with a firm, "No."

Kaos decided to let the subject drop. Obviously, the house and garage were surrounded in mystery and the realtor was not going to discuss it any further. He surmised she probably didn't want to lose the sale and saying nothing was better than saying too much. Besides, the asking price didn't offend his budget.

After the purchase of the property went through, Kaos had to get the garage up and running. Slim had either forgotten or intentionally left inventory on the dusty shelves, and he didn't know how old the parts were. Sure, it was possible some parts could be used on cars but upon closer inspection, he identified the parts as belonging to motorcycles. Vintage parts were getting harder and harder to find if one wanted to remain a purist. Prudence dictated that it would be wise to keep these. He could order new parts for newer bikes, but vintage models…he would need old parts.

The more he looked around, the idea came to him that he could build a bike out of these left behind pieces. He'd have to find a frame but that was also the thrill of the hunt. There were places where no one suspected vintage parts could be found. Sometimes they were buried under layers of vegetation, and they were there for the asking. Kaos wasn't too proud to ask, and he didn't mind digging up, dragging out, or climbing over piles of junk to find treasure. He didn't care what kind of frame he found because that was the challenge of marrying parts according to their functionality.

There had been some great vintage bikes and every model seemed to be an improvement upon a former model. But vintage bikes, aw… vintage bikes were something special. Kaos didn't need to be reminded of that as he remembered the sign hanging in Slim's Garage.

THERE ARE TWO KINDS OF PEOPLE.
HARLEY PEOPLE AND EVERYONE ELSE.

Kaos returned to his house on Arlanda Drive around four in the afternoon. As soon as he unlocked the front door, he could see Tim reaching into the refrigerator, oblivious of his arrival, retrieving the pizza box from the night before.

"Hey, did you save a slice for me?"

Startled, Tim dropped the pizza box on the floor. "Kaos, don't sneak up on me like that!" Kaos chuckled, "Why, are you afraid of ghosts?" Tim bent down and picked up the pizza box. He looked up at Kaos, "No, I'm not. I didn't know where you went, and I was hungry."

"No problem, Bud…I…mean Tim."

"Do I look like Bud?"

"No, can't say you do, but I have been thinking about Bud's last wishes."

"Oh, what did he want?"

"Tim, he didn't really have any other than he wanted to be cremated. I didn't take him to be a religious man."

"I don't remember him as such, why? What are you thinking?"

"I've been thinking since Bud, sorry, your dad and mom died on the same day, maybe their ashes should be interred together somewhere. Maybe I am assuming too much, I didn't ask you what your mom wanted."

"No problem, Kaos, I didn't tell you. My mom had specific wishes I need to honor. The cremation part is the same, and since my dad really didn't care, other than to be cremated, that's a good idea. They should be together in perpetuity, mix their ashes together, bury them or do what my mom wanted."

"What did she want?"

"She wanted to dance on sunbeams."

"Maybe we should say a few words, Tim, before we do that. I'm assuming you mean scattering them to the wind."

"That does sound kind of impersonal without some sort of ceremony. They were born, they lived and died. They were people who loved us. We should honor them in some way."

"Did your mom like poetry?"

"Wow Kaos! For a crusty guy you surprise me."

"Sorry to burst your bubble, Tim. I am cultured despite my appearance."

"In answer to your question, my mom liked Kahlil Gibran. I haven't a clue about my dad."

"What did she like about Gibran?"

"Because of her final wishes, dancing on sunbeams."

Kaos offered, "I have a few favorites, even if Bud didn't. I like the poet Rumi. He has profound thoughts on goodbye, and Antoine de Saint-Exupery has a specific thought as to why people run into each other. I'd like to read something from those before we scatter the ashes. Maybe you could read that poem about dancing on sunbeams."

"Sounds good to me," answered Tim. "Listen, I need to go home, get showered and come back. I also need to make sure Kauffman's has picked up my mom's body and see when I can have her back. Where did my dad's body go?"

"Same place. Kauffman's."

"That certainly wasn't a coincidence," Tim surmised.

"But their dying on the same day was, Tim?" Kaos inquired.

Tim hesitated, not sure what he believed about coincidences. Looking down at his watch, he wondered how the day passed by so quickly? It was almost 5 p.m. and he still had things to do. He reminded his friend, "Kaos, I have to make that call, and you can make yours. Then we shall wait for a brilliant, sunny day for our impromptu scattering of their ashes. I don't care for gloomy days at all."

"Nor do I."

"Alright my friend, I will be back in an hour or two."

"Tim, if I'm not here when you get back, I'll be at the garage."

"Ok, sounds good, Kaos."

Tim made his phone call to Kauffman's and was relieved that his mother's body had been picked up and that her cremains would be available on that Friday afternoon. He was sad that his mother was gone physically, but he had made peace with the fact that she had checked out mentally years before, even though he never gave up hope that she would have a glimmer of a memory of her son. Clearly, Mary Jane remembered his dad, which gave him a different perspective on life and the hereafter.

Maybe there was something more, Tim thought. He was not a selfish, evil man, and he treated his clients fairly. But maybe he should do more with his life.

He would describe himself as lukewarm in his relationships with most people, other than Helen Trenton. Her flirtatious advances were benign. She knew and Tim knew that they fed off each other. Tim helped her feel alive again, and Helen helped Tim feel like he was important to someone. Perhaps it was time to change and that woman in the red dress was the proof he needed.

Tim arrived at his home in time to watch the horizon from his lanai transform into spectacular bursts of red and orange and then soften into hues of lavender and deep purple until there was nothing but a black void staring back at him. He lingered in the darkness thinking about nothing until his automatic garden lights illuminated the pea gravel paths that led to his bedroom from the lanai. His feet crunched under the pea gravel as he walked to his house.

When he pushed open his bedroom door, he noticed a blinking red light on his answering machine but chose to ignore it. Whatever the problem was or whomever it was, could wait. He told Shelly he was taking a few days off and he meant it.

He gathered extra casual shirts and jeans, boxer shorts, and a freshly dry-cleaned black suit and white shirt. He glanced at his tie drawer, then decided he didn't need a tie, as the ceremony for his parents was not a formal event. Tim packed his clothing and toiletries in a leather valise.

Before heading down the stairs, he took a second look at the blinking red light on the answering machine, choosing to ignore it for a second time. He looked at it again, feeling conflicted, because he was not in the habit of ignoring phone messages. Tim let out a deep sigh; whatever the problem was could wait.

He descended the stairs into the kitchen and turned on a small light on the back counter before strolling down the open hallway leading to his front door. Satisfied when he heard the automatic lock engage, he walked briskly to his car as the motion sensor lights came on.

The black sky sparkled with myriads of shimmering lights while a gentle breeze swirled around him. The night air was clean and crisp, a rarity for Southern California. Tim didn't feel the need for music as the silence he experienced gave him a sense of tranquility and peace, unlike the silence he experienced after a long day at the bank.

When Tim arrived at Kaos' house an hour later, he wasn't surprised there were no lights on. Kaos said he would be at the garage, so Tim decided to meet him there. When he arrived, the office lights were on and the door was unlocked, which surprised Tim. He wasn't used to working alone but obviously Kaos was. Hearing a ding overhead, Kaos came out of the bay area, wiping his hands on an oily cloth.

"I see the travel fairy was good to you. Honestly, I thought you wouldn't return until tomorrow." Tim chuckled, "Yes, the travel fairy was."

Kaos, wondering why Tim preferred sleeping on his couch rather than staying at home, asked, "So, you don't mind the couch for another night?"

"Nope, the couch will be just fine."

"Mi casa es tu casa," Kaos said smiling. He was extremely glad Tim had come back; he enjoyed his new friend's company more than he realized. It was as if a part of Bud was still around, and he didn't hesitate to invite Tim to a longer stay. "You know Tim, you are welcome to stay here as long as you want."

"Thanks, Kaos, I appreciate your offer. I will have to get back after our service of sorts."

"I thought you were taking some time off?"

"Kaos, I am. It's just that there was a message on my answering machine that I didn't retrieve. I will have to go back and respond to the message. It probably has something to do with a client from the bank. By the way what did you find out about my dad's ashes?"

"I can pick them up Friday. And you, what about your mom's?"

"Same as you. So, if Saturday's weather cooperates with what my mom wanted, I would like to get this over with."

"Saturday, works for me."

On Saturday morning, there was not a cloud in the sky. A perfect day, as Mary Jane would say, since she wanted her ashes sprinkled through the whispering pines along the coast, and Tim intended to honor her wishes. So when he announced this was the day, he and Kaos quickly got themselves physically and mentally prepared for the service and secured both Mary

Jane and Bud's ashes in the passenger seat of Tim's car.

Kaos followed Tim on his motorcycle.

As Tim drove out of Culver Heights with Mary Jane and Bud's ashes secured in the seat, he thought how his parents had lived in that area, and now he was escorting them out. Sadness enveloped him because this chapter of his life had closed. He looked in his rearview mirror checking to see that Kaos wasn't far behind on his motorcycle, and he was glad he wasn't.

At the last minute, Tim decided to stop by his house; he didn't think he needed to wear his suit, and he knew his mom really wouldn't care. So when he activated his left turn signal alerting Kaos to follow him up a gravel driveway, Kaos was surprised. Tim pulled up to the covered walkway that ran from the garage to his house. Then Kaos pulled alongside him and turned off his motorcycle. He looked around in awe of how Tim lived. "Some place you got here, Tim! Is all this yours?" He got off his motorcycle, took off his helmet, and placed it under his arm.

For the first time, Tim felt embarrassed about where he lived so he downplayed his response. "Yeah, Kaos, it's all mine." Kaos laughed. "Maybe that pretty woman in the red dress you talk about will make this her home?"

"That would be nice, Kaos. But what are the chances of that happening?" Then he motioned his head for Kaos to follow him. While gaining access to his house, Tim asked, "Kaos, you want a drink or something before we head up the coast?"

"Just water. Thanks, Tim."

Tim pushed the hammered metal door open, entering the foyer, before making a sharp left turn that led to his kitchen. He laid his freshly dry-cleaned suit over a stool next to the counter that served as a breakfast bar. Ambling to the refrigerator, he reached in and pulled out two bottles of water and placed them on the island between the refrigerator and the sink. "I'm going to put my suit away. I don't think Mom would mind me wearing jeans, and I doubt she'd remember me in a banker's suit."

Kaos added to Tim's conversation, "Bud never saw me wearing a suit.

He'd probably say, 'Lighten up, you look like you're going to a funeral.' I'm sure of it."

"That's funny, Kaos!"

"Well, what I have on will have to do, Tim. Too bad my bike isn't made for two people."

"It's fine, we're going in my car. I can secure the urns in the back seat. You can sit in the front with me. Where would we put the ashes on your bike, anyway? I can see them flying out of their containers because we didn't secure them. And we would be none the wiser. However, I don't think that was Mom's idea of dancing on sunbeams."

Kaos thought that would certainly be amusing; a stream of ashes flying out behind the motorcycle landing who knows where. "I'm thankful we aren't. We should try to honor funeral decorum."

"Kaos, I haven't been to many funerals, so your guess is as good as mine. I don't make a habit of going to client's funerals." Tim retrieved his dry-cleaned suit from the bar stool and dashed up the stairs to put it away.

Kaos didn't have much experience either. The only funeral he could remember, and that was barely, was his mother's. The social worker thought that his fostering family should help him find closure by going. It was a blur and not a happy thought at all. Just a dark pit of nothingness. Kaos shuddered as Tim came bounding down the stairs.

"Your choice, as far as the ceremony goes. Are you ready to go, Tim? Do you know what you are going to say?"

"I almost forgot. Thanks for the reminder. You can go on out to the car. I'll be there shortly."

As Kaos turned to leave the house, Tim walked to his bookshelves staged against a brick wall under the open slatted staircase. He pulled a book off the shelf and turned to a poem his mom would have liked and folded the page at the corner so he could easily find the poem before her ashes were released.

While Kaos waited by the car, he was lost in his own thoughts about the ceremony for Bud and his wife. Bud had many followers in his day and now there were only two who would mark his passage from this earthly place.

Perhaps that was the way it was supposed to be. Kaos always believed there was no such thing as coincidence. Tim running him off his bike was not one, just as the woman in the red dress was not happenstance.

After they got into the car, Kaos asked, "Tim, do you know where you are going to do this? Do you have a special place in mind?"

"Not really, other than a spot near pine trees overlooking the Pacific."

"So we're just gonna drive along the highway?"

"Yes," was all Tim said, engaging the engine. He put the car in reverse to back out of his parking spot, turned around, then drove slowly down the gravel driveway until his car met the street. After looking both ways, he turned left and zoomed out onto Highway 1.

They drove in silence, each to his own thoughts. Tim didn't know where he was going to stop until he heard his mother's sweet voice from somewhere inside him, "Pull over here."

Tim turned to Kaos, "This is it; this is the spot."

"How do you know, Tim?"

"Because I do," was all he offered.

Tim pulled over to a clearing on the right side of the two-lane highway. Crossing the highway could be tricky any day of the week, but today the traffic was minimal. After he got out of the car, he reached into his backseat and picked up his father's brown urn, handing it to Kaos. Then he picked up his mother's urn that was just as plain as his dad's. There was no reason to buy ornate urns when there would be no cremains in them for perpetuity.

They waited for a couple of cars to pass before sprinting across the road and climbing up a small embankment covered with pine trees. They came upon a flat spot in a clearing overlooking the ocean.

"You want to go first?" Kaos asked Tim.

"No, you go ahead."

Kaos handed the brown urn to Tim, holding what was the last remainder of Bud. He took a folded piece of paper out of his pants pocket. "I have two verses I would like to read for Bud." Tim nodded, indicating Kaos should continue.

"Every person that comes into our life, comes for a reason; some come to learn, and some come to teach." Then he turned toward the brown urn in Tim's hands and said, "Thank you, Bud for coming into mine."

Kaos paused as he brushed away the uncontrollable tears that had suddenly began flowing from his eyes. Tim waited, then asked, "What's the second one? I thought you said you have two." Kaos wiped the last set of tears from his cheeks, taking a second piece of paper out of his pocket. "This second one is also from the poet Rumi. I like to think of it as my philosophy on life and death. 'Goodbyes are only for those who love with their eyes. Because for those who love with heart and soul, there is no such thing as separation.' I'll be seeing you, Bud."

Then Kaos said, "Now it's your turn, Tim."

Tim handed Kaos both urns. This was more difficult than he thought it would be until he heard her still small voice say, "Let me go."

"My mom liked Kahlil Gibran, so I'm reading his thoughts on death." Pausing, Tim swallowed the lump that had suddenly risen in his throat. Then he began.

"For what is it to die but to stand naked in the
wind and to melt into the sun?
And what is it to cease breathing, but to free the breath from its restless
tides, that it may rise and expand and seek God unencumbered?
Only when you drink from the river of silence shall you indeed sing.
And when you have reached the mountaintop, then shall you climb.
And when the earth shall claim your limbs, then shall you truly dance."

Tim took his mother's urn from Kaos. Together they opened the vessels that temporarily contained Tim's parents and Kaos' good friend.

Turning to the breeze that had suddenly swirled around them, they opened the vessels so the ashes could flow out. As the wind caught the ashes comingling, Tim said,

"Dance on the sunbeams, Mom. I love you."

12

HELEN TRENTON

By the time Tim and Kaos returned from their mission, the late afternoon sky was a scatter of blue and yellow lights that left a red hue in its wake. The events of the day had turned out to be more emotionally draining than either of them expected. Once the ashes were dispersed into the wind, they were momentarily at a loss in what to do next.

Tim suggested they drive to his dad's favorite seafood joint that overlooked the Pacific Ocean. After feasting on an assortment of fruits de la mer, they decided on a glass of wine, a toast to those who were now carried in their hearts. Tim took a sip looking out over the ocean from his seat next to the railing of the pier's restaurant.

Kaos noticed Tim's faraway look. "Where did you go?"

"Kaos, do you believe in an afterlife?"

"Weren't you listening today?"

"I was, but I wasn't hearing you."

"What I said was, when someone we love dies, we never really say goodbye to them because they live on in our hearts."

"Yeah, I heard that part."

"Alright then, let me ask you this, Tim. How did you know where to stop?"

Tim took a deep breath, deciding how to explain. "It's strange. I used to think death was the end, nothing more. My parents were not religious. But the events of the week have led me to believe otherwise. For example, when Mom died, she was reaching for something or someone. The nurses said she kept repeating my dad's name all day. And today as we were driving, I didn't have a location in mind. I knew what my mom wanted, and that was to dance on sunbeams. So, when I heard a still voice from within me say, 'This is the spot,' I knew I should stop. Who else could that have been?"

"Then it was your Mom."

Tim thought that if he replied in the affirmative, he would be admitting he believed in the hereafter, and that was a huge step. Taking the leap, he said, "Yes, I believe it was."

"I've told you, Tim, there is no such thing as coincidence."

Tim looked at his glass, swirling the remaining claret liquid pooled at the bottom before sipping it down. Then, looking at Kaos, he asked, "You ready to go?"

"Yeah, it's been an exhausting day."

"You can stay over at my place, Kaos. I have a guest room; never used. You will be my first guest."

Kaos thought a moment before accepting Tim's invitation. "Thanks, I appreciate your offer."

"No problem, my pleasure," he said as he signaled the server. "I'll take our check, please."

After paying the bill and handing their server a generous tip, they left the restaurant and drove to Tim's house. By the time they got to the driveway, the sky had turned dark red. Tim smiled as the pea gravel crunched under the weight of the car singing, "Welcome home, welcome home." Tim pulled to the front of the breezeway and turned the engine off. "Here we are. Home."

"That has a nice ring to it, Tim. Home."

"Yeah, it feels like home with someone other than me to wander through it. You can stay as long as you want."

Tim opened the front door to the house, letting Kaos walk in before him. For the second time that day, Kaos marveled at the space in front of his eyes. Tim walked past him into the kitchen, opened the refrigerator door, and asked, "You want a drink, Kaos?"

"Water will be fine, thanks."

"Suit yourself," Tim said, pulling out two bottles of spring water. I need to go upstairs and check on some mail."

"I thought you were taking the day off."

"I am."

Tim retreated upstairs to his bedroom and saw the blinking red light on his answering machine. He was tempted to listen to the message but, again, chose to ignore it. Whoever and whatever could wait until tomorrow. He pulled open the double glass doors that led to the lanai. As soon as he stepped onto the gravel, a soft breeze surrounded him like a fluffy blanket. His shoes sloshed as he walked on the rain-soaked gravel path; it occurred to him that he hadn't noticed the water on his driveway. He didn't mind the rain. Someone once said that rain was a good omen.

Kaos finished his 16 oz. bottle of spring water before realizing Tim had been gone a while. Kaos ascended the stairs and found his friend standing outside, looking over his garden wall into the night sky.

"What are you looking at?"

Tim pointed to the sky. "Do you see these stars?"

Kaos, thinking Tim must be making a joke, responded, "I see lots of stars."

Tim pointed to two very bright stars. "Look, do you see them now?"

Kaos saw, among the millions of stars in the sky, the two Tim had focused his attention on.

"Yeah, I see them."

"Do you know that these two stars burned out lifetimes ago, and this is what's left of them? It is a puzzle how their brilliance remains."

"I'm not an astrophysicist, Tim, but I would like to think those stars are a sign from Bud and your mom they are together."

"Maybe. I'd like to think that too; that they are a sign. As you say, Kaos, there's no such thing as coincidence."

Kaos yawned, "I don't know about you, but I'm tired. I'd like to get some shut eye if you don't mind."

"I'm tired, too. I'd better show you to the guest suite."

Kaos followed Tim into the house and down the hallway to the guest quarters. When Tim opened the door, Kaos noticed that his room had its own separate door to the lanai. His room was not as large as Tim's, but whoever designed it gave the room as much detail as they did to the master suite.

The walls were painted a soft dove gray, complimented by white moldings. A predominantly red oriental rug covered the middle of the floor. Upon the rug rested a queen -sized bed. The linens were a gray and white ticking pattern, covered with a white duvet. A black leather chair and a sleek stand-alone brushed nickel floor lamp were in one corner of the room, overlooking the lanai. On the other side of the chair, a small blue-gray table held a single red rose in a glass vase. Against a wall leading to the hallway, a wardrobe fit neatly in an alcove. It was uncluttered; a simple-elegant design.

"Will this do?" Tim asked.

"Are you kidding, I feel like a king. This is nice. I might stay indefinitely."

"As I said before, Kaos, you are welcome to stay as long as you want."

"Thanks, Tim. Good night."

Tim exited and closed the door to the guest bedroom suite. He was not as tired as he alluded and the blinking red light on the answering machine would not go away. Tim rarely received messages on his home machine, but since he had taken time off and did not want to be disturbed, this was the only way he could be contacted. He pushed the button to activate the message that was left on Wednesday. Tim stood back from the answering machine with his arms crossed, listening to the unfamiliar voice on the recorder.

"This is Dr. Franklin from General Hospital. Please return my phone call at your earliest convenience. I am allowed to tell you this is in regard to Helen Trenton. If you call the hospital, they will transfer you to my office." BEEP. Tim hit the button again for the second message. "This is Dr. Franklin, please return my phone call immediately." BEEP.

The second message alarmed Tim. As he dialed the number Dr. Franklin left, anxiety and waves of nausea overcame him, so he quickly hung up the phone. When the episode was over, he dialed the number again. As soon as the voice on the other end said, "Hello," Tim blurted, "This is Tim Hurst; I am returning Dr. Franklin's phone call. He says it is urgent."

"One moment, please," the voice replied.

While Tim waited for Dr. Franklin, he walked down the stairs into the kitchen and then to his bar, where he pulled out a bottle of bourbon and poured a generous shot into a glass tumbler. Finally, he heard a man's voice on the other end of the call.

"Mr. Hurst, this is Dr. Franklin. I am deeply sorry; your friend, Helen, died of a massive stroke. We did all we could to save her. I am contacting you because your name was on her directive."

Tim was stunned. The last thing he expected to hear was that his client, Helen Trenton, was dead. He was speechless.

"Mr. Hurst...I am very sorry," Dr. Franklin repeated.

Slowly, Tim's presence of mind returned and as it did, he asked, "When did this happen?" Dr. Franklin paused since it was obvious Tim had just heard the message.

"Last week, on Thursday. In her directives, she stated that you would fulfill her wishes. You need to contact her attorney, Phillip Hartson at Hartson and Hodges."

The only words Tim managed to say were, "Thank you, Doctor."

Tim poured another bourbon but did not drink it. He carried the tumbler upstairs to his bedroom and placed the glass on his nightstand. Walking to the glass doors, he stared out into the black night. Kaos, unable to sleep, noticed Tim's bedroom light shining on a swath of the garden's path and thought Tim might need to talk. It had, after all, been a hard day.

Kaos walked down the hallway to Tim's bedroom and knocked on the door leading to the master suite. Standing at the closed door, Kaos asked, "You ok?" Tim answered from the other side, "Not really." Wanting to respect Tim's space, Kaos didn't want to pry, but something was amiss with his host so he asked, "You want to talk?"

"I don't know, Kaos."

Kaos slightly opened Tim's door, peeking his head in.

"What's going on?"

"Helen is dead!"

"Who's Helen?"

"She was my client at the bank. I saw her recently; she didn't appear ill."

"Was she ill, and maybe you were not aware of it, Tim?"

"Not that I know of. She had a stroke."

"I am very sorry about that. Were you two close?"

Tim thought for a moment about how he would answer Kaos' question. Anything he said would sound unscrupulous.

"She was my client; we had an understanding."

Suddenly Tim's emotions got the best of him, and he began to sob. Kaos stood by helplessly, not knowing how to console his friend. When Tim regained his composure, he explained, "The last time I saw Helen was at the gala, the night I ran into you. I left her at The Jackson Hotel in the early hours of the morning. She thought I was going to sleep with her."

"Did you?"

"No, Kaos, I always let her think I would, though."

"Tim, why would you do that if you had no intention of following through?"

"Because she wrote big checks!"

"TIM!"

"I suppose you think the worst of me now, Kaos."

"No, I don't think that. I am just surprised."

Tim felt that Kaos needed more of an explanation into the relationship between himself and Helen Trenton. "As I said before, Helen and I had an understanding. I think she knew I would never go that far with her. I gave her the attention she needed, and she made me feel like I belonged."

"Like family?"

"I guess that sounds messed up, like an Oedipus Complex?"

"No it doesn't. Bud made me feel like I belonged."

"I have lost everyone close to me in a matter of days, Kaos."

"What are you going to do, Tim? And why did YOU get the phone call about Helen? Didn't she have a family?"

"I'm not aware of any. I was told to see her attorney regarding her final wishes."

"That's a lot to ask of you."

"She could trust me, Kaos. I suppose that's why."

"I know that's a lot to think about, but you should try to get some sleep."

"Yeah, I will try. Thanks, buddy."

The next morning, Tim made the phone call to Phillip Hartson. It was not hard tracking down the phone number, as the firm was known as the most reputable Estate Planning Law Firm in the greater Los Angeles area, which was about an hour's drive north of Culver Heights. He let the phone ring several times before someone finally picked up. After the voice on the other end identified the firm, Tim said rather briskly, "I'd like to speak to Phillip Hartson, please. This is Tim Hurst." The voice pleasantly answered, "Mr. Harston is with a client. May I take a message?"

"Yes, tell him I am contacting him via a mutual client at the behest of Dr. Franklin at General Hospital."

"Thank you, Mr. Hurst, I will make sure Mr. Hartson receives your message."

Tim hung up from the phone call having accomplished his first order of business for the day. Suddenly, his head felt a tad murky, realizing he had not had his morning elixir.

"Coffee. Coffee is what I need right now."

Opening the refrigerator door, Tim peered inside and located a glass mason jar that contained what looked like ground coffee. When he removed the lid, the bold flavor of coffee awakened his senses. He no sooner set the coffee maker to brew than the phone rang.

"Hello, Tim Hurst here."

"Mr. Hurst, this is Phil Hartson returning your call. Helen Trenton is, excuse me, was my client and has asked me to read her will. I have an opening on my schedule this afternoon at two."

Since Tim had no plans to go into the bank, he agreed to the afternoon appointment. "I'm available. I'll be in at two today."

Tim ended the phone call just as Kaos came downstairs, yawning, as he sniffed the wafting scent of bold coffee and chocolate with a hint of orange.

"Sure smells good, Tim. Better than that old stuff I've been drinking."

"Help yourself. The coffee mugs are in the cabinet above the coffee maker. How'd you sleep, by the way?"

"I slept like a king, thanks."

"That's great, Kaos. Nobody's ever slept in that bed, so that's good to know. Hey, listen, I have to attend a meeting this afternoon at two. I'd like it if you could stick around."

"Yeah, sure no problem. I'm not in a hurry to do much at the garage since Bud passed."

"Good because the appointment involves my client, Helen, and I have an unsettled feeling about her directives."

"I don't mind sticking around, but why would you feel that way?"

"She never mentioned beneficiaries. If she has any coming out of the woodwork, her estate could get messy. I'm not that naïve."

"Tim, stressing yourself will not do you any good. Go to the appointment, find out what her specific directives are, and go from there. Then and only then can you decide if the directives are worth stressing about."

"Thanks doc. I'll take that under advisement."

"Where is the appointment? Is it far from here?"

"Far enough, considering there is always traffic."

"You have a driver, don't you?"

"Yes, but I gave him a few days off. I'll drive myself. I need a diversion to think about on the way back."

"Oh," Kaos smiled wickedly, "like the woman in the red dress?"

"Exactly. Like, I'll never meet her. Thanks a lot for reminding me. As if I don't already have enough stress."

"You will meet her. Not sure when or how, but you will. There are no coincidences."

Tim thought about what Kaos said, hoping it was true. Then he looked at his watch, "I better get a move on, Kaos. Make yourself at home. The doors lock automatically, so if you go out while I'm gone; you might not get back in."

"I'll hang out on the lanai. I'll be fine."

"Alright, see you in a bit."

"Yep, I'll be here."

Tim poured coffee into a travel mug and headed out the front door. Kaos watched him get into his car and start the engine, put the car in reverse and spin around, spitting pea gravel from the tires. The sound of the deep, throaty engine was like no other car. Kaos opened the front door to watch Tim, admiring not only the design of the car, but also the sound of the powerful engine as it zoomed down the street. "That's some machine!" he exclaimed, as he closed the front door.

The drive to Hartson and Hodges took as long as Tim had expected. He arrived a few minutes before his appointment, thankful he wasn't late. The receptionist's voice was recognizable as she greeted him, "Mr. Hurst, would you like a beverage?"

He replied, "Some water would be nice, thank you."

The receptionist disappeared and then reappeared carrying a tall glass of cold water with a slice of lemon floating on top. She handed him the glass. "I will be happy to give you a refill, if you need more." Tim accepted the glass of water, doubting the sincerity of her hospitality, taking it as a flirtatious overture. Normally he would have responded with something equally witty, but today was not that day. He had more pressing matters than fueling coquettish advances.

After a few more minutes, Mr. Hartson came out of his office, whispered something in his receptionist's ear, then vanished back into his office. "Mr. Hurst," she called softly, looking directly at Tim. He immediately stood up from his chair, handing her the empty glass. "Mr. Hartson will see you now."

"Thank you, Ma'am," he said, looking straight through her.

The receptionist swooned as a sudden burst of crimson radiated across her pale cheeks. Tim had that effect on women without even trying. Sometimes it was a blessing, which served his purposes as the women he met at social functions were constantly vying for his attention. He waited for the receptionist to open the door to Mr. Hartson's office. Observing her reaction to his gaze, Tim winked at her before entering.

Mr. Hartson's office was conservative in design, typical for a law firm. Behind his wide oak desk were bookshelves that housed volumes and volumes of red law books. When the attorney saw Tim enter the room, he came from behind his desk and extended his hand to Tim. After a business handshake, he gestured to one of the two leather-back captain's chairs in front of his desk signaling Tim where to sit. Then Mr. Hartson returned and sat in the chair behind his desk, producing a manilla envelope and handing it to Tim. "Helen wanted you to have this. Take your time reading it. I will wait for you to finish and avail myself for questions."

Tim took the contents out of the envelope, surprised to see a letter.

My Dearest Tim,

Because you are reading this letter, you know I am deceased. I am sorry dear, that is an unpleasant fact; we eventually die from something. I trust my demise was quick. Do not be sad for me; maybe a little sad. And when you feel sad, remember the good times we shared, even though I never got to show you my "etchings."

I have left you, knowing there will be someone in your life who can make you happy. I say this because I observed your attentions on the woman in the red dress from the gala. I am certain that at the right time, you will find each other. There are no coincidences in life.

I decided to write this letter after I returned home from my stay at The Jackson Hotel. You should not have indulged me with such luxury. However, I would be remiss if I did not mention that I enjoyed my stay, your company, and the champagne. Thank you very much, Tim.

Now on to the business portion of my document. As you know, I have no living heirs, at least none that I am aware of, who will contest my directives. With that said, I bequeath to you the remainder of my estate, valued at one hundred million dollars. I have a charity near and dear to my heart that, while I have given you the estate, I would like you to honor my wish that some of the money be given to Children's Hospital. I had a child with Howard who died from a blood cancer, so a portion of my estate should be made in an endowment. No child should ever be denied treatment based on an inability to pay. I know in my heart you will do the right thing for me.

Tim, if I were to say you were like a son to me, that would not be true, even though a son has a place of *honor in a mother's heart. You were more than that. You gave me life. You made me feel beautiful, even though I am wrinkled and old. And you were kind to me. Compassion goes a long way. Never lose sight of that, my dear. Always strive to do what is best for the people who provide you with the very clothes you wear and the fancy car you drive. People are important, Tim.*

And lastly, do not tarry finding the woman in the red dress. There is no guarantee that one will have tomorrow. Make the most of today. I believe you deserve to be happy.

With all my love and affection,
Helen

Tim stared blankly at the letter in his hands, shocked that Helen had left him her estate. Mr. Hartson let him collect his thoughts before asking, "Mr. Hurst, do you have any questions?"

Tim mumbled, "One hundred million dollars!"

"Yes, Mr. Hurst, that is the sum Helen left you."

"I don't know what to say."

"You don't have to say anything, Mr. Hurst. It's all yours."

"Mr. Hartson, are you positive there is not some long, lost relative that will come out of the woodwork, so to speak?"

"I assure you, Mr. Hurst, there is not."

"Mr. Hartson, as Helen's investment banker, I know where some of her money is invested. Do you have a list of all her assets?"

"I do."

"In that case, I would like to retain your services."

"It will be my pleasure, Mr. Hurst."

Tim stood up and they exchanged another handshake. "Thank you, Mr. Hartson. I will be in touch for a review of Helen's assets."

Tim was still in shock when he left the law offices of Hartson and Hodges. Had he known the nature of the appointment, he would have asked Terrance to drive him. But since he had given his driver the day off, he had to regain his presence of mind because he felt a sharp, stabbing pain in his chest.

Sitting in his car, Tim took a few deep breaths thinking the pain would go away but becoming more light-headed with each breath. "This is ridiculous," he said out loud. "I'm not having pain in my jaw or running down my left arm. I'm not having a heart attack."

Convincing himself that he was fine, Tim pressed the ignition button on his car. As he drove along the highway, he thought about Helen. He didn't expect her to die, at least not so suddenly. He thought she would be old and die in her bed, that she would not wake up one day and that would be it. But not so unexpectedly. She was only seventy-five. That was not old.

Why did she have a stroke? Why did she leave him? Now, everyone he loved was gone. For the second time in his life, Tim felt alone, and it was not a pleasant feeling. Even though death was certain, it had come upon him like a thief in the night and he was unprepared.

The sharp pain returned, continuing to squeeze his chest. "This is serious," he thought, pulling to the side of the road and turning the car's hazard lights on, hoping the pain would go away. As another sharp pain came, Tim slumped over the steering wheel as he cried out, "Oh God, am I dying?"

A state trooper, traveling the same stretch of highway, noticed the blinking hazard lights. After pulling the patrol car to the side of the road, he got out and approached the car. When he saw the man resting on the steering wheel, the officer rapped on the driver's window, which startled Tim who had enough presence of mind to place his hand on his chest.

The trooper immediately called in on his radio, "I've got a possible heart attack victim; I need a bus. I'm on Highway 3, just north of exit ten." Then the officer returned to Tim, making a rolling motion with his index finger indicating for Tim to roll down his window, if he could. As the window was lowered, the officer reported, "I've got an ambulance coming in about five minutes. Hang in there. Anybody I can call for you?"

Tim nodded his head as he picked up his phone with his right hand, punched in Kaos' cell number, and handed the phone to the state trooper. "His name is Kaos."

Noticing the number on the screen was Tim's, Kaos answered his phone. "Tim?"

The officer quickly identified himself. "This is Office Cunningham. Your friend is in distress and is going to the hospital. He wanted you to know." Kaos was alarmed. "Wait… what…where's Tim?"

"I suspect your friend is having a heart attack. I've got an ambulance on the way. You should get his car towed. Don't want to leave it unattended too long or it will be stripped in no time."

Kaos regained his composure, quickly inquiring about his friend. "Will he be alright?"

The officer saw that Tim was breathing, but couldn't offer anything other than to say, "So far…he is hanging on. Ok I see the ambulance. Your friend will be taken to General Hospital."

"Ok, thanks, where is the car?"

"Highway 3, just north of exit 10 on the side of the road."

"Got it," Kaos said, then ended the call. He was glad Tim was alive; relieved actually. He wasted no time getting a tow truck to Tim's parked car, giving instructions to have it towed to Slim's Garage, even though it was an hour's drive away. Then he collected his few belongings and headed out on his motorcycle to meet the tow truck at the garage to help unload and store Tim's car inside the bay doors.

In the meantime, Officer Cunningham kept Tim awake by giving him a minute-by-minute account of the ambulance's whereabouts until the shrill siren and flashing red lights could be seen and heard. The ambulance pulled in front of Tim's car and stopped. Two EMT's jumped out to quickly assess him before putting him on a gurney and loading him into the back of the ambulance. The state trooper watched until he saw the flashing red lights disappear, then walked back to his patrol car and wrote up the incident report. Just as he finished the report, he could see a tow truck approaching from behind. He was relieved that the "friend" had acted quickly dispatching a truck to the scene. Satisfied, he turned on his left signal then entered the sea of traffic.

The ambulance wasted no time navigating through the parted sea of cars, arriving at General Hospital within minutes. While Tim was being transported, his vital signs were monitored by a twelve lead EKG. The EMT looked over the printout once it was completed, asking Tim the same questions over and over.

"Do you have any nausea? Do you have any radiating jaw pain? Does your left arm hurt? Do you feel lightheaded? Do you feel fatigued? Do you have pain between your shoulder blades," to which Tim replied, "No."

The EMT had no sooner asked Tim the same questions again than it pulled up in front of the emergency entrance to the hospital. The driver got out, opened the back doors of the ambulance, and helped the EMT assistant lower the gurney onto the sidewalk in front of the doors. Wasting no time, they transported Tim back to the treatment area while an attending physician met them enroute. The EMT who had been attending Tim called out, "57-year-old male, possible heart attack, vitals stable." Then he handed the EKG printout to the attending physician after they had wheeled Tim into a treatment bay. The attending doctor took the printout, saying, "Thanks, I will take it from here."

After getting Tim settled, the physician immediately ordered nitroglycerine. When the nurse brought the medicine to Tim, she said, "I want you to place this tab under your tongue. It should help with the pain you are having."

Even though Tim had said "No," the tremendous pain he had experienced earlier was not dismissed by the ER staff. He had no choice except to comply with the doctor's orders. While the medicine worked its magic, another staff member came into the bay to admit him into the hospital. When Tim was asked who his next of kin was, the only person he could name was Kaos. Suddenly, the gravity of Tim's life hit him like a ton of bricks. Other than Kaos, he had no one else to list. He was alone and this made him think about the possibility he would be alone for the rest of his life. He had better make plans for that.

After collecting pertinent information from Tim, including next of kin, health insurance, and whether he had a living will, the admitting staff member left Tim's bay. The attending physician came back into his room, "Mr. Hurst, I want to admit you overnight for observation. I also want to do a complete blood profile on you, and I want you to see our cardiac guy tomorrow. Do you have any questions?" Since Tim was his captive audience, he mumbled, "No."

"Alright then, my nurse will be back to get your blood."

The attending had no sooner pulled the curtain around Tim's bay than the nurse came in with her partitioned blue caddy containing collection tubes and paraphernalia to draw his blood. She looked at his arms, deciding on a generous vein in his left arm. "I think I'll use this one," she said with a smile. "Looks juicy."

"If you say so," Tim replied. "Some way to get a vacation."

While the nurse swabbed his arm with an alcohol wipe, she asked, "Mr. Hurst, do you have any issues with needles?"

"Not that I am aware of," then joked, "Should I?"

The nurse smiled again as she tied a six-inch flat rubber band around his arm above the area she was about to stick with a needle. Before she did, she gave the vein of choice a smack. Tim was intrigued. "What did you do that for?"

"I wanted to irritate the vein, make it inflamed so I could get a good placement the first time."

"What do you mean, the first time? Have you done this before?"

The nurse stopped what she was doing, looked at her patient and calmly said, "Mr. Hurst, I have done this many, many times." She wiped the area again with an alcohol spritzed cotton ball and waited for it to dry before she advanced the needle two degrees into his arm.

"You might feel a little pinch."

Tim felt a sting, but that was about it. Once there was blood, the nurse flushed the tubing, then hooked up a collection tube and untied the rubber band from around his arm. His rich, red, blood flowed easily into one tube, then another, and lastly into a third.

"Geez," Tim remarked. "Did you leave me any? Oh yeah, I'd be dead if you took it all," he joked.

The nurse teased, "I assure you, Mr. Hurst, I left you with some. I am not that cruel." She placed a folded two by two gauze pad on top of the needle and gently rolled it out. Holding the pad firmly with her fingers, she secured it in place with a self-adhering bandage. "Try to get some rest while we wait for the results of your labs. We should have those shortly."

After she left, Tim closed his eyes, but he could not rest, as he had many thoughts running through his mind about his end-of-life needs, which, up until the last twenty-four hours were not a concern. Ten minutes later the nurse came back to check on him.

"Is there anything I can get you, Mr. Hurst?"

"Water would be nice."

"Let's wait on that for a few more minutes until your labs come back, then I can get you whatever you want."

"Hm…a bourbon would be nice!"

"I am sure it would, but we don't have a bar on the premises. Perhaps you can think of something else."

Tim paused. He had been thinking about some decisions he would have to make. "Actually, I do have some questions. What if I get incapacitated? I don't have anyone to help me at home. What if I get sick with terminal cancer, where is the nearest hospice? I have some serious decisions to make."

"Mr. Hurst, let's see what your blood work says first, then we can go from there. It's important you are thinking about these things, and since you asked, we recommend Tri-County Hospice. It is very close to our facility."

"How convenient," Tim said sarcastically.

"It is, Mr. Hurst. Now try to get some rest."

13
THIS MUST BE HEAVEN

$\mathcal{T}$im stared at the ceiling above his bed attempting to block the thoughts that were keeping him from sleep. He wished he had asked for a sedative, but since his blood work was still being processed, he would have to wait. Finally, he decided to call Kaos.

"Hey, buddy," he said as soon as Kaos picked up the call.

"Tim, it's good to hear from you. What's going on?"

"Well, I'm not dead! I'm talking to you!"

"Very funny, Tim."

"Sorry, Kaos, it's not funny."

"I'm glad you called because I had your car towed to Slim's Garage. Well, it's my garage now but somehow, I don't feel inclined to change the name. Slim's is how I will always remember the garage, and I want new life breathed into it."

"Thanks for towing my car to the garage. It's reassuring knowing it's not sitting on the side of the road stripped down."

"No problem, Tim."

Tim continued, "You can rename the garage. Why don't you see what kind of business you get once people realize Slim's is open."

"Yeah, I guess."

"Hey, I'm supposed to get out of here tomorrow. Can you give me a lift?"

Kaos smiled, "Sure, I'll pick you up in your car."

"Alright, I'll give you a call when I'm ready to spring this joint."

Realizing how relieved he felt to hear from Tim, he added, "I'm glad you are ok, I really am. What happened, Tim? Did you have a heart attack?"

"I won't know until my labs come back. The doc gave me some good meds; I feel fine now."

"Medicine saves lives, Tim."

"Yeah, but I don't want to depend on medicines for the rest of my life, if I have a broken heart."

"You mean that figuratively or literally? Still thinking about the woman in the red dress?"

"YES!"

"Medicine can fix part of your problem if that's what happened to you. Only time can fix the other problem."

Tim chewed on his friend's words for a moment, then asked, "Kaos, have you been in love?"

"Is that what you think you are feeling, Tim?"

"I can't get her out of my mind."

"You don't even know her. How can you think it's love?"

"It's a feeling I've never had before."

"I know you don't believe me, Tim, but I do read poetry. There is a verse by the poet Rumi that I think sums up what you are feeling. 'Love is an open secret, the most obvious thing in the world and the most hidden, with no why to how it keeps its mystery.'"

"Hmmm…"

"We can talk about motorcycles, Tim, take your mind off of her.

"Sure, what are you thinking about, Kaos?"

"Remember when you said you wanted to build a bike in Bud's memory."

"Yeah, I remember."

"Well, I have been thinking about the kind of bike Bud liked the best. Even though he had trick bikes, he really loved a Harley."

Tim replied, "I guess he was a Harley guy, after all."

"Yeah, but what if we combined the best parts of different kinds of bikes."

"What would you start with, Kaos?"

"I think the Commando is one of the 'coolest' in the history of cycles."

"Which one are you talking about, the Dominator or Commando?"

"I like the Commando, Kaos. Anyway, I read a newer version has a 961-cc air/oil-cooled parallel twin engine."

"What kind of gear box?"

"Five-speed."

"Steel frame?"

"Yep, steel frame."

"I like those features."

"You know, Tim, Kawasaki has a cool frame that might be able to accommodate that engine."

"Yeah, but I think my dad's all-time favorite motorcycle was the Knucklehead."

"You're talking the 1936 EL?"

"Is there any other?"

"Just making sure. Why did he like that one?"

"For one thing, it's a classic Harley, a one-seater, and he liked the sturdy fenders over the wheels. He said, there's nothing worse than taking a drive when you hit some water and mud flies up the back of your shirt."

Kaos pondered Tim's thoughts about fenders. "That's interesting Bud would say that."

"Yeah, I learned the importance of fenders."

"Your dad let you have a bike?"

"Not exactly. I had a bicycle and I wanted it to look cool. I begged my dad to take the fenders off. He advised against that, but I insisted. He said, 'You will see there's a function for fenders. They are not just for looks.' Then he took them off."

"And?"

"It had rained the night before and there was this massive mud puddle on our driveway. I thought it would be fun riding through the puddle as fast as I could, splashing water everywhere, and it was. I rode through the red clay mud until all the water was gone. By the end of the day, you couldn't see a speck of white on my new shirt. Mom washed it, but the red clay stains didn't come out. She said, 'Tim, you'll just have to wear your shirt like that to school.' I wasn't happy about that."

"Did you? Wear that stained shirt to school?"

"No, ruining one shirt was lesson enough."

Tim had just finished his sentence when the nurse came back. "Time to get another set of vitals, Mr. Hurst."

"I got to go now, Kaos. I'll call you when they let me out of here tomorrow."

"I'll be waiting for your call."

The nurse waited for Tim to put his phone down before taking a blood pressure cuff from the wire basket behind his bed and wrapping it around his upper arm. She put a pulse ox meter on his index finger and pushed the activation button on the automatic machine. After a few minutes, the monitor beeped, signaling the end of the cycle. The nurse looked at the readings and wrote them in Tim's chart, then she unwrapped the cuff from his arm, rolled it up, and put it back in the wire basket. She smiled at Tim, "Get some rest, Mr. Hurst."

Tim felt restless after his chat with Kaos. Just thinking about the motorcycle made him anxious to get out of the hospital. After the shift change at eleven that night, a new nurse came on duty. She poked her head in Tim's door, "Sorry to wake you, Mr. Hurst, I'm Brenda and I need to get a new set of vitals."

Tim didn't say a word and, without making a production, stuck out his left arm for the blood pressure cuff. Brenda smiled, "Looks like you've done this before," she said as she wrapped the cuff around his upper arm and started the monitor. She waited for the cycle to complete but it set off an alarm ending its cycle. Tim's pulse, she noted, was not rapid nor was his SpO2 low. Tim glanced at the machine, then asked, "What's SpO2 mean?"

"It means the amount of oxygen circulating in your blood, furthest from your heart."

"Oh…" Tim responded to her explanation.

"Mr. Hurst, are you having any pain?"

"No."

"I need to recheck your blood pressure."

"Why?"

Brenda didn't want to alarm Tim so she said, "Sometimes the readings can be off. We always do a second set." Satisfied with her answer, Tim said, "Ok, go ahead then. I wasn't sleeping anyway." When the monitor finished the cycle, Tim's blood pressure was still high. Not dangerously high but high enough. After Brenda unwrapped the cuff and recorded the set of findings in his chart, she sat on the chair next to his bed. "Mr. Hurst, is something bothering you?"

"Why do you ask?"

"Your readings are higher than we would like. Perhaps you would like to try some relaxation to lower it."

"Like what?"

"I want you to close your eyes and think of a time when you were the happiest. You don't need to tell me what or when this was. I want you to recall every detail. What did you see, smell, and touch? Can you do that for me?"

"I'll try."

Tim closed his eyes, recalling the moment he saw the woman in the red dress enter the ballroom at The Jackson Hotel. She was a flash of red, enough to turn his head. Then he remembered when their eyes met; an exquisite shade of blue looking through him. He felt new life surging in him, thinking about her. Tim recalled the sweet scent in her hair when he bent over her chair, and let himself think of lying next to her, with his face buried in her blonde hair. When the blood pressure machine finished its cycle, Tim's blood pressure was still elevated, but not as high as the reading taken before. Brenda looked at the numbers on the monitor.

"Mr. Hurst, your numbers are better, but higher than we'd like to see. Make sure you keep your appointment with the cardiologist tomorrow."

Tim looked at her, chuckling, "Do I have a choice? I'm kind of a captive here."

"You always have a choice," she answered. "And if you need additional tests, the cardiovascular doctor can order them and help you live a long time, because whatever you were thinking, certainly worked. Keep thinking those thoughts and your numbers may be exactly what we want to see in the morning. Try to get some rest, Mr. Hurst."

While his thoughts about the woman in the red dress were somewhat calming, in other ways they were not. She was his life's breath, and this unsettled him because no other woman had that kind of power over him. Then he remembered the poem Kaos told him about love. "Love was an open secret, obvious and hidden. And no why to how it keeps its mystery." This summed up his feelings and he didn't understand why. Sleep would not come easily and, try as he might, he drifted in and out of questionable slumber.

After a restless night, Tim was more than ready to go home. As much as he wanted to discharge himself, he had to wait for his consult with the resident cardiothoracic surgeon before getting discharged, if he could get discharged, and that was something he definitely wanted. He didn't have to wait long before he heard a knock on his door. A young doctor wearing a white lab coat over freshly laundered scrubs waited for Tim to acknowledge him. "Come in."

"Mr. Hurst, I'm Dr. Adams. I have been looking over your lab work."

Before the doctor could say another word, Tim spoke up, "Good morning to you, too, Doctor. As you can see, I'm not dead." Dr. Adams chuckled. "If you were, I wouldn't be talking to you. There would be a slab in the morgue with your name on it."

"Very funny, Doc," Tim countered back.

"Actually, Mr. Hurst, heart disease is no laughing matter."

"Is that what I have, Doc?"

"Your labs look good, so no, I wouldn't say that you do from those. However, there are other factors that can contribute to cardiovascular disease."

"Like what?"

Dr. Adams paused before continuing his discussion. He sensed he needed to tread lightly but not mince words with his patient. Taking a deep breath and letting it out, he began. "There are four main lifestyle factors that can affect your heart. They are diet, exercise, stress, and weight."

"I don't know, Doc; my diet is fairly healthy."

"What about exercise? How often and what kind do you do, Mr. Hurst?"

"I have to be honest; I don't have a regular exercise routine."

"Perhaps you could find some time to get to the gym? Lift some weights?"

Tim paused before answering. Since he came into Helen's estate, he didn't have an excuse not to go to the gym. "Yes, I suppose I could make the time."

"What about stress, Mr. Hurst. Been under a lot of stress lately?"

Suddenly, Tim became noticeably quiet. He didn't feel like talking about his recent traumatic events of the past two weeks.

"Mr. Hurst, did you hear my question?"

Tim became irritated, "Yes, yes, I have been under a significant amount of stress. Too much, really, in a short period of time."

"How did that make you feel, Mr. Hurst, the reason for your stress?"

Tim thought for a moment. If he talked about the things that stressed him, they would be real and the loss of them would be hard to bear. But if he was going to stay out of the hospital, now was the time to be honest with his feelings. He vacillated before answering Dr. Adams' questions.

"For starters, Doc, I met the woman of my dreams, but I don't even know her name."

"Do you have a plan to meet her, Mr. Hurst?"

"I have been told there is no such thing as coincidence. So, I trust I will meet her."

"What about other stresses?"

"You don't think that is enough stress, Dr. Adams?"

Dr. Adams chose his next words carefully. Getting his patient to acknowledge his cause of stress would go a long way toward his health. His patient clearly didn't need surgical intervention. "It says in your medical chart that you lost your parents recently."

"Yes, I did. On the same day! I had not seen my dad in years, and I literally ran into this guy on a motorcycle who knew my dad. Talk about serendipity," Tim said, looking away from Dr. Adams.

"That must have been a shock, but I'm not sure I follow you. I don't want to pry, but what happened to the motorcyclist you hit?"

Tim looked at Dr. Adams, "If you think I killed the guy, I would be in jail for manslaughter, not here."

"I don't judge, Mr. Hurst. I'm trying to help you. Tell me more about this motorcyclist."

"It was a shock that he knew my dad, especially when I learned he had been my dad's surrogate son. I was upset when I found out, because my dad had me, his real son, and I hadn't seen him in years."

"That is certainly a reason to be stressed. Are there any other stressors you can think of?"

"Yes, an exceptionally good friend of mine died just a few weeks ago. We had an understanding; she was much older than me."

"Oh…"

"I was her financial advisor; I invested her money. She had many philanthropic interests."

"I take it her death was unexpected."

"Very unexpected, Dr. Adams. In her will, she left me her estate."

"That's a lot to take in."

"It sure is, Doc."

"Mr. Hurst, after what you have told me, I don't think a CT scan is necessary. However, we should talk about ways to help minimize your stress. Do you have any hobbies?"

"Not really, I work long hours at the bank because I don't have anyone to go home to."

"I see. I want you to think about this, Mr. Hurst. Your body is a car. The engine is strong, but the chassis is falling apart. Maybe not immediately, but that will happen if you don't make some changes. I recommend practices like Yoga and Tai Chi. Believe me; you can get a good workout from those disciplines. The idea is to work your muscle groups while keeping the organs soft with breath. There is a beautiful flow to the practice."

"Sounds like you are partial to those, Doc."

"I am, but there are other things that can be just as beneficial. You can write poetry, listen to music, calming music, like nature sounds in a rain forest or anything like that. Or go for long walks along the beach."

"I do like long walks along the water's edge, feeling the sand between my toes and the cold water washing over them, even though it's freezing."

"The idea is to get a meditative attitude, Mr. Hurst."

Tim thought about the suggestions before commenting, "I can do that." He really didn't have an excuse not to.

"Ok, it's good you heard me because I think you can get out of here. You don't need my services. One thing though, you should have a plan for the rest of your life, a living will, instructions for your end-of-life care."

Suddenly Tim became alarmed. "You said I was ok!"

"What I said, Mr. Hurst, is you need to take care of your body and make plans. It is smart to have a support system in place. You might want to think about visiting Tri-County Hospice across the street."

"That's for cancer. I'm not planning on getting cancer."

"Nobody does, Mr. Hurst. Hospice isn't just for cancer end-of-life care. I have patients go there for cardiac care. They get better and go home. Think about Tri-County. It's very close by.

After writing the notes about what they had talked about in Tim's chart, Dr. Adams stood to shake his patient's hand and said, "That does it, Mr. Hurst. You can get dressed now and get out of here."

"Will do, Doc, and thanks."

After Dr. Adams left, nurse Brenda returned to go over Tim's discharge instructions. "Mr. Hurst, do you have any questions about your instructions?"

"No, not really. Doc Adams said I have a clean bill of health."

Brenda smiled because she had heard that line before. She gently reminded Tim, "If you want to keep that clean bill of health, Dr. Adams wants you to focus on practices to relieve stress. Do you have any questions about those suggestions?"

"No, not really."

"Ok, then Mr. Hurst," Brenda said as she handed him a pen. "I will need you to sign here that you understood everything we went over."

"I understand," Tim said taking the pen from her. "I will focus more on relaxing."

He thought about Tri-County Hospice across the street as he finished getting dressed. He understood pre-planning because he had helped clients pre-plan for retirement. On occasion, a client would cash in a mutual fund to help pay for long-term care and even hospice.

Tim didn't have a heart attack, but what if he did? In his experience, one usually died from something. He had provided for his mother, so he should set up plans for himself. Then his mind turned to the woman in the red dress and her reasons for attending the gala. Maybe hospice care wasn't a bad idea, after all. So, before he called Kaos to pick him up, he decided to investigate Tri-County Hospice across the street.

The outside of Tri-County Hospice looked like a modern hotel with a trellis of magenta bougainvillea on either side of the automated double glass doors. The building was three stories high, each room had large windows letting in lots of sunlight if the blinds were open.

Tim stood in front of the glass doors for several minutes before a middle-aged couple exited. Now he had no reason not to go in. The doors opened automatically, just as they had for numerous others. Some folks entered and exited as they pleased. For some, Tim surmised, these would be the last set of doors they would go through in a physical state. This was an epiphany as Tim didn't know what to expect on the other side of the doors he gingerly walked through.

Pleasantly surprised, gone were the sterile walls and the hospital disinfectant that permeated one's clothing, a scent that would never go away no matter how many times clothing was laundered. There was nothing pleasant for Tim to connect the hospital disinfectant to. It would always remind him of death.

Today the sun was shining through Tri-County's tinted glass windows and there was a feeling of peace and calm. It was vastly different than the hospital he had been a guest in overnight. Tim stood motionless soaking in the atmosphere when someone asked, "May I help you?" He turned to what he thought was an ethereal voice, relieved to see a live person sitting behind a receptionist's desk. "Are you visiting someone?" she asked pleasantly.

Tim tried in vain to produce the appropriate words explaining the reason he was there but could not. So, he said what was on his mind. "No, I'm not visiting anyone. I want to check the place out. Do you give tours?" The receptionist smiled. "We do. We have a lovely nurse, Miss Warner, who oversees community education and usually gives these tours. We are lucky to have her on staff. All her patients fall in love with her in their last days. She is a treasure."

Tim smiled, "She must be a rare gem."

"Nurse Warner is that indeed. Would you like me to see if she is available to give you a tour, or do you want to schedule an appointment and come back at another time?"

"I can wait while you check with her. I'm not in a hurry to go anywhere."

The receptionist smiled while dialing the telephone. After a few minutes, she put the receiver back on its cradle. "You are in luck," she said with a grin. "Nurse Warner is with a family and will be out shortly. You may have a seat in our living room."

Tim chuckled at the irony of the description. "Oh, is that what you call it? I thought people came here to die."

"They do," she said, "but their loved ones go on living." The receptionist's matter of fact response to life and death made Tim feel slightly uneasy. "Hmmm," he muttered, turning his back from her.

"Sir, I need you to sign the visitor's log, and you need a visitor's tag. There is a basket of them next to the sign-in book. Pick any one you like."

Tim thought she must be joking. The visitor designation on all the name tags attached to the green lanyards looked the same. He picked one out and hung it around his neck, then sat down in an oversized chair in the living room opposite a flagstone wall that boasted an inset gas fireplace. Above the oak mantle hung a large painting of children clad in short, white gowns in a field. Some were playing chase and laughing while others picked yellow daisies. The sky was a cloudless, brilliant blue and, while there was no obvious sun, the sunlight was there.

Tim got up from his chair and walked over to the painting. The longer he stared at it, the more he felt the warm sunshine on his face. He was no longer an observer as a smiling child handed him a flower. He forgot where he was until he heard someone call his name, "Mr. Hurst." Tim nearly jumped out of his skin at the sound of her voice. Something about it sounded familiar, but he could not place where he had heard it. "I see you have been transported," she said. "People tell me they are taken away somewhere special when they gaze at this painting long enough."

"I must have been. I thought I was." Tim said, still engrossed in the painting.

"That's what the artist wanted," the woman said. Without turning around Tim continued the conversation. "Do you know who painted this?"

"Yes, one of our clients. She had a dream, and this was where she went in her dream. This is what she saw. She said she was in that field."

"I felt like I was in that field."

"A lot of people say that." The woman waited for Tim to finish looking at the painting before she said another word.

"Mr. Hurst, I understand you would like a tour."

"Yes," he said with his back still turned away from his tour guide.

"May I ask, any reason why? Have you been in a Hospice facility?"

"No, other than a gala I attended for a hospice fundraiser, that's all I know about hospice. Well, that is not entirely true. I had clients withdraw funds from their retirement investments to pay for hospice care."

"I see…" she said.

Tim continued, "I lost both of my parents recently. If I got terminally ill, I wouldn't have anyone to take care of me. So, I thought I should decide on a plan for my end game."

"You are wise to have a plan. Would you like to go on your tour now, Mr. Hurst?"

"Yes," he said, turning away from the painting. He didn't see her face because she had turned to talk to a nurse who had suddenly appeared, but something about her took his breath away. Only one other person had done that to him. Without turning to face him, the nurse said, "Excuse me, Mr. Hurst. I will be right back."

Tim was clearly out of his element. Something about his brief encounter with his tour guide made him feel alive again. "She said she would be back," he repeated to himself over and over. Then he sat in a wing chair and stared at the picture of the children playing in the field. Suddenly, he wanted to be a child again; to be with people he loved. Now they were gone. He didn't like this new feeling. He had clients die but that did not impact him the way his parents and Helen's deaths had. He was alone and didn't know if Kaos would be with him in the remaining years of his life. Then he thought about Shelly at the bank. She liked him but he didn't reciprocate those same feelings. Something about this woman, her voice, made him feel alive. So he waited for her to return, but she did not. After what felt like an eternity, the receptionist came to where he was seated.

"Mr. Hurst, I am terribly sorry. Nurse Warner has been detained and sends her apology. She says she hopes you understand. This is the nature of our business. Sometimes a situation changes rapidly, and we think we have more time, and we don't."

Tim felt his breath catch in his chest like he was gut punched. He couldn't make demands that Nurse Warner leave whatever she was doing and attend to him. He was the intruder.

"I understand. I would like to come back tomorrow, if possible."

The receptionist wanted to accommodate Tim, so she suggested, "Mr.

Hurst, since you are here, I can see if another qualified staff member can show you around and answer your questions."

Tim politely replied, "No, thank you. I will come back tomorrow."

The receptionist returned to her desk and pulled up the nurse's schedule for the following day. She looked up from the screen, "You are in luck, Mr. Hurst. Nurse Warner has an opening right before her lunch break."

Without hesitating, Tim replied, "Pencil me in." Then changed his mind and said, "Better yet, inscribe my name in ink." The receptionist smiled. "You don't have to worry; I made the appointment with Nurse Warner."

"Thank you," Tim replied. Then he walked toward the automated glass doors and pressed the button, smiling as the doors magically opened, leading him out into the sunshine.

What Tim didn't know was that Nurse Warner had been called to her pediatric patient, Susie, who had suddenly become lucid after being unconscious all day. "Tell me your dream again, Susie," Kristen asked. Normally, she could remember every detail her patients recounted, but now she was distracted, which was unusual. While Susie was important and could transition quickly, she had left a potential client who clearly needed to have his mind put at ease about hospice care. There were other qualified staff, but Kristen felt particularly drawn to Mr. Hurst and she did not know why.

Susie was her ten-year-old patient who had a history of headaches. When she was finally diagnosed with a glioblastoma and had not responded to radiation and chemotherapy, her parents wanted to take her home, but Susie refused, saying she wanted to stay near Nurse Warner.

This was hard for Susie's parents to accept. Kristen not only had Susie as a patient but also Susie's parents, who were present with their daughter most hours of the day and night. Their needs were just as important as their daughter's. Knowing this might be the last time her parents would hear her voice, Kristen encouraged the young girl, "Susie, tell Mommy and Daddy your dream." Susie was lucid and her pain was controlled even though her voice was barely above a whisper. Kristen whispered into Susie's mother's ear, "You can lay down next to her, there is enough room."

There were no wires, flashing red lights or monitors that beeped every five minutes to prevent the mother from laying close to her child. Kristen looked at Susie's mother again and said, "It's ok, you will not hurt her, she needs you." Her mother nodded, climbing onto the bed. Then cradling her daughter in her arms, Susie closed her eyes, took a deep breath, then opened them and began. "Mommy, I was flying high in the sky on a trapeze. The higher I got the more the sky opened up. It was a blue sky with puffy white clouds that looked like cotton balls, like the ones you cleaned my scraped knees with. Then I looked below, and I could see you and Daddy and all kinds of people cheering me on to fly higher and higher, 'Fly Susie,' they said. But I was afraid. I didn't want to go that high because you were not there to catch me."

Susie's mother's eyes filled with tears. She hugged her daughter closer to her breast and whispered in her ear, "I will always catch you, my darling."

That was all Susie needed to let go, dying peacefully in her mother's arms.

14
DISCOVERY

A peds death was never easy. Wiping away her own tears, Kristen turned to the young girl's mother. "I am so very sorry, Mrs. Kline. Take all the time you need."

Kristen walked out of her patient's room, closing the door behind her. She had been so consumed with Susie's last minutes that she had completely forgotten about Tim until she walked into the living room and saw the painting above the fireplace. Bursting into tears, she valiantly tried to brush them away, but to no avail.

Susie's death was one of many that Kristen had attended during her career at Tri-County. But for some reason, Susie's death hit her hard and left her wondering if she should continue her work. It was an honor and a privilege to serve as a "midwife" for souls, but how long could she continue in this role until she lost all passion for life? She had to live for herself and not just for the dying.

Kristen brushed away the tear streaming down her cheek in earnest hope it was the last one. She turned away from the painting and walked to the receptionist.

"There was a gentleman here, did someone else take him on a tour?"

The receptionist paused, "You mean, Mr. Hurst?"

For some unknown reason, Kristen hoped he had not gone on a tour. She felt a connection to him even though their meeting had been brief. She swallowed the lump that had risen in her throat, not really wanting the answer. "Yes, did he?"

"No, Nurse Warner, he made an appointment for tomorrow. He wanted you to take him."

Kristen was relieved. "What time did he make the appointment?"

The receptionist was amused that Nurse Warner was so interested, as this was a little unusual for her.

"He made the appointment before your scheduled lunch break."

Kristen smiled, elated with this news. "Thank you" she said, looking directly at the receptionist.

While Kristen had been attending to Susie and her family, Tim left Tri-County deciding it was time to call Kaos. He dialed the number, then waited. When the phone rang for a fifth time, Tim started to end the call. It was obvious Kaos wasn't going to answer until he heard, "Tim?"

"Hey, buddy, I'm ready for my chariot. I'll be waiting outside Tri-County Hospice."

Kaos was gob smacked. "Wait…what…why did you go there? Is there something you aren't telling me?"

"I'm fine, Kaos. Just checking out my options, you know, for the future."

"Oh, ok that's good to hear. I'll be there as soon as I can."

"I'm in no hurry, buddy. Take your time."

When Tim made his next appointment with Nurse Warner, he had an ulterior motive in mind, which was to take her to lunch. He wanted as much time with her as her schedule would allow, and he doubted she would say no. If he took her away from the facility, that would be even better. A recon of nearby restaurants was Tim's first priority.

A block away from Tri-County Hospice, Tim was delighted to discover a little café with a small courtyard. Inside the courtyard, a fountain in the shape of a pineapple stood in the middle, surrounded by a circle of tables and chairs. "This will be nice," he said out loud, "as long as it doesn't rain." He was hopeful the sunny weather would continue while he enjoyed his stroll back to Tri-County Hospice. He couldn't remember the last time he took a day off work; the pressure to make money for the bank always came first.

Thinking about work, Helen came to the forefront of his thoughts. She had left him her estate. Her directives were comprehended and would be distributed accordingly. She had taken care of him, now he would take care of her posthumously.

As Tim neared the hospice facility, he noticed a bench outside the building next to a bus stop. Deciding to wait for Kaos in the warm sunshine, he got comfortable on the bench, closed his eyes, and thought about the hospice gala and the last time he had seen Helen. A feeling of remorse crept over him. His unscrupulous actions toward her were appalling, but that was the nature of his business toward his clients with deep pockets. He was becoming tired of the pressure to perform. Thanks to Helen, he did not have to. He wished he could see her one more time. Then, a voice stirred him from his thoughts.

"Do you mind if I share your bench?" the voice inquired.

Tim opened his eyes. A gray-haired woman who looked to be in her seventies stood beside him. "I don't mind," he answered.

"Thank you, I want to enjoy this lovely day for a bit longer. I don't get out much."

Tim was tempted to ignore her benign interrogatory but had second thoughts as he pondered the consequences of his actions if he did. Helen's passing and his recent "event" had given him a new lease on life. He was not as unfeeling as he once thought. Some people lived their lives tenuously while others robustly. He wanted to make every moment count from here on out. Deciding to give her his full attention he asked, "Why is that?"

The woman paused, taking a hankie out of her small black clutch purse, and began wiping her eyes.

"My Lewis passed recently. He used to drive me everywhere. I never learned to drive."

Tim was surprised. He wondered if she was a patient, "Oh…do you live here? I don't mean to imply you are sick."

The woman laughed heartily. "Oh no, dear, I am not ill. I ride the bus because I don't want to be a prisoner in my house. I can be independent without Lewis."

"I have a driver; his name is Terrance. I like having a driver," Tim volunteered.

"I see," said the woman. "Are you by chance ill?"

Tim was shocked the woman spoke plainly regarding his wellbeing. "No, I'm not ill. I was thinking of a dear friend. I miss her."

The woman looked at Tim, then asked, "Am I correct to assume she is no longer with you?"

Without hesitating, Tim answered her question. "She was my client, and I was not always nice to her. We had an understanding. I flirted with her, and she gave me lots of money to invest, and I acted only in my best interest. I wish I could tell her how sorry I am for my behavior."

The woman listened attentively to his every word, nodding her head in agreement to the things he was telling her. Something about her prompted him to share his thoughts, which was unfathomable when he suddenly realized he was telling a complete stranger about his relationship with Helen Trenton. But Tim continued, "She left the remainder of her estate to me. I don't deserve it." The woman smiled, "She must have loved you."

"I think I reminded her of the child she had who died very young."

"There is always that possibility," she said. "Women are wise, you know. I am sure she understood there would never be anything amorous between you two. She must have enjoyed your company and wanted to take care of you. There is always a give and take when it comes to relationships."

"You think so?" Tim asked.

"I know so. Lewis and I were married for fifty years. It was not all roses and champagne, but most of the time it was. Sometimes I did want to go out by myself, but I didn't have a license. He never objected to driving me. He would sit patiently in the car, no matter how long I took in the store." Tim found himself astonished that a man would do that because he had no example of that growing up. He responded, "Really!"

"Lewis didn't mind," she said.

"I would mind," Tim replied.

The woman smiled, acknowledging his response, then added, "You probably would because you were born in a more independent decade. This is what I knew, and I was happy."

Tim was so drawn into her conversation that he didn't see or hear the oncoming bus. When it came to a hissing stop, the woman turned to him and patted his hand, "Looks like my ride is here. I am sure your friend forgives you." He watched her rise from the bench and walk to the bus, then climb the few steps into the cabin. Before she walked back to her seat, she turned in the doorway and waved. Then the bus driver closed the doors and, with a hiss of the hydraulics, pulled away from the curb.

There was something oddly familiar about the woman who shared his bench, and he wondered where she came from. Tim wondered why he felt so comfortable with this stranger. Then it dawned on him. "There is no such thing as coincidence." Perhaps Helen was watching over him.

The bus turned the corner and disappeared down the street just as Kaos pulled up in Tim's car. He started to get out, thinking Tim would want to drive, but before he opened the door, Tim had already opened the passenger door. Kaos looked at him in astonishment. Tim chuckled at Kaos' surprised gaze.

"You can drive. I don't feel like it."

"Are you sure, Tim?"

"Absolutely!"

They drove in silence, each with their own thoughts, until they both spoke out loud in unison. "You will not believe what happened to me today." Kaos chuckled. He was beginning to feel like Tim was becoming his twin, with their likes, but yielded, "You go first."

"You are not going to believe this, I'm not even sure I do." Kaos interrupted, "What did you give away? Your inheritance? Not that it is any of my business."

"No, I made a date."

"With whom?"

"A nurse at the hospice."

Kaos was surprised at Tim's announcement of a date. He really didn't know anything about Tim's private life and, up until this point, his friend had never said there was anyone. Kaos also noticed that Tim's house, albeit luxurious, was lacking a woman's touch. He responded, "That's interesting." Tim, not in the least daunted by Kaos' lack of enthusiasm, continued, "There's something familiar about her. I was going to go on a tour of the facility with her when she got called away. She said she would come back, but whatever she was doing took a long time, and that gave me a reason to schedule an appointment with her." He sat pensively for a moment and then asked, "By the way, what's your news, Kaos?"

Kaos was more interested in Tim's auspicious date than his own news, "Mine can wait. Tell me more about yours."

"I made an appointment for tomorrow right before lunch. I'm going to take her to a little café I found within walking distance. I don't want to miss out on a single second of her time."

Kaos thought better than to bring up the woman in the red dress since it was obvious Tim had decided to move on. That sounds like a nice plan."

"Yes, it is. I'm happy, and I hope the weather holds out."

Kaos drove in silence until Tim remembered Kaos had some news.

"Kaos, what's your good news?"

"I found a Knucklehead!"

"No kidding, what are you going to do with that?"

"I'm going to keep it as a show piece; draw people to the garage. Maybe I can eventually have a custom bike business."

"That sounds like you will need financing; a custom bike venture."

"Tim, I'm not asking you for money."

"I know. Don't forget, I like bikes the same as you. And I don't have to go back to the bank to work."

Kaos thought for a minute about Tim's offer, then asked, "Do you think Helen would want you to spend your inheritance that way?"

Tim was surprised Kaos would even consider Helen's thoughts. Then he decided to tell him about the woman he met outside Tri-County Hospice. "It's interesting you would bring Helen up."

"Why is that?"

"I was sitting on a bench outside Tri-County Hospice waiting for you when a lady stopped and asked if she could share my bench."

"What did she look like?"

"Seventy-five-ish, same age as Helen. Come to think about it, she even looked like Helen, except there was an overall brightness to her appearance."

"What did she say?

"She got me to talk about myself. I don't know why, but I was so comfortable talking with her that I told her I missed Helen and wished I could tell her how sorry I am for the way I treated her."

"Are you? Sorry?"

"I am, Kaos. It was as if she knew why I had conducted myself in that way. This is the most interesting part of the conversation. Before she got on the bus, she said, 'I'm sure your friend forgives you.' Talk about coincidence, Kaos."

"There is no such thing as coincidence, Tim."

"I'm starting to believe that."

The next morning, Tim was up before the sun. Out of habit, he had set the coffee maker on auto the night before. The bold scent of percolating coffee wafting up the stairs awakened his senses. His usual shower could wait while the coffee brewed. Today, he was a man taking his time. He waited until the whole pot of coffee finished brewing before pouring a generous serving into an oversized white ceramic mug. He took a sip of the steaming liquid, satisfied it was brewed to perfection, then carried the mug upstairs to the lanai where he listened to the cheerful notes of the awakening birds.

This was a novelty because, in the past, he took the birds chirping for granted, not really paying attention to their singing. This morning though, Tim noticed the chirping of the birds was not one big cacophony but distinct notes. He closed his eyes as the sun rose in the east, straining to hear each polyphonic chirp blending into a homorhythmic serenade.

After the sun broke through the clouds, Tim decided it was time to begin his day in earnest. But first, a shower and a second cup of coffee were in order. After his shower, Tim rummaged through his closet looking for a freshly laundered white oxford button down shirt. He didn't have much in the line of casual clothes as his daytime attire often overlapped into the evening. The white shirt and pair of jeans would have to suffice.

Tim opened a bottom dresser drawer and pulled out a neatly folded pair of jeans and a mahogany leather belt, then remembered he had a pair of unworn loafers on a shelf in his closet. Comfortable in his choice of attire for his date with Nurse Warner, he didn't think she would have a problem with his casual outfit. He never really cared what people thought because he was always impeccably dressed for work. This was different. Today was different, and he totally felt out of his element. Though he didn't like that feeling, he had no control over it and decided he may as well get used to his new lifestyle and think of it as a new beginning. After all, new beginnings were always filled with trepidation.

On the same morning, Kristen reviewed her notes before stopping by the room that had been occupied by her pediatric patient. She watched as Susie's mother folded the pink and white gingham quilt that had covered her daughter's bed. On the windowsill stuffed into the corner sat Teddy, a bear with a red heart sewn on its left side. Kristen remembered the day she gave the bear to Susie. Mrs. Kline observed her staring at the bear. She turned her tear covered face toward Nurse Warner and asked, "Do you want Teddy back?" Kristen thought for a moment before giving Mrs. Kline an answer, "No, I think you should keep him."

"I can't, Nurse Warner. It's too painful to have anything from here that reminds me of my daughter."

"Alright then, I will keep Teddy, as long as you don't mind."

Truth of the matter was, Kristen didn't want the bear either and for the same reasons. It was too painful! That was why she found herself questioning whether she should continue to give her heart to her patients through her work. Was she getting burned out? She never thought she would, but Susie's death stung as if she had been her own child. She took Teddy off the windowsill cradling him in her arms. Then looked at the grieving mother. "I am so sorry, Mrs. Kline, I truly am. Taking care of your daughter was an honor and a privilege."

"Thank you for your kindness, Nurse Warner," was all Mrs. Kline said, before turning her back on Kristen to continue folding the quilt.

There was nothing Kristen could say to ease Mrs. Kline's grief. In all her years of training and of the experiences she had, she was at a loss. Susie's dream must have had some meaning. She was going somewhere high in the sky but needed to know her mother would always catch her.

What did that mean? Could it be that Susie's ethereal nature was watching? Would she send a sign confirming that her life continued? Kristen left Mrs. Kline to her tasks. The room wasn't needed, and she thought the grieving mother should not be rushed as she closed a chapter of her life. Some things were better left unsaid. Kristen closed the door behind her and walked down the hallway and out into the living room of the facility. She stopped at the receptionist's desk and asked, "What time is my appointment today?" The receptionist looked up from her computer screen. "I made it for eleven this morning, right before your lunch break. I thought if your tour overlapped, you wouldn't mind."

"That was very considerate. Thank you, Hilda."

Turning away from the receptionist, Kristen walked down the hall to her office and sat at her desk, stuffing Teddy into the corner of her chair. She stared at her computer screen, unable to perform her usual tasks of the day. Because she stayed at work every afternoon until her paperwork was done, nothing was pressing that needed her immediate attention.

Today was different, she thought. She could not concentrate, thinking about Susie and her appointment with Mr. Hurst. She felt a good cry coming on and wanted to get it over with before her appointment. Kristen got up from her desk, picked up Teddy and stuffed him into her oversized purse. Putting on her sunglasses, she walked out of her office, shutting the door behind her. Before exiting, she made a stop at the receptionist desk.

"I'm going to sit outside for a while, in case anyone needs me."

"I will make a note of that, Nurse Warner, enjoy the sunshine."

"Thanks, I will."

Outside the main entrance to Tri-County Hospice, Kristen noticed a bench next to the bus stop. She had not taken notice of the bench because she often arrived before the sun was up and left after the sun went down. She thought it was convenient for her purposes and convenient, in general, for family members visiting a loved one who didn't have any other means of transportation. Sitting on the bench, Kristen took Teddy out of her purse and held him tightly, turning her face into the sun. The feeling that came over her was indulgent and novel. She had never taken time to sit quietly before a shift. There always seemed to be someone who needed her. Up until now, Hospice had been her life.

As she sat oblivious to everyone and everything around her, Tim pulled into a parking space next to the bench. Recognizing the figure on the bench as Nurse Warner, he let the car idle. Tim only watched her for seconds, then the purr of the car's engine caused Kristen to look in its direction.

He got out of his car and walked toward the bench, "May I sit?"

"Sure," she answered. "You don't happen to be my eleven o'clock, do you?"

Tim thought of something witty to say, then changed his mind. "If you are Nurse Warner, then yes, I am."

"Do you want your tour now?" she asked.

"Do I have a choice?"

"You always have a choice, Mr. Hurst."

"In that case, Nurse Warner, how about an early lunch?"

Kristen hesitated until Tim reassured her that he was not a miscreant.

"I know a place within walking distance where we can grab a bite to eat so you don't have to worry I'm going to abduct you."

"You're funny, Mr. Hurst. That wouldn't be a bad idea though."

"Oh really?" Tim replied.

"My answer is yes. I would love to take a walk because the sun is shining, and I don't get out at midday very often. Actually, I never do, but a ride in your car sounds even lovelier. I'll take you on your tour when we get back."

"Alright, let's get out of here."

Kristen rose from her seated position on the bench with Teddy still clutched under her arm. While gazing at the bear, Tim opened the car door for his date. "For me? You shouldn't have."

Kristen was impressed with Tim's attempt at humor. "This old bear," she began to say, but her voice started to quaver. She swallowed the lump that had risen in her throat because the morning's interaction with Mrs. Kline was still raw. "Teddy belonged to my last patient, a ten-year-old girl."

"Why didn't she keep it?"

"Sadly, she died." Kristen tried to say while wiping away a tear that had rolled down her cheek.

"That must have been extremely sad."

"It was, until you came along."

"Am I that charming?" Tim chuckled.

Kristen smiled, "That you are, Mr. Hurst."

The lively banter between two people who hardly knew each other could not have been more heaven sent. The conversation was relaxed and unassuming. Kristen felt something stir inside her heart that made her happy in Tim's presence.

He helped her get into the car because she didn't object to his opening her door. Then he went around to the driver's side and got in. Reaching behind his seat, he retrieved the retracted seat belt and secured it around his body, snapping into place. Then, before starting the engine, he turned to Kristen, making sure she had fastened hers. "You ready?" he asked. "I am," she said, smiling at him.

They arrived at the café within minutes. The car barely got out of fourth gear before Tim downshifted, pulling into a parking spot near the café.

"Are we here already?" Kristen complained.

"We are," Tim answered. "I thought you would want to be close to work."

Kristen let out a sigh. "I did, but today is so lovely. I don't have any patients who need me, so I don't have to rush back. Besides if anyone questions me, I will say I'm on a PR assignment."

"Is that what you think this is?"

"Is it?" Kristen countered.

"It is whatever you want and need this time to be, Nurse Warner."

"That works for me, Mr. Hurst."

"Since we are here, we should eat. How about I grab some sandwiches. Are you familiar with this café, Nurse Warner? It's vegan oriented, kind of reminds me of a hippy hangout. You know, tie dyed clothing, loose flowing skirts on women wearing peasant blouses. I don't know what any of the male staff wear. I'm assuming jeans and a bandana around their dreadlocks."

Kristen laughed. Tim's appearance was not that of someone who would embrace the hippy culture. "I have eaten here. It's good, I can assure you of that. One feels nourished after a meal, not bloated and icky."

Tim thought about Kristen's description of the food and thought he'd give it a try. "How about this idea. We will order sandwiches to go, and I will drive you anywhere you want to go away from here."

"Sounds lovely. I'll take a hummus, grated carrot, spinach, tomato, and alfalfa sprouts on whole wheat with hibiscus tea."

"As you wish, Nurse Warner." Since they had driven with the convertible top down, Kristen asked, "Do you mind if I wait out here?"

"Not at all," Tim chuckled. "Besides, you don't want Teddy jumping out and running away, do you?" Kristen laughed, "No I don't."

"Alright, you stay here. I'll be back with the food."

Kristen laid her head back on the head rest, closing her eyes and savoring the warm sunshine. This was a different kind of happiness. One she had not felt in a long time, as the feeling was somewhat reminiscent of her happy days with Stan. She opened her eyes when she heard Tim walking toward the car. He stopped by her side, handing her the drinks to put in the cup holders. Then he handed her the bag of sandwiches.

"Where to?" he asked, after getting into his car.

"Anywhere far away from here."

"Nurse Warner, that sounds like you want to run away," Tim joked.

"Actually, Mr. Hurst, that would make for a quick exit."

"Don't you love your job? I mean your patients?"

"I do, Mr. Hurst, but life is short I am realizing, and I don't know how long I can keep up with this kind of work. I think I should have more in my life than work. What about you? Do you think about what you want out of life?" She hesitated and then continued, "I apologize. I shouldn't be so straightforward asking you such a personal question. It's just that I feel so comfortable around you even though we've just met. It's like I've known you my entire life."

Tim paused before answering. Truth be told, he felt a connection with her too. He just couldn't understand why. And since she asked him what he wanted out of life, he decided to tell her.

"Recently, Nurse Warner, a former client from the bank left me in a very comfortable position. I thought I'd have to work for a few more years and I am grateful I do not. I have always wanted to take a cross-country trip. For the longest time, I thought it would be a solo trip but now, as you say, and I agree with you, life is short. It can be snatched away like a thief in the night. So, more and more, I'd like to share that cross-country trip with someone. And I do not want to have an itinerary of two weeks. I want to go and stop whenever we want and see whatever we want."

"That sound's lovely, Tim. I really think it does. No time constraints, no commitments."

Tim filed away Nurse Warner's thoughts. She was beginning to sound like someone he would enjoy that kind of trip with. He asked, "How about a drive up the coast?"

"Sounds lovely."

"Alright, then, let's go," he said, as he put the car in drive and zoomed onto the highway.

Tim didn't have any place in mind until they arrived near the cliff where Bud and Mary Jane danced on sunbeams.

"How's this?" he asked, turning off the car.

"It's lovely! Because I work inside, I have missed so much. Look at the water and the sunlight. Oh, how I can imagine dancing on it!"

Tim didn't know what to say since Kristen's words were exactly what his mother had said. This couldn't be coincidence, could it? Or was his mother sending her blessings? All he could think to say was, "I'm hungry, how about you?"

"I'm very hungry," Kristen replied.

"I know a spot where we can sit but it's across the highway."

"That's alright, Mr. Hurst, I'm feeling adventurous."

They got out of the car with food and drinks. Tim watched until all cars had passed in both directions before they crossed the highway. Kristen followed him as he led the way through the pine trees to a boulder a short distance from a cliff overlooking the ocean. There didn't seem to be a need for conversation, even when Tim took the sandwiches out of the bag and placed them on the makeshift table. He offered Kristen his hand, helping her sit on the boulder, then sat next to her. They consumed their impromptu picnic in silence, enjoying the sunshine and the whispering wind as it wove in and out of the pine boughs overhead.

After they finished eating, they sat quietly, each to their own thoughts, looking out over the horizon on the sunbeams that sparkled and glittered on the water below. Tim broke the magic of the moment, "I think I should take you back to work, even though I could sit here all afternoon."

"What time is it?"

Tim looked at his watch. "Twelve-thirty."

"Oh no! I forgot about your tour."

"No need to fret, Nurse Warner. You were on a PR assignment, don't forget."

"That's stretching the truth, Mr. Hurst."

"Not really, Nurse Warner. You were getting to know a potential client; oops I mean patient."

"I hope not for a very long time."

"I don't intend to get sick. But if and when I do, you can be my nurse."

Tim helped Kristen up from the boulder. They cleaned up their wrappings, taking them with them as they left the pine grove overlooking the ocean. The whizzing of cars flying by on Highway 1 took longer to clear than normal, but finally there was an interlude in the flow that allowed them to cross safely. Kristen smiled at Tim as she got into the car. She secretly hoped she would get to know him long before he became her patient.

The drive along the coast back to Tri-County Hospice didn't take as long as it did to arrive at their picnic spot. Perhaps it was because Tim opened up the engine full throttle as the car twisted and turned in one smooth motion along the circuitous highway. He down shifted as they approached the parking lot of Tri-County, pulling into the same space he had when he arrived for his tour.

After Tim parked the car, Kristen took off her sunglasses for the first time that day, looking directly into Tim's soft brown eyes. "I had a lovely time. Thank you very much, Mr. Hurst." When Tim saw the exquisite color of her eyes, he knew he had found the woman in the red dress.

15
METAMORPHOSIS

$\mathcal{A}$s he watched Kristen walk back into Tri-County Hospice, Tim sat in his car, stunned, for what seemed like an eternity as he pondered the phrase Kaos used to explain the unexplainable: "There is no such thing as coincidence."

He had found the woman of his dreams. In the natural order of things, so he thought, how likely was it that he found the woman he could only dream about. He was not a religious man; his parents did not bring him up in any denomination, but they must have believed in something because he could not help recalling a phrase he read: "A coincidence is a small miracle when God chooses to remain anonymous."

Was this God's hand? Did life continue in a different form once the last breath was drawn? Tim was beginning to believe it did. Who was the woman at the bus stop who seemed to understand him without ever having met, except by chance? And what about his parents? His mother called out to his dad hours before she passed. The nurses said she had been reaching for someone. She must have been, because she appeared to have left with him.

These were questions he decided he should take up with Nurse Warner. He couldn't keep addressing her that way, or should he? They had spent an intimate moment together. Surely, that qualified as being on a first name basis. "Flowers, I should send flowers, and ask for a second date," Tim said out loud. Nurse Warner seemed to enjoy his company. He knew he wanted hers. But what would be appropriate?

This was the first time he was at an absolute loss in what to do. He was used to being in control because women fawned over him, and he held the upper hand. But the trajectory of this woman's arrows went straight through his heart.

Tim decided flowers would be appropriate, but what kind? He was tempted to do something outrageous and bountiful, but maybe that would be too much, and he didn't want to scare her off. Then he thought, "What if she doesn't like flowers? Who doesn't like flowers?" All the women he knew loved flowers, so Tim decided to gamble on sending a bouquet of something to Nurse Warner, care of Tri-County Hospice.

The florist Tim patronized when his mother was alive was located a few blocks from Tri-County Hospice. The low brick building with green houses behind it was hard to miss because it advertised the seasons with tasteful and expensive displays that were a delight to young and old alike. The day Tim stopped in to order flowers for Nurse Warner, a large green topiary rabbit sat upright on its hunches holding a woven basket of colorful pansies.

When he bought flowers for his mother, he knew what she liked and what might peak her memory. But this situation was different. Tim frowned as he walked up and down the aisles of pre-made arrangements. Nothing seemed to suit.

Seeing the customer might need help, a florist approached, "Mr. Hurst, I thought I recognized you. I haven't seen you in a while. How is your mother?"

"My mother passed away a few weeks ago."

"I'm sorry to hear that."

"Thank you."

"Is there anything in particular you have in mind? You seem lost, if you will permit me to say."

"I am in a quandary, of sorts," Tim replied.

The florist smiled. He was not the first person she helped who hadn't the slightest idea how to speak the love language of flowers. "How may I help you?"

"I met a woman, took her to lunch, and I want to thank her for a nice afternoon. I want to see her again, but I don't want to scare her off."

The florist paused, "Does she feel the same way toward you? Forgive me for overreaching, but the right kind of flowers send the right message. Sending the wrong kind can be disastrous, trust me."

"I have reason to believe she does. If I didn't get that 'vibe,' I wouldn't be here."

The florist smiled. "Then may I suggest something simple. That is a good rule of thumb, as we say in the flower business."

Tim laughed, "You mean green thumb, don't you."

The florist chuckled at his attempt at humor. When she didn't offer an explanation, Tim frowned because he was thinking roses, but didn't get the impression this was what the florist had in mind.

"You mean like a single red rose for something simple?"

"Oh no, not for this occasion, Mr. Hurst. Red roses mean passion, for an anniversary or Valentines Day. Or any time the occasion calls for that. I mean those are reserved for down the road, if you understand what I am saying."

Tim sighed, "Oh, I do. Loud and clear. Alright, what do you suggest?"

The florist walked over to a small mixed bouquet of colorful daises, tulips, and lilies. "I'm thinking something like this." Tim looked at the flowers but wasn't sold on them. He eyed the refrigerated case with buckets of fresh cut flowers of all shapes and sizes, stopping in front of a large case.

"Can I choose something from these cases?" he inquired.

"Of course you may. We have a variety of cut flowers that I can arrange for you, that you may deliver yourself."

Tim was taken aback. "I'm not going to deliver them! You still have that service, don't you?"

"Yes, Mr. Hurst, we do. When do you want the flowers sent?"

"Tomorrow."

The florist smiled knowingly, "Mr. Hurst, I will personally make sure the flowers go out for delivery tomorrow."

"Thank you."

The florist started to walk over to a case and noticed Tim was not following her. She walked back to where he stood transfixed.

"Let's get started, Mr. Hurst."

In another refrigerated case, there were more buckets of flowers waiting to be arranged in spectacular designs for all occasions. There were buckets of peach, white-lemon-colored roses, and deep velvety looking red ones. Tim started to reach into the case when the florist cleared her throat.

"Mr. Hurst, those are not for you. Remember, later. You do not want to make every effort to impress and then have nothing in your back pocket, so to speak."

"But they are so pretty, they look like velvet."

"Yes, they do," the florist agreed, then reminded him. "For another occasion, I'm hopeful you will have more."

"So am I."

The florist opened the door to a case holding buckets of fragrant Asiatic lilies, tulips, and colorful daises. "Mr. Hurst, is there something that catches your eye?"

"I like the lilies, tulips, and daisies. I can't decide on one type."

"They are all very pretty on their own, or they can be mixed together. Remember, keep it small."

Tim decided on the colorful daisies, choosing several variegated varieties of yellow petals with deep blue centers and peach petals with dark brown centers. Then he chose a pink fragrant Asiatic lily that complimented the bouquet.

"How about these?"

"You have made an excellent choice. I will make sure they look lovely. I may add some deep purple statices if you don't mind. Statices are straw-like flowers that, when added to an arrangement with greenery, give a pop of color that pulls the arrangement together. I assure you; your bouquet will be exquisite."

"You're the expert. I will leave the details to you."

Tim started to pull his wallet out of his pocket, then remembered he should write a note. "Do you have little note cards?"

"Yes. They are up at the counter. There are several to choose from, but remember, keep your message simple."

A simple ecru colored card caught his eye. It had a tiny white lily of the valley embossed on the upper left corner. He wrote something on the card that the florist strained to see. She hoped Tim had remembered to keep the wording simple. When he finished, he put the card in its envelope and handed it to the florist.

"Please deliver these to Nurse Warner at Tri-County Hospice at your earliest convenience. Thank you." Then he queried her a second time. "Can you make sure they are your first delivery of the day?"

"Let me check out deliveries for tomorrow, Mr. Hurst. I think we may be able to squeeze in an early morning stop at Tri-County."

Tim didn't want to be pushy, but his logic told him Tri-County was close by so surely they could be delivered first. He held his breath while the florist looked at the deliveries.

"You're in luck. We can get your bouquet delivered as our first stop."

Tim smiled. Feeling light in his heart, he thanked the florist, then walked out to his car.

Kristen felt happy when she awoke the next morning. Her lunch date with Mr. Hurst, while unexpected, gave her a new perspective and put a spring in her steps that had not been there for a long time.

She realized that her past experiences had left her heart with no room for anyone other than her patients, but the previous day's interactions with this man was different. How would she know if he felt the same? Would she see him again?

Then she remembered that Mr. Hurst hadn't taken his tour of the building. If he had already rescheduled, she would see him again. If he hadn't, she decided it would be appropriate to contact him to set up another date and time. This was a bold move as she would normally let providence intervene on her behalf.

As soon as Kristen entered Tri-County Hospice, she stopped at the receptionist's desk to make the inquiry.

"Good morning, Hilda, are there any messages for me?"

Hilda smiled because Kristen never asked about messages. When calls did come in, Hilda either sent them directly to Kristen's voice mail or, occasionally, if it were an older caller who didn't want to go into voice mail, she would record the caller's name, phone number, and message on a pink "While You Were Out" slip of paper and slide the message into Kristen's mailbox.

"Good Morning, Nurse Warner. I haven't received any calls for you or placed any messages in your mailbox this morning. And since it's only a little before nine and the mail doesn't arrive until noon, your mailbox and voicemail should both be empty."

"Oh…ok, I'll be in my office in case anyone needs me. I should try and get some work accomplished."

Hilda noticed something different about Kristen and asked, "Nurse Warner, is there anything I can do to help you?"

"No Hilda, not really."

Hilda knew her supervisor better than Kristen would admit. Her boss was a creature of habit and had put her heart and soul into her work. However, she did notice that Kristen had taken a real interest in Mr. Hurst. She couldn't blame her. He was handsome, polite, and engaging. She smiled at Kristen before saying, "I'll let you know if anything comes up."

"Thank you, Hilda," Kristen said, then retreated to her office. The wonderful "high" she had been on since her lunch date with Mr. Hurst was beginning to wear off. She didn't like the feeling of loneliness that was trying to return; she wanted this newfound hope to stay on her heart. Realizing she was distracted by and attracted to a man with only a last name, she turned on her computer and stared at the screen. When would she ever feel again the way he had made her feel? How had he so quickly brought down the walls of protection she had built around her heart? What about him was so familiar that she immediately trusted him and now wanted to escape with him? Lost in her thoughts, she jumped when the phone rang. It took three rings before she could pull herself together enough to answer the call.

"This is Nurse Warner."

"Nurse Warner," Hilda began, with a slight lilt in her voice. "Can you please come to the front desk?"

Kristen's heart skipped a beat. She was used to events changing rapidly in her line of work, but as far as she knew, there weren't any patients' needs she was aware of, and she didn't have any appointments with potential clients.

"I'll be right there, Hilda."

Hanging up the phone, Kristen headed to the receptionist's desk, wondering what could be taking place at the front of the building. The morning sunlight streaming through the glass doors at the main entrance was almost blinding. Squinting her eyes, she walked several more feet thinking how patients loved the alcove where Hilda's desk was situated. It was against the wall to the right of the living room as one entered the main doors, but it offered just enough privacy so conversations could not be overheard.

As Kristen turned the corner, she blinked to help her pupils readjust to the office lighting, and gasped when she saw a lovely bouquet of flowers on Hilda's desk. As she approached, Hilda pointed toward the notecard attached to a plastic pick holder inside the arrangement.

With a mischievous grin, Hilda asked, "Your name is Nurse Warner, is it not?"

Kristen's hands trembled as she took the notecard and opened it.

> *Dear Nurse Warner,*
> *Thank you for a lovely afternoon.*
> *Sincerely,*
> *Tim Hurst*

Kristen tried to hold back her emotions and whirling thoughts as she placed the card back into the envelope and returned it to the pick holder in the arrangement. So, his first name was Tim. Tim Hurst. Kristen repeated his name a few times in her mind, thinking what a nice ring it had to it. Tim Hurst.

Turning to Hilda she explained, "These are from Mr. Hurst thanking me for a lovely afternoon yesterday." She inhaled the fragrant Asiatic lily in her bouquet as she looked at the address of the florist. At the very least, she thought she should send a thank you note to Tim.

Hilda could not take her eyes off Kristen's flowers, "Oh my, your bouquet is lovely. I would certainly thank him if I were you."

"Hilda, that's exactly what I'm planning to do."

Kristen picked up the arrangement and walked back to her office with a lift in her heart and her step. Once inside, she set the flowers on her desk and stared at the bouquet.

Left alone with her thoughts, she felt this was an answer to her questions before the phone call from Hilda, but was she right? Was he truly interested in her from a romantic standpoint? Was this a sign he felt the same way toward her as she did for him? The flowers would indicate that he did. Kristen didn't want to get her hopes up; she had been hurt so many times. But maybe it was time to stop trying to control her future and to allow fate, or chance, or whatever was happening, to take its course. Maybe it was time for her to move forward.

But she also had to stay in the present, put those thoughts away for a while, get on with her day, and check in on her stable patients. She was happy that not every patient who came to hospice died. Some cardiac patients recovered and went home. Other patients diagnosed with an illness, who had no one to care for them, would come to hospice to be validated and shown love as they worked through their illness and the treatments. This was the current situation at Tri-County, which allowed Kristen to take her lunch break away from the facility. So, when her paperwork was caught up for the morning, she decided to take an early lunch.

Before exiting the building, she stopped by the receptionist's desk. "Hilda, I will be out for my lunch break. If you need me, call my cell phone."

Hilda grinned, "I will, Nurse Warner. By the way, here's the address for the florist."

Kristen turned a bright shade of red. "Nurse Warner," Hilda began, "I know how important thank you notes are. I thought I would save you time."

"Thank you, Hilda. I will be back in an hour."

Kristen drove to the florist, arriving in minutes. Her heart was beating violently in her chest thinking of Mr. Hurst. She did not want to appear too eager, nonchalantly walking up and down the aisles of flowers. The same florist who had attended to Tim the day before suspected who this wanderer was.

"Excuse me," she said. "Is there something that I may help you with?" Kristen blushed, "My request is a little unusual."

"Enlighten me," the florist responded. "Nothing surprises me anymore." Kristen took a deep breath, exhaling slowly. "I received a lovely bouquet of flowers today and I would like to thank the sender, especially since I don't know if I will have the opportunity to personally thank him. I am wondering if you would be so kind as to provide me with his address."

"We usually do not give out our client's personal information. What arrangement did you receive? Can you describe it?" the florist asked.

"There was a fragrant lily and peach daisies with brown centers, and lemon-colored daisies with deep blue centers, and I think there were several deep purple straw-like flowers mixed throughout."

The florist smiled. So, this was the woman who had captured Mr. Hurst's heart. "I will make an exception and honor your request. but please do not share with anyone that I gave out the address." The florist turned and walked to the front desk, followed by Kristen, who answered, "I will not betray your trust. I know how important personal information is."

She waited while the florist shuffled through the stack of invoices piled on the corner of the space. Finding the correct one, the florist quickly jotted down the contact information for Mr. Tim Hurst and handed it to her.

"Thank you," Kristen replied, taking the information from her.

Kristen could hardly wait for her workday to be over. Normally, she would stick around and visit her patients with their families. Sometimes she ate dinner with them, but not today. She could have written a personal note and popped it in the mail, but this felt different. Instead, she decided to do something completely out of character and take a chance. Feeling afraid and bold at the same time, she drove to the address that had been provided by the florist.

As she pulled into the driveway, her tires crunched on the steep pea gravel driveway as she inched up, stopping on the flat. Then doubt started to set in and, second guessing herself, Kristen wondered why she didn't call first. Why did she brazenly think it was ok to drive to the house of someone she had only met once without waiting for an invitation? He had not invited her; she had invited herself. Maybe she misinterpreted the flowers? Was he just being polite? Maybe she should leave before anyone noticed her car in the driveway.

While contemplating the latter, Kristen heard footsteps approaching her car. Now it was too late to save face and leave. She stared down at her steering wheel hoping the footsteps would go away, but they continued coming closer, stopping next to her car. Embarrassed, she kept her head down, not wanting to look out the car window to see who was standing next to it.

Terrance had been watching from the garage where he was polishing Tim's black BMW. As Tim's driver, part of his official responsibilities was to keep the car clean and ready for service within a moment's notice. But, as a close friend, he felt his unofficial responsibilities included providing a sense of protection for his employer. Seeing unfamiliar cars and people on the property always brought out the defensive side of Terrance, and Tim always gave him a heads up when he'd be entertaining a client, which was not very often. So, when he saw the young woman turn into the driveway, he came out to meet the uninvited guest.

"May I help you?" he asked, in a tone that sounded more like a security guard than a driver. "Are you lost?"

Sheepishly, Kristen replied, "No, I'm not." Then, taking a breath and regaining her courage, she asked, "May I ask, do you live here?"

"Not exactly," Terrance replied. "But I spend a lot of time here. Who are you looking for?"

Kristen decided it's now or never. I've come all this way, so I may as well go for it. So, taking off her sunglasses, she looked at this man standing beside her car and explained, "I was hoping to see Mr. Hurst. I wanted to thank him for the flowers he sent this morning."

Terrance, always the guardian, hesitated to give out any information about Tim or his whereabouts. But, looking into her eyes, he suddenly remembered what Tim had said about the woman he had met at the gala. She had been wearing a red dress, but he also described her with an exquisite shade of blue eyes. He had to admit, these were the most exquisite eyes he had ever seen. Coming to his senses, he softened, "Oh…that is a pity. Mr. Hurst is not here at the moment."

Kristen, slightly embarrassed, deeply disappointed and just a little bit relieved, apologized, "I shouldn't have come here uninvited. I am so sorry to have barged in on you like this."

"Not a problem, Ma'am," Terrance said. Then offered the platitude, "I'm sure Mr. Hurst will be sorry he missed you, too."

Kristen was distraught that she had driven all the way to his home only to discover Tim was not there. But that wasn't the only reason she was feeling overwhelmed. The mixture of emotions from the days gone by including Susie's death, the grief of her parents, and her stupidity in thinking she could just drive to a man's house and find him there, arms outstretched, suddenly brought an overflow of tears that streamed down her cheek. She wiped them away as quickly as she could, not wanting a complete stranger to witness her outburst, but it was too late. Terrance, a bit confused by her display, looked upon her with compassion. Was she as taken by her boss as he had been the night of the gala?

Not knowing what else to do, he asked, "You ok to drive?" "Yes, I'm fine. Thank you. Goodbye," she answered. Then she activated the ignition of the car, put her sunglasses on, turned around and slowly drove down the driveway. Kristen fought back the tears she desperately tried to squelch, but it was no use. Again, they poured uncontrollably from her eyes as she stopped at the end of the driveway before pulling onto the street. The happy bubble and the feeling of hope that had surrounded her all day had burst. A sad, vacant feeling swelled within her chest wherein, just twenty-four hours earlier, there had been a joyous feeling of endless possibility. Hopelessness set in again as she thought, I met someone with whom I felt connected and now he is gone. What are the chances he will come looking for me? Kristen knew she might be overreacting because her expectations were not met. She had expected Mr. Hurst to be home and for him to meet her at the car in a warm embrace, to rescue her from her loneliness, and for them to live happily ever after. It was the fairy tale she and her brother, Harry, had played out in their childhood. Harry was her prince, her rescue. She was aware she was hoping Tim would be her prince, her rescue, so when disappointment set in, it seemed everything else came crashing down too.

Life just wasn't fair. She knew that as so many patients and their families articulated these thoughts to her. She knew that because of her brother's motorcycle accident and her first love, Stan. People she loved left too soon from her life. Kristen also knew that life had happy, little moments and she should hold onto those moments before they became a distant memory. She had to or she would die herself.

On the morning of the floral delivery, Tim called the florist to make sure the bouquet had been delivered. When she assured him that his arrangement was the first stop on the route, he was both relieved and anxious.

When Tim wanted to be alone with his thoughts or needed to work out a problem with a client, he would go for long rides on his motorcycle. This was one of those times. Terrance was well aware of his friend's tendency to disappear into solitude when something was bothering him.

"Terrance, I'm going for a long ride."

Terrance, suspecting Tim needed to seek a resolution for his angst, asked, "Anything on your mind, Sir?"

"Yes, Terrance, there is."

"Care to share, Sir?"

Tim thought for a moment before relaying the news to his loyal friend. "You aren't going to believe this, Terrance. I found the woman in the red dress."

Terrance frowned, trying to recall who Tim meant. "What woman, Sir?"

"Terrance!" Tim exclaimed. "The one from the Hospice Gala."

Terrance suddenly remembered, "Oh...that one."

"Yes Terrance, that one."

"What's your plan, Sir, if I may ask?"

"I don't know. I sent her flowers and a note thanking her for our lunch date yesterday."

"Oh, really? I didn't know you had a date, much less with the woman of your dreams. Was it a chance meeting or was it really a date?"

"Well, in all truthfulness, I made an appointment with her the day before, but at the time, I didn't know who I had made the appointment with."

"I am so confused. You made an appointment with a woman you had never met, and you took her on a date, but you're not sure if it was a date, and then you sent her flowers. Let's back up a minute. What kind of an appointment did you make with her?"

"It was at Tri-County Hospice."

Terrance, alarmed, blurted, "ARE YOU SICK?"

"Relax, I'm not, but with both of my parents dying at the same time and losing Helen Trenton unexpectedly, I became painfully aware that I didn't have anyone to take care of me or my needs if something were to happen to me. And if I were to become terminally ill, I would need a plan in place for my care. I don't have a family to help me in that situation."

Terrance, relieved that his friend wasn't in need of hospice care at the moment replied, "That's true."

"Sadly, it is. I wanted to tour the hospice across the street from the hospital."

Terrance looked at his employer with consternation as Tim continued, "You know, so I would have an idea of what to expect, what the place looks like. I mean, if that's where I'm to go out."

"SIR!"

"Terrance, I'm being pragmatic."

"Yes, you are practical, and truthfully your life has provided me with amusement."

"I'm glad you find me amusing. However, as a financial advisor, I saw the importance of what end of life care means for people."

"I trust you saw the place? Took a tour? Met some of the staff?"

"No, Terrance, I didn't. My tour guide got called away before I saw her face; all I saw was her back walking away from me. She said she would return and complete the tour, but she didn't come back. The receptionist said Nurse Warner had been detained and offered to have someone else give me the tour, but I declined. There was something about the voice of the woman that felt familiar, so, I made another appointment, which happened yesterday."

"When you went back for the tour, were you so impressed with the place that you sent flowers?"

"I never saw the place, Terrance."

"Really? Why not?"

"Because Nurse Warner was sitting outside, waiting, when I pulled into the parking lot. As I drove up, I recognized her by her shape, not by her face. I asked if I could sit with her on the bench, and she asked if I was her 11 a.m.

client wanting a tour guide. As we talked, she looked a bit distraught and said she didn't want to go back into the facility, so I suggested an early lunch."

"Were you prepared for that?"

"Of course. I knew I wanted to take her to lunch and was planning on asking her after my tour. We had an impromptu picnic instead. Nurse Warner said she had her reasons for wanting to stay outside. I didn't pry, although she mentioned that a one of her young patient's had died and she wanted to get away."

"You enjoy her company, Sir?"

"I did, I do! I want to see her again, so I sent her flowers."

"Oh, so you don't know how she feels. That's the reason for the bike ride."

"You figured that out, Terrance."

"Just be careful, Sir. I will see you when you get back."

"I'll be back, and I will stay safe. I want to see her again."

Tim slowly rolled down the driveway on his motorcycle, stopping just before the driveway met the street. While he had somewhat of an idea where to ride, he contemplated if he should turn right or left. Turning right would take him into town. Turning left, the road would take him out along the highway that paralleled the ocean. He decided to turn left.

Driving along the oceanside was good for Tim as he processed his thoughts. It had been a long time since he had taken time away from work, and having free time to do anything he wanted was proving to be relaxing and productive, but also reminded him how alone he was.

His thoughts turned to Nurse Warner. No longer was she the woman in the red dress; now she had a name. At least he knew her last name. No longer were her eyes just an exquisite shade of blue; now they carried in them compassion, care, and he thought he had seen a glint of pain and loneliness. Was he just making this up, or was there something there, pulling him in.

Was this the magnetism pulling them together? Loneliness? And maybe it wasn't. Maybe it was a soul connection. That was a kind of loneliness until you found the other half of you, the part that felt lonely, wasn't it?

As the sun started to set, Tim noticed the beautiful hues of orange and purple. As he turned his motorcycle toward home, he determined to take one more risk in reaching out to Nurse Warner. Maybe, just maybe, she was playing it cool and waiting on him to reach out again to reschedule the tour for a third time.

By the time Tim returned home, twilight had faded into darkness. The beam from his headlight was a beacon along the vacant streets until he turned onto his driveway. The bike hesitated before jumping the tiny curb between the street and the driveway. Riding slowly up the gravel drive, he pulled into the garage, alerting the motion sensor which automatically turned on the overhead light. As Tim parked the bike next to his BMW, he noticed something in the back seat but wasn't sure what it was until he turned the engine off and dismounted his bike. On closer inspection, he discovered Teddy, the bear Kristen had accidentally left behind, or had she? Tim was beginning to believe there was no such thing as coincidence. Tim reached into the back seat, gently picked up the bear, tucked it under his arm, and walked into the house.

When he entered, Terrance was waiting.

"How was your ride, Sir?"

"It was good. Nothing like a long ride to clear your head. How was your day? Anything to report?"

"You had a visitor."

"Oh?"

"Yes, a pretty little gal with the most amazing blue eyes. Never seen anything like them."

Tim tried to act composed even though his heart was beating out of his chest. He hoped Terrance didn't see him grab the counter for balance, as he suddenly felt unsteady. "What did she want?"

"She wanted to thank you for the flowers, Sir."

"She came all the way out here to personally thank me for flowers?"

"She was terribly disappointed that you were not here, crying and all."

"Terrance, why did you let her go?"

"What was I supposed to do? I didn't know she was your person of interest."

"She's more than that. I want to spend the rest of my life with her."

"Sir, you went on one picnic lunch, and you want to spend the rest of your life with her?"

"I knew from the moment I saw her at the gala."

"I won't doubt your judgment, Sir. By the way, I see you found the little stuffed bear that was hiding in the back of your car."

"Yes, this is Teddy. Nurse Warner was holding him when I met her outside Tri-County Hospice"

Terrance thought for a moment. He knew of the dalliances his employer had in the past. None of them compared to this woman. "Other than your tour, Sir, I think you have a good reason to go back there."

"Yes, I do, Terrance. Yes, I do."

16
NEOPHYTE

Kristen was beside herself. How could she have thought that personally thanking Mr. Hurst by driving out to his home, uninvited, was a good idea! And then to find he wasn't at home was even more embarrassing. As she drove home, Kristen pounded on the steering wheel shouting, "STUPID, STUPID, STUPID!" Truth of the matter was, she wanted to see him again.

After her tirade, she decided that if he had any feelings for her, he knew where to find her. Sure, he had sent flowers and thanked her for a lovely afternoon, but the flowers were simple, the note was simple, and neither gave any indication of his intentions or interest. Only that he was thankful he had someone to share lunch with. He hadn't called to schedule another appointment for a tour, as far as she knew, and maybe his gestures were out of kindness rather than romantic interest. So, if indeed he did have interest, he could come to her.

That had to be enough to satisfy her uncertainty. She had to let the issue go and not beat herself up over something she had no control over. Mr. Hurst would be interested in more or he would not. It was simple, no gray area, not maybe. It would be yes, or it would be no, and providence would be left to determine their fate. She arrived home as the sun was setting, determined to get a good night's sleep and let things roll out as they were going to, rather than trying to will things into existence. If there was to be a relationship with Mr. Tim Hurst, it was his turn to take the next step.

The next morning, Kristen pulled into the parking lot at Tri-County and took her car key out of the ignition, pausing briefly before grabbing her purse from the back seat and heading into work for another shift. Today was a new day. She would put on her happy face; she didn't want her personal life, or lack thereof, interfering with her patient's needs. "All will be well," she told herself.

After passing through the double glass doors, Kristen stopped at Hilda's desk summoning up as much cheerfulness as she could manage so as not to betray her true feelings.

"Good morning, Hilda."

Hilda smiled back, "Good morning, Nurse Warner."

Hilda sensed a change in her boss, that her faux cheerfulness was a definite disconnect from her joyous self of yesterday, to which Hilda inquired,

"How was your evening?"

"It was fine, simply dandy," Kristen answered sarcastically. Hilda decided to leave well enough alone. Perhaps things did not go well with Mr. Hurst, she surmised. If Nurse Warner wanted to talk about what was bothering her, she would.

"I'm glad to hear that. Have a nice morning."

"Thanks Hilda," Kristen said, then she turned and walked down the hallway and retreated into her office.

There was always paperwork to be done, phone calls to be made, and note cards to send. But before Kristen started her routine, she re-read the note sent along with the flowers, lingering over the words, "Thank you for a lovely afternoon." If Mr. Hurst didn't enjoy her company, she surmised, he wouldn't have sent flowers. That was all she needed to get started on a stack of unopened mail.

Most of the letters were from senior citizens inquiring about the services

Tri-County Hospice provided. Halfway through the pile, Kristen discovered a small, white envelope. She opened it carefully, finding inside a note from the family of Susie Kline, her last patient. The note read.

Dear Nurse Warner,

The parents of Susie Kline personally invite you to a celebration of life service for our darling daughter. We are at a loss for words to thank you for your care and concern during Susie's illness. She was very fond of you, and we know you helped her in ways we could not.

As a final gesture of farewell, we are releasing doves at the end of her service. I know Susie would have wanted you to be there and would like you to release the doves on her behalf.

The services will be held at

St. Marks Catholic Church,
1022 Apostle Way,
Culver Heights
Saturday the 10th of April
10:00 a.m.

Sincerely,
Esther Kline

Kristen put the note next to the vase of flowers, juxtaposing life and death, and stared at them for a long time. She would honor Mrs. Kline's invitation even though funerals and celebration of life services were not something she made a habit of attending.

Tim woke in a cheerful mood. He had good reason to begin his day, remembering that Teddy needed to be returned to his owner, Nurse Warner. Surprisingly, he had a restful night's sleep; surprised because sound sleep had eluded him in the past.

Looking at his watch, Tim noticed it was too late to invite Nurse Warner to lunch. He could, however, extend an invitation for dinner. He looked at Teddy lying on the pillow next to him, grateful he had been left behind. After showering and putting on fresh clothes, he again grabbed Teddy, tucking him under his arm, and headed outside. He didn't bother to stop for a cup of coffee, even though Terrance had put some on to brew. Tim found his driver outside waiting, and both got into the car.

"Where to, Sir?"

"Tri-County, please."

"Yes Sir."

Terrance started the ignition, then drove slowly down the driveway. He liked the sound the gravel made crunching under the tires. When he got to the end of the driveway, he turned right and headed into town. Terrance drove in silence while his employer looked out the window, obviously lost in his own thoughts. Tim doubted that Nurse Warner would turn down his invitation to dine with him that evening, since she drove out to his place to personally thank him.

"Who does that?" he pondered. "How does she know where I live?"

He smiled thinking that Nurse Warner must have her sources and admired her inventiveness. Her interest in him was justification enough. He'd let well enough alone; she obviously liked him.

Since it was past midday, the drive to Tri-County Hospice didn't take long because the route was not a slow-moving parking lot. Terrance stopped the car next to the doors of Tri-County Hospice, letting the car idle.

"Sir, we're here," he announced softly. Tim seemed to be unaware they had arrived at the destination. Coming to his senses, he turned to Terrance, and said, "I won't be long."

"Take your time, Sir. I'll be waiting."

Tim grabbed Teddy and, without looking back, walked through the glass doors in front of him. He paused in front of Hilda's desk, who recognized him from a few days earlier, but didn't see his name on the appointment calendar.

"Sir, do you have an appointment?"

"No, I don't. I'm here to return something to Nurse Warner. Is she, by chance, available?"

"I will check, Mr. Hurst," she said, remembering his name. Then she picked up the phone and dialed Kristen.

Kristen let the phone ring until she finished compiling her thought into a patient's folder, then looking down, noticed the call was coming from the receptionist.

"Hello Hilda."

"Nurse Warner, there is a gentleman here to see you."

Kristen paused, "I didn't think I had any appointments today."

"You don't, Nurse Warner. Do you want to come out or should I send him back?"

"I'll be out in a minute, Hilda. Thank you."

Kristen quickly fluffed her hair, then opened her side drawer and took out her compact and a tube of lipstick. She had just bought the new frosted pink tint and wanted a reason to try it.

"I will have to do," she said, looking at her reflection in her compact mirror. Then she closed the lid, shoved the compact back into her drawer, and walked out to meet her visitor. When she rounded the corner to the living room, she was more than surprised to see Mr. Hurst standing at Hilda's desk, clutching Teddy.

"Mr. Hurst, I'm surprised to see you," she said as calmly as she could without betraying her elation. Tim's smile made Kristen swoon. She tried to remind herself, to no avail, that he was a client, not her boyfriend.

"You forgot someone. I thought you would like to have him back."

"Yes, thank you. He is a very special bear."

"I'm glad you think he is because yesterday, he didn't get that impression."

Kristen smiled at Tim. "Mr. Hurst, would you like to come back to my office?"

"That would be nice, thank you."

Tim followed Kristen into her office. He observed the flowers on her desk before sitting down in the chair she offered.

"I see someone sent you flowers, or did you buy them for yourself," he teased.

Kristen decided to play along with his attempt at humor. "I think Teddy did because I left him by himself all night somewhere in a cold garage, and he didn't know where he was. He must have thought I was angry, and these are apology flowers."

"Is that what you think?" Tim asked.

"No, I should be the one apologizing to you."

"Why do you think that, Nurse Warner?"

"Because I drove out to your house uninvited, and you were not home. That was presumptuous of me, and I am sorry. I've never done anything like that, but I wanted to thank you in person for sending me such a beautiful bouquet of flowers."

"I heard I had a visitor, and I am sorry I wasn't home. But I'm here now, and you can thank me if you feel the need."

Kristen looked deeply into Tim eyes, "Thank you, Mr. Hurst. The flowers are fragrant and beautiful, and I also had a lovely afternoon with you."

Tim paused for a moment, then, taking the risk he was prepared to take, he clearly stated what had been on his mind.

"Now that apologies and thank you's are out of the way, Nurse Warner, perhaps we should be on a first name basis."

"I thought you wanted a tour. I never call any of my patients by their first name until…"

"Until what Nurse Warner?"

"Until they are my patients that I take care of in their last days, and they tell me to call them by their first name."

"Do you think I will change my mind about you being my nurse because we are on a first name basis?"

Kristen was taken back by Tim's direct question. She tried to answer him but couldn't find the words.

"I…" she stammered, "I don't want you to be my patient."

"Oh really, why is that, Nurse Warner?"

Kristen blushed, then turned away and said, "I may not be here when you become a patient."

"Why do you say that? Are you ill?"

"No, Mr. Hurst, I'm not ill. I need a break. I don't know for how long, or if I will come back. Nursing has been my whole life, but I can't keep living for my patients. I must live for me."

"You have a point there. Still, I'd like to know your first name." Nurse Warner turned to face him. "My name is Kristen, Kristen Warner." Tim extended his hand. "I'm Tim. It's nice to meet you, Kristen. By the way, would you like to have dinner with me tonight?"

Without a pause, Kristen replied, "Yes, yes, I would love to Tim."

"What time do you get off work?"

"Barring any unforeseen events, my workday ends at five o'clock."

"Would you like me to pick you up here around that time, or meet you at your house?"

"You can meet me at my house, it's not far from here. The address is 285 Barlow Street."

"Very good. Your house. I will see you at six."

Still clutching the bear, Tim remembered his initial reason for the visit was to return Teddy.

"Before I forget, this guy belongs to you," he said, handing her the bear. As Kristen reached for Teddy, their hands touched, and a spark of electricity shot through Tim's hand. Surprised, he told himself, "This is not a coincidence."

"I'll be going. Don't get up, I know the way out. I'll see you at six."

Kristen felt like her heart would explode in her chest. She was smitten with Tim and had good reason to believe he felt the same about her. What could possibly go wrong.

Terrance was excited when Tim returned to the car. He could tell by the gleam in his eyes that the plan for dinner was confirmed.

"Sir, how did it go? Did you have a chance to talk with Nurse Warner?"

"I did. She apologized for coming to the house unannounced, she thanked me for the flowers, and I returned Teddy to her, safe and sound. After business was finished, I asked her to go with me to dinner tonight. I'm picking her up at her house at 6 p.m."

"Sir, do you need me to drive you and Nurse Warner?"

"No, Terrance, but thank you. I plan on picking her up myself. And, by the way, we are now on first name basis. Her name is Kristen."

As Tim readied for his date, he didn't want to appear too formal, so he picked out a pair of jeans, a casual short sleeve button down shirt the color of blue gray that matched her exquisite eyes and pulled on a pair of low-cut leather bike boots. These, he thought, would work for their first dinner date – not too dressy, not too casual. And they would be fitting for taking his motorcycle. He was excited to have her riding behind him, arms around his waist, as they took the bike from her house to a nearby restaurant.

Tim arrived at Kristen's house promptly at six o'clock via his motorcycle. The sun was shining, and the air was warm. A perfect night, Tim thought. He also brought along an extra helmet for his passenger.

Kristin arrived home shortly after five and picked out a pair of jeans and a white T-shirt, then slipped on a black linen blazer. Tim didn't say where they were going, but she was confident her outfit would suffice for wherever he had in mind.

She didn't hear him pull up in front of her house, however, she did hear a soft chime from the doorbell announcing a visitor. Remembering she had a pair of dark brown, almost black, ballet flats under her bed, she quickly pulled those on, completing her outfit. Then she slipped silver hoop earrings into the tiny holes in her ears and fluffed her hair before quickly applying a neutral shade of lipstick.

Tim felt like he had been standing on the porch for eons. He was certain he had the correct address. When she opened the door and smiled at him, all thoughts of waiting too long vanished.

"Hi Tim, did you have trouble finding the place?"

"No, not really. Boy, you weren't kidding that you only lived a few blocks from Tri-County. Was that planned, your location?"

"Come on in, and I will answer your questions." Kristen said, holding the door open for him. Once Tim stepped inside the tiny foyer, he noticed it was obvious she didn't spend much time there. Her home wasn't messy, just sparsely furnished. That was ok with him because he didn't care for clutter and was pleasantly surprised.

"Tim, may I interest you in a glass of wine or beer?"

"Just water, thanks, since I thought we would go for a ride first."

"Sure thing, coming right up," Kristen said cheerfully as she took a pitcher of filtered water out of the refrigerator and poured him a glass. She handed him the water and asked, "Where do you have in mind?"

"Sometimes I let the bike take me."

Kristen's ears perked up when she heard the mention of a bike. Surely, he didn't mean a bicycle built for two.

"What do you mean, a bike?" she asked.

"A motorcycle, Kristen. Is there any other kind?"

A wave of nausea swept over Kristen, as though she was going to pass out. Just the mention of the word *motorcycle* put a tremendous fear in her. Tim noticed the instantaneous change.

"Don't you like motorcycles?"

Kristen didn't answer his question. Instead, she said, "Maybe us going out is a bad idea, Tim. I think you should leave."

Tim, deeply hurt and confused, answered, "But I just got here."

"I know, but I can't go out with you."

Tim was shocked.

"Kristen you are a grown woman. What's gotten into you?"

"I can't get involved with someone who rides motorcycles," she said, walking toward the door and opening it.

Tim didn't argue or try to convince her to let him stay. Whatever it was that spooked her must have been traumatic. Instead, he walked out the front door without looking back.

Kristen closed the door behind him, listening to the motorcycle roar off down the street. She collapsed, sobbing, with her back to the door. She liked Tim. Now he was gone before they even had a chance.

Kristen realized that she needed to figure out a way to heal from the fear, trigger, and trauma that connected motorcycles with loss. Everyone she had loved and lost had been involved with motorcycles. First it was her brother, Harry. Then Stan, even though he didn't ride one, his brother did. Now she had pushed away Tim, whom she felt a deep connection with, because he rode a motorcycle.

She could hear her dad's voice. He had constantly drummed into her head not to get involved with anyone who had anything to do with motorcycles. He had said more times than she could count, "You'll end up with a broken heart, or dead, like your brother." Without warning, all the pain she had felt from Harry's death came flooding back, crashing down like a heavy weight thrust upon her shoulders, making her fall to her knees in grief.

Kristen didn't know how long she stayed that way, but when her knees started to hurt, she got up from the floor, walked to her couch, and sank into it, staring blankly at the wall in front of her, feeling both numb and exhausted. It was just a little after 6 p.m., which was too early for bed, but she didn't have other plans, so she thought maybe if she took something to help her sleep, she could end the night early and wake up realizing this had been a bad dream.

Remembering she had wine on hand for special occasions, which would have been this evening had things turned out differently, she removed the cork, tilted the bottle to her lips, and took a large swig, not caring that the burgundy liquid didn't make it into a wine glass. Kristen carried the bottle by the neck into the living room and sank back into her couch. Returning the bottle to her lips, she guzzled the contents. As her body and mind relaxed, other memories came flooding back.

Kristen had chosen hospice care for a reason, having endured far too long the abuse of a narcissistic boyfriend she had met after graduating from nursing school.

In the beginning, he was charming and attentive. It didn't take long for his true colors to surface. He used alcohol, especially wine, to make her feel inadequate, ugly, and a drunk. She knew her limit, but he would encourage her to drink more than she could tolerate. Then, when she stumbled into the doorway of their home, he would call her a lush and a drunk and chide her that no "self-respecting nurse would do such a thing." On occasion, he would grab her so hard, he would leave bruises on her arms and, to "teach her a lesson," he would hit her. The abuse took its toll on Kristen. She no longer felt attractive nor desirable, and when she tried to confront him, his reaction disoriented her because he would twist her words to make himself appear the victim. At times, she thought she might be losing her mind or her grip with reality.

One night when they were at a local establishment, the boyfriend disappeared leaving her alone at the bar. The bartender, wondering why someone so enchanting and pretty was left alone, made conversation with Kristen as he poured drinks for her and others. He noticed bruises on her arms and a bruise on her face, slightly visible through her makeup. As they talked and laughed, Kristen's self-esteem began to surface as she realized she might be desirable after all. It was then her boyfriend returned, enraged to find her talking to someone else. Glaring at the bartender, he commanded his bill and, as he reached into his wallet for cash, the bartender discreetly slipped Kristen a card with the phone number for battered women.

On the drive home, the narcissist pulled into a dimly lit parking lot, stopped the car, and hit Kristen across her face. Forcing her down on the seat, he shoved her dress up over her hips, tore her lace panties, and climbed on top of her with the intent of rape. She came to her sensibilities enough to thrust her knee into his groin, and as he moaned and rolled onto the floor, Kristen sat up, pulled down her dress, grabbed her purse, shoved open the car door, and ran.

Now, she couldn't erase this horrific experience from her mind. It seemed she was destined to be hurt by every man she came into close relationship with. Harry's death had broken her heart, and she had never been able to get over the pain. Stan, her first love and closest male friend, had shown her the wonder of what it felt like to have a connection with someone who made her feel important and seen. Then, there was the narcissist. The pain he put on her was intentional, selfish, emotional, mental, and physical. It took a restraining order and police escort for Kristen to get moved out of the house they had shared, and after blocking his phone number and refusing his many attempts to reconnect, he finally found another love interest and disappeared from her life. But the scars were there, and they were deep and attached to a lot of trauma she had been working through for years. Still, she realized trusting another love interest would take a while and barriers she had built around her heart would need to be broken down. She thought Tim might be someone worth the effort to open her heart again, but now, with her fear of motorcycles and lashing out at him, she had ruined that chance.

Coupled with the agony and grief over the loss of Harry, Stan, and Tim, one bottle of wine quickly became two, until a black void overtook her, making the memories disappear, at least for the time being.

Tim rode his motorcycle home in shock, completely shattered by the abrupt end to their evening, but in his mind, he was determined he wasn't going to let Kristen get away. He had found the woman of his dreams. He wanted to help her overcome whatever it was that triggered her trauma.

The next morning, Kristen was awakened by the sunlight streaming through the crescent shaped window in the front door. Still laying on the couch, she realized the two bottles of wine must have tucked her in for the night. With a splitting headache from the overindulgence, which ended up being a poor attempt to placate the emptiness she felt, her cell phone started ringing insistently, bringing her out of the grogginess. Turning onto her stomach, Kristen fumbled for her phone that was lying on the floor beside the couch. After locating it, she mumbled, "Hello."

"Nurse Warner," the voice inquired, "Is something wrong?"

"Hilda? I'm not feeling well. I'm going to take a few days off so don't worry about me. I just need some space."

"We were worried about you. It's not typical of you not to be at work or even to arrive late."

"I know, and I'm sorry," Kristen repeated, then ended the call. She struggled upstairs, clad in her jeans and T-shirt from the night before, and stumbled into the bedroom. Her bed looked so much more inviting than the couch.

Turning off her cell phone, Kristen laid it on her nightstand, closed the room darkening curtains, then pulled back the fluffy duvet cover and climbed in, covering her body from head to toe in her warm cocoon where nobody could intrude.

All she wanted to do was sleep and dream about Harry and Stan and Tim. She wanted to dream about adventures with Tim, knowing she would probably never see him again. Dreams were all she had left, and dreamland is where she decided to stay. Not sure whether it was day or night, Kristen didn't get out of bed. She would wake up long enough to take a sip of water, to guzzle down enough wine to keep her in a numb slumber, or go to the bathroom, but then she would climb back into her cocoon. As she snuggled deep within the covers, she remembered how her lifetime had been spent serving others, pushing aside her own needs and emotions, and barely taking time to grieve the loss of family members, patients, and love.

Now, with the disappointment she felt about pushing Tim away, everything from her past seemed to be cascading down, wanting her to face it head on. She knew grief and loss could take the energy out of a body, but she had never dealt with this feeling of being so overwhelmed, so discouraged, so lost. Sleep, or so it seemed, was the only answer she had, and she allowed it to overtake her and hold her there for as long as it could.

The day after their failed date, Tim decided to give Kristen enough space to work through her thoughts and to calm down. The following day, he tried unsuccessfully to contact Kristen on her cell phone, and each call went straight to voice mail. After two days of reaching voice mail, he decided to try to track her down and make sure she was ok.

"Hello, Tri-County Hospice, how may I help you?"

Tim wasted no time with pleasantries. "Hilda, this is Tim Hurst. Is Nurse Warner there?"

"Mr. Hurst, Nurse Warner is not in today. Is there something I may help you with?"

"I'm concerned about Nurse Warner; she hasn't answered my phone calls in two days."

"Mr. Hurst, I will let her know that you called when I see her," was all Hilda offered.

Tim was not satisfied with the brevity of his conversation with Hilda. After she hung up, he decided to take matters into his own hands. Something was amiss with Kristen, he was certain. She had said her patients were her life, and he couldn't imagine she would abandon them without an explanation. He was slightly irritated that Hilda would not divulge any helpful information regarding Nurse Warner and he needed to figure out what to do.

As Tim stepped through the door of his house onto the pebble driveway, Terrance asked, "Where to, Mr. Hurst?"

Tim thought for a moment. "Terrance, I would like to drive myself today. You can have the day off, with pay, of course."

"Are you sure, Sir?"

"Yes, I'm certain, Terrance, enjoy your day."

"Thank you, Sir," Terrance said, handing out the car keys for Tim to take. But before his boss could take the keys, Terrance saw a look in Tim's eyes and snatched them away. "Sir, are you sure you want to drive yourself?"

"I'm fine," Tim reassured his driver, reaching out his hand for the keys.

"Alright, then, Sir. You seem a bit distracted, so please be careful driving."

Tim knew exactly where he was going; Kristen's house. He didn't want Terrance driving because he didn't know how well he'd be received, what he might find, or how long he would be gone.

A balmy breeze swirled around Tim as he drove his car with the top down. He decided it would be rude to show up empty handed. Remembering a coffee shop about a block before Kristen's house, he pulled into the drive-through and ordered two large coffees. He also asked for cream on the side and a packet of sugar. While he drank his coffee black, he didn't know how Kristen would take hers. "Better to be prepared," he said out loud.

Kristen woke up to the sound of pounding on her front door. She threw back the duvet that had been her cocoon and struggled down the stairs. Her hair was a mess, and she had not showered in three days, nor had she changed her clothes from the night Tim had left her house. Furthermore, she didn't care. When she cracked open the front door, she was surprised to see Tim standing on the porch with a large cup of coffee in each hand.

"Aren't you going to ask a guy in? I was worried about you, Kristen."

"Why do you care?" she retorted sharply.

Tim didn't make a fuss over her terse remark. He figured from the looks of her she probably had one heck of a hangover, even if he was being presumptuous.

"Because I like you. Hilda said you were not at work. From your appearance, I'm guessing it's been a few days."

"Yeah, I guess. I really don't know how many days, Tim. Well, this is the worst it gets. You can leave if you want."

"Why would I do that, Kristen? I drove all the way out here because I'm concerned about you! I like you; I want to get to know you. The choice is yours. By the way, coffee's getting cold."

Kristen opened the door and stepped aside, letting Tim enter. He handed her a cup of coffee. Normally, she would say, "Thank you." She was fixated and shocked about what he said, despite the fact she had dismissed him from her life. He liked her and wanted to get to know her. After Kristen closed the door, she remembered to say, "Thank you."

"You're welcome, Kristen."

Tim glanced around the living room noticing several empty wine bottles on the living room floor.

"When was the last time you ate?"

Sheepishly Kristen replied, "I don't know. I drank my meals."

Tim didn't say anything for a few minutes. "It does look that way. How are you feeling now?" He didn't wait for her answer because a loud, rumbling, gnawing sound came from Kristen's direction. That was answer enough.

"Why don't you take a shower so I can take you to lunch."

"Ok," Kristen meekly replied.

After a shower and clean clothes, Kristen felt more like her old self; the person Tim came back for. That was proof he cared. She smiled at him as she walked down the stairs, refreshed in mind and spirit.

"I'm starving."

Tim agreed, "I'm sure you are. How about we go to that vegan restaurant a few blocks from Tri-County? We can sit outside and talk."

"I'd like that, Tim. You drove your car, didn't you?"

"What do you think, Kristen?"

"Silly question, wasn't it."

Tim winked, "I'm not that good that I could balance two cups of coffee on the handlebars."

Kristen smiled. She liked his attempt at humor, trying to imagine the scenario.

They didn't say much on the short drive to the restaurant. When Tim parked, he noticed they could have the courtyard all to themselves. After stopping his car, he turned to Kristen and asked, "Outside or inside?" Before she could answer, she glanced into the courtyard.

"How about outside."

"Alright, your choice. I'll order if you grab a table. You never know who or how many will swoop down and congregate around all these tables if we don't claim one first."

Kristen laughed at Tim's witty sense of humor. She chose a table while he ordered their food. He already had an idea of what she liked and didn't ask her what she wanted. It wasn't that he wanted to be controlling, but that Kristen was probably still recovering from her binge and may not be able to decide from the menu. Besides, she didn't object to him ordering for her.

Tim brought their food out to the table and set it down before Kristen realized he was there. She was enjoying the warm sunshine on her face. The aroma of the sauteed peppers, onions, and garlic caused her to salivate.

"Tim, I didn't think I was this hungry, but I am. Thank you very much. In fact, if you hadn't come back, I don't know when I would have eaten, nor if I would have returned to normal, whatever that is."

"Kristen, normal is you and me. That's what I think, anyway. I like you; I care about you. So, when you are ready to talk, I'm here to listen. I assure you; I'm not going away."

Kristen was lucid enough to ponder the magnitude of what Tim was saying. Could he possibly be so caring and honest? Taking a chance, she didn't hesitate to ask, "Really, Tim? No matter what I tell you, even if it involves something you love?"

"The only thing/person I care about is you."

Kristen let Tim's words sink in before she took a sip of the herbal tea. Tim came back to her. She owed him an explanation. After a long pause, she began. "My brother was fifteen years old when he died in a motorcycle accident. I was ten at the time. I felt like my life was over because Harry was gone…I didn't think my heart would heal. Then, in my freshman year of high school at St. Ambrose Academy, I met Stan. I liked Stan. I guess you could say he was my second love after my brother, Harry."

Tim wondered if Stan also died tragically. "Did Stan die in a motorcycle accident?"

"No, he was sick. But his brother rode a motorcycle and my dad made Stan guilty by association. My dad also constantly berated Mr. Slim, who owned Slim's Garage and worked on motorcycles. His son, Mitch, died in a motorcycle accident, and was also responsible for my brother's death."

"How so?"

"I thought Mitch was a bad influence on my brother."

"Why, Kristen? Because he liked motorcycles?"

"He liked fast ones."

"I can understand that."

Kristen's eyebrows furrowed. She was completely lost in her thoughts until Tim lightly touched her hand.

"One night, Harry sneaked out of the house and went on his first and last motorcycle ride."

"I'm so sorry," Tim said, as Kristen fought back tears. He put his arms around her and let her cry. He felt protective of his fragile, priceless gem. He wanted her to feel safe in his arms. And she did feel safe as he held her. She could tell his kindness was sincere, so she lingered in his arms for a while, allowing her tears to fall. When she finished crying, she wiped her eyes, "I'm so sorry, Tim."

"You don't have to apologize, Kristen. Do you want to talk about it some more?"

"I would like to, but not here. It's not very private; people could come in at any minute and I don't want to be seen crying."

"Fair enough," Tim said. "Where do you have in mind that's away from prying eyes?"

"My place."

Tim paused before answering. He didn't want to do anything Kristen suggested without confirming that was exactly what she wanted.

"Sure, that sounds nice. As long as you are sure."

"I'm sure," she said looking into his eyes.

Tim's heart leaped in his chest. There was one other time she had given him that look; at the gala. He wondered if she understood what her eyes communicated.

Kristen scooted her chair from under the table, got up and took a step toward Tim. He stood up, ready to leave, but didn't offer her his hand and didn't want to assume she would take it. He was letting her lead with her emotions and didn't want to jeopardize anything with her by acting hastily.

They walked in silence to his car. He opened the passenger door, helped her get in, then he closed the door, walked around and got in the driver's seat. After he started the engine, Kristen laid her head back on the head rest and closed her eyes, letting the warm breeze smack her in the face as they made the short drive to her house. She didn't realize Tim had stopped the car until she heard him say, "Here we are, home sweet home."

Kristen, realizing her house was in complete disarray from her binge, said, "Tim, before we go in, I want to apologize for the mess you saw in there. Are you sure you want to come in?"

"I'm sure Kristen. As long as you are inviting me."

From the outside, Tim liked Kristen's one and a half story bungalow. It had two bay windows on either side of a buttercup yellow front door. The shutters on either side of the windows were a gray blue that provided a lovely contrast to the yellow door without overpowering it. The punch of yellow was pleasing and not too bright. It made one feel happy. That was the feeling Tim got, anyway. Once they were standing on the front porch, Kristen patted her pockets, searching for her house keys.

"Looks like I forgot my house key, Tim. Would you mind stepping off the mat so I can get my spare?"

Tim was shocked. "You keep a spare key under your door mat, Kristen!"

"Doesn't everyone?"

"I don't."

Tim thought as his relationship progressed with Kristen, there were some fundamental things he'd like to change for her safety. The first being where to hide a spare key. As Kristen unlocked the front door, Tim remarked, "By the way, Kristen. I like your yellow front door; it has a happy feel to it."

"Thanks, that was the vibe I was going for when I picked the color."

"Do you own this place?" he asked.

"No, I'm renting but could have purchased it by now. I just didn't want the hassle of having to sell or be responsible for major repairs. I'm not here much."

"Oh, so you can pick up and leave anytime you want?"

"Not exactly. I have to give a month's notice, but that's all."

Tim didn't comment on the terms of Kristen's living arrangements. He filed the thought away that this would be convenient when "things" became more serious between the two of them. As Tim stepped into the house, Kristen apologized again for the empty wine bottles.

"I'm not this messy, really Tim, I'm not. I was in a bad way; I thought I had lost you and I drowned my sorrows instead of dealing with them more maturely."

"You are human, Kristen."

Kristen started to pick up the empty wine bottles that were strewn on the floor. "Make yourself comfortable while I dispose of these."

"Thanks. The couch looks comfortable." Then he teased, "I guess you are not up for another glass of wine."

"Not today! Maybe not for a while."

"I didn't think so, Kristen."

"Tim, would you like a glass of lemon water?"

"Yes, that would be nice, thank you."

Tim heard the empty wine bottles clink in the recycle bin. He closed his eyes, listening to the sounds of activity in the kitchen. He heard her take glasses out of the cupboard and close the door. He heard the refrigerator door open and the clink of a glass pitcher on the counter. Then his senses awakened to the fresh, clean biting notes of lemon as Kristen sliced it. He also caught the scent of something strong and sweet that was both herbal and slightly citric. It was not overpowering, and he guessed she had prepared sweet basil for the water as well.

After Kristen finished preparing the flavored water, she carried the pitcher and two tall glasses into the living room on a mint green, gold-edged curved tray that had white hydrangeas painted on its surface. She set the tray in front of Tim on her round marble surfaced coffee table.

"May I pour you a glass?" he asked.

"I should be pouring you a glass, Tim. After all, you are my guest."

"I am your friend, Kristen."

Kristen sat next to Tim on the couch after he had poured her a glass of lemon-basil flavored water, then he filled his own glass. Before he took a sip, he reminded her, "You said you wanted to talk privately. Can't think of any place more private than here."

Kristen swallowed the lump that had suddenly risen in her throat. She didn't want Tim to go away because of her fear of motorcycles and she didn't want to push him away because of her trust issues. She owed him more of an explanation than she had previously given.

"After my brother died, my dad never got over his death. As I said before, my dad blamed Mr. Slim for Harry's death. I felt sorry for Mr. Slim. I would go and sit with him on his front porch whenever my dad got into one of his tirades. We would sit quietly, let our hearts talk. But one day, he packed up and moved without telling me goodbye. He took away my memories for a long, long time."

"And those memories just happened to come to the surface recently, Kristen?"

"I guess your motorcycle triggered something, Tim. Call it PTSD or whatever."

Tim said, "Kristen, I haven't told you about how motorcycles impacted my family. My dad loved to ride. He was part of a group who rode for thrills, he was in a lot of accidents and had a lot of injuries. When I was young, he would let me get on the back of his bike and he would take me for rides, which always made my mom angry. She was afraid I was going to die from a motorcycle accident with my dad driving. She was never able to get over that fear. Then, after my dad had been through so many accidents and broken bones, my mom decided she could not be married to him anymore, so they were divorced. For the longest time, I thought it was my fault."

"Oh wow, I had no idea other people had the same fears or experiences with motorcycles. I am sorry you thought it was your fault."

"Yeah, it was hard. When I got my first motorcycle, my mom was upset with me, but I told her it wasn't the motorcycle that hurt my dad, it was his reckless riding and hunt for the thrill that turned his bikes over. I helped her work through her fear just by letting her talk to me and by listening to her. She never stopped loving my dad, she just stopped wanting to be in the middle of the threat of her family being hurt."

Then, looking at Kristen, he added, "Would you like me to help you with your fear?"

"You don't think I'm hopeless, Tim? Not worth your time?"

"Kristen! Didn't you hear me when I said, I'm not going anywhere? I liked you from the moment I first saw you. I felt something."

"When was that? At Tri-County?"

"No, Kristen that wasn't the first time. I had no idea that was you. It was at the Hospice Gala for Rory's Place. I saw you, our eyes met, and I sat next to you at our table. You wore a red dress."

"THAT WAS YOU!"

"Yes, that was me. We briefly met, you had to leave unexpectedly, which might have been fortuitous, in retrospect."

"Why do you say that?"

"There was another gentleman at our table who obviously tried to compete for your attention."

Kristen thought for a moment, remembering the event. "Oh, Tim, he was not a competitor, but my patient was."

"Is that why you left so abruptly?"

"Yes."

"Would you like to enlighten me as to why, Kristen?"

"I suppose I can. My patient who I will call L, was getting close to transitioning."

"Transitioning? How do you mean?"

"Transition is a term we use in hospice care when someone is getting ready to pass. We often refer to this as a laboring mother in transition just before her baby is born. It's a change from one state to another. A baby transitions from inside its mother to live independently on the outside once it's born. A soul transitions from the physical body to a spiritual one."

Tim tried to comprehend transitioning. He was at a loss, not having the experience of a laboring woman. "Oh…I'll take your word for that, since I don't have experience with birth."

"As I was saying, L kept saying she had to get into a boat. She insisted she get in that boat. I asked her if there was someone in the boat. She said, no, but someone was on the shore waving to her to get in. I asked L if she knew the person on the shore. L said it looked like her Jeremy."

"Who was Jeremy?"

"I'm presuming her husband who had passed several years before."

"So, what did you say to her after she told you it was Jeremy?"

"I said, don't keep Jeremy waiting."

"Is that why you left, Kristen. To be with her?"

"Tim, before I got ready for the gala, I told her goodbye. I hoped she would be there when I returned but, deep in my heart, I knew that would be the last time I saw L alive."

"Oh…"

"Death is an experience. One minute the patient is present in body and spirit and in the next second, gone. It's distinct, there is no maybe. While the body is present, its essence, its spirit, its soul has vacated."

Tim remarked, "That's amazing. My dad was like that. He waited until I arrived at the hospital. And that certainly wasn't by coincidence. I told him I loved him and forgave him. Then he was gone."

Kristen thought about her end of life and, since they were on the subject of death and dying, added, "That's why I don't want a viewing, Tim. I don't want people weeping over a shell of what I was. I want to be remembered as vibrant and alive."

"So you believe life goes on after we die?"

"I do."

"Are you positive about that?"

"Yes, Tim, I am, and I will tell you why. Not only do I believe as a Christian, but I also believe scientifically. I have been present at so many deaths. Patients, people, are never alone. Someone is always waiting on the other side. They know the person who is waiting for them."

"Did your brother come back to visit you, Kristen?"

"My mom said she could feel his presence, but as soon as she acknowledged him, he was gone. It was as if he was granted a limited amount of time, maybe it took a lot of energy for him, I don't know."

"I don't know either. I never thought about dying much until recently."

"Really? Why is that?"

"I had clients that went to hospice, but I never went to see them or attend their funerals. So, death didn't affect me. My dad wasn't around, so what was there to miss? My mother had Alzheimer's. She was physically present but mentally absent. It's interesting, though, because the nurses said my mom kept calling for someone the last day she was alive. They said she called for Bud."

"Who was Bud?"

"My dad."

"Tim, did she, your mom, say anything else?"

"Yes, she did. The nurses said they heard my mom say just before she passed. 'Bud, I knew you would come back for me.' My parents died on the same day, maybe even minutes apart."

"Oh, Tim, I'm sorry to hear that. Losing them both on the same day must have been so hard on you. But how beautiful they were together and that your dad left first and stopped by to get your mom. You know, Tim, I don't believe there's such a thing as coincidence."

"I'm beginning to believe that, Kristen."

Kristen and Tim sat quietly for a few minutes, content in being together while processing the depth of the conversation and death. Then, both sensing the need to move to a lighter topic, Kristen asked, "How about a movie?"

"Sure, got any suggestions?"

"I'm thinking of an old one."

"Kristen I'm not in the mood for Fred Astair and Ginger Rogers or even Bogey and Bacall."

"I'm thinking of Easy Rider with Peter Fonda."

"Sure, that's a good one."

Before the movie ended, Kristen had fallen asleep curled up next to Tim. He turned the television off and closed his eyes. He didn't know how long he had been asleep until he felt a light tugging on his sleeve and the sound of Kristen's voice.

"Tim, I'm so sorry I fell asleep. I have no clue what time it is?"

Tim yawned. "I really should be going."

"No, it's too late. Stay here with me. I'm not comfortable with you driving this late at night." Tim chuckled because he had been in the habit of driving late at night when something was on his mind, and the last time he had something on his mind, it was Kristen.

"Are you sure?"

"Yes, I'm certain. Come upstairs with me."

Tim had his reasons for declining her offer. Normally, he wouldn't think twice about an invitation such as this, or was this the kind of invitation he thought it might be?

"Maybe I should go home." he repeated.

"Tim! It's late. My bed is more comfortable than the couch, although I certainly didn't mind it during my event."

"I'll stay here on the couch, Kristen. Do you have an extra blanket I could use?"

"I do, Tim. I'll be right back."

What Kristen really wanted was to sleep in Tim's arms, but he made it clear he would sleep on the couch. She pulled her fluffy duvet off her bed and trudged down the stairs with it stuffed into her arms. Miraculously, even though the comforter obstructed her view of the steps, she didn't fall. When Tim saw her precarious situation, he met her on the steps, taking the comforter from her.

"I think this will keep you cozy," Kristen said.

"Thanks, Kristen, good night. I wish you sweet dreams."

"Good night, Tim."

He had his reasons for choosing the couch, she surmised, even though she had no intention of doing anything other than sleeping. When she got to the top of the stairs, she pulled a down-filled quilt out of the closet on the landing and wrapped it around her. She didn't turn on her bedroom light as she plunged onto her bed, immediately falling asleep.

The morning sun shone brightly through the bedroom window, awakening Kristen from her dreams of Tim. She didn't remember he had stayed overnight until, from the top step of the landing, she saw him asleep on the couch. She smiled because Tim wasn't a dream, he was here with her.

"I'll make coffee," she whispered in his ear.

A slight smile crinkled at the corners of Tim's mouth. He hadn't been sleeping; he just pretended he was.

While the coffee brewed, Tim dressed in his jeans and T-shirt, then strolled into the kitchen where Kristen was watching the pot brew.

"Smells wonderful, Kristen. I could get used to this."

"So could I, get used to this."

When the pot was filled to the six-cup line, Kristen took two thick white mugs out of the cabinet above her coffee maker.

"Coffee's ready, how do you take yours?"

"Black is fine, thanks."

After Kristen poured the coffee, she suddenly remembered it was Saturday, Susie Kline's celebration of life service.

"Tim, what time is it?"

"8:30. Why?"

"I almost forgot! Today is my pediatric patient's celebration of life service and I'm expected to be there."

"What time does it start?"

"Ten."

"You don't want to be late, do you?" Tim, realizing he needed to get going, asked, "Do you have a to-go cup I can put this in?" Kristen smiled at his consideration for her getting to her engagement on time, then reached into the cabinet and pulled out a Styrofoam cup and lid, handing it to him. After transferring the hot liquid into the cup, he handed Kristen his empty mug. "I'll be on my way so you can get ready."

"You'll come back later, today, won't you?"

"I'll be back, I promise. How about we go to my place."

"I'd like that, Tim."

"Great, I'll see you in a few hours."

Kristen walked Tim to the door and watched him put on his shoes. He stood up, kissed her on the cheek, and walked out the door. Then he was gone. This wasn't like the last time Tim walked out. She knew she would see him again.

While she felt sad about Susie, she felt joy in her heart. Perhaps she would need to rely on this joy to get her through Susie's celebration of life. Foregoing breakfast, Kristen raced upstairs with her mug of coffee, to quickly shower and get dressed. She didn't want to be late.

The drive to St. Mark's Catholic Church was bittersweet. Kristen felt honored to be participating in the services, but she was in a quandary. In some respects, Susie was her last pediatric patient. Her death was difficult, even though death was the door, Kristen believed, to be far better than what one experienced when terminally ill.

Susie's death was a wake-up call. Maybe it was Kristen's own mortality that reared its head. Her biological clock had run out of time. Perhaps this was a godsend because she would never have to bear a child only to face the possibility of losing the child to cancer. The disease was all too familiar as it robbed families of their loved ones, and they never had enough time. Losing a child would be devasting. She couldn't think about the what ifs; she needed to stay positive for the Klines.

St. Mark's Catholic Church was not more than a small chapel built on a hill overlooking the Pacific Ocean. Kristen opened the door to the chapel and stood in the back, looking for Mr. and Mrs. Kline. When the service started, rays of sunbeams shone through the clear ceiling to floor windows that surrounded Susie's small, white cloth draped casket in a golden glow.

Kristen barely heard the priest speaking words of comfort, specifically, that Susie was playing in lavender fields in the heavenly realm, when he invited the family and their friends to join him outside for a last earthly farewell. Mrs. Kline gently nudged Kristen's arm, reminding her it was time. She followed the priest to the front of the chapel and out a side door from the sacristy to where two caged turtle doves waited to be released.

When all the attendees had gathered, Kristen opened the cage door and watched as the doves took flight up into the sky and disappeared. She set the cage down, valiantly trying to wipe away tears rolling down her cheeks. She had no sooner dried her tears than a little girl in a red dress appeared from nowhere, handing her a tissue. "Thank you," Kristen said, as she turned to look at the child. But just as suddenly as she appeared, the little girl had disappeared. "There is no such thing as coincidence," Kristen told herself.

Susie had wanted her to be part of her last send-off before her remains were interred in the ground. It was easier for Kristen to think of her playing in lavender fields. But the stark reality of mortal remains felt like a hard blow to her lungs, comparable to a fall that knocked the wind right out of her chest. Mrs. Kline found Kristen staring up into the sky. She lightly touched her arm so as not to scare her.

"Thank you, Nurse Warner. Somehow, I think Susie was here, watching."

"I think so too, Mrs. Kline."

"Goodbye, Nurse Warner. Thank you for everything you did for our Susie."

"It was an honor and a privilege, Mrs. Kline. You're welcome."

Then Kristen left Mrs. Kline standing on the hill overlooking the Pacific Ocean. She couldn't imagine the heartbreak Mrs. Kline must endure over the next weeks and months and years.

She was relieved that Tim would be picking her up soon and taking her to his house. Otherwise, she might have sunk into a deep, dark depression with no way to crawl out.

17

LIKE RIDING A BIKE

Kristen returned home in the early afternoon half expecting Tim to be there, which was silly because she didn't give him a key to her house. He would come back. He said he would.

She was starting to get hungry but decided to put her efforts and attention into getting ready for her date before Tim arrived to pick her up. As she changed her clothes from her church attire, she thought about Susie. Her memory haunted Kristen. Not that she saw an apparition, because others would describe an apparition as the appearance of something remarkable, unexpected, or even a ghostlike image. But more so as confirmation by the little girl in the red dress whose appearance was fleeting once she fulfilled her purpose. If this was Susie, then she possessed a real lifelike form that hinted of her personality. Whereas Kristen had taken care of her, the little girl was now the caretaker through a simple act of kindness.

Kristen contemplated the magnitude of Susie's death. For a ten-year-old girl, she left an indelible impression that resonated with her. Although, as a hospice nurse, Kristen had experienced many terminal patients and helped them transition, Susie's case was different. She was not just another case or a patient, none of them were. These were people she had loved and cared for when they were most vulnerable. Vulnerability was something Kristen had to be watchful for in her terminal patients. Some had already passed through the stages of grief before arriving at her front door. However, families were not always prepared for the process of dying and that was why they were more vulnerable.

She remembered a family member who insisted she suction the patient because the pharyngeal rales were tortuous. Kristen agreed it was not easy listening to the rales as a bystander, but gently reminded the family that their loved one was not bothered by the rales and suctioning would be far more traumatic for the patient. When she explained why, they were more accepting of the process that was taking place before their eyes, no longer able to deny this was the end of their loved one's earthly journey. If the kidneys had started to fail, she would explain that the patient no longer needed fluids. They didn't need secretions caused by the fluids to contend with while dying. Sometimes a little bit of phlegm remained and that was what was creating the raucous. Kristen would do what she could to lessen them by repositioning the patient. Sometimes, she administered medications that helped the body relax even more.

Occasionally, a family member would be adamant that tube feedings be given, "to keep their strength." Kristen gently reminded them that feeding tubes and IVs robbed their loved one of peace. It was her job to educate the family as much as possible about the things to come. Many times, a family member would leave in tears because they felt extreme detachment from their loved one. Kristen would encourage them not to take it personally. This was necessary because the patient could not focus on where they were going if they felt bound to stay attached to their family.

Maybe this was why Susie's death was so difficult. Her passing didn't have all the usual events that Kristen experienced with other patients. Susie was there and then she was gone. Brooding over the events of the morning would not make Susie come back. She was playing in lavender fields in the sunshine. That vision had to be enough, which brought Kristen back to the subject of her job.

She truly needed time to think about her future now that there was someone else in her life. She had allowed Tim in; she was not going to stay married to her job. That would not be fair to her patients, or so Kristen thought, and it certainly wouldn't be fair to Tim. Since this was the weekend and she was not on call, what to do about work could wait. She was happy Tim would be over soon to pick her up.

Kristen raced back upstairs, quickly throwing some necessary items into an oversized purse. She didn't want to presume he would invite her to spend the night, even though waking up with Tim was a happiness she wanted every day. He said he could get used to that, too. Her connection with and trust in someone she had known only briefly surprised her. She had waited a long time to find her perfect match, and she wanted to throw all caution to the wind and see if he was the one she had been waiting for.

Kristen had no sooner finished packing than the doorbell rang. Giddy with excitement, she leapt down the stairs in seconds. Her heart was beating a mile a minute when she opened the front door, barely able to speak above an audible, "Hi Tim."

Tim was surprised to see and hear Kristen out of breath, offering the explanation, "Am I that breathtakingly handsome?" Without skipping a beat, Kristen responded, "Yes, you are, Tim." Then she quickly added, "Do you want to come in?"

Tim had other things on his mind and politely said, "For a few minutes, Kristen. I thought we'd pick up some lunch and head over to my place."

"I can make us lunch here, although I haven't been to the grocery store in weeks, and I honestly don't know what I'd make."

"That's ok, Kristen. We can get something on the way or stop at the grocery store, pick up a few things to prepare at my place."

"Let's make something at your place. I don't feel like being around people."

"Suits me fine, Kristen. Are you ready?"

"Give me a minute. I have to dash upstairs to get something."

Kristen grabbed her oversized bag from her bed. She saw that she had not hung up her clothes from the morning, but that could wait; she didn't want to waste a second. When Tim saw the oversized bag, he didn't think much of it. Women were mysterious and what they chose to include in a large purse just added to the puzzle.

"Ready?" he asked again.

"Yes, I am."

"Alright then, let's get out of here," Tim said as he shut the door behind Kristen. She was relieved to see he had driven his car. She knew his motorcycle was important to him, and she would have to face her fears sooner rather than later if she wanted to be in his life. She sensed his bike wasn't negotiable; it was as much a part of Tim as the sand was to the beach.

"I'm glad you picked me up in your car." Without hesitating she added, "I know your motorcycle is an important part of who you are. I would never ask you to give that up."

Tim let Kristen articulate her thoughts without responding. He didn't intend to give up his motorcycle or love of it, no matter how much he liked Kristen. He didn't see that ever being an option. He could, however, be patient with her.

On the outskirts of town, as they made their way to the grocery store, they passed boutiques, antiquities, and other shops filled with ephemera.

"Tim, did you see that storefront with the stack of old magazines? Who would want those?" Tim smiled, thinking about the stacks of old telephone directories in Slim's Garage still there after Kaos bought it and his intended purpose for keeping a few.

"You'd be surprised, Kristen. People collect all kinds of things, like bookmarks and art and sometimes people like to collect signed plates. You might even be able to find someone's old memorial mass card because people just can't throw stuff away. Many people like to collect oddities."

"I'm glad I don't," Kristen said. "Because I think of all that stuff as clutter."

Tim chuckled again. "The stacks of old telephone directories my friend Kaos found in a garage he purchased served a purpose at one time. Kaos thought, well I thought, I could find you through one of those old yellow pages. But having a near heart attack saved me the trouble."

"Did you have a heart attack."

"No, I was under a lot of stress. Meeting you is the best thing that has happened to me."

"Was I the reason for your stress?"

"Truthfully, Kristen, yes. You could say that."

"Why?"

"Because I never thought I would find you."

"Well, here I am in the flesh!" she joked.

"I'm glad you are not an apparition. People would think I was ridiculous."

"Speaking of apparitions, Tim, this morning at Susie's service after I released her doves, I couldn't stop crying. Out of nowhere, a little girl in a red dress handed me a tissue. When I looked to see who it was, she was gone. She didn't have the appearance of a ghost, but she appeared out of nowhere. Her essence was that of Susie. It was surreal, to say the least."

Tim started to say something, then stopped, reconsidering what was on his mind.

"Kristen, I am beginning to believe there is no such thing as coincidence."

They drove in silence until the town came into view. Tim drove two more blocks to the grocery store. He passed several parking spaces in front of the store, then pulled into a space far removed from other cars.

"I hope you don't mind walking."

"I don't mind. I park away from other cars and under a light, for obvious reasons."

"I guess I take being a guy for granted. I don't have the same worries as you, and I have a driver."

Kristen chose not to say something sarcastic and instead explained.

"I park where and why for my safety. I park away from other cars so nobody can sneak up behind me unnoticed. I lock my car doors so nobody will be in my back seat. I park under a light so I can be seen. And I leave space around me to run if I must."

Tim was impressed with her thoughtfulness about safety in parking lots as he remembered the house key she kept under the mat on her front porch.

One safety issue at a time, he thought to himself. Dealing with the issue at hand, he asked, "Kristen, do you carry mace?"

"I should, but I don't. I had pepper spray once."

"Really…"

"Yes, I sprayed it in someone's eyes who tried to hurt me."

"Do you want to talk about that?"

"No! He's not worth talking about."

"An old boyfriend?" Tim asked, pushing Kristen for an answer.

"Yes." Kristen's curt answer meant she didn't want to talk about the old boyfriend.

Since Tim was familiar with the grocery store, there was no need to protract the excursion, as he wanted to get home as soon as possible so he could have Kristen's attention all to himself.

They stopped by the deli counter and purchased a premade turkey wrap for a light snack. "Thanksgiving rolled up," Tim called it. Then they checked out of the grocery store and drove to his house, which didn't take long. He pulled onto his gravel driveway and slowly drove up the incline to his garage, purposely leaving the car in the open. After stopping the car, he got out, walked around the car and opened Kristen's door, taking the deli bag from her. They walked side by side, feet crunching in unison on the pea gravel that led to the porch.

Tim pushed a series of buttons on a side panel that magically opened his hammered metal front door, then stepped aside to let Kristen enter first. Closing the door, he took her hand and led her into the kitchen. As they unpacked the food, Tim took two plates off a neat stack on the back counter and handed the plates to Kristen. She placed the wrap on the top plate and grabbed a sharp knife from the caddy next to her, cutting the wrap in half and putting each piece on a plate, thankful they were having a light lunch.

Her excitement over being with Tim in his house was curbing her appetite. She didn't need much; just enough to quiet her growling stomach.

"Tim, where are your napkins?"

"There should be some cotton ones in a drawer by the silverware."

"Where's that, the silverware?"

Tim laughed, then he walked over to the drawer that housed his silverware. "Won't be long until you know where I keep everything. There's not much to discover, as you will find out."

"Oh, so you're planning on my staying here with you," Kristen teased back.

"Would that be such a bad idea?"

"No Tim, I could get used to that."

Tim smiled. That was what he wanted to hear. But he decided to give her an "out," even though he doubted she would want one.

"Let me take you on a tour first, Kristen. Then you can decide."

He picked up a plate and napkin and handed them to her. Then he grabbed the same for himself.

"You will have to follow me upstairs for the best part."

"Just what do you have in mind, Mr. Hurst?" Kristen asked.

"It's not what you are thinking, trust me. You can't see the view unless you go through my bedroom to the lanai.

"Lead the way, Mr. Hurst," Kristen replied laughing.

"Are you afraid of these slatted stairs? They are a tad formidable."

"No Tim, I'm not. Just anxious to see what's up there."

"I trust you will be delighted," he said with a smile.

When they reached the top of the stairs, Kristen gasped at the enormous bedroom in front of her. She couldn't help marveling at Tim's excellent taste in his surroundings. The bedroom was not overly masculine. She liked his color scheme of grays with a pop of burgundy. It was nice and comfortable. Best of all, there was no clutter anywhere. Tim walked to the double glass doors leading to the lanai.

"My Lady," he said as he opened the door. "The best part is out here."

Once through the doors, another world appeared before Kristen's eyes. Tim's flower beds were meticulously kept, and the pea gravel made a delightful crunch under her feet as she followed him toward two chaise lounge chairs.

"This is lovely. Do you sit out here often?"

"Truthfully, I don't when I'm working at the bank. I am always in a hurry, always attending functions, like boring galas where the person I want to sit next to the most disappears."

He took her plate and set it down next to his on the wide arm of one of the chaise lounges. Pulling her close, he whispered in her ear, "And what do you know, here she is."

Kristen laid her head against his chest, savoring the moment with Tim's arms around her, again feeling safer than ever. After a moment, he released her and walked to the outer wall of the patio garden that overlooked the city and ocean. Looking out over the horizon, Tim said, "I have the best of both worlds in this spot."

"How so?" Kristen asked.

"I have spectacular sunsets. And when the sun has sunk into the ocean, the lights from the city below sparkle, lighting up the darkness. But there is a brief magical interlude, twilight, when no sun shines and no artificial lights come on. That's my favorite time of the evening. You will have to see it for yourself, Kristen."

"Is that an invitation, Tim?"

"Yes, that's my invitation to you. I want to show you something else, though. We have a few hours before twilight. It's in the garage."

"What's in the garage?"

"You'll see," was all Tim offered. Then he handed Kristen her plate and they ate in silence. Kristen wondered what Tim could possibly want to show her in the garage. When she finished her last bite, he took their empty plates and Kristen followed him through his bedroom and down the stairs to the kitchen. As they passed through, Tim laid the plates on the counter, stopped, then paused briefly before saying, "Follow me."

Kristen obediently followed him through a side door that connected the house to the garage under a covered walkway. Tim paused and then slowly opened the door. Waiting for her reaction, he noticed she trembled as she stammered, "It's a…it's a motorcycle."

Tim quickly added, "It's not just any motorcycle, Kristen. It's a Norton Commando."

"I don't know what to say Tim, part of me wants to throw up."

Tim looked at Kristen sympathetically and said, "That's ok, get it out of your system. You can throw up."

"I won't do that here, Tim. This is not a laughing matter."

"I know, remember I said I would help you get over your fear of motorcycles?"

"Yes, I remember."

"Kristen, this is step one. All you need to do is stand in the same room as the motorcycle. It won't bite you. It's a machine. It doesn't have a mind of its own. The person who turns on the motorcycle has a mind and that is what makes the machine go fast or slow."

Suddenly it dawned on Kristen that, after all these years, she never comprehended that the operator of the machine was responsible for accidents.

"You're saying it wasn't the motorcycle that killed Mitch and Harry."

"That's correct, Kristen. It was the operator of the motorcycle."

"I was ten when Harry was killed. I didn't know who was operating the motorcycle. I didn't ask a lot of questions. I knew my brother was hurt and in the hospital."

Tim paused before asking his next question. He wanted her to be comfortable talking about motorcycles first, as there was more work to be done to help her overcome her fears.

"Kristen, do you know what kind of motorcycle they were riding?"

"I think it had a name like a super something."

"Sounds like a Super Blackbird. That was a powerful bike, certainly not for novice riders."

"Obviously not!" Kristen shouted at Tim. Thinking about her brother's death touched a raw nerve that set her off. Tim was sensitive to her feelings. He didn't want her to backslide and then decide she didn't want to be with him, after all.

"That's ok, Kristen. I think you have had enough for one day."

He put his arms around her to calm her trembling. She agreed, "I think so, too."

Tim took her hand and walked toward the garage door. "Let's get out of here," he said. "I have another idea I think you will like."

Kristen took a deep breath as she started to calm down. "As long as it doesn't involve…"

Tim chuckled, "Don't worry, you will like my idea."

They walked hand in hand back into the kitchen where Tim suggested they relax with a bottle of wine. He realized only a couple of days had passed since her "event," but perhaps enjoying a glass of wine with someone else would appeal to her more than using it as a numbing mechanism to escape reality. "Kristen, what kind of wine do you like?"

"I usually prefer red, Tim. I tell myself it's healthy for my heart. Truthfully, I like a full-bodied smooth red."

"I've heard, Nurse Warner, that wine has heart healthy benefits. I have a Cabernet."

"Sounds perfect."

"I'll be right back."

He disappeared through a narrow door under the staircase and reappeared with a bottle of Cabernet Sauvignon in one hand and two wine glasses in the other.

"Yeah, I have an extensive wine collection down there, but I want to go up on the patio."

Tim turned and started up the staircase with Kristen in tow. They passed through his bedroom a second time, then through the glass doors and out onto the patio. There was a harmonious crunching of pea gravel under their feet as they moved toward one of Tim's favorite spots. "How about here?" he asked. Kristen looked around, noticing the furniture. There were several sitting areas in Tim's garden that looked like they had never been used, in addition to the chaise lounges they sat in earlier in the afternoon.

"Tim, how long have you had this furniture; it looks new?"

"It is sort of. Before my parents died, I worked all the time and never had time to myself. I didn't entertain very often. Other than clients, I did not, do not, have many friends."

Kristen was shocked to learn that Tim lived a solitary life. She assumed he had an extensive social life and was surprised he was as married to his job as she was.

"Tim, you sound a lot like me. I don't have many friends either, if any, actually. I give my heart to my patients. It's easier that way."

"Why do you do that?"

"After nursing school and the fiasco of a narcissistic relationship, the old boyfriend I didn't want to talk about, I didn't want to get hurt anymore and I doubted whether I would ever be able to trust anyone again, if I were even able to find someone."

"You don't have to worry about that, Kristen. I would never hurt you."

"I'm glad to hear that," she replied.

Tim poured the vinaceous liquid into their stemware. After handing Kristen her glass, he clinked his to hers. "Here's to more days like this," he said. Kristen smiled as she took a sip of the smooth, full bodied Cabernet Sauvignon. They sat in the warm sunshine savoring the beverage, making small talk, and enjoying their surroundings. Tim poured the remainder of the wine into their glasses just as the afternoon sun was retreating over the horizon, painting the clouds in a warm palette of orange and pink. It was nearing the time of day Tim liked the most.

"Come look at the magic, Kristen."

By the time they stood at the wall overlooking the city, the sun was almost below the horizon. The fading light created a lavender, rose and gold band stretching as far north and south as the eye could see, while the sky above was neither light nor dark. Twilight, when time stands still; when one holds their breath for fear that the slightest wind of change will hasten the encroaching darkness.

"It's magical, Tim, just like you said it would be."

When the sun slid over the horizon and the sky turned the clouds overhead a deep purple, tiny white lights from the city below began to dance and flicker before their eyes. Tim whispered in Kristen's ear, "Savor the magic, it's almost over."

Within seconds the sky became dark and Tim's garden lights came on, lighting a path from the patio to the bedroom. As they walked back into the house, Kristen remarked, "I can't believe you didn't take advantage of this more often."

"I have on occasion, that's why I wanted to share the magic with you. Are you hungry?"

Tim's stomach started to gurgle and rumble. Kristen smiled. "I am ravenous, which is unusual. I don't know why?"

"Probably all the fresh air and my good company, Kristen."

"You think so?" Kristen teased. "Probably just the fresh air."

Tim thought about what he had in his refrigerator to prepare for dinner.

"I have some steaks we can grill. You do eat meat, don't you? That could be a deal breaker if you didn't?"

Kristen laughed, "Of course I do. I feel better when I eat red meat, although I really can't remember the last time I did."

"Interesting," Tim responded, then quickly added. "Kristen, would you mind throwing together a salad? I have some fixings in the refrigerator."

"I don't mind, as long as you don't mind me rummaging through your fridge."

"Not at all. Remember I said before too long you will know where everything is kept."

She smiled, then buried her head in Tim's refrigerator, looking for the right selections of produce. She made herself at home in his kitchen while Tim cooked the steaks to perfection.

The kitchen space was neat, orderly, and not replete with unnecessary implements, which was something Kristen appreciated. Occasionally, Tim glanced in her direction while she prepared the salad. When their eyes met, he knew he could get used to her being with him in his house. After the steaks had been grilled and the salad made, they sat together at the kitchen bar. Tim opened another bottle of wine and slowly poured the mellifluous liquid into Kristen's glass.

When their sumptuous feast had been consumed and the bottle emptied, Tim broached the subject of overnight accommodations. He was in no condition to drive, nor did he want Kristen to leave. Everything they did together, thus far, felt easy and natural. He wouldn't let himself imagine more because that would be torturous. Instead, he would enjoy the surprise of each moment as it came.

"Kristen, we didn't finish the tour. Would you like to see the guest suite?"

At this juncture, Kristen was very relaxed, if not tired. "Yes, that would be a good idea, I'm rather tired. Maybe I'm very, very relaxed, which is something that has eluded me for a long time and," Kristen paused, "I don't feel like going home."

Tim was glad to hear that. "Nor should I drive. So it's settled. You will spend the night."

Suddenly Kristen remembered she didn't bring anything to sleep in. "Tim, I didn't bring anything to sleep in. I didn't want to assume I would be invited to stay over."

"Come with me. I'm sure I have something that will work for you."

Kristen grabbed her oversized bag and followed Tim upstairs into his bedroom and sat on a chair in the corner while he disappeared into his closet. He emerged a few minutes later with a soft, white oxford shirt that, while clean, had somehow missed the laundry bag and a stiff starching.

"You're in luck, Kristen. I think this will work."

"Thanks."

Then Tim offered to show her the guest suite. "If you are ready, My Lady, I will show you to your suite." Kristen followed him as he made a left turn down the hallway and stopped in front of a closed door. After Tim opened the door, Kristen noticed it was decorated the same as the master suite, but on a smaller scale. She even had her own ensuite and a door that led outside to the lanai.

"This is beautiful! Thanks, Tim. I think I'll call it a night."

"Good night, Kristen, sleep tight."

"Good night, Tim. I had a lovely day."

Tim shut her door, then walked down the hallway to his bedroom. He was happy Kristen was in his house, but was restless, tossing and turning, thinking about her sleeping only a few feet away in another room.

He intentionally didn't make sexual overtures to her during dinner. If she were of the same inclination, that would be at her invitation. He finally fell asleep under the full moon that had risen in the sky. He was oblivious to the moon's beams that cast a silvery light in his room until he awakened to see Kristen standing by the window. She turned to him and said, "I can't sleep." Tim looked at her wrapped in the moonlight and, rather than do what was on his mind, which was to get out of bed and wrap his arms around her, he asked, "Do you want something to help you sleep? I might have some pills in my bathroom that I have used on occasion. I can personally vouch for their effectiveness as a sleep aid."

"No," Kristen mumbled.

"Then what is it?" Tim asked.

"I...can't sleep."

Tim propped himself up on his pillows and pulled back the comforter that had been covering him. He patted the space beside him, like he had seen his dad do while he was recovering from his first major accident to console his mother. He opened his left arm inviting her to lay on his chest, then pulled her in closer, inhaling her herbal scent of eucalyptus and sweet herbs.

They fell asleep and stayed in that position until Kristen rolled to her side, away from him. Tim turned on his left side. Her perfect curves dovetailed into his body, and he could not resist wrapping his arms around her waist. He sighed and closed his eyes. He no longer had to dream about the woman in the red dress. Here she was, in the flesh, lying next to him. She chose him. She wanted to be near him, next to him in his bed. How much longer could he resist the temptation to consume her? That would be her choice and he would wait.

It was mid-morning when Tim woke up. He whispered in Kristen's ear, "I'm going to brew some coffee. Stay in bed if you want. But if you decide to join me, there is a white terry cloth robe hanging in the bathroom. Help yourself to it."

He sat up, stretching his arms above his head, releasing kinks in his muscles that were new to his body. He pulled aside the comforter and got out of bed clad in his boxers. He bent over Kristen and kissed her lightly on the cheek. "I do not, have never, entertained a woman in my bed. I hope you don't mind my poor manners, not wearing anything else."

"I don't mind, Tim. I like looking at you, and, for your information, I never entertained anyone in my bed either." Then she became serious. "This is not entertainment; you and I both know that."

Tim smiled, then went downstairs to check on the coffee that was set to automatic brew. He took two white coffee mugs from the cabinet and carried them to the coffee maker while waiting for it to finish its brewing cycle. Then, after filling the mugs, he carried them upstairs, hoping Kristen would still be in bed. Instead, he found her in the garden, wearing his white bathrobe, gazing over the outer wall toward the ocean in the distance. He handed her a mug and asked, "What would you like to do today, my love?"

"Hmmm...I'll give you one guess."

"I give up, Kristen. Although I can think of something."

"It's a beautiful day, Tim, and I would like to take a drive down the coast to the ocean. I can't tell you the last time I dipped my toes in the Pacific Ocean."

"Alright then, do I get a raincheck on my first guess?"

"Of course, Tim."

Kristen held her coffee mug between her two hands while gazing out over the city. There was a calm to their morning and a peacefulness in saying nothing, sipping coffee, while enjoying each other's presence.

When Kristen had taken her last sip, Tim suggested they have a light brunch, get dressed, and go for the drive Kristen asked about earlier. While she dressed, Tim toasted bagels and set out smoked salmon, sliced red onion, tomatoes, cream cheese, and capers. Then he quickly showered and dressed. Kristen, in the meantime, had come downstairs and poured another cup of coffee and set out plates, silverware, and napkins. Tim smiled when he saw that she had made herself at home. He liked having her with him and wanted nothing more than to wake up every day with her.

When Kristen saw him come down the stairs, she got up from her seat at the kitchen island and poured another cup of coffee for him. She walked to the island and handed him the mug saying, "I made myself useful. I hope you don't mind."

Tim chuckled, "Remember yesterday when I said it won't be long until you know where everything is? I meant that."

Kristen smiled, "We should eat. Shall we take our plates upstairs, go out on the lanai. It is such a pretty day."

"That's a great idea. That's what the lanai is for. To enjoy mornings like this. We really don't have to be anywhere or do anything. I like your idea, though, about going for a drive to the ocean."

They ate in silence, savoring the melted cream cheese on the bagel with the saltiness of the smoked salmon, the pungent capers, and the sweet tomatoes. When they had finished their bagels, Tim took Kristen's empty plate. She followed him through the house and downstairs to the kitchen. After they had cleaned up, Tim took her to the garage and slid open the doors, revealing the Norton Commando. He turned to Kristen and said, "I know yesterday was hard. Today will be easier."

He walked toward the Commando motioning Kristen to come with him, stopping in front of the bike and stroking the gas tank and leather seat.

"See, it doesn't bite. It's a machine that I can control. Touch it."

Kristen felt panic in her body as she stiffened. She could hear her dad's voice telling her to stay away from motorcycles. She was standing closer to a bike than she had in her entire adult life. And now she was being encouraged to touch it. Closing her eyes, she whispered, "The bike won't bite me. It's a machine. It doesn't have a mind of its own. The person who turns on the motorcycle has a mind and that is what makes the machine go fast or slow."

Taking another deep breath, she repeated, "The bike won't bite me. It's a machine. It doesn't have a mind of its own. The person who turns on the motorcycle has a mind and that is what makes the machine go fast or slow."

Taking a step closer, Kristen did something she never imagined she would do. She slowly and gently slid her hand across the soft leather seat of the motorcycle. It was not like a dog that would move; it stayed in the same position. "It won't hurt me. It's the rider who makes the decision to go fast or slow." Then she thought to herself, "If I can trust the driver, then I can trust the bike."

"Can I sit on it?" Kristen asked, sheepishly, not sure where this courage was coming from.

"Sure. First, let's see if your feet touch the ground."

Kristen slowly straddled the seat of the Norton. Her feet touched the ground, which helped her feel a little more in control. Again, she encouraged herself with this whisper, "It's the driver who decides whether to go fast or slow." She took a deep breath in and let it out. In some odd way, sitting on the seat was reassuring, not threatening. Tim could tell her mind was racing and wondered what she was thinking about. Her panic seemed to be easing but he didn't want to push her over the edge. He was patient and there was no rush in getting her comfortable being around the Norton.

"Maybe this is enough for today," he said.

Kristen surprised him by asking, "Tim, what does the engine sound like?"

"You want to hear it?"

"Yes, I do."

"Alright, you have to get off, though."

Kristen swung her leg over the saddle of the motorcycle, then stood next to it as Tim cycled through the start-up procedure, finally turning the engine on. Not sure whether the sound of the engine would cause the panic to surface again, Kristen wanted to run and hide, but confidence and courage told her she could trust this man, and she wanted to stay close to him. The closer, the better, she thought.

"Can I get on behind you, or is this a one-seater?"

"You can get on."

After Kristen was seated, Tim pointed to the footrests. "You can put your feet on these."

Kristen placed her feet where he motioned, she took another deep breath, listening to the purr and whir of the engine as Tim revved it just a little. She could feel the vibrating of the bike as it revved, and wondered what it would be like to go for a ride. Gulping in another shot of courage, she asked, "What does it feel like when it's on the road?"

"It's kind of like riding a bicycle, only better."

"Oh..."

"Do you want to go for a little ride?"

Kristen hesitated because she still wasn't convinced that she wouldn't get killed, though he didn't know her self-talk was telling her the same thing. She didn't know if she could trust herself, but she was certain she could trust this man who held her tenderly and spoke truthfully. Tim sensed her quandary. He offered her a solution. "You don't have to go for a ride today."

"I want to, Tim. As long as you are in the driver's seat."

Tim was elated that Kristen's fears were less than yesterday and that she trusted him. She had made significant progress in a very short period of time. He handed her a helmet saying, "Let's see how this fits."

Kristen put the helmet on, and Tim helped her adjust the chin straps. He put on his helmet and cycled through the start-up. Engaging the bike in first gear, he slowly rolled out of the garage and onto the gravel driveway, then he stopped the bike and turned around halfway to face her.

"See, this isn't so bad, is it."

Kristen decided that she wanted to go for a ride. That she wasn't going to die, and that Tim was a safe driver. "No, Tim it's not scary, let's go somewhere."

"A short ride will be enough for today, Kristen."

"Ok," she answered.

Tim drove his Norton down the driveway until he stopped at the end where it met the street. He turned halfway around in his seat and asked Kristen a second time, "Do you want to go out on the roads?" Kristen gave him the thumbs up. "Yes, Tim, I'm curious. I want to know what it feels like to ride on a motorcycle."

"Alright, hold on to me firm then."

Kristen put her arms around Tim's waist. He patted her hands, then put his hands back on the handlebars, engaging the throttle. After a few blocks, Kristen lightened her death grip around Tim's waist and started to relax. She put her head on his left shoulder, enjoying the view ahead. While they rode along the quiet streets, Tim pointed out interesting things for her to see. Then Kristen tapped his shoulder, giving him the thumbs up again that she wanted to go faster. He smiled, shifting the bike into higher gear. They rode along the highway in quiet solitude, each to their own thoughts.

An hour later, Tim turned the bike in the direction toward home. Once they were parked back inside the garage, Tim asked, "So what do you think, Kristen?"

"I enjoyed the ride a lot more than I thought I would."

18
TWO WEEKS

After spending the weekend with Tim, Kristen didn't want to go home. They drove in silence, not because they were at a loss for words, but because individually, they were pondering the next step in their relationship.

In the past, Tim would have taken the weekend for granted and then moved on without any kind of closure for the recipient of his attention. But that was the last thing he wanted to do with Kristen, who didn't want the weekend's magic to be over. Somehow, she felt strange going back to her cottage. It was as if the few days she spent with Tim had become a lifetime. Her home was now a foreigner, not in a strange new land, but in a land that no longer had a reason to exist. She had fallen in love with Tim.

The drive to Kristen's house took them through palm tree lined streets and power lines, past boutique shops, antique galleries, and nondescript storefronts advertising oddities that, while unappealing to Kristen, were another man's treasure. She felt conflicted. Just hours earlier, she had felt joy and happiness. Now, the feeling of being made whole was beginning to fade, and that was not a feeling she welcomed.

Tim had not invited her to stay and, while she hoped he would, she had to get back to work and, after missing a week of work to hide away and rest, she would be behind as soon as she got there. It might take her two or three days to catch up on everything. In addition, she was on call for the next two weeks, which meant she had to be available at any hour when a patient was in transition. This was important because Kristen believed that no one should be alone when they stepped through the curtain of earthly existence into something better. Like her patient, Lottie, who insisted she had to get in the boat because her Jeremy was waiting for her on the other side of the water.

Kristen wondered about the patients who would need her during the next two weeks. She had always put them first. But now there was Tim, and he was not a ticking time bomb; he was alive, vibrant, full of all the things her heart had been missing, even though unaware they were absent until this past weekend.

When Tim pulled up in front of Kristen's house, her heart sank. She didn't want to be here. Tim sensed a change in her demeanor instantly but chose to say nothing. He stopped the car and got out. She sat in the car, staring blankly at the street in front of her. When she saw Tim coming around to her side of the car, she unbuckled her seat belt. The weekend was over.

Taking hold of Tim's hand as he helped her out of the car, she didn't let go as he walked her down the neatly trimmed sidewalk. He noticed that the lawn in front of her house had been mowed and the bushes in front of her windows trimmed, thinking it was a good thing she rented and that whoever her landlord was understood the demands of her job. When they stepped onto the porch, before Kristen unlocked her front door, Tim pulled her close, taking her face between his two hands and gently kissed her lips. As their kisses became more passionate, Tim suddenly stopped. "I should go now, Kristen." He turned and walked away.

Kristen felt like her heart would break. Suddenly the certainty of the weekend became uncertain. She ran after Tim. He turned around, surprised. Then to lighten the dark cloud hanging over them, he jokingly asked, "Miss me already?" Kristen could feel tears forming and falling onto her cheeks, so she quickly composed herself and said, "Yes, I do." Tim brushed aside another tear that had fallen down her face with his fingers. "I will be back, I promise you, Kristen."

"But if you leave, I am afraid things will not be the same."

"What are you talking about?" Tim asked. In his mind, things were solid between the two of them.

"The magic."

"I assure you; I will keep the magic going."

"Do you promise?"

"I promise, Kristen. We will always have the memories of our first nights together. That will never change. What will change is that it gets better. Have faith, you will see."

"I'll try."

Tim kissed her lightly on the forehead, saying, "That's my girl. You better get inside before I change my mind."

"I wish you would, Tim."

Tim had an idea he wanted to share with her but wasn't sure how she would respond. Pausing before speaking what he had been muddling over, he said, "Kristen, listen to me. You need to figure out what you want. Do you want to continue working with the dying, or do you want to travel with me?"

Kristen was gob smacked. "Really, do you mean that, Tim?"

"If I didn't mean it, I wouldn't have said it. That has been my plan all along, that when I retired, I would take a cross-country motorcycle trip. Thanks to a client, my retirement from the bank and that journey will happen sooner rather than later. Kristen, my plan is to go into the bank tomorrow and submit my two-week notice. And then I plan on packing my bags and enjoying that trip!"

"And you want me…to join you?"

"Kristen, you are not afraid of a motorcycle. I suspect you thoroughly enjoyed the ride we took today, and it was your idea. We would ride a bike built for long-distance cruising so you would be comfortable. I am thinking we could start at the Pacific Ocean, dip our toes in, then drive across to the Atlantic. We could discover lakes and rivers in between. And when the weather is inclement, we will hole up somewhere in a rustic cabin, not too primitive; it will have some luxurious amenities. I'll let you imagine those as I'm a pretty basic kind of guy, but what you want is what's important. I doubt we will be at a loss for something to do."

"That sounds nice, Tim."

"It will be if you decide to join me."

"That's not a hard decision. I think you know what I will say."

"I really don't, Kristen, because you will have to give up your job. I know how committed you are to your patients. I know that sounds harsh and I don't mean it to come out that way. So let me explain my thoughts. The cross-country trip I am envisioning wouldn't have any time constraints. I don't want to have an itinerary, and that is why I suggested you give up your job, to have the freedom to travel with me. You don't have to worry about money. Trust me I have plenty for both of us. I also appreciate your independence and respect your career. I can't ask you to give that up and I understand why your patients fall in love with you, even for a short time."

Kristen thought about her last patient, Susie Kline, and hesitated before responding to Tim's conditions. "I know I don't want to experience another peds death." But then she thought she heard Tim say he loved her. Was he in love with her?

Tim thought about what Kristen had just said. Then firmly, without mincing words, he said, "I'd like you to think about this over the next two weeks. I'm not giving you an ultimatum; I'm giving you a choice."

"I know," Kristen responded.

Tim let his words sink in before he left her standing on the porch. "Take your time, but don't take too long. Good night, Kristen." He quickly turned and did not look back. She watched him get into his car and drive away.

Walking into her house, Kristen closed the heavy oak door behind her. She paused, looking in the mirror in her tiny foyer. Noticing a pallor on her face where there had been a bloom, she thought she felt fine until fatigue and syncope overcame her. Luckily, she was able to stumble to a chair before collapsing on the floor beside it.

Tim's departure from Kristen left him feeling unsettled. He didn't want their first memories to be tainted because of his ultimatum, even though he told her it was a choice. More importantly, Tim wondered, what if she chose her patients over him? Her life up until now had been her patients and these were not patients that got well and went home. They were people whose earthly journey had come to an end, and she was instrumental in assisting them and helping their loved ones move on. Was it reasonable to ask her to give it up? They were not young, nor were they old. But the reality was their length of days ahead of them were shorter than what they had left behind. That was a sobering thought, one that had surfaced when his client, Helen Trenton, died. There were no guarantees that tomorrow would come, and one must not waste the precious time one had left.

Thirty minutes after Tim walked through his front door, he decided to follow his instincts and check on Kristen. He dialed her number but the phone rang and rang. Thinking she was indisposed, he left a voice mail. "Hi, it's Tim, just checking in, call me." BEEP. Then he walked aimlessly through his house, waiting for her to return his call. There was a distinct stillness that surrounded him, one he had not noticed until Kristen came to fill the void. There were times when he enjoyed the quiet, especially after a busy day talking to clients when he desperately wanted the noise to go away and solitude to be his comfort. But now that he had allowed her into his heart, the stillness was overwhelming.

Tim dialed her cell phone again, still no answer. He decided to let well enough alone as his phone calls were not helping her with a weighty decision that was hers alone to make. Instead, he sought solace in a bourbon neat, then climbed the stairs to the second floor into the bedroom where, just hours before, Kristen had been laying with him. She was not there now, and he felt empty. With his drink in hand, Tim opened the doors leading to his lanai and surrounding gardens. When he walked along the pea gravel paths, one set of footsteps crunching on the gravel only confirmed what he felt in his heart. He wanted to spend the rest of his life with the woman in the red dress who had captured him from the moment their eyes met. She was all he could think about. He strolled over to one of the chaise lounges, thinking about the phone call, and not caring if his call swayed her to his way of thinking. He decided to dial her again. Still, no answer.

Something was amiss. Kristen usually returned his calls. Surely, she had enough time by now for a shower or a long soak in her tub, so he thought. Rather than second guessing himself, Tim left the glass of bourbon on the chaise lounge. He stood up, patted his pants pockets to confirm his car's fob was still there. Then, running along the garden path to his bedroom through the glass doors and down the stairs into his kitchen, he paused briefly before bolting through his front door, not checking to make sure the heavy metal hammed front door latched behind him. He was in a hurry to get to Kristen. Something was wrong.

The car's powerful engine roared, and his tires spun out as he fishtailed, spitting pea gravel behind him. He reached the end of his driveway turning onto the street. This was not a leisurely drive, and he was glad for the dearth of cars on the road.

He reached Kristen's house in fifteen minutes. When he pulled up, he noticed the lights were not on. Dashing out of his car and up the steps to her porch, he furiously knocked on the front door. Even though his pounding was relentless, Kristen did not come to the door. Tim's anxiety became alarming. He looked in her front windows, grateful the bushes had been trimmed. Every hair on Tim's head stood up as a chill descended down his spine when he saw Kristen lying motionless on the floor. He immediately dialed 911. A dispatcher answered on the second ring.

"This is Monica, what is your emergency?"

"Please hurry! My girlfriend isn't moving."

"Sir, are you with her?"

"No, I'm outside her house. I can see her lying on the floor."

"What's the address? I will send an ambulance."

Tim couldn't remember the address. All he could remember was Barlow Street, two blocks from Tri-County Hospice. He told the operator that the ambulance would see his BMW in front of the house, adding that the front door was painted a buttercup yellow.

Then Tim remembered Kristen hid a key under the mat. He retrieved it and quickly shoved the key into the lock, gaining access inside the house. He tried to quell his fears that something tragic had happened. "No, we can't end like this, WE CAN'T!" he shouted.

Within minutes, Tim heard the wailing sirens rise and fall. The ambulance had no sooner pulled up in front of the house than an EMT jumped out and ran inside the door Tim had left opened. "I can take it from here," he said. The EMT checked for a pulse, noticing it was thready. Then he checked for breathing. Satisfied that Kristen was alive, he turned to Tim, "What's her name?"

"Kristen, Kristen Warner," Tim replied.

The EMT called out her name several times. Finally, she opened her eyes, looking quizzically at the man in uniform. In a raspy voice, she asked, "Why are you here? What happened?" The EMT explained, "Your boyfriend called us. You are lucky he did." Kristen heard him say "your boyfriend" and spoke, "Tim…Tim, are you here?"

"I'm here Kristen. I'm not leaving you."

The EMT waited for their exchange then said, "Ma'am we need to take you to the hospital to get checked out. My partner has already called this in."

"I think I can stand," Kristen said, trying to stand up.

"I prefer that you do not," the EMT said.

Kristen didn't have a choice other than to acquiesce with the EMT's orders. Tim watched helplessly as they loaded her onto a gurney. She looked fearful.

"I'll be right behind you in my car," he reassured her. "I will meet you at the hospital."

After the EMTs loaded her in the ambulance, Tim closed and locked the front door, returning the key to its place under the doormat, relieved he had not yet suggested she find a better hiding place.

On the way to the hospital, the EMT cross typed Kristen's blood. There was a reason she had passed out and he wasn't going to make any assumptions. It was wise to do what they could and give the ER team as much information as possible to make a diagnosis.

The ambulance arrived at the hospital in a matter of minutes. While Kristen was admitted to the ER, Tim parked his car, assuming he would only have to give her name to be taken to her in the treatment area. But when he inquired at the admissions station, the staff inquired, "Sir, I can't let you go back without proper identification. What is the patient's date of birth?"

"I don't know?"

"Then you will have to take a seat in the waiting room."

Tim was angry. He didn't want to sit. Instead, he paced back and forth. Back and forth. There was nothing he could do to get to Kristen except wait. So, he waited, though not patiently. After what seemed like years, he heard someone speak his name.

"Mr. Hurst? How may I help you?" Tim was surprised to hear his name called by someone other than the admissions staff. When she saw that he could not place her, she gently reminded him, "I'm Cheryl, I took care of your dad."

"Yes, I recognize you now. You did take care of him. But right now, I need to get back to the treatment area. My girlfriend was just brought in, and I don't know what happened to her."

"What is her name?"

"Kristen Warner. She was brought in about an hour ago."

The nurse disappeared for a few minutes while Tim continued to pace back and forth, hoping upon hope that she would be able to get him back to be with his beloved.

Appearing from behind the heavily guarded doors, Cheryl appeared carrying a visitor's badge, which she handed to Tim. "Mr. Hurst, you need this." As Tim fumbled with the clasp to get the badge attached to his shirt, the nurse said, "Come with me. I will vouch for you." Using her magnetic key card, Cheryl opened the double doors into the hallway leading to the patient bays. "Stay here while I find out where your girlfriend is being treated." As she walked away, Tim took a deep breath, thankful to have gotten behind the iron curtain of the hospital.

Tim didn't have to wait long for Cheryl to return. When she did, he followed her to bay three. Before going through the dividing curtain, he turned to Cheryl, "Thank you for this courtesy. I was out of my mind with worry."

"You're welcome, Mr. Hurst." Then she took him aside and reminded him, "I bent the rules because I know you. But you must get your next of kin in writing if and when there is a next time. I cannot do this again."

"I will. We will. Thank you, Cheryl."

The nurse pulled the curtains around Kristen's bay and walked away.

The first thing Tim saw when the curtains were drawn was the rich, red blood hanging from a bag and an IV tube going into Kristen's arm. He reached across the gurney and stroked her forehead, but she didn't wake up. A nurse came in shortly after his display of compassion to check the flow of blood into the IV.

Tim asked, "What's going on with her?"

The nurse explained that, upon arrival, Kristen was distressingly anemic, which was one of the reasons she had passed out. She said that, because the EMTs had cross typed her blood before arriving, the hospital staff was able to quickly start a blood transfusion.

"How long has she been asleep?" Tim asked. The nurse looked at Kristen's chart. "We started the drip about an hour ago. These procedures usually take four hours. Why don't you try and get some rest? You can sit beside her, if you want."

"Thanks," Tim said. He sat in the chair, laid his head between his arms on the bed next to Kristen, and closed his eyes.

He had no idea how long he had been asleep until the same nurse returned, "Time to check," she said pleasantly. Upon inspection, the nurse observed that the bag of blood had emptied completely. She deftly removed the IV, the tubing and empty bag, and disposed of the items without waking Kristen.

Then she turned to Tim, "Let her sleep while I get the discharge and after care papers ready."

Within a few minutes, the nurse returned. "You can wake your friend up now." Tim gently shook Kristen's arm, "Kristen, wake up. It's time to go home." Slowly, she opened her eyes, then dozed off again. Tim let her sleep for a few more minutes before again encouraging her to awaken. "Kristen, I need you to wake up so we can go home."

Kristen finally opened her eyes and began to awaken. When her nurse saw she was fully awake, she went over the discharge instructions.

"You are anemic and need to be mindful of your iron intake. You were extremely low, dangerously low. Dr. Anderson wants you to take the day off. You can go back to work tomorrow. Make sure you eat iron rich foods and take a B12 supplement. Be careful with the iron supplement and purchase one that is slow release. And if constipation becomes a problem, stop, drink lots of fluids and take psyllium."

Tim was able to follow along with the instructions until the nurse mentioned psyllium. "What's psyllium?"

"It's a fiber product easily mixed with water. It can be immensely helpful for stopped up plumbing."

By the time the nurse finished the instructions, Kristen wanted to go home. "Alright, when can I get out of here?" she asked, as she started to get out of bed.

"After you get dressed, you can sign your name by this arrow. I'll leave you now. Just open the curtain when you are ready?"

Confused, Tim asked, "When did the doctor check her out?"

"Dr. Anderson was here before you came back to the bay area. He had labs drawn and orders prepared," replied the nurse.

"Oh, ok, then can we go?"

"Yes, as soon as Kristen signs the orders."

Tim turned to Kristen, "Did you hear that? No work today." Kristen looked at Tim quizzically. "When did yesterday turn into today?"

"A few hours ago."

Kristen didn't waste any time getting dressed. The blood transfusion left her feeling fresh and energetic. She opened the curtains around her bed, then she signed her name by the arrow, indicating she was aware of Dr. Anderson's instructions. She knew how these procedures worked. The nurse came back into the bay area and handed Kristin a copy of her discharge instructions. Kristen politely thanked her, then followed Tim out of the ER and to his car.

Within minutes of leaving the hospital, Tim parked in front of Kristen's house. The wee hours of the morning were upon them, and the sky was still wrapped in a cloak of darkness. He took the key from under the mat, unlocked the door, and stepped to the side so Kristen could enter.

"Kristen, doctor's orders, no work today. Why don't you call off before going back to bed." After he said these words, he made no attempt to follow her into her house. Kristen noticed and asked, "Aren't you coming in?"

"Do you want me to?"

"Yes, Tim, I do."

He followed Kristen into her house and reminded her, "Don't forget to call Tri-County."

Kristen walked into her kitchen and threw her purse on the counter. Then she took out her phone and dialed Tri-County. Even though it was early in the morning, the hospice was staffed around the clock. She knew Hilda was not going to pick up, so she left a message. Then she trudged up the stairs with Tim close behind.

She no sooner entered her bedroom than fell fully clothed onto her bed. Tim was tired as well and made no attempt to get out of his clothes. He laid beside her, pulling the comforter up around them.

It was late afternoon when Kristen woke up. "What time is it?"

"It's 4:00. You slept most of the day."

"I hope I will be able to sleep tonight."

"I'm sure you will, Kristen."

"I know I will if you are beside me."

Tim didn't say a word. Kristen still had a decision to make, and his being with her might give her the idea that she could continue to work and have him, too.

"We better get something to eat, Kristen."

"I think I have something to prepare for us."

Tim didn't know what Kristen had in her refrigerator. She didn't have much that he recalled, which was her choice because she spent most of her time at Tri-County. "Don't worry, I'll pick up some groceries." He got out of bed and left to go on a light grocery run.

While Tim was running the errand, Kristen took a shower and set the table. Then she put a set of clean sheets on the bed. Having Tim with her felt natural. She didn't want this to end; it needed to continue without interruption but, in the back of her mind, Kristen knew she had to go back to work the next day.

Tim returned with the grocery items.

"Kristen, do you have a grill?"

"No, I don't. I mean, not an outdoor grill, if that's what you asked. I have one on the stove."

"Have you ever used it?

"No. I spend most of my time with my patients. Even when I'm off work, I find a reason to go in. I don't have a life. Didn't have a life outside of work until now."

"That has been your life, hasn't it?" Tim reminded her.

"Yes…" she mumbled, peeking into the grocery bags delighted to see Tim had picked up freshly made burger patties.

While she was busy preparing lettuce, tomato and onions for the burgers from the items Tim had purchased, he took the burgers out of white butcher paper and seasoned them with salt and pepper. Then he fired up the indoor grill. When it was hot, the burgers made a sizzle and hiss as he laid them out on the hot grate.

As Tim cooked the meat, Kristen finished assembling the "fixin's" and carried them to her dining table. She heard Tim call, "Burgers ready." Then she took two plates out of the cabinet next to the sink and handed them to him. He placed a burger on a bun on each plate and carried them to the table. They sat quietly together for a moment before Kristen looked at him and smiled.

"You know, Tim, this is the first time I have used this table."

"Why is that?" he asked, even though he had a pretty good idea of what she was going to say.

"I usually eat with my patients."

Tim said nothing. He decided to use this as an opportunity to paint a picture of what she would be giving up if she traveled with him.

"Do you think you will miss that kind of intimacy with your patients?"

Kristen thought for a moment before answering him. "Yes."

"Hmm," Tim responded. At least she was candid with what she would miss, Tim surmised. He truly hoped she would choose him. They ate together in silence until their plates were empty. Kristen finished chewing her last bite, swallowed it, then looked at Tim and said, "You sure know how to cook a good burger. Thank you."

"You're welcome, I'm glad you enjoyed the meal."

"I did, very much."

"Alright," Tim said as he got up from the table. "I'll help you with the dishes and then I'm going home."

Kristen really thought he was going to stay over. Dejectedly, she said, "Oh…"

She was confused but said nothing. When the last dish was dried and put away, Tim turned to Kristen. "You have some decisions to make, and that is why I am not staying with you. Please don't misunderstand. I am serious about our future, and I know how much your patients mean to you.

But I don't want time constraints. And remember, you wouldn't have to worry about money. Although, I am guessing money is not what your career means to you."

Then he opened his arms for a hug. Kristen didn't protest. She tilted her head for a kiss. As their lips touched, their chemistry ignited, passion aroused in Tim, but he withdrew his affection before there was no turning back. This was difficult, maybe even cruel, but Kristen needed to know what she would be missing. He took her arms from around his waist and placed them at her side. "Good night, Kristen, choose wisely." And then he was gone.

Kristen watched as Tim's BMW pulled away from the curb in front of her house. She couldn't believe Tim had left her when, clearly, he had wanted to stay. Why was he making this so difficult? She felt dejected, even embarrassed, that she let her desire for Tim, for everything about him, cloud her judgment. Why did love have to hurt so much?

19

LEAP OF FAITH

Kristen closed the door once Tim's car was out of her sight. She had an unsettled, empty feeling whenever she was away from him. Was love supposed to be a host of emotions, like a ride on a roller coaster? Terrifying, exhilarating? Why couldn't love be easier? Did Tim love her? She suspected he did even though he had not come out and said, 'I love you.' Maybe she was reading more into their relationship then she should. But he did say he wanted her to travel with him. Surely, that meant more than a platonic relationship. She was being silly; she was being insecure. If Tim only wanted a one-night stand, he could easily have that. But she knew better.

He said she would have to quit her job, and the idea of doing that was beyond her comprehension. She always worked, always had a paycheck. Thankfully, she didn't have to worry about a mortgage payment. She had significant savings but what about health insurance? Her recent "event" that caused a hospital visit was an indication she would need some kind of medical coverage. It wasn't prudent to blindly quit her job and lose its benefits. But he said money wasn't an issue. And what about her patients? They had been her life, however briefly they were in it. Recalling Susie's death, Kristen knew she could not do another peds death.

She had no idea of Tim's financial status even though he said he had plenty of money. He was planning on retiring from his job at the bank, so he must be doing ok. But there were things they still needed to discuss. Was taking a leap of faith out of the question? She needed a sign; she needed something to confirm that traveling with Tim was what she should choose.

When the idea of a sign entered her mind, Kristen felt better about her situation, and said out loud, "Yes, a sign will appear somehow, and I will know what to do. It will be clear, I will not second guess, but it will be a sign, it must be a sign."

Since it was getting late and the morning would soon be upon her, Kristen decided to take something to help her sleep. She didn't do that very often, but when she was anxious or restless, she was relieved knowing that sleep would not elude her. She reached into her bathroom cabinet and took out prescription strength sleeping pills and popped two of the tablets into her mouth followed by a glass of water. She was sure she would get a solid eight hours from the medicine. Then she stood in the doorway of her bedroom and stared at the bed, looking at the spot where Tim had laid with her. She remembered how she felt cuddled in his arms and waking up next to him. She let her mind drift to the weekend she spent with Tim at his house.

Being around him felt natural. There was an ease in conversation up until this evening. Surely, they would have that again. For now, sleep would be the darkness she would escape into so her mind could rest.

The shrill chirping of birds outside Kristen's window awakened her before her alarm rudely disturbed her slumber. She preferred waking up to the birds' sweet tweets, chirps, and even their shrill notes rather than being jolted out of a deep sleep. Usually she could remember her dreams, but not this morning. Her sleep had been deep, no memory, no anything, just a dark place where singing birds suddenly lifted her out of an abyss.

Kristen grabbed her silky, lavender bathrobe that had been lying at the foot of her bed and let it slip over her shoulders. She tied it at her waist before standing up. While she had been away from Tri-County for only a few days, two of which were the weekend, emotionally, she felt as though eons had passed, bringing her to this morning.

"Coffee. Coffee is what I need right now," she said out loud as she trudged down the stairs. Still somewhat foggy from the sleeping pills she had taken the night before, she entered her kitchen that was neat and tidy, almost too clean she mused, as if nobody lived there. While she prepared her coffee and waited for it to brew, Kristen looked at the dining room table from her kitchen and was reminded of unsettled business. She didn't want to lose Tim, nor did she want to abandon her patients. These thoughts tumbled around in her head as she drank her morning elixir.

After finishing the last sip in her mug, she put the vessel in the dishwasher and turned it on, forgetting that the dishes were already clean from dinner with Tim. Noticing the time, Kristen decided to get moving because there were patients to take care of at Tri-County. After dressing, Kristen retrieved her white lab jacket hanging in the coat closet. Before leaving, she turned on a light in the kitchen because she anticipated working late and didn't want to come home to a dark house. She turned on her porch light, shut the door behind her, and drove the short distance to Tri-County.

The short drive didn't give her much time to think. As soon as she parked her car in the employees parking lot, it was as if she suddenly changed gears, forgetting about her dilemma. There were patients and their families to take care of, which was all she thought about as she walked through the glass doors of Tri-County Hospice.

Kristen stopped at Hilda's desk before going back to her office. "Good morning, Hilda. Do you have mail for me?"

"Good morning, Nurse Warner, are you feeling alright?"

"Yes, I am. Thank you for asking. I am ready to be of service. Do we have any new admissions?"

"As a matter of fact, we do, Nurse Warner."

"Do we have an intake form ready?"

"Yes, I put the information on your desk for review."

"Oh, ok, has the patient been admitted?"

"Yes, he has."

Kristen smiled at Hilda, "I'll be going now, call if you need me."

"I will, Nurse Warner," Hilda replied. "I'm glad you are back with us."

Kristen walked to her office and tossed her keys on her desk before sitting in front of her computer. The flowers Tim had given her were dried and crumbling. She picked up the vase and threw the dead flowers into her trash can. Then she took the can and the vase to the staff kitchen used not only for lunch breaks but when they were on call. Kristen emptied her trash into a larger receptacle and left the vase in the sink. Then she brushed her hands together ridding herself of any remaining dried particles of flowers before returning to her office.

Walking out of the staff kitchen, down the hall, and back into her office, she noticed her new patient's admission file. Kristen read his diagnosis and saw that her new patient had been admitted with stage four pancreatic cancer. While some patients miraculously got better, it was doubtful this patient would walk out on his own. She decided to pay a visit to room 113.

Kristen knocked on the patient's door before going in, giving the patient the dignity and respect he deserved. "Hello, Mr. Castro," she greeted the man lying in bed. He immediately smiled from ear to ear. "Hello, Nurse, come on in. You must be new?" Kristen smiled at Mr. Castro, then said, "No, I have been here at Tri-County for a while. I was away the day you were admitted. It's so nice to meet you, Mr. Castro."

"Call me Damian. Mr. Castro is too formal for my taste. I'm just an ordinary guy who happened to end up here."

"I'm glad you ended up here, Damian," Kristen said with a smile.

"And what is your name, now that you know mine?" Damian asked.

"I apologize, Damian. I should have introduced myself. My name is Kristen. Kristen Warner."

"It's nice to meet you, Kristen. I think we shall be good friends."

Kristen had to catch herself. Damian was charming his way straight into her heart and she knew his time was short. She couldn't let herself get too attached. But there was something about him, his cheerfulness, despite a terminal diagnosis. She liked being around him even though they had just met. Kristen quickly detached herself from her emotions because she was there to help her patient.

"Damian, is there anything I can get you?"

"No thanks, I'm fine for now. I think I'd like to take a nap. Will you come back later?"

"Of course, I will. I will stop back this afternoon. Have a nice nap."

Damian smiled. "I will now that I have met you. Would you mind closing the door on your way out?" Kristen smiled back at him, then instinctively straightened his blankets and repositioned his pillow. "Thanks Kristen, "he said.

"You're welcome, get some rest, Damian."

"I will have a date with a pretty nurse later today. I may need my strength."

Kristen chuckled at Damian's attempt at humor. "Is that a fact?" she said.

"Yes, now get out of here, Kristen, I need to sleep."

"Yes Sir," she said. Turning away, she closed the patient's door softly behind her. All thoughts of Tim had evaporated during her conversation with her new patient. "This is why I love my job," she said out loud as she walked down the hallway and back to her office.

The morning soon became the afternoon before Kristen realized she had not eaten a meal. Breakfast, if she could call it that, had been consumed hours ago. She remembered her doctor's orders to take care of herself. She had better, since Damian was relying on her and she didn't know how long he would be at Tri-County.

She popped into the staff kitchen and rummaged through the refrigerator. She didn't find a single morsel to her satisfaction. Since the vegan restaurant was a block away, picking up something wasn't out of the question. Kristen stopped by Hilda's desk before leaving.

"Hilda, I am going to the vegan restaurant, do you want anything?"

Hilda thought for a moment before answering. "I would love one of their banana nut muffins, please. That is, if I have a choice."

"What if they are out of those, do you have a second choice?"

"Hm…maybe the pumpkin spice."

"Ok, I will be back shortly, Hilda."

Kristen pushed on the revolving doors following the semi-circle of glass that led outside. The air was clean, and the sun was shining in a cloudless, brilliant, blue sky. For the moment, she felt happy, but the happiness of the moment disappeared once she stood inside the vegan restaurant and peered into the courtyard where she and Tim had shared a meal. She felt conflicted and sad. A woman standing in line nudged Kristen, waking her from her melancholy thoughts.

"I believe you are next," she said.

The young man taking orders winked at Kristen. "I'm ready to take your order if you know what you want."

"I do," she said. "I'd like a banana nut muffin, no make that two please, and I will also have your Mediterranean salad with lots of leafy greens, Kalamata olives, feta cheese, red onion, cavatappi pasta, and red beans. And I would like your house dressing on the side, please."

"Coming right up and, just so you know, you get the last two banana nut muffins for the day!" Kristen thought that maybe she should take a pumpkin one since she didn't want to take the last two banana nut in case someone else wanted one.

"Excuse me, may I change my mind about the muffins?" she asked the young man at the counter. "Maybe I should take one of your pumpkin spice instead of the two banana nut ones."

"Too late," the young man said. "They already have your name on them. Don't worry, the pumpkin spice is a good second choice for those who don't get here early enough for the banana nuts."

"Thank you," Kristen replied, as he handed her a carryout bag with her order.

Once outside in the warm sunshine, she felt a little better but thoughts of Tim tore at her heart. Kristen's cheerful disposition was left behind at the restaurant by the time she returned to Tri-County. Hilda noticed the change in her.

"Nurse Warner. Are you ok?" she asked nonchalantly.

Kristen paused before answering her. "Yes, I'm fine, Hilda. Thanks for asking." Hilda chose not to pry. If Nurse Warner wanted to confide in her, she would, and if not, she would respect her privacy. Perhaps her recent absence had more to do with a personal issue than an illness.

Kristen handed Hilda the banana nut muffin saying, "You are in luck!"

"Thank you, these are my favorite."

"You're welcome, my pleasure."

Hilda started to reach into her purse to pay for the muffin. Kristen put her hand up. "No, I don't want any money. Pay it forward when you have the opportunity."

"I will, Nurse Warner, thank you."

Kristen smiled, then took her salad and the muffin to the staff kitchen. She ate half of her salad, saving the other for dinner later that evening. Then she took the muffin to Damian's room.

"Knock, knock," she said poking her head in the door.

"Kristen, I've been expecting you, come in."

"I've brought you a surprise, Damian."

Damian looked at the bag in her hand, then turned away. Kristen noticed a faraway look in his eyes.

"What is it, Damian?"

He turned back to face her. "Oh, let me guess. From the looks of the bag, I'd say you were at the vegan restaurant everyone raves about."

"Guilty as charged, Damian. Do you want to guess what's in the bag?"

"Hmmm…," Damian dragged out his answer. "Maybe one of their famous banana nut muffins?"

"How did you know?"

"Oh, I know a lot of things, believe me, Kristen."

"Maybe I should let you read my palm, tell my future?"

Damian became quiet, choosing his next words carefully. "I'm not a crystal ball, but I can read people's hearts."

"Oh…" was all Kristen said.

Damian could tell something weighed heavily on Kristen's heart. He knew he had a few weeks left to guide her in the right direction. Hopefully, she would be willing to listen. He took the bag from her. Before he opened it, he said, "Let me see if I guessed correctly." Damian let out a squeal of delight when he opened the bag. "I haven't had one of these in a long time."

Kristen was surprised at his response. "Other than being sick, Damian, why is that?"

Kristen noticed Damian's faraway look returned. She waited until he wanted to talk. "I used to go there with someone special."

"Really!"

"Yes, Kristen. This special person and I went there when the restaurant first opened up. People were not exactly into vegan food. We were pioneers, you could say. Hippies would be a better description."

Kristen's interest piqued with this newfound knowledge. "What was the restaurant like back then, Damian?"

"You make me sound ancient. I'm not that old."

Kristen wasn't sure of her patient's sense of humor because of how he had responded. So she offered to make amends. "I stand corrected. You are not old, my apologies."

"Kristen, I am that old, I was teasing you."

"That's a relief," Kristen chuckled. Then she added, "You know what I like about the place, Damian?"

"No, what?"

"It's the scent of it; you know what it smells like when you first walk in. After a while you feel different."

Damian smiled, then he said, "It's like walking in a pine forest. I believe it's because of the chemicals called terpenes that you encounter through the olfactory nerve. I love that earthy scent, Kristen. I think I will miss that the most."

Then Damian looked at Kristen. "I think this is too big for me to eat. Why don't you take half of it."

Kristen divided the muffin, giving Damian the half in the muffin paper. He closed his eyes like he was remembering something. "What is it, Damian?" Kristen asked. He opened his eyes after chewing a bite of muffin. Then he asked, "Have you ever smelled something or eaten something or looked at something, that reminds you of something entirely different?"

Kristen thought for a moment before answering, "The end of summer always reminds me of someone I really liked from a long time ago."

"Who was that, Kristen?"

Kristen's voice trailed off as she answered, "My friend, Stan." Damian noticed her reluctance to add more detail but prodded her anyway to divulge more. "I see. Is this a sad memory or a happy one?"

"I guess you could say, Damian, a little of both."

When Kristen did not comment further, he didn't push her for more. Instead, he waited patiently until she summoned the courage to talk about Stan.

"I met Stan in my freshman year of high school at St. Ambrose Academy. We were in the same room taking a test. You know those horrible, standardized tests that are given during the hottest time of the year."

Damian chuckled, "I take it you don't like taking tests, Kristen?"

"I don't have a problem taking them. I earned a scholarship to St. Ambrose because I scored the highest on the entrance exam in the history of the school. No pressure, I'd say. I was so bored I was tempted to throw off the scoring algorithm by alternating my answers. You know like A,B,C,D, D,C,B,A. But I couldn't justify that because clearly the answers were wrong."

"What about the boy, Stan?"

"He sat across the aisle from me. He almost finished the test. We ate lunch together that same day. After that he met me at my locker every morning before classes and after school every afternoon. We liked each other without saying it. One day Stan asked to come to my house after school."

"Did he?"

"Yes, he did."

"Smart boy, I would have asked, too."

"Damian, I think he had a motive for coming over and it wasn't just me."

"Why do you say that?"

Kristen wasn't sure she wanted to talk about Stan's ulterior motive because it would make her think about her brother. "It was rumored that the house across the street from my house was haunted."

"That's interesting, Kristen. Do you believe in apparitions, you know, ghosts?"

"No, but I think Stan did, and that is why he wanted to come over. He wanted to explore the house across the street. You should have seen his face when I scared him."

"Was that a nice thing to do, Kristen?"

"At the time, I thought it was funny. I hid behind the side of the porch while he looked in the windows. I threw a rock behind him. You should have seen him jump!"

Damian thought this was interesting. "Tell me, Kristen. Why was the house haunted?"

"That is a sad story, Damian. Are you sure you want to hear it?"

"I'm sure."

Kristen swallowed the lump that had suddenly risen in her throat. She thought she was over her brother's death, but since Damian was interested, she continued. "My brother Harry was killed in a motorcycle accident."

"How old were you when your brother died?"

"I was ten."

"Hmmm, I see, you loved your brother very much, didn't you?"

"Yes, I did."

Damian let her words sink in, carefully choosing his next question. "How did the accident happen? Does that have something to do with the house across the street being haunted?"

Kristen paused before answering. "Damian, people used to say the house was haunted because my brother was friends with Mitch who lived there. His dad owned Slim's Garage. Everybody took their cars there for repairs. But Mr. Slim really liked working on motorcycles. Mitch was a few years older than Harry. One day, Mr. Slim got a special motorcycle. From what I was told, Mitch and Harry went for a midnight ride while everyone was sleeping. They never came home."

Damian noticed tears welling up in Kristen's eyes as she talked about her brother. He handed her a tissue from a box that was on the sliding table across his bed. Then he said, "Oh, so because Mitch lived in that house and died, people automatically assumed it was haunted."

"Yes. It gave people closure over an impossible situation. I used to go and sit with Mr. Slim after the boys died. My daddy never forgave Mr. Slim. I knew it wasn't his fault. We never said much, actually we never said anything at all. We let out hearts talk."

"That's a rare gift, Kristen, being able to hear what someone's heart is saying."

"I guess. But one day Mr. Slim up and moved without saying goodbye. I was sad for a long time."

"Hmm," Damian said. "So, what happened to Stan. Did you marry him?"

"I'm not married, never have been. I am more married to my patients, Damian."

"I see," he said. Then Kristen continued her story about Stan. "After I scared Stan and he forgave me, he built a bench for me in the backyard of the haunted house. We sat on the bench for the longest time. That is when Stan gave me my first kiss."

Damian let her reflect on her memories before speaking up. "Kristen, I am getting tired; do you mind if we pick this up tomorrow?"

Kristen was surprised when he ended their conversation. Embarrassed, she said, "Damian, I'm so sorry. I have been talking about me instead of learning about you."

"No Kristen, you did exactly what you should have, and that was to tell me about yourself."

"Thank you, Damian."

Kristen straightened his blankets, fluffed his pillow, and helped him lay back. She refilled his water glass, making sure the straw was secured and would not spill water everywhere when he took a sip.

"I will be back tomorrow, Damian. I promise."

Then she waited until Damian closed his eyes before exiting his room, closing his door softly behind her. When Damian heard the door close, he opened his eyes. His mind wandered as he thought about their conversation.

Kristen did not come across as lucky with love. He would help her find a way to love again. He understood why she felt abandoned by her brother, maybe even Stan. Although she didn't say what happened to him, she never married, and yet chose to be married to her dying patients.

Kristen tried not to think about Stan or her brother. Talking with Damian about the people she loved was like pouring salt into a wound and it stung! She decided she would be more guarded the next time Damian started asking her questions.

Since she was on call, Kristen decided to stay overnight at Tri-County. Going home only made her choices more difficult because she didn't have patients there to distract her from the "elephant in the room."

In the middle of the night, the call button came on in room 113. Kristen's heart stopped beating for a minute, then she collected herself because she had been dreaming about Stan, and she couldn't ascertain whether she was dreaming or awake.

The buzz of the call button removed all doubt. She rushed to Damian's room only to discover there was no emergency. His light was on, and he was sitting up in his bed grinning from ear to ear like a cheshire cat. When Kristen walked into his room, he said, "I'm glad you answered my call. I'm awake now. I thought we could talk some more."

Kristen was relieved that this was not a distress signal because she liked her patient, and she was not ready for her friend to leave. Damian patted the bed. "Come sit," he said. "Tell me more about Stan."

"Where did I leave off, Damian?"

"I recall something about your first kiss."

Kristen remembered to be guarded before offering information about Stan. She looked at Damian.

"I invited Stan to stay for supper, but he said he would have to be going. I can still see him waving to me before he turned the corner. He said he would see me at school the next day. But I never saw him there again."

Damian's brow furrowed, "Why?"

"I didn't know Stan had a disease called aplastic anemia. I found out when I volunteered as a candy striper at St. Joseph's Hospital, and that was serendipitous because I was asked to take some mail to the Ped's floor. I saw Stan because I had mail for him."

"Hmm," Damian murmured. "How did it make you feel when you saw Stan?"

"Relieved!"

"Go on, tell me more, Kristen."

"The first thing Stan said was how sorry he was that he couldn't take me to the dance."

"What dance was that?"

"Homecoming! The only dance underclassmen could go to."

"How did that make you feel?"

"I told Stan I didn't mind. I was glad I finally found out why he wasn't in school. He told me he had been sick for a while. After that, whenever I finished my shift or was on lunch break, I would eat with Stan in his room. On days when he was feeling strong, we would walk to the end of his hallway and look at the clouds in the sky. Stan would hold my hand and say, 'Let's go for a walk on the clouds.'"

"That sounds like it was a precious time for you two. What was your heart feeling?"

"Love? I suppose, Damian."

"You didn't tell me what happened to Stan?"

Suddenly, Kristen's eyes filled with tears. Damian waited until she was ready to talk.

"One day, when my shift was over, I went to Stan's room, but he wasn't there. The bed had been stripped and someone was mopping the floor. I never saw him again."

While Damian listened to Kristen's story, he wondered about her reasons for choosing hospice care. "I have a question to ask you. Why did you choose hospice care?"

Kristen didn't answer Damian's question. Instead, she said, "It's late, I need to get back to sleep." Damian nodded and then turned off his light. "Good night, Kristen. See you in the morning."

"Good night, Damian, I wish you sweet dreams."

"You too, kid!"

Damian knew why Kristen chose hospice care. He assumed she was not present when her brother died. She didn't say if she was or not, and he assumed Stan had died as well. For some reason, every patient she took care of was Harry or Stan. Perhaps someday, someone would say they saw Harry and Stan waiting on the other side. Perhaps that was the sign Kristen needed to move on.

Over the next two weeks, Kristen was a frequent visitor to room 113. Damian never talked about himself; he always got her to talk. One day fairly close to the end, he brought up the subject of what was weighing heavily on her heart.

"Kristen, I never asked, but I think there is something you're not telling me. You know I'm not going to be here much longer."

"I know... and for the second time this makes me incredibly sad. I don't know how long I can keep doing this, Damian."

"You don't have to, Kristen. So, what's keeping you here?

"I suppose this sounds silly, but I'm waiting for a sign."

"Is that right?"

"I'm in a quandary, Damian, because I love my vocation."

"Do you love it for the right reasons?"

"It is an honor and a privilege to be on this journey with the dying."

"Is that the only reason, Kristen?"

Kristen felt her heart stop beating in her chest. Damian had touched a nerve!

She was angry but decided against being angry with him. "It is easier to love those who are going away, whose journey with me is short. And yes, it hurts. It is going to hurt tremendously when you pass. But I don't know if I can love someone for a lifetime and be happy only to lose them."

"Do you have faith in love, Kristen?"

"I want to, Damian."

"Is there someone you have grown close to?"

"Yes."

"It shouldn't be a difficult choice then, should it?"

"I guess not."

"Choose love, Kristen. Always choose love."

The next morning when Kristen checked in on Damian, he had been drifting in and out of consciousness and was restless until she sat at his bedside. Someone from the previous shift, Kristen noticed, had opened his window. When she started to close it, Damian tried to put his hand up to stop her, then closed his eyes. Kristen held his limp hand in hers and kissed it gently. Damian struggled to open his eyes with the last ounces of strength he could muster. He was holding on for her, because there was something he still needed to do even though his voice was raspy.

"I knew you would come."

"Of course, I came. I am not leaving your side, Damian. Would you like me to tell you a story?" Damian blinked two times. Kristen thought for a moment, then remembered the story she told Harry minutes before he died. She thought a rendition of that story would be fitting.

"Once upon a time, there was a brave man named Damian. He was a free spirit of his day, and he was kind. His heart was full of love, but he had not found anyone who wanted his love. He was sad until he saw a woman in a white peasant blouse and a long skirt that floated around her legs when the wind blew. She was standing outside a new restaurant. She was so pretty that he walked right up to her and invited her to join him in the restaurant. The woman felt an instant connection to Damian and accepted his invitation. When they stepped inside the restaurant, they thought they were in a pine forest that smelled like freshly baked muffins. Damian asked the woman what kind she would like? Did she have favorites? She said her favorite was banana nut.

"So, Damian bought three banana nut muffins and tea, and they went on a picnic. They sat in the lush green grass, nibbled the muffins, and drank hibiscus tea. The third muffin they shared with the woodland creatures who came out of the forest to greet them. When they had all eaten their fill, Damian and the woman lay down in the soft, green, grass and fell asleep."

When Kristen finished the story, Damian moved his head so Kristen could hear him speak.

"See someone," was all he said.

"You see someone?" Kristen repeated.

Damian tried to nod. Then he made a motion with his fingers indicating two, then a single motion indicating one. Kristen asked, "You see two, three people?" Damian nodded. Kristen knew that patients in transition were met by someone they knew. She had experienced this over and over in her career and, even though Damian never talked about anyone other than the woman he met at the restaurant, she wondered if this was who he saw.

She asked, "Do you know these people?" Damian moved his head as much as he could from side to side, indicating he did not. "Do I know them?" Damian nodded. Kristen wondered who it could be. Could this be the sign she had been waiting for? Her heart skipped a beat in anticipation of her next question.

"Is it Harry?" Damian blinked two times. Kristen's heart began to beat fast.

"Is Stan with him?" Damian blinked three times.

"And Mitch? Is he with them?" Damian nodded one time.

"Are they saying anything?" Kristen asked. Damian nodded.

"Can you tell me what they are saying?"

Damian tried to nod, and he desperately tried to form words but couldn't. He looked straight at Kristen, letting his heart tell her what his words could not. "Choose love."

Damian had no sooner conveyed his thoughts when a slight breeze flapped at the sheer curtains over his opened window. Kristen turned her eyes toward the sound of the curtains. When she looked back at Damian, he had floated out on the gentle wind and was gone.

Tears erupted from her eyes, spilling down her cheeks in a waterfall. She held his limp hand against her cheek, wanting him to come back just one more time, sobbing and sobbing. Her heart was broken into pieces. Kristen didn't know how long she had been sitting with Damian's lifeless body until another nurse entered the room and lightly touched her arm.

The nurse put her stethoscope in her ears and the bell on Damian's chest. She listened intently for breathing sounds but there were none to be heard. She turned to Kristen, confirming what she already knew.

"He's gone. I know you cared for Damian. We all knew you cared deeply for him. Write your end notes, I'll do the needful so you don't have to."

While the nurse was preparing Damian's body for removal, Kristen wrote her end notes in his chart and handed his chart to her co-worker. She walked out of her deceased patient's room without as much as a backward glance. Hilda saw her coming down the hallway from room 113 and watched her walk into her office.

This business of caring for the dying was hard and it took a special person to be able to do this day in and day out, year after year as Nurse Warner had.

Hilda knew Nurse Warner deserved more and she wouldn't be surprised if Damian was the last patient where she served as mid-wife for the soul. So, when Nurse Warner walked out of her office with her purse over her shoulder and without as much as a goodbye, Hilda knew Nurse Warner would not come back.

Kristen heard a rumble as she walked to her car and got in. Just as she had turned the engine on, rain poured down in buckets. Before putting her car in drive, Kristen thought about what Damian had said. He had made it clear that life goes on. He had seen Harry and Stan and Mitch. They all wanted her to be happy, they wanted her to choose love. Even though she wasn't sure where she was going at first, thinking about the sign made up her mind. She would choose love, and she didn't care that she was not invited to Tim's house. Why would he invite her since she had not spoken to him since he left her house two weeks ago. Kristen was not going to let that stop her. She couldn't get to him fast enough driving in the blinding pouring rain.

Tim had been sitting in his leather chair in the corner of his room, staring out the windows, watching the rain fall. He had resigned from his position at the bank, worked his two week notice, and was relieved to have that behind him. It would be a major adjustment to learn how to live without work being his focus. He had also resigned himself to the fact that Kristen had not chosen him, and he was deeply hurt. The rain didn't help either. It was gloomy and he was alone. He started to get up and walk down the stairs when a flash of a car's headlights caught his eye. He wasn't expecting anyone, but then for the briefest of seconds, his heart leaped in his chest thinking that maybe Kristen had come to a decision. But then he thought how plausible was that. Who was he fooling? He stood up listening to the car's tire slosh on the wet gravel until it stopped in front of his garage. He couldn't make out the car because the rain was coming down in torrents. Then he saw a woman get out of the car.

Who could this woman be? he wondered. Tim turned away from the window and walked through his bedroom to the open slated stairs. He quickly descended the stairs that opened to his kitchen and walked through, down the hallway, and out his heavy metal hammered front door.

He looked and then looked again, recognizing Kristen standing motionless in the pouring rain. His heart began to beat wildly as she shouted above the pounding rain, "I choose you, Tim, I choose you!"

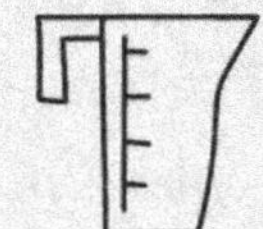

Recipe

Blue Eyes, Red Dress
The Hopeful Romantic Series

Sylvia's Chocolate Chip Cookies

Ingredients

- 2 cups all purpose flour
- 1 cup rolled oats
- 1 tsp baking soda
- 1 tsp salt
- 1 cup softened butter
- 3/4 cup white sugar
- 3/4 cup brown sugar
- 2 large eggs
- 1 tsp vanilla
- 2 cups chocolate chips

Directions

1. Preheat oven to 375 degrees F.
2. In a bowl, combine flour, baking soda and salt. Whisk together and set aside.
3. In a large mixing bowl, beat butter, sugars, eggs, and vanilla. Add flour mixture, mix well.
4. Add oatmeal and chocolate chips; stir.
5. Bake for 9-11 minutes. Let cool 2 minutes before removing from baking sheet.

Recipe

Blue Eyes, Red Dress
The Hopeful Romantic Series

Banana Nut Muffins

Ingredients

- 1-1/2 cups all-purpose flour
- 1 tsp baking powder
- 1 tsp baking soda
- 1/2 tsp salt
- 3 large bananas, mashed
- 3/4 cup white sugar
- 1 egg
- 1/3 cup butter, melted
- 1/2 cup chopped walnuts or pecans

Directions

1. Preheat oven to 375 degrees F.
2. Spray muffin tins with cooking spray or use cupcake liners.
3. Sift together flour, baking powder, baking soda, and salt. Set aside.
4. In large mixing bowl, combine bananas, sugar, egg, and melted butter.
5. Mix well then add flour mixture, incorporating into a smooth batter.
6. Add chopped nuts.
7. Bake in preheated oven 20-25 minutes for large muffins; 10-15 minutes for mini muffins.

Recipe

Blue Eyes, Red Dress
The Hopeful Romantic Series

Pumpkin Spice Muffins

Ingredients

- 1-1/2 cups all-purpose flour
- 1 tsp baking powder
- 1 tsp baking soda
- 1/2 tsp salt
- 1 tsp ground cloves
- 1 tsp ground cinnamon
- 1 tsp ground ginger
- 1/2 tsp nutmeg
- 1 cup canned pumpkin, packed
- 3/4 cup sugar
- 1/2 cup cooking oil
- 1 large egg

Directions

1. Preheat oven to 350 degrees F.
2. Spray muffin tins with cooking spray or use cupcake liners.
3. In a large mixing bowl, sift together first 8 dry ingredients. Set aside.
4. In another bowl, combine pumpkin, sugar, cooking oil, and egg. When well mixed, add to dry ingredients. Fold until smooth.
5. Scoop into muffin tins and bake for 15 minutes. For large muffins, bake 25-30 minutes.
6. Muffins should spring back when tapped lightly.

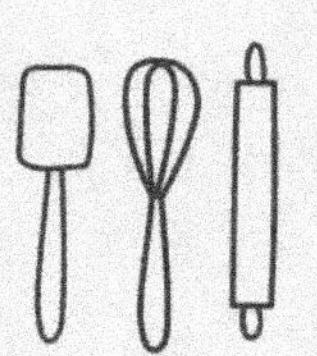 

Recipe

Blue Eyes, Red Dress
The Hopeful Romantic Series

Mediterranean Salad

Ingredients

- 2 cups washed and dried leafy greens (romaine lettuce or any combination of greens)
- 1/4 red onion, sliced
- Kalamata olives, as many as you want
- 1/4 cup Feta cheese
- 1 cup cooked Cavatappi pasta, rinsed and drained
- 1/2 cup cooked red beans

Directions

1. Assemble lettuce on a plate.
2. Add pasta, red beans, Kalamata olives, red onion.
3. Top with Feta cheese
4. Dress with Greek olive oil and balsamic vinegar, salt and petter, or Gazebo Room Greek marinade and salad dressing.

Recipe

Blue Eyes, Red Dress
The Hopeful Romantic Series

Vegetarian Wrap

Ingredients

- Any wrap of your choice: tomato basil, spinach, whole wheat
- 1/3 cup red pepper or garlic hummus
- 1/3 cup matchstick carrots
- Sliced Campari tomatoes
- Alfalfa sprouts
- Cucumber slices

Directions

1. Spread hummus on wrap.
2. Layer ingredients and roll up.
3. Cut in half on the diagonal and secure with toothpicks.
4. For extra protein, add cheese slices.

Keep reading for an excerpt from my forthcoming novel, WAYNE'S CREEK. A coming-of-age story about a runaway from the foster care system who overcomes adversity, challenges, and isolation through love and motorcycles.

WAYNE'S CREEK

The afternoon sun was beginning to change into that magical time of day known as twilight. Kieran found himself sitting on the banks of Wayne's Creek thinking about his present circumstances. The air was so still not a ripple of current disturbed the clear glass surface of the water, which reflected the sky and trees to the point where one could not ascertain which was real and which was the mirror image. The wonder of seeing where heaven meets earth, in a dream when nothing matters, as the sun casts a spell over the sky, mixing shades of pinks and oranges and violets. The beauty of the fleeting minutes of glory paralyzed Kieran. He was a captive to the magic created around him.

The old wooden dock on his right creaked, reminding Kiernan of the things he would miss. Every summer, for as long as he could remember, he had played with his friend, George, on that pier, wearing a pair of cutoff jeans from the previous school year and nothing more, not even a t-shirt. They would fish for hours in their bare feet, catching minnows then throwing them back, arguing over who caught the biggest.

Sometimes they would tie a chicken neck to a heavy string and go crabbing. Crabs were clever and not easy to catch. One had to be quick with the net, scooping them up before they slipped off the string. As the tide ebbed, the chicken neck would become a dark, green, almost black, slimy mass that no bottom dwelling scum sucker would touch. But that was the fun of crabbing.

Sometimes he and George caught crabs to eat. They would collect them in a bucket filled with creek water until there was enough to make a meal. After that, George would dump the live crabs into a Styrofoam cooler, and they would haul the cooler into George's mother's kitchen. George would fill a large stock pot with fresh water and crab boil seasonings. After bringing the water to a boil, he would dump the crabs into the bubbling liquid.

Kieran hated the sound of the crab claws scratching on the underside of the lid. Sometimes George would hold the lid down with a kitchen towel so the crabs could not get out, knowing they would succumb to their demise in a matter of minutes. Kieran loathed the process of hearing the crabs suffer.

One afternoon, he asked, "George, isn't there a more humane way to cook 'em?"

George frowned. "This is how my mother always cooked them."

Disturbed, Kiernan replied, "I think it's barbaric."

George was slightly irritated with his friend's questioning. It was hot and humid, and his mother's kitchen was not air conditioned. "Do you have a better idea?"

Kieran thought about the question, then remembered something he had heard. "Yes, I do. Why don't we dump the crabs in warm water then bring it to a boil. That way, as the water heats up, they go to sleep permanently."

"Yeah, I suppose we could do that next time. If we are lucky enough and there is a next time."

As Kiernan thought back over that conversation, he was overtaken by sadness, knowing there wasn't going to be a next time. George was losing his friend. Kieran was being forced to move, which weighed heavily on his heart as he watched the sun sink lower and lower behind the trees across the creek. The second he thought the sun would sink for good, it popped up in a fiery ball before dipping again, transforming into a glowing ember just above the tree line.

Kieran loved this moment when the trees across the creek became a thin dark line wherein the space above the trees colored the sky magenta and the space beneath the trees reflected magenta on the water's still, smooth, glassy surface.

He found some comfort remembering something he had read from the poet Kahlil Gibran. "When you are sorrowful look again in your heart, and you shall see that in truth you are weeping for that which has been your delight." Then he thought about the creek and what he would miss. Like the poet said, "The feelings we live through in love and in loneliness are simply, for us, what high tide and low tide are to the sea." He would have to be content knowing that life goes on even though his teenage years were coming to an abrupt halt. This was his sixteenth year. He should be learning to drive a car. He should be going on double dates with George if either of them were lucky enough to have girlfriends.

Kieran couldn't blame his foster parents for putting him in this predicament. He knew that going into their care could be temporary. Edith and Randy Morrow were much older, as foster parents go. They didn't want a baby; they wanted an older child. One old enough to enjoy playing ball with Randy or go fishing with him.

The Morrows had not always lived on Wayne's Creek. So, when the adoption agency contacted them about fostering an older child, this was an opportunity to buy a home on the water and start over as a family. No one needed to know differently as the stigma of remaining childless would not be an issue.

Kieran had been in and out of foster homes when the Morrows found him. Most couples wanted a baby, not an older child with scars or one who could hardly remember who his real mother was.

As he sat, deep in thought, the rustling of dry grasses in the dark night alerted Kieran. His ears perked as he listened for the distant slithering of a water moccasin, known to live on the banks of Wayne's Creek. When he felt a thump between his shoulder blades, he nearly jumped out of his skin. While he couldn't say in the moment it was an actual snake bite, the pressure of the thump was enough to make his heartbeat wildly. "I'm gonna die," he moaned.

Without warning, George started laughing hysterically, which kicked Kieran's sympathetic nervous system into overdrive, necessitating a change of his pants.

"Ha, ha, ha, you should have seen you jump!"

Kieran was angry. He was terrified of water moccasins and George knew that.

"THAT'S NOT FUNNY GEORGE! What if it had been a snake?"

"Relax, I've never seen one around here. Have you?"

"No, but I heard they've been found on Wayne's Creek."

"That's what you've heard, not seen, right?"

"Yeah."

George was curious. His friend was sitting in the dark on the banks of the creek. He had finished supper and wanted to get out of the house before being asked to help with dishes.

"What are you doing out here anyway?"

"I could ask you the same thing, George."

"If you must know, I'm hunting water moccasins, ha, ha."

"I wish it was that simple; hunting snakes."

"What are you talking about?"

Kieran wasn't sure how he would tell his friend about his recent turn of events, and it made him sad. He and George had been friends for a long time, and he would miss him very much.

"If we got bit by a moccasin, my mom says we could die and that might be simpler than me having to think about moving away from here." Kieran sighed then put his head between his knees.

"You're being overly dramatic, don't ya think? Why do you have to move?"

"Randy had a stroke, he's real sick and Ethel can't take care of both of us."

"You call your parents by their first name? Besides, what kind of parents can't take care of their kid? None that I know of from around here."

Kieran frowned; he didn't know if he should share the next thing he was going to say with George. Sighing, he began. "They aren't my parents."

George was dumbfounded. "You never said they weren't your parents. I just assumed they were since you were the new kid on Wayne's Creek. Most families grew up here, like, generations of families grew up on Wayne's Creek."

That was true, George wasn't making that up. It was rare to find a newcomer to Wayne's Creek, which was good and bad, because Wayne's Creek bore the stigma of exclusionary; they didn't like outsiders.

"George, Ethel and Randy are my foster parents. My mom died from a drug overdose. I never knew my dad."

George was bowled over by this new information. It shouldn't have mattered, but he conveyed his thoughts anyway.

"Kieran, this is a lot to take in. I don't want you to move. You are my best friend. What are you going to do?"

Kieran hadn't really thought much about whether or not he had a choice. All he knew was the foster system and it looked like he might be going back into it.

"I don't want to go back into the system, that's for sure, George."

The boys sat quietly with their thoughts until George said, "Maybe you don't have to."

Kieran's ears perked, "You got an idea?"

"Yeah, I do. You can run away, disappear. Nobody has to know where you are." For a sixteen-year-old-boy, the idea of running away always solved the problem, initially. And while that sounded like a brilliant idea, Kieran was of sound enough mind to ask.

"Where am I gonna run to?"

George was excited to share his plan with his best friend. "You can live in the loft above my dad's garage."

Kieran began to smile; all was not as hopeless as he thought. "For real?"

George patted his friend on the back, "For real. I wouldn't kid you."

Then Kieran thought about the changing seasons. "George, what about during the winter? It gets cold and damp."

George chuckled, "It's heated, has a heater anyway for the winter. My dad made that a livable space a long time ago. Sometimes he just liked to be by himself. This was his get-away-space, it's nice. C'mon, I'll show you."

ABOUT THE AUTHOR

Stephanie Jack, Ph.D. is a professional writer with a heart and soul for storytelling that inspires and uplifts. Her life experiences provide the background for her characters, and her love of teaching is evident as she intricately weaves tidbits of nutrition, research, and history throughout each novel.

Her first published book, *Food for Thought, Energizing Busy Professionals,* is a nutritional reference book for busy professionals. She is a featured author in Natural Awakenings magazine and Therapeutic Thymes. Stephanie has also written two novels, *The Day the Train Stopped* and *The Secret in the Letter."* She is currently working on her fifth publication, *Wayne's Creek.*

Stephanie lives in East Petersburg, PA with her husband, Terry, and cocker spaniel, Leila.

To contact the author: sbjack2022@gmail.com
Follow on Facebook: thehopefulromantic and Stephanie Butterfield Jack
Follow on Instagram: @sbjack2011
Follow on Tiktok: The_hopeful_romantic
Follow on Threads: @sbjack2011

ACKNOWLEDGEMENTS

Perhaps I should thank COVID when the world was in lockdown and I was isolated. Social media became my link to people I never even hoped to meet, and yet it did, giving me inspiration to draft this book. Thanks goes particularly to Madeleine R. who gave me the knowledge, thrill of motorcycles, and book title: you have my eternal love, and to GH.

I owe a great debt of thanks to several incredible nurses whom I have worked with throughout the years. Snippets of your personalities manifest as the main character in this book. Special thanks to KW, KR and AW.

In addition, there are two people who gave me the generous gift of their time to collaborating with me to create plausible characters. First, I am grateful to my mentor, CKR. You have won my everlasting gratitude and affection. Second, to my editor and publisher, Mary Ethel Eckard. Without you this book would not have come together so perfectly. You patiently read each revision giving your insights into parts of the book wherein I was at a loss. We are a perfect match in the literary world. I am indebted to you and look forward to our journey ahead because there are stories waiting to be told.

Lastly, I would be remiss if I did not thank my husband, Terry. You listened to each page I had written and gently commented with encouraging words, even when I did not want to hear what you had to say. Your critique and thoughts helped make the characters come to life and I wouldn't be able to write without your love and support.

KEY SOURCES

ALEX HARVIL https://www.tzm.com/2021/06/17/Alex-harvil-dare-devil-dead-28-failed-world-record-jump.

ANTOINE DE SAINT-EXUPERY, A-Z Quotes.com, Wind and Fly, LTD, 2022. https://www.azquotes.com/author/12890-Antoine_de_Saint_Exupery. Accessed 03-30-2022.

APLASTIC ANEMIA IN CHILDREN https://www.urmc.edu/encyclopedia/content.aspx?contentTypeID=90&contentDPO2312#,~text=aplastic%zoa. Accessed 01-12-2022.

BMW@MOTORRAD/Sports Model/bmwmotorcycles.com. https://www.motorcycles.com/sport. Accessed 11-16-2022.

BRAINY QUOTE.COM. "Love is space and time measured by the heart." Marcel Proust. https://www.brainyquote.com/quotes/marcel_proust_118197. Accessed 03-09-2022.

BROWN, ROLAND. "Motorcycles (Dream machines)." Barnes & Noble Books, January 1, 2003.

CALLANAN, MAGGIE AND KELLEY, PATRICIA. "Final Gifts: Understanding the Special Awareness, Needs and Communications of the Dying." Simon & Schuster Paperbacks, New York, 1992

CANDY STRIPER UNIFORMS Images Mary Frances Salone Konecy. https://www.pintrest.com/konecky0004/candy-striper-uniform/.

CHANCE, COINCIDENCE, MIRACLES, PSEUDONYMS, AND GOD https://quoteinvestigator.com/2015/04/nocoincidence. "A coinci dence is a small miracle when God choses to remain anonymous." ~Albert Einstein

CHERRY, KENDRA. "Maslow's Hierarchy of Needs" www.verywell-mind.com THEORIES BEHAVIORAL PSYCHOLOGY. "The Five Levels of Maslow's Hierarchy of Needs" by Kendra Cherry, retrieved by David Sussman, on June 3, 2020. Updated 04/02/2024. Accessed 12-19-20 and 07-24-2024. https://www.verywellmind.com/what-is-maslows-hierarchy-of-needs-4136760

CYCLEWORLD.COM. Norton Motorcycles. https://www.cycleworld.com/new-norton-motorcycles. Accessed 02-27-22.

DREGNI, MICHAEL "The Harley-Davidson Reader," Motorbooks, First Edition, 2006. pg. 231; pg. 244.

GIBRAN, KAHLIL, AZQuotes.com, Wind and Fly LTD, 2022. https://www/azquotes.com/quote/569180. Accessed 03-09-2022.

HARLEY DAVIDSON PARTS DIAGRAM https://www.bing.com/images/search?q=Harley-Davidson+parts+diagram&form Accessed 02-27-2022.

KALINA, KATHY. "Midlife for Souls" Spiritual Care for the Dying." St. Paul Books & Media, 1993.

KENDALL R. www.classroom.synonym.com. "Sending a Girl Flowers After a First Date" 09-20-2017. https://classroom.synonym.com/sending-a-girl-flowers-after-a-first-date-12079597.html. Accessed 12-19-2020.

LEAP, ERWIN, M.D., Emergency Medicine News: "Revolutionizing EMS Code 20-203." November 2005-volume 27-issue eleven pages 24-35.

MORALES-BROWN, PETER. "How Long does a Blood Transfusion Take, and How Long Does it Last?" www.medicalnewstoday.com. https://www.medicalnewstoday.com/articles/318984. Accessed 05-23-2022.

MOTORCYCLE PARTS SCHEMATICS https://bing.com/images/search?view=detailY2&accid=NZrkbTqe+id=979ECD769CD208183E9ICCE948F8E9545E4F121A5+th. Accessed 02-27-2022.

PLAIT, PHIL, "Are the Stars you See in the Sky Already Dead? Slate.com. https://slate.com/technology/2013/98 are the stars you see in the sky already dead? Accessed 10/02/2022.

ROADRACERZ.COM. "Motorcycle Crash and Safety Statistics" updated December 2020. https://roadracerz.com/motorcycle=accident-statistics/. Accessed 02-27-2022.

RUMI – https://AZQuotes.com/author/12768-Rumi. "Goodbyes are only for those who love with their eyes. Because for those who love with the heart and soul, there is no such thing as separation."

VERYWELL.COM. "Law of Attraction (What is the)." https://www.verywell.com. Accessed 12-19-2020.

WWW.THEHEALTHBOARD.COM. "What is a Candy Striper?" https://www.thehealthboard.com. Accessed 12-19-2020.

WHAT HAPPENED TO THE SOUL AFTER WE DIE? Personal conversations with Rev. C. Anthony Miller, Saint Patrick Church, York, PA, 2001.

WILLIAMS, J.E. "Prolonging Health: Mastering the 10 Factors of Longevity. Hampton Roads Publishing Company, Inc. Charlottesville. 2003. Pgs. 78-80, 82, 220-223.

WINES.COM. Champagne. www.wines.com by Lamborghini.com. https://www.wine.com/search/Lamborghini/0. Accessed 03-09-2022.

WHO IS ENTITLED TO READ A WILL AFTER DEATH https://www.co-oplegalservices.coUK/media-center/articles-may-aug-2019/who-is-entitled-to-read-a-will-after-death/. Accessed 03-09-2022.

YOUTUBE. Keanu Reeves Shows Us His Most Prized Motorcycles | Collected | GQ. https://www.youtube.com/watch?v=O4iGNXsqghs. Accessed 03/09/2022.